As this book is the third in an ongoing series, please allow me to introduce you to the characters central to the story. Of course you may already have met Harriet and Mark Glover in my first novel, 'A Question of Answers' where the scene is set. Harriet and Mark first meet at university, in the supplies store. Behind each other in the queue they discover they share the same surname, 'Glover'. Herein lies the problem. This coincidence serves only to reinforce Mark's need to remain single. Serves only to reinforce Harriet's desire for marriage and one more baby. Frustrated, she finds herself falling for her boss, the head of her school; the charismatic, charming Mr. Sanderson.

And so we have:

Harriet and Mark and their two daughters Rachael and Clare, both in their early twenties and newly married, living down South.

Harriet's mother Frances, intent on impressing all her WI friends with her social standing, lives constantly in fear of Harriet dragging herself and her husband George down to a level from which they'll never recover. Frances is a snob and can't deal with the changing mores of everyday life. Harriet struggles to please her. After all her brothers have managed marriage. James to posh Geraldine. They have a married daughter Clarissa. Paul married Susan whom Harriet envies. She had another baby last summer. And they already have four children!

Mark's mum and dad, Shirley and Harold aren't too sure about Harriet, either. Oh they were delighted when their own daughter frothed her way down the aisle in a cloud of white netting but no, they're more than happy Mark has never made the same commitment to Harriet. They are good, solid down-to-earth people. Not short of money since they've spent a life-time watching it very carefully.

Mark is a scientist working on global warming along with Geoffrey and Melissa, married only briefly. Melissa is now leaning heavily on Mark as she recovers from a quick divorce. Harriet can't stand Melissa Scott having rightly or wrongly suspected something going on between her and Mark for some time.

Harriet teaches at Stetmead Street Primary school. This school has many disadvantaged children and Harriet works very hard to redress the balance. The children love her, as do the parents. She's acquired a certain authority; a certain influence over them that Mr. Sanderson and Mr. Whittle the Area Chief Inspector of Schools find difficult to deal with. Not to mention Mr. Brown, the caretaker. He's convinced Harriet has it 'in' for him and he's constantly threatening her with legal action, always consulting Mr. Potts the union man much to Mr. Sanderson's fury.

Mr. Sanderson relies heavily on his newly appointed deputy Lucinda Lawton, as he is frequently absent attending to various business interests, the main one being Starboard Marine North West. A skilled yachtsman he saw the need and opened the business just over a year ago. Never still, last Christmas he installed a coffee shop after buying out an American coffee franchise company. The place is now well frequented by the parents, as intended. The aim being to lift the life chances of both children and parents alike. Courses of all kinds are run there, including many related to sailing.

A much respected member of the sailing club, Mr. Sanderson has managed to gain cooperation from Tarquin Bridgewater the commodore and most of the club members to give his school children and their parents the opportunity to learn the skill. It's flourishing. It seems the whole of Steatmead is thriving under the direction of the charismatic, wealthy Joris Sanderson.

Not surprisingly, his parents, Olivia and Charles are very wealthy, too. They have long-standing friends with one daughter, Belinda Oxfordshire, who grew up with Joris. She's completely obsessed with him, as many women are. She's aware of Harriet's feelings for him and stops at nothing to put her down. Belinda Oxfordshire is classically beautiful. Harriet and Tricia can't stand her!

Harriet and Mark know Tricia and her husband Bob through the sailing club. Long time friends, though initially Harriet saw Tricia as a threat. Her unrelenting flirting with Mark constantly irritated her. However they both do have one thing in common, their attraction to Joris Sanderson. Almost opposite characters, yet this attraction serves to bond them into a friendship which deepens as Harriet comes to understand her better.

Finally I turn to Harriet's dearest friend, Pepper, her cat. Pepper is central to Harriet's well-being, though she has a mind of her own! This little black cat licks and purrs comfort into Harriet when there's no one else to turn to.

Now, I hope you've learned enough to make you want to read 'A Question of Answers' followed by 'Ne Obliviscaris: Do Not Forget', before this one.

The first book spans ten months, from new year to late autumn. The second continues on through Christmas to the following June. This one covers the next three turbulent weeks in Harriet's life.
However all the books do stand alone as new strands feed into the ongoing story of Harriet, enabling each book to conclude in its own particular way.

Contact via websites:
www.margarethendersonsmith.co.uk
www.aquestionofanswers.com

John

my reason for being
also for

Jane & Richard Gail & John
Pat & Howard

and all our sweet rosy apples for when they've grown up

Jack
Lucy
Anna
Rose

Never forgetting dear rellies

Elizabeth & Derek
Gill & Malcolm
Peter
Janet & Alex
Jenny & David
Mary & William

and dear friends present
Roy
Lynne & Malcolm
John
Jean

and dear friends and colleagues past
Ted
Raymond
Edna
Isabelle

All for different reasons inspiring
&
brought to mind with love, affection & thanks
Also

My thanks and appreciation to Richard Franklin of arima publishing for his
unfailing help and patience in getting my work to print.

Also by Margaret Henderson Smith

A Question of Answers   *arima publishing 2008*
Harriet's life is going nowhere! Tired of trying to get her commitophobe partner to marry her, she finds herself falling for her boss, the gorgeous six foot blonde in charge of her school, only to discover she's not the only one! She soon learns he has fingers in other pies and dubious friends in high places.

This is a contemporary novel sparking off the conflicts between the differing worlds of the haves and have nots. Live the highs and lows of Harriet's dilemma as she takes you on a passionate yet humorous journey in pursuit of her dreams.

The Bookbag: review extract
    "Margaret Henderson Smith has to perfection Harriet's feeling of being completely enraptured by the man and there were times when my heart ached for her."
    "I hope that we'll hear more from Margaret Henderson Smith - and Harriet Glover."
Sue Magee: reviewer

The Writing Pad: review extract
The book is well written and has been well proof read, which makes a pleasant change. It's a promising debut from this new writer and we look forward to seeing more.
David Carter: reviewer

Ne Obliviscaris: Do Not Forget   *arima publishing 2009*
    Harriet. Caught between the steady and the charismatic. Wavering. Two very different men. She's trouble. Can't stay out of it. Still digging away. In serious danger of collapsing the fragile corners of her triangular existence into one big hole.
    Can Mark really put his fear of marriage behind him? She's only looking for one answer. Unless of course 'that gorgeous hunk of a blonde' in charge of her school gets there first. Him? Unlikely. Different worlds. Too many questions.
    A weft of answers weave their way through the story. In and out. Criss-crossing the threads of rivalry, jealousy, anger, passion and desire. Ride all Harriet's emotions as she takes you on the rest of her journey. Then ask. 'Was she ever in control of her dreams?'

The Bookbag: review extract
    "I enjoyed the story, particularly when we got towards what turned out to be a nail-biting finish."
Sue Magee: reviewer:

A Flight of Fancy!   *arima publishing 2010*
A collection of writings from 'The Big 40 Blog'

San Marco the End of the Road

Margaret Henderson Smith

Edited by Jane A. Williams

Published 2010 by arima publishing

www.arimapublishing.com

ISBN 978 1 84549 468 1
© Margaret Henderson Smith 2010

Printed and bound in the United Kingdom

Typeset in Garamond 11/14

Swirl is an imprint of arima publishing.

arima publishing
ASK House, Northgate Avenue
Bury St Edmunds, Suffolk IP32 6BB
t: (+44) 01284 700321
www.arimapublishing.com

Chapter 1

Just the odd sob now. Almost silent but still shaking her ribs sideways. Forcing her to look out of the window. Her side. Trying to keep it from him. This gorgeous, gorgeous man. She could feel his hand catching hers. Squeezing it tightly. She closed her eyes hard in an attempt to focus on the incredulous change just beset them both. Inside this car. His car. She could scarcely believe it. Catching her breath. Breathing in hard. Taking in the unmistakable smell of expensive pale grey leather. Feeling it connect with every last pang her mind, her body had refused to relinquish. She felt strangely removed. As if in a film. A film about somebody else.

She slipped her hand into the side pocket of her dress. Felt the ring against the paper. Against the note Mark had given her. She knew at some point she would have to read it. She'd promised Mark that. But just now the thought was too painful. She looked across to catch Mr. Sanderson's gentle smile. Caught more than a hint of concern in those deep blue eyes.

'Are you still OK about the reception, Harriet? We can go along. Make our excuses. They'll all understand.'

'No. I'm sure I'll be alright, thank you Mr. Sanderson.'

She watched his smile broaden.

'Now Harriet. Try saying my name.'

She could feel herself blushing. She didn't know how. They might just as well have been standing in his office for all the chance there was of her being able to do that. Their brief affair in some strange way had only served to reinforce this formality thing. Besides there had been no need. She'd had to get her head round the fact she would be marrying Mark.

She had tried so hard to lose those brief exquisite moments shared with this gorgeous, gorgeous man. Moments conspired by the evening sun and lapping tide. Just the two of them on the beach that hot summer evening a little over two weeks ago. She was oh so receptive. Even now she could see the sheltered cove. Still hear the cry of the gulls circling low, skimming the shimmering crimson sea as the sun kissed the horizon in magnificent consummate splendour. Her hair matted with the wet sea salt she'd tasted on his lips. Smelt on his arm as he'd brushed his hand across her breast and lifted it to his lips. Oh how hard she had tried to forget those moments when they'd lain on the warm sand. Moments when she opened to the full force of his body, penetrating deep inside her. Her body, mind and soul fused with his in an exquisite expose of submissive bliss. Shared moments. Precious and beautiful. She'd tried so very hard to rationalise them. Lose them to the depths of her mind. Tried so very hard to forget.

'Just once, it was only the once,' she'd reminded herself so many times. She knew it had to be. That was all she had asked for. Just to be made love to once by this gorgeous man before she married Mark. She'd had to return to school after that. She had done her best to stay out of his way. Kept well away from his office after that. Just scurried past his closed door when taking the children down to assembly. Of course it was unavoidable. It was the only way to the hall. She had only seen him once during that time. Just once when he'd strode into her classroom to return the bag of heart-shaped tomatoes she'd left in his car on their return from that fateful trip to Falmouth. He'd breezed in and out of her room. She knew he had been avoiding her. She knew she should never have allowed herself the emotional freedom to go there. She didn't know how impossible it would be to rein it in. To rein it in against the tightening harness of yearning, aching need he'd left her with. Her boss. The head of her school. She could hardly believe she had done absolutely nothing to stop him slipping her out of her blue lace panties. Her boss! Mr. Sanderson! She could hardly believe how exposed, how vulnerable she'd felt after that. She knew only too well the deep hole she'd managed to dig for herself. She didn't know quite how deep it was until last night. Until she'd tested for pregnancy. Pregnant by this man. Her boss! Pregnant, yet hardly broken the formalities. Hardly closed the distance born of being subordinate to him. No. In the space of forty minutes or so it was almost impossible to call him anything other than Mr. Sanderson. It was the only way she knew.

She looked across at him. His thick blonde hair tousled by the wind. The curl still defiant, just resting at his collar. His profile strong, handsome. She followed it down to the damp patches she'd not long made on his pristine white dress shirt. Large ovals of wet sitting below his black bow tie. She was trying desperately hard to unravel the mix of emotion inside her. This handsome, gorgeous man. Marrying him? Pregnant by him? Mark kept cutting across her thoughts. He'd let her down. Stood her up at the church. Her breath caught again. She felt Mr. Sanderson's hand instantly on hers. Her mind now racing.

'Melissa Scott. Pregnant? Was she pregnant too? It's in the note. It must be in the note. How could he do that to me?'

She could feel her eyes filling and spilling with tears again. She could just about see the traffic lights ahead. Blurred, magnified now to a distorted fudge. She watched him change gear as he slowed down to stop. The lights now changed to amber.

'Amber.'

She'd been on amber so many times. For a fleeting moment it crossed her mind sometimes she had just wanted to stay there.

'You're not alright Harriet. You are not alright at all. Look we'll go to the hotel and I'll just pop in to explain. They'll get on well enough at the reception without us.'

'Are you sure Mr. Sanderson? I don't want to let you or anyone down.'

'Absolutely Harriet! We'll drive back to yours. Try and put some kind of perspective on it all. You'll be fine. You can't expect to come to terms with it all just like that. Now wipe your eyes. There's a pack of tissues in there.'

Harriet watched the steering wheel slip through his hands as they turned right at the lights. She felt the firm clasp of his hand on her knee as she wiped her face and blew her nose. She just caught his smile as she looked across and up at him. The last time they'd been on this road together it was *her* steering wheel he was slipping through his hands. When he'd needed a lift after school. When he'd driven them both to his grand, magnificent house in her car. The very first time she had seen it. She drained at the thought now triggering her nerves to knots deep inside her stomach. She could feel her weakening body collapsing under wave after wave of unrelenting, penetrating anxiety. Now swamping her every thought, leaching all stability from her mind.

She watched him drive on. Somehow the roads seemed longer, endless. She kept glancing across, unable to absorb the new reality she'd almost impulsively dug for herself. He'd intoxicated her mind, her body, her soul with every breath she'd taken. On the point of letting this compelling man go. On the point of telling Mark this man had made her pregnant. At least she'd been spared that before wavering in and out of consciousness on the edge of that very deep hole she'd dug for herself. And now on the point of marriage again. Deep in turmoil, her mind offered no stillness in which to settle her thoughts. Her eyes closed now. Her hand clasped tightly in his. The car engine, barely discernable, hummed to the change of gear as he put his foot down on the empty country roads. She opened her eyes to see the lane go past that would have taken them to the house with the 'For Sale' board on the corner. The last house before his. She grasped a fleeting moment of comfort as she glanced back. They were climbing. She could just see the detached house nestling between the trees. Molly's house. Comforting Molly. She tried to hold the thought hard against the next gathering wave of fear, already smashing away the last threads of coherences from her thinking. Fast losing resistance, her subconscious preparing her body for flight, she wanted to run. She touched at her face, felt her legs rise towards her chest. Then taught, tense, barely able to move. She caught his face. Serious, almost stern. She looked back. The hills steady against the fast moving clouds, scurrying towards the tiny patch of elevated land looking out to sea. Stranded in the sand, impatient for solitude. Impatient for the tide to make it an island again. It felt like she was watching a film. She felt like she was in a film losing control of her part. She wanted to be there. She desperately wanted to be there. She wanted to be there on her own and just left to die.

She sensed Mr. Sanderson pull the car over to the left. He stopped, opened his door. Marched quickly round the front to open hers. Dazed, she felt him reach for the clasp on her seatbelt. Her body now leaning into the strength of his arm round her back, easing her forward. Before her eyes, colour indistinct, everywhere fading, coming and going, like she was still standing on the church path, on the edge of that black hole.

'Get your head down between your knees Harriet. As far as you can.'

The pale blue silk wrapped against her face as she lowered her head into the fullness of fabric dropped by its length between her open legs. His hand, spread wide against her back, gently moving, spreading warmth through her shivering body. A few moments feeling like forever. Time bending and stretching painting her world white.

'Feeling better now Harriet?'

'Yes thank you Mr. Sanderson.'

'Good! Now come up slowly and gradually take deeper breaths.'

Her head cradled in his shoulder. His touch gentle, stroking away the hair from her eyes. She felt the brush of his hand against her right breast as he bent forward to clip her seatbelt back. Just as she did the very first time she'd got into the car. Into *his* car. Into *this* car. This top of the range silver Mercedes. He'd met them getting off the ship. Taken her to the field of flowers. Laid her down in the meadow. Bared her breast and lifted it to his lips. Harriet caught her breath again. Pressed her hand hard against her stomach. Shocked at the capability of her adrenaline saturated body to gather yet again that drawing aching need for him, pulling intensely, low down between her hips.

'Nearly there Harriet. Feeling a bit better?'

Harriet smiled. Nodded.

'You're looking a bit more like it now. I suggest you stay in the car whilst I pop in to explain. Then we'll take you home.'

Chapter 2

'Home without Mark.' Harriet was still trying to get her head round it as Mr. Sanderson pulled to a halt outside the house. She looked down to the ring he'd placed on her wedding finger. Thought of the words running the inner face. Words engraved.

'Our perfect day' *Ne Obliviscaris' JS*.

They'd sat in just this spot when he'd slipped it on to her right hand. His words:

"This hand for the moment. Just for the moment Harriet."

She could scarcely believe how things had moved on. She looked out of the window. The two cars still on the drive. Mark's car still there. The 'For Sale' board sporting its achievement. Just reading 'SOLD' now. The removals firm due on Wednesday. Same day as completion. She took a deep breath and swallowed hard. She wasn't sure how events could have overtaken them all so quickly. In a returning surge of nervousness she followed Mr. Sanderson to the front door. Turned to him.

'I don't know where my keys are. I just don't remember having them at all. Unless Daddy put them in his pocket. Yes that would be it. He was the last out.'

'Spare set Harriet. Somehow they didn't get returned to the agents.'

She breathed a sigh of relief as he waited for her to go through. Boxes everywhere. The cat brushed at her long silk dress, trying hard to weave its way in and out of her legs. She lifted it to her face. The soft fur pressing hard against her cheek as she sniffed back the tears. She watched its head stretch full back, tipping its soft wet nose into the palm of Mr. Sanderson's hand as he stroked it.

'Cup of tea Harriet? You sit down and tell the cat all about it whilst I make us both a nice cup of tea.'

Harriet sank into the sofa. The cat sat on her lap, purring loudly. She reached for the box on the side. Felt the soft white tissues disintegrate as she tried to dry her eyes.

'I've still got *you* Pepper! Of course I've still got you. You're still the same. You haven't changed.'

She'd heard about the therapeutic value of pets. Now she knew why. In the few seconds she'd had the cat pressed to her cheek she was feeling better. Calmer now. The affective, emotional torrent easing back to allow her mind spasms of clarity. Still the soft black fur warm and damp against her cheek, she drew in what remained of the familiar. Every corner of the room, every last woven slub in the curtains. The light fittings. The fireplace. All exuding comfort. Drinking it in like some strong, cathartic cocktail mixed to ease her mind. Her thinking stronger now.

'Grow up Harriet! Just grow up. Move on. Just move on. Move on from amber to green. You can't stay on amber all your life!'

She reached over. Grabbed a handful of tissues. Tried to lower the cat to her lap.

'No, that's Mark all over! He never, ever got his head round the way I felt about marriage. He's kept me on red ever since I met him. Ever since I got pregnant with Rachael and had to give up university. Oh no! He thought it was enough just living together. Well it wasn't. And it never would be. But why did he ever let it go as far as this? To this day. To our wedding day?'

She swallowed hard. Took a deep breath. Blinked away the excess moisture stinging at her eyes.

'Anyway Mark's been away a lot. What's different? It's not the first time I've been on my own here with the cat. The first time it was all off and this time it was supposed to be all on. On enough to be getting married, anyway.'

She looked down to the ring on her finger again. Then she'd only wanted Mr. Sanderson to marry her. She hadn't a clue Mark would return to ask her instead. She'd leapt at the familiar. The safe. The steady. She knew she'd be pleasing everyone else, even Mummy, if she married Mark. In any case how long could she wait for Mr. Sanderson? He'd asked her to wait, but for how long?

'Men like that don't do marriage. Especially to the likes of me,' she'd thought.

She felt her cheek warm and damp as the cat stepped across the back of her neck to scramble down her chest onto her lap. She turned her head sideways, brushing its tail away from her face.

'Oh how wrong I was Pepper. How very wrong I was. It's men like Mark that don't do marriage, Pepper. Especially to the likes of me!'

She'd found her voice, but hushed. Didn't want Mr. Sanderson to hear that. She called through.

'Would you like some help Mr. Sanderson? Can you find everything?'

'Not quite at the "lapsus memoriae" stage yet Harriet. I've done this before. Remember?' He laughed.

She smiled at the Latin. Guessed at the meaning. Thought back to that time before Christmas. Of course she remembered. He knew just where everything was. He'd well familiarised himself with the kitchen just a couple of weeks before Christmas, last year. The time Mark had been in Newcastle. The time she'd thought she might be having a miscarriage.

She sat back. The cat yawned then shifted itself round to face the window. Harriet fidgeted to accommodate its bottom, the cat budging itself until there was no further maximisation of comfort to be had.

'There you go Harriet. I'll put it down there.'

Mr. Sanderson stretched across to place the cup on the small square mat sitting on the adjacent coffee table. He sat down on the opposite sofa, in his usual place by the door. Placing both hands round the mug he bent his right leg lifting it over to rest his foot on his knee. Harriet reached for hers, looking down at the cat as she did so. Sipped at the mug of hot tea, letting its warmth ease its way down to her over-churned stomach.

'Are you feeling any better Harriet?'

'Yes I am thank you Mr. Sanderson. I'm feeling really bad about it all now.'

'Nonsense Harriet. Given the situation, anyone would have reacted in such a way. You've had a tremendous shock you know. I can't begin to imagine how you felt discovering you were pregnant on the eve of your marriage. That in itself must have been considerably traumatic. Just wondering how you were going to deal with it. How you were going to tell Mark. It's a bad time anyway, the very early stages of pregnancy. Hormones in uproar and natural fears kicking in. That's something you must bear in mind Harriet, especially right now.'

Harriet looked across. Hardly able to believe he was there. Looking gorgeous, handsome, feeling his presence permeating her senses. Slowly releasing her from the familiarity fix she'd been desperately clinging to, the turmoil just beginning to ease away now.

'I'll need to speak with Mark, Harriet. It's completion on Wednesday, isn't it? We can't be doing with this place being cleared out just at the moment. I expect it will be a little while before you're ready to move into Lower Tideside.'

The cat shifted on her lap, momentarily bounced by the flop of relief instantly collapsing the still tensed muscles gripping her stomach.

'Unpack Mr. Sanderson? I'll need to unpack most of it if we're going to be here for a while.'

She watched him flick his thick layers of blonde hair to the side before nodding his head.

'Just let me get hold of Mark first. Have you got his mobile number Harriet?'

She caught the cat in a sideways glance of disgust as she gently nudged it away. It stretched long, catching its claws in the low cut pile of the cushion before curling up into a disinterested ball.

Harriet stood. Her long blue bridesmaid dress looking incongruous now. Her eyes still swollen, set pink against her colourless cheeks.

'Pop up and get changed first Harriet. You'll feel a lot better out of that.'

Harriet opened the top drawer of the dressing table. Felt in her pocket. The edges of the diamond ring caught in the folded square of paper. Caught in the note from Mark sitting in the pocket at the side of her dress. She sat on the bed. Mark's pillow. She swallowed. Bit hard on the temptation to bury her face in it. Tried to rationalise his actions against her own as she clutched the small paper parcel squeezing it hard to the palm of her hand. She held it close to her chest before hiding it somewhere between her pants, bras and socks at the back of the drawer.

Chapter 3

'Far more suited to a Saturday morning Harriet! Or is it lunch time?'

Mr Sanderson, still in dress shirt, drew back his immaculate white cuff to check the time. Harriet pulled her lacy black angora jumper down, stretching it long over her faded denim jeans. She went to her bag hanging heavy by its long strap from one of the row of silver coat hooks in the cupboard under the stairs. Her elbow sliding down Mark's bulky waterproof jacket as she struggled to release her address book jammed into the pocket lined into her bag.

She opened it at the back, letting the pressed buttercups slide into the palm of her hand. She smiled. Pushed away the jacket. As if pushing away the rising irritation with Mark. He'd ducked out. She didn't want this sense of recovery to be overtaken by anger. She'd wished them both well on her return to the church with Mr. Sanderson. She replaced the buttercups between the last page and the cover of her book vowing to control the swing of emotions that wanted to keep her on amber. A place she knew only too well didn't exist any more.

'No good hiding in the cupboard Harriet. How long does it take?'

Mr. Sanderson strode into the hall, laughing. She blushed as she passed him the book, opening it at the first page as she did so, not realising she'd been so lost in thought.

'That's his mobile number. The one at the top.'

She watched one eyebrow pucker slightly as he raised the other. His laughter now relaxed to a broad smile. She fixed her eyes to those elongated dimples running both sides of his strong, handsome face. Drawn to those white almost perfect teeth.

'Oops! There you go Harriet. We don't want to lose these!'

'No, most definitely not Mr. Sanderson.'

'As I recall this was the exact jumper. Ah, yes, I remember now, I almost got it confused with the cat.'

She felt his eyes resting on her breasts. He slipped the top two buttons away from their buttonholes and gently kissed into the parting he'd made.

'Now Harriet. I can't possibly stay in these all day. I'll take this if you don't mind. I'll pop back and get changed. Give Mark a call from there. Do you fancy a trip back to Lower Tideside with me, or do you prefer to stay here?'

'Oh, I'll be just fine here, thank you Mr. Sanderson.'

'And what about tonight Harriet? Would you like me to stay or would you prefer the space? Maybe time on your own might help you come to terms with all you've just been through? Perhaps?'

Harriet thought for a moment. The cat sauntered in meowing its way into the question.

'Of course I'd love you to be here, but you may be right. It would give me a chance to stand back from it all. A chance to talk it through with Pepper.'

'Splendid Harriet! Sound thinking!' He looked at his watch. 'I suggest you get some lunch and I'll do the same. There are one or two things I need to attend to back at Lower Tideside, anyhow. I should be back before two.'

He kissed her forehead as he took the keys from his pocket. She stepped out to watch him stride towards his car. In an instant he'd turned it round, waved and driven off. She hurried down the drive just in time to see his silver Mercedes turn right at the end of the road. Followed the cat back into the house and closed the front door with her left hand for fear of damaging the precious, fragile buttercups he had just given her.

Chapter 4

'Right Pepper, we've been told to get some lunch. You first and then me.'

The cat jumped, brushing at her feet. Hastily she shook the dry pellets into the bowl as she opened the fridge for the milk.

'Oh! Hang on Pepper, it's the phone. Out of there. Shoo!'

She pushed the cat away from the fridge shoving the bowl under its nose before answering it.

'Ooh `arriet! You're there! Ooh `arriet I'm so glad you're there. I `ope you're feelin` better and I do `ope you don't mind me phonin` you `arriet. Are you with `im?'

'Oh Tricia, it's lovely to hear you. Yes thanks I'm glad to say I'm feeling a bit better now. Mr. Sanderson's just gone back to Lower Tideside to get changed. It's just me and the cat.'

'Ooh that's good `arriet. You're not still callin` `im Mr. Sanderson are you? Or `ave you finished with `im already?'

'I don't think I'll ever be able to call him anything else. I just can't bring myself to say his name.'

'Oh you will. You're going to `ave to try `arder. After all in three weeks time you're goin` to `ave to be sayin` it. Ooh `arriet, you are lucky! I wish it was me. I wouldn't `ave been too upset to go to the Gerald Roper `otel if it `ad been me. You're far too sensitive. If Bob `ad done that to me and our friend Joris `ad stepped in to save me, I'd `ave been there like a shot showin` off my new `usband to be.'

Harriet laughed. Tricia always made her feel so much better.

'Anyway `arriet. Why I'm phonin` you. On this occasion it was probably just as well you weren't there.'

'Why Tricia? What do you mean? What's happened?' Harriet couldn't get the words out fast enough.

'Well, you know I told you Bob `ad disappeared to go and find Mark?'

Harriet put her hand to her stomach. Didn't want that sinking feeling again.

'Yes Tricia, I remember.'

'Well `e did `arriet. `e did and `e brought `im back.'

'What Tricia? You mean they both came back to the Gerald Roper Hotel while the reception was going on?'

'That's exactly what I mean `arriet. `e was gunnin` for Joris. Mark and Bob crashed through those doors. I thought they were comin` off their `inges. Everyone gasped. They were lookin` around then Bob spotted me. They were marchin` towards me then Belinda Oxfordshire suddenly jumped up and got `old of Mark. She took `im back right outside so goodness knows what she was sayin` to `im `arriet. I told Bob that Mr. Sanderson `ad only just left. I told `im `e'd been in to explain that you weren't feelin` well enough to come. Ooh `arriet it's a good job `e `ad left. Bob thought Mark was goin` to kill `im!'

'Hang on Tricia. I don't get this. It was Mark that did a runner. Mark that said Melissa Scott needed him more than me. Oh Tricia, it's because Mr. Sanderson stepped in straight away. It's got to be. It won't stop him marrying her.'

'Well that's it. That's exactly it. `e's not goin` to marry `er `arriet. `e told Bob `e'd given you a note to read. `e told Bob `e just couldn't come to terms with `is phobia about gettin` married. `e told `im that Melissa was `avin` very serious problems since `er divorce and `elpin` `er out `arriet `ad `elped `im to take `is mind off marryin` you. `e said `e wouldn't be marryin` `er either. It was just somewhere else `e could be, away from you.'

'Oh Tricia. Gosh! And Mr. Sanderson's going to phone him when he gets back to Lower Tideside.'

Harriet could hardly believe all she'd just heard.

'Ooh you're goin` to `ave to get `old of `im. Warn `im `arriet. I can tell you Mark was in no mood for messin` about.'

'He'll still be on his way Tricia. I'll try and get him on his mobile. Oh gosh Tricia I can't even do that. I don't even know his mobile number.'

'Just a minute `arriet, I think I've got it. `e gave it me in case `e was ever needed urgently at Starboard Marine North West.'

Harriet clutched nervously at the receiver wishing Tricia would hurry up.

'Sorry about that `arriet. `ave you got a pen?'

'Oh Tricia, I think he's back. The door's opening. Look I'll ring you back.'

She turned as she put the phone down. She jumped. Shocked at standing face to face with Mark.

Chapter 5

'Oh! Bloody hell Mark! That's a bit off. Where did *you* come from? You've just frightened the life out of me!'

'I'll more than frighten the life out of you Harriet! Where is he? Where is that fucking fat arse of a lard ball you've decided to marry?'

'Mark! I think you've forgotten something. It actually is none of your business now. You've just turned me down remember? This morning. On the church path. Melissa needed you more than me. Remember?'

'The note Harriet. I gave you a note. You promised to read it. You obviously didn't. Couldn't do that one last thing for me. Couldn't wait to throw yourself into his sodding arms.'

'Hang on a minute Mark. I don't get this.'

'You might do if you'd read the bloody note Harriet.'

Harriet looked down. She knew she had to pull back for fear of sending him completely over the top. Frightened. On her guard. She definitely couldn't afford to let the fact she was pregnant slip out.

'Look Mark. We've both been traumatised and we're only talking about this morning. Just a few hours ago. That's all it's been. I'm about to put the kettle on. Where's Melissa, anyway? How did you manage to escape?'

'Likewise, that's also none of your business Harriet.'

'Well what's it all about then Mark? What do you want to see Mr. Sanderson for?'

'There's a couple of things I want to get straight with him Harriet. You think you know him, but you don't. And he's already involved with the family as from today.'

'As from today?' Harriet blanked.

'Yes Harriet. The girls. You haven't forgotten them already have you?' He looked at his watch. 'They'll be well married by now.'

Harriet felt dreadful. How could it have so completely slipped her mind?

'They'll all, no doubt, become involved in this Starboard Marine North West thing. I don't want him exerting any influence whatsoever over them. He can leave my daughters out of his wheeler-dealing.'

'My daughters still, Mark. They haven't suddenly just become yours. Anyway you've got it so wrong. He's not a wheeler-dealer. If you'd heard his mother like I did on Christmas day, you'd know just why they're so well off.'

'Rubbish Harriet! If he keeps just this side of the law, I'd be surprised. I have it on good authority.'

'Whose authority Mark?'

'Let's put it this way. Belinda Oxfordshire knows him a damned sight better than you. I'll fill him in if he treats you the same way as he's treated her.'

'Whatever it is she's making it up Mark.'

'Oh I wouldn't be so sure of that Harriet.'

'But she still wants him. She wouldn't if he'd treated her that badly.'

'Don't be so sure Harriet. Anyway how do you know she still wants him? The woman must be off her head if she still wants him after that!'

Harriet went quiet. She poured the boiling water over the teabag in each mug and opened the fridge for the milk.

'Oh sorry Pepper!' She filled the cat's saucer first.

'Sit down Mark. Drink this.'

They sat either end of the kitchen table. The atmosphere a strange mix. He'd set her wondering. She fought the urge to lay into him, now on both counts. She knew he wanted to keep her guessing. He wasn't about to say any more. But looking at him. His elbows driving into the hard table. His head in both hands. All her instincts pulling her towards him. She sat hard on the urge to cradle his head to her chest. Drowning in the overwhelming need to stay on amber. Now feeling sick at the thought of being pregnant, again she knew amber wasn't a place she could be.

'Come on Mark, it's only fair to tell me what you know. Try to make some amends for dumping me at the church will you? For making me look so stupid. You've just walked out of my life and now you're back here telling me this.'

'It's a warning Harriet. I didn't ask for it. I've no wish to become embroiled either. If it ever got out, she'd point the finger straight at me. You've made your own bed. It's up to you if you choose to lie on it.'

'Thanks Mark. Thanks a bunch. Don't you think you've done enough damage for one day?'

'No Harriet. No I don't. This house sale. I've instructed the solicitor to pull out.'

'You've what Mark? I don't believe I'm hearing this. You can't do that. We've signed contracts. It's completion on Wednesday. How can you do that anyway without joint permission?'

'I've done it Harriet. If one party in a joint ownership reneges then the other has no choice but to go along with it.'

'Mark! It's going to cost a fortune! We'll have to pay a penalty percentage to either side. What about the house we've bought? What's going to happen to those people? It's going to have a knock-on effect right up the chain. You just can't do it Mark. Have you lost your mind or something?'

'No Harriet. Just the opposite. Melissa's parents are buying it for her. Initially, anyway. All the legal work's already been done. They're happy to go along with that. The new contracts have been drawn up already and they're probably signing them right now. Lard ball's not the only well-heeled one on the planet.'

Harriet took a gulp of tea. She looked around her. Packing boxes everywhere.

'So what about Mr. Sanderson, Mark? He's expecting this to be transferred to the business portfolio on Wednesday. What are we supposed to do about that?'

'You don't have to do anything Harriet. His solicitor will have informed him by now. My parents have agreed to meet the financial penalties of the withdrawal.'

Harriet was absolutely stunned.

'I don't get it Mark. If you're going to be living in Millington with her, why are you so desperate to hold on to this?'

'Because that fucking arse hole isn't getting his hands on it Harriet. You've declared your hand. You're committed to marrying him. You'll be going to that medieval gingerbread house of his. You'll be hearing from my solicitor. If it takes every last penny I earn I'll buy you out!'

Harriet panicked. The stability she'd managed to achieve rested on staying just where she was.

'No Mark. No! I don't want you to buy me out!'

'Oh so that's it Harriet. You know damned well you'd never fit in with that place. Belinda Oxfordshire was right. It was never anything to do with keeping her on board, buying this. He had it all worked out. It was the perfect answer for him Harriet. You, his bit of stuff here. No doubt you'd be living here on your own at his beck and call.'

'Stop there Mark! Stop just right there! He's marrying me Mark. The first banns will be called in the church tomorrow. Didn't Bob tell you that?'

'Of course he told me Harriet. I got the lot right down to every last mushy detail.'

'Then there's your answer Mark. Married people tend to live together.'

'Don't bank on it Harriet. You might just be digging the biggest hole you've ever got yourself into.'

He stood up. His face drained, white with fury.

'You've just ditched me Mark. You've ditched me for Melissa bloody Scott!'

'Come off it Harriet. She barely figures in this.'

'Barely figures in this? When she was waiting at the church gate with your parents? She needs you in a way I don't? What do you take me for Mark?'

'I take you for the fool you are Harriet. Bloody Dame, to boot! You were careful not to mention that one.'

She raised her hands to her face. Tried to cover the flush to her cheeks.

'Going with him to Falmouth, helping him to sort his yacht! Two weeks before our wedding.'

'Belinda Oxfordshire. She threw the lot at you, then.'

'I'd have soon found out Harriet. I understand it's all over the sailing club. What kind of a fool would that have made me look today?'

'Don't use me as an excuse for your phobia Mark. You ducked out before you knew any of this.'

'Oh I've had my suspicions Harriet and well you know it.'

'You've had your chance Mark. We're not married! You're speaking as if we were. There's never been any marriage vows to break.'

'You and that sodding piece of paper Harriet. What difference would it have made? Isn't it all about love? Couldn't you have seen that Harriet? I thought you loved me enough to understand this sodding phobia. Who asks for them? Who wants to admit to them? It's as irrational as being terrified of a bottle of tomato ketchup, which happens. Who can understand that? Who can understand mine? I sodding don't that's for sure!'

'I presume Melissa Scott does, Mark. Or has she sufficient attributes to enable you to overcome it?'

'That remains to be seen Harriet. That remains to be seen.'

Without realising it they'd moved to the hall.

'Anyway, this lot's not going anywhere.' He kicked the corners of the cardboard box at his feet. 'I've phoned the removals people. Wednesday's cancelled. You might just as well start unpacking.'

Harriet jumped. Mark's mobile ringing. She hadn't got round to mentioning the call.

He fished inside his jacket.

'Pass it over Mark. I'll answer it. It's *him*. He was going to ask you about all of this.'

She reached for the phone. Mark held tight. Swerved away. He wasn't letting go. Faintly she could just hear Mr. Sanderson speaking in the background.

'That's where I am right now. She's here. She's just told me she doesn't want me to buy her out. You'd better ask her yourself.'

Mark promptly cut him off.

'Why did you tell him that Mark?'

'Because it's what you've just bloody told me Harriet. Remember?'

'What else did he say?'

'Oh, the ever rational gentleman and I don't think. He doesn't give a damn about compensation. He doesn't give a damn about shagging my bride-to-be either. He did, didn't he Harriet? On that sodding great yacht of his.'

Harriet looked down to her feet. The colour in her cheeks intensifying.

'You were never going to marry me Mark.'

'You didn't know that at the time Harriet.'

'And what about you Mark? Just don't try telling me you haven't done it with her.'

'OK Harriet, so we're quits. We've both had a last fling before our wedding day. But I haven't committed to sodding well marrying her Harriet. He might have jacked you up a couple of notches in the social stakes with this damehood thing. He had that one planned, too. But for goodness sake Harriet you're not one of them. You'll go under trying to keep up with the likes of him. Just think of the circles he moves in. Anyway, he's on his way back. I'm off!'

'Mark, I thought you wanted to see him. That's why you went to the Gerald Roper hotel, remember?'

'I went there to fill him in Harriet. It's a damned good job you'd both left. I couldn't control myself. I'm going now, before I land him one at the front door.'

'What about tonight Mark? Where will you be tonight?'

'Right here Harriet. It's where I live. Remember?'

Chapter 6

The front door banged closed as Harriet went to the small window in the hall. He'd screeched his car off the drive. Went without looking sideways. For all she knew Melissa Scott could have been sitting outside. Someone must have given him a lift.

'Melissa Scott! So he *has* done it with her!' The thought sent her into complete fury. She couldn't rationalise her own behaviour against it. A stinging sense of betrayal overtook her only slightly tempered with the relief of knowing he wasn't on the verge of marrying her.

'Not phobia busting material Melissa. No obviously not! She hasn't got whatever it might take for Mark to get his head round that one either.'

Her thinking was fast. Mark wasn't forcing her to sell. She was so grateful to him for that. Just now she needed the house more than she needed either of them. She clung hard to all around her, desperately hoping the indicator to be misreading her pregnancy, desperately trying to get back to amber. 'And you Pepper. Of course I need you. I need you more than anything.'

She hugged the cat hard against her chest, flopping onto the sofa, unable to let go. Unable to move as the phone started ringing. She heard it click. Waited for the voice.

'Oh hello Harriet. It's Mummy here. Just a quick call to see how you are. Daddy and I do hope you're feeling better. Who would have thought the day could have turned out this way Harriet? It was only this morning Daddy and I were taking you to the church to marry that totally irresponsible good-for-nothing. I had my misgivings Harriet but at least after all these years he was going to be doing right by you. Then to leave you like that. It's preposterous Harriet! Daddy's stopped me more than once from phoning his parents. Fancy raising a son to have him behave like that. Parents should definitely take responsibility for the way their children turn out Harriet. Oh! But then I had you! Still, it might have taken a very long time Harriet but you've finally come to your senses. Do you know Harriet, Mark came rushing into the dining room of the Gerald Roper hotel with the husband of that common girl. He looked positively demented. That poor girl Belinda got off her seat and took him outside to calm him down. Such a kind girl. You know Harriet you are most fortunate Mr. Sanderson could well have married her. I can't believe he broke off his engagement to her. I can see now why his mother was so upset. Yes Olivia was distraught when it happened. Belinda would have made her such a sweet daughter-in-law. When I think about the way she's been treated. Still I'm sure Mr. Sanderson had his reasons. Anyway I do hope she meets a nice man, Harriet, like you have. Daddy and I couldn't be more pleased for you both. We're so looking forward to the wedding in three weeks time. Now don't you be doing anything to put him off Harriet. Oh I must go. It's James and Geraldine back for tea. My word have we all got something to talk about today. Now don't forget to return this message Harriet. Not this evening, I'm busy now. Tomorrow morning will do.'

'Tomorrow morning will have to do. Mummy's all we need just at the moment, Pepper. Wouldn't you say?'

The cat yawned then licked away at her right paw before stretching her claws and closing her eyes. She looked across to the window. Over the hedge a slip of silver, the roof of Mr. Sanderson's car gliding to a halt. She watched him, tall, tossing his mop of blonde hair to the side as he looked across before disappearing up the drive. She heard the key in the lock and then the door close firmly behind him.

'No Harriet. Don't get up. You both look comfortable there.' Concern in his voice. 'I'm sorry Harriet. A totally inopportune time to leave you alone. I had no idea Mark would be showing his face here.'

'No. Please don't worry. You did ask me if I wanted to go with you. I'm OK, really I am. How about you? It must have been a shock picking up that message from the solicitor.'

'Oh it had already crossed my mind Harriet. I didn't expect an easy ride. In many respects you can't blame him. I've dealt with phobic patients. Most cases ended up as referrals. It must be hellishly difficult trying to deal with intensely irrational fear on one's own. Though I feel in his case it's not necessarily all about that. No Harriet. I fear he's out to make life as difficult as he can. We'll just have to work our way round this one. Now! Have you lunched?'

'Oh I just couldn't now, thank you.'

'Nonsense Harriet! We've all got to eat. Stay there. I'll sort you something out.'

She watched his face break now into that most gorgeous of smiles. He didn't deserve this. Mark stepping it up. Being bloody-minded. Just arriving, like that. She was angry at him admitting being with Melissa. Sleeping with her. Being ditched. Angry that he'd never felt able to share his deeply held fear with her, always passing it over, moving it along. Never allowing the question of marriage the benefit of discussion. Taking it right to the day. This day. Waiting until she was outside the church to dump her. And now this! Holding onto the house when all she needed was space. Her stomach churned again.

'There we go Harriet. Eat that sandwich. I'll just get the tea.'

'Ah, thank you Mr Sanderson. As you've kindly made it I'll do my best.'

The cat jumped down to stare at its usual spot by the fireplace. Then in spite of the missing rug, curled up to go to sleep just opening one eye to Harriet as she came back from washing her hands. Mr. Sanderson was already seated in his usual place by the door.

'Now Harriet. In view of changed circumstances I suggest you spend at least tonight with me at Lower Tideside. I can't say I'm terribly happy at the thought of leaving you here on your own. It could well be very difficult should Mark decide to turn up.'

Harriet bit into her sandwich. The bread wouldn't go anywhere and then she finally managed to swallow it.

'Oh no! He's not doing that Mr. Sanderson. I know for sure he's not doing that.'

'Really Harriet? Now how can you be so sure?'

'No. He said that. He said just that. He told me to get on with unpacking because he'd be moving back here only when Melissa Scott gets sorted and settled in Millington.'

She knew there was no way she could prevent the flush of colour to her cheeks.

'Are you sure Harriet? You wouldn't lie to me would you?'

'No. No I wouldn't do that. No most probably not. No, I mean most definitely not

Mr. Sanderson. Oh, I've gone all hot. It must be the tea and this jumper's making me itch.'

'Now Harriet, I want the truth. I don't want you to have to undergo any needless stress. That's why I originally wanted you to have the choice. You've had an extremely traumatic experience and we mustn't forget you're pregnant. You could well have miscarried the last time Harriet. You're at a very vulnerable stage just now and without doubt there's a correlation between high stress levels and loss in the first twelve weeks and particularly in the first three. It may or may not be directly causal but the outcome's the same Harriet. I think you should bear that in mind just now.'

Harriet bit her lip.

'No, really Mr. Sanderson but thank you. I know I'll be alright. Yours is just a bit big and scary at the moment. I'll get my head round it all.'

'Right Harriet. No unpacking mind.' He looked at his watch. 'Phil Davenport's coming round later to go through this mess. He went to see your solicitor Harriet as soon as he got the call this morning. Mark's certainly taken this thing to the wire. Anyhow I'll need to get back, if that's OK with you. I'll pop back later this evening just to make sure everything's alright.'

'No, really Mr. Sanderson. You've done nothing but chase around today. It's been a pretty traumatic day for you too. I'll be alright. I'll get a very early night. We'll both feel better for a good night's sleep.' She watched him stand, mug of tea in hand. Tall. Commanding. He moved towards her.

'If you're absolutely sure Harriet. Now...' He slipped his hand into the back pocket of his jeans. Took out her address book. 'There you are Harriet. You'll find both my numbers on the back page. Now I want you to call me on the landline before you turn in. Oh and you'll need these.' He went to pass her the spare set of keys.

No you keep them Mr. Sanderson. I'm sure we had more in the top drawer of the filing cabinet. Somewhere.'

'Better check Harriet.'

'Oh golly. Can't open it. No key. I wonder where that's gone now?'

'Here Harriet, let me try this. It usually works.'

He unhooked a piece of bent wire from his own bunch of keys. Jiggled it in the lock.

Almost instantaneous. He pulled the drawer open. Rummaged towards the bottom. Brought out the keys.

'Oh thank you Mr. Sanderson.'

'Hang on to that. You'll need it. Swift's got a couple of spares. Never fails!'

'I will. I'll put it with these right now. Thank you for doing that.'

She went to the back page of her address book. Found his numbers.

'I'll phone. Will *you* be answering it? It won't be Mrs. Harris will it?'

'No, no! She doesn't bite either, you know. But yes, to answer your question. I most certainly will Harriet. Now, get the rest of your lunch.'

Both hands around the mug he lifted it to his lips and downed the rest of his tea, almost in one.

'Now just try to relax Harriet. One step at a time, remember. I'll speak to you later. I'll see myself out. Don't get up.'

Already at the window she heard the front door close. She just caught his smile and a quick wave as he turned. She went back to her lunch hoping against hope Mark would change his mind about coming back tonight.

Chapter 7

'Get from under my feet, will you Pepper? You've been following me round ever since you woke up. I'm not going anywhere.'

Yet again she shoved the cat outside with her foot, only for it to come back in through the cat flap.

'There, now that's the phone ringing and I'm closing the kitchen door on you.'

'Ooh, `arriet, it's me again. I've been waitin` for you to phone me back. `ave you got `im there or `as `e gone `ome again?'

'No, it's OK Tricia, they've both gone now.'

'Both `arriet? Who `ave you `ad? Oh no, you `aven't `ad them both scrappin` it out `ave you? Oh `arriet I do `ope you are alright.'

'Yes thanks Tricia, I'm OK, apart from feeling a bit surreal every now and then. Yes I'm alright. No, it was Mark coming in when you were about to give me Mr. Sanderson's number. He came in blazing.'

'Ooh `arriet, I was frightened of that. I saw `im before that long drink of iced water got `old of `im `arriet. Did she not manage to put `is flames out? Oh `arriet there you go, I've really got the `ang of these metathingies now. `e was `arriet, `e was burnin` with rage. Oh there I go again `arriet! Sorry `arriet, what were you goin` to say?'

'Oh Tricia. Have I ever told you what a tonic you are? How much better you always make me feel.' Harriet could feel the tears welling in her eyes again.

'Oh `arriet. Now don't you be so silly. You're not cryin` are you? I know you've `ad a day of it. Now just you calm down and tell me all about it.'

'Sorry Tricia. It's just that I've been a rotten friend. You've always been open about your feelings for Mr. Sanderson and I've always tried to hide mine. And now here you are, just the same as before. You being so kind after having to listen to all that in the church this morning.'

'Listen `arriet, do you think I never guessed you felt the same way about `im as me? Of course I did `arriet. Who wouldn't feel like that about `im? Us girls I mean `arriet. I don't think Bob and Mark fancy `im very much.'

Harriet laughed.

'There now `arriet. That's better. That's much better. Never in a million years was `e ever goin` to `itch `imself to me. Couldn't you just `ave seen all those posh friends of `is disappearin` arriet, if `e `ad done that. No `arriet, that's why `e `ad you lined up for that `onour. Oh, I don't mean that you didn't work very `ard for it. I know `ow `ard you worked when Mark was away canoodlin` with `er on that ice. No `arriet it served `im both ways. `e got credit for the school. Or `e will `ave when the press get `old of it and at the same time `e was makin` sure you `ad the same status as `im in your own right `arriet before `e married you.'

'Oh Tricia, I didn't realise you had such a handle on it all.'

'Oh I make sure I get an `andle on most things `arriet and I make sure I `ang on. I've got one big `andle on Bob and Miss Snootypants at the moment. `e's tryin` to tell me `e's only `elpin` `er out. Mendin` this that and the other for `er. `e thinks if `e tells me `alf the truth I'll swallow the rest. Fat chance `arriet. I'm sick and tired of `im. Do you know `arriet? Do you know those white lacy knickers I `ad ready to wave at your Mark? Well, as Mark was supposed to be marryin` you I put them on in bed one night with my best lace nighty `arriet. I thought I would give `im one last chance. `e got into bed and I said "Don't turn over Bobsy I've got a little teeny weeny surprise for you." Well `arriet `e started to smile and when I slowly lifted my nighty to show `im my knickers `e said "What are you doin`? Where's my surprise then? I thought I was gettin` a present!" "Like what?" I said. And do you know `arriet `e thought I'd bought `im another bottle of that designer aftershave so `e could wear it at your weddin`. For `er, of course! `e's run out `arriet because `e's been smotherin` `imself in it every time `e sees `er. I was furious `arriet. I pulled the duvet off `im and slept on the sofa. We `aven't really been on speakin` terms since. Only when we `ave to, do we say anythin`.'

'Oh Tricia, I'm really sorry.'

'Oh don't be `arriet. I couldn't `ave `ad any better news than I've `ad today. Well I don't mean your weddin` not goin` ahead of course. But if you really `ave finished with Mark and `e's not thinkin` of marryin` whats `er name then that's got to give me a chance with `im `asn't it `arriet? I always felt your Mark `ad a fancyin` for me. But of course `avin` Bob round my neck would put anyone off makin` a move wouldn't it `arriet? Now your Mark's free again. You do know what I mean, don't you?'

'Of course I do Tricia. Do you know Tricia, you and Mark, well I actually think you'd be brilliant together. In fact it wasn't that long ago he told me he thought you were a very bright girl.'

'Oh `arriet. `e didn't say that to you, did `e? Your Mark said that about me? Ooh `arriet, now that would be somethin` special. You marryin` our friend Joris and me marryin` Mark.'

'Yes Tricia. You might just be the one that means more to him than his phobia. Let's work on it shall we?'

'Can't wait! Now I'm sorry `arriet. I've gone right off the subject. I think you were goin` to tell me all about it before you sidetracked yourself tellin` me what a rotten friend you think you are. Anyway `arriet, I want you to know you're my very best friend and I never want to `ear you talk like that again. Now what was my Mark doin` round at your `ouse `arriet? I `ope `e wasn't lyin` in wait for our friend Joris.'

'No Tricia. He left to get out of his way. He swore he'd land him one if he met him on the doorstep.'

'Ooh `arriet. It's just as well then.'

'He came to let me know he's pulled the plug on the house sale.'

'You what `arriet? `ow can `e do that? I thought you were supposed to be movin` out on Wednesday. You can't pull out once you've signed the contracts `arriet, not unless you're prepared to take the consequences.'

'Precisely Tricia! And he is! He wants to buy me out!'

'Oh well that's alright then. If `e's payin` all the compensation and you're not losin` out, it won't make much difference to you, will it?'

'Oh Tricia, you wouldn't believe the wobbles I've had today. Just being here in this house has been the only thing able to calm me down. I can't bring myself to go and live in Lower Tideside just at the moment. It's a huge big house Tricia. He's got a housekeeper and a gardener. I can't go and live there yet. It's all been such a shock. It's the very last place I want to be.'

'Ooh `arriet, you `ave got a problem, `aven't you? I know I'd feel just the same if it was me. Well you don't `ave to agree to `im buyin` you out `arriet. You can always refuse. So what's goin` to `appen to the `ouse you were goin` to buy then? You were supposed to be movin` in on Wednesday. What's goin` to `appen to those people?'

'Melissa's parents have stepped in. Those people have agreed to transfer the sale to them. Of course all the paper work's already in place. I'm not sure when exactly completion will be but they will have signed the newly drawn-up contracts already I think, by now.'

'Oh so I'm not goin` to stand a chance with your Mark after all `arriet. `e'll be goin` to live with `er then in that `ouse. I'll never even get to see `im `arriet.'

'No Tricia. It doesn't look like he's planning on doing that at all. He's talking about living here.'

'Oh that's not very good, is it? Whatever are you goin` to do? Does our friend Joris know about all this?'

'Oh yes he knows alright Tricia. His solicitor's already been on to him. In fact he's got a meeting with him very shortly.'

'Ooh `arriet and does `e know `ow you feel about movin` in with `im?'

'Well he guessed it Tricia because he asked me what I wanted to do. It wasn't a problem whilst this was belonging to Starboard Marine North West.'

'Oh no `arriet. Of course it wouldn't `ave been. Ooh `arriet I do `ope Mark isn't plannin` on movin` back tonight.'

'That's just it Tricia. He is! He was most emphatic he'd be coming back here tonight.'

'Well you'll just `ave to go to `is `ouse `arriet. It won't be very good you bein` there with Mark tonight. I think that would be very difficult to say the least.'

'No Tricia, I just can't go there. I've already told him. Not about Mark coming back though. I couldn't tell him that. What am I going to do?'

'There's only one thing for it `arriet. We've done it before you and me. Remember?'

'No Tricia. I'm sorry I don't know what you mean.'

'`arriet, we're both goin` to `ave to sleep in your shed again. As soon as Bob goes out I'll drop the kids off with my mum. I'll leave `im a note `arriet and tell 'im I'm 'avin' a secret night away as I've 'ad enough of 'is behaviour. That'll shock 'im. 'e won't be so keen on mendin' things for 'er if 'e thinks I'm playin' 'im at 'is own game. It'll give us chance to chat 'arriet. Chance to decide 'ow you're goin' to 'andle all this.'

'Oh Tricia, you're an angel. I'm absolutely desperate for a solution tonight. It may be mad but I'm going for it Tricia. You give me a call once you've dropped the kids off and I'll come and pick you up. I can run you back home again tomorrow. Mark's bound to be off early for Melissa's mummy's wonderful full English breakfast. I'm beginning to think it's her he's fallen for Tricia. He's not exactly rushing off to live with green Melissa, the froggy one.'

'Ooh does she look like a frog 'arriet? That 'as cheered me up. Now where was I? Oh yes, tonight. Right 'arriet. It's decided. This is goin' to 'elp us both out. That'll give Bob a shock. The first of many 'arriet.'

'Right Tricia. I'll go and make a bit of room in there. See if I can get enough space for the sun loungers to open right out. Yes, I'll do that and then get some bits and pieces together.'

''ave you got any wine 'arriet?'

'Too right Tricia. We'd stocked up to celebrate. I'm not even leaving one bottle in the house for him.'

'Oh I'm really lookin' forward to it 'arriet. What a day this 'as been. Who'd 'ave thought we'd be doin' this tonight? Oh, just one thing 'arriet. What if Mark decides to go in the shed, or 'e spots a clue from your kitchen window? What will we do then?'

'Oh I don't think he'll be going in there Tricia. Everything's packed away ready for the move. We'll lock the side gate and then we'll lock the back door and leave the key in. He won't be able to open it then.'

'Ooh 'arriet what a good idea. I'll make us some sandwiches in case we get 'ungry in the night. It's very excitin' 'arriet. I can't wait to come round. I'll go now and start gettin' ready. See you later.'

'See you later Tricia and I'll make the sandwiches. It's the least I can do. You've saved my life.'

'Oh 'arriet, just one last thing. What 'appens if Mark comes 'ome before we get back? It might be better 'arriet if I come in my car and park it out of sight. If I see 'is car I'll come straight round the back 'arriet on my 'ands and knees. You crouch under the kitchen window sill and I'll push a long piece of card under your gate. You tug on it three times 'arriet and then I'll know it's you. Then you can open the gate and we'll escape into your shed.'

'Good idea Tricia and if Mark decides to come back any time between now and then I'll tell him there's been a call from Tarquin Bridgewater to go down to the sailing club straight away to look at the boat. That'll get rid of him. Once he gets down there he always forgets to come back.'

'Good thinkin' 'arriet. Now let me see. Bob's usually out by a quarter to seven. Look out for me at about half past seven 'arriet. That'll give me chance to drop the kids off and get back. Ooh 'arriet. I can't wait. It's a good job it's the middle of summer though.'

Harriet put the phone down. It was the only solution she had. She opened the back door and went straight to the shed. Relieved it was so tidily packed. There was more than enough room for the sunloungers full stretch. She returned to the kitchen and then back to the shed, carrying the first of the wine bottles through. She was feeling surreal again. The final bizarre act to end this totally unreal day.

Chapter 8

Crouched beneath the kitchen window sill Harriet looked at her watch. It was fast approaching seven-thirty.

'Sod off Pepper, won't you? Just sod off! You're making that much noise you'll be giving the game away!'

She grabbed it, turned the key in the back door with just enough time to push the cat in and close it again. She thought she could hear the front door opening.

She turned the key in the lock and left it there. Her heart pounding as she crawled back to her place under the window sill. She hoped against hope Tricia would be late. The possibly of Mark watching them both disappear into the shed from the kitchen window was just too awful to contemplate.

She sat crouched, staring at the gap between the path and the side gate. She jumped as a thin strip of white card began poking its way through.

Steeped in panic she lay herself against the side of the house then wormed her way past the corner along the return wall before the gate. Lying flat, she stretched her arm out to reach it. Then she tugged as best she could, three times.

'Tricia, it's not safe,' she whispered as loud as she'd dare.

'Bloody `ell `arriet just let me in will you before Mark comes back.'

Harriet shot up, sliding the bolt back hard as Tricia pushed the big solid gate forward.

With break-neck speed they were in the shed. The door banged closed.

'Tricia. I thought I heard Mark coming in.'

'No `arriet. That was the paper-boy. I saw `im comin` arriet. I've been on my `ands and knees under your `edge pretendin` to tie my shoelaces I `aven't got `arriet, waitin` for `im to get to yours with `is bloody paper. `e's really dozy that one. I don't know `ow `e ever got the job!'

Harriet smiled, relieved that at least they'd made it before Mark.

'Did you lock the gate again `arriet? We don't want Mark comin` round the back findin` us do we?'

'Oh gosh, no Tricia, just let me do it.'

'`ang on `arriet? `ave you got a key for the padlock `angin` loose on the back of this door?'

'Here Tricia.' Harriet took the bunch of keys from the back pocket of her jeans.'

'It should be next to the back door key.'

'No `arriet. It's not this funny little thing is it? It looks like a bit of wire. Oh `ere it is. It'll be this little one. Is that it `arriet? Your back door key's stickin` out of the door, `arriet! Remember?'

'Sorry Tricia my brain's given up. You can't lock it without locking yourself out.'

'That window. Does it open `arriet? Come `ere, let me give it a shove. There 'arriet. 'elp me back in will you?'

She pushed hard against the window causing it to fling wide open. With barely chance to panic Harriet struggled trying to pull Tricia up and in from the bench below. Tricia just managed to angle her small frame almost diagonally through. They both landed on the floor knocking the loungers sideways. Quickly Harriet got up to close the window.

'Are you OK Tricia? I'm sorry I had to tug so hard. I really thought you were going to get stuck at one point.'

'Oh I'm alright, thanks 'arriet. Just pour us both a glass of wine. In 'alf an 'our or so we won't be feelin' a thing.'

Harriet rearranged the loungers, unfolding a small garden table to place between them.

'There Tricia, I've made us some sandwiches and there are crisps and other stuff in here.'

She sat down plonking the carrier bag on the table.

'Now Tricia, a glass or a bottle?'

''ere 'arriet just pass the bottle! I see you've brought quite a few. Plenty to see us through the night.'

'Too right Tricia. I don't think I've ever needed a drink more.'

'Me too 'arriet. I can't tell you 'ow good it feels to 'ave escaped from my, er, 'er Bob.'

'I can't tell you how good it feels to have escaped from today Tricia. Do you know this has got to be the best part of the day.'

'It will be once you've unscrewed the lid off that bottle 'arriet. Oh look, I'm well past the neck. Come on 'arriet you've got just a teeny weeny bit of catchin' up to do, I would say.'

'Oh these are lovely sandwiches 'arriet. Ooh 'arriet. 'e must 'ave come back. I'm sure I 'eard a car door bang just then. Did you 'ear it? Oh 'arriet I've gone all nervous.'

'Me too, Tricia! Oh no! Bloody hell Pepper will you sod off! Tricia look, she's stretching up at the window. If Mark sees her the game's up.'

''ere 'arriet. Let 'er in. Let me just get to that window. 'ang on 'arriet. Oh she's gone again. No, we'll 'ave to leave it now. Let's just 'ope she's gone for good.'

Harriet unscrewed the lid from the wine bottle cradled against her chest. She drew it slowly in and let it roll round her mouth before swallowing hard.

'Tricia, just what am I going to do? We can't do this every night.'

'Of course we can't 'arriet. We're only 'ere like this because you've most probably 'ad the very worst day of your life. Tomorrow you'll feel very much better. I'm sure you'll get used to 'is posh 'ouse in no time at all. Now don't forget what I said. It's goin' to give you the best chance ever to find out what's really goin' on with our friend.'

'Tricia it could just be a bit late by then. I'm supposed to be marrying him three weeks today. The first set of banns are being called in the church tomorrow morning.'

'Sorry `arriet, it's the wine already. Look, I've got past the label. I think it's the sandwiches `arriet. You don't realise `ow much you've drunk if you're eatin` as well.'

'Just let me catch up with you Tricia. You've got to come up with an answer by the time I'm down to mine.'

'Now `arriet, did I just `ear you say your *supposed* to be marryin` `im in three weeks time?'

'Did I just say that Tricia? Oh no, I've not started on Freudian slips now, I hope.'

'Who's `e arriet? I `ope you `aven't been `avin` a go at someone else now since that caretaker of yours keeps runnin` away when `e sees you. I `ope you `aven't tripped this one up as well. Who is `e anyway? I can't say I've ever `eard of that name before.'

'No Tricia it was Freud who came up with it years ago. It's just something people say now.'

'Oh so it's been turned into one of those metathingies `arriet, just when I thought I `ad the `ang of them. Now what was I sayin`? Oh yes! You said *supposed* to be marryin` `im. Are you not sure `arriet?'

'I'm not sure of anything right now Tricia. I want the whole day to go away. I just want to stay on amber.'

'Who's Amber `arriet? Will she be able to put you up until you make up your mind?'

'Amber Tricia! Like the traffic lights. Not stop and not go. At the moment I just want to stay somewhere in between.'

'Sorry `arriet! I don't seem to be able to concentrate very well. `ere, a drop more of this might just clear my mind.'

'Oh Tricia what am I going to do?'

She needed an answer before Tricia blotted out completely.

'Oh gosh Tricia, I'm supposed to be phoning him about now. I don't want him phoning and Mark answering it. I'm supposed to be in there on my own tonight. You haven't got your mobile in there have you?'

Harriet pointed to Tricia's handbag.

'I `ave `arriet, but I `aven't got `is number. I left it by the phone waitin` for you to call me back.'

'I've got both his numbers Tricia, but they're in my bag, in there.'

Harriet sank the wine bottle into her mouth. By the time she'd emptied it she didn't care.

Chapter 9

Sunday morning now. Early. Harriet woke and looked up to the window to see the sun glinting off the water droplets hanging either side of the cat's whiskers. Her little mouth opening wide, stretching her tiny pink tongue between the long incisors and the short row of tiny white teeth underneath. Her head throbbing, she wondered if Mark was still inside. She eased herself up from the only position the lounger would allow and then fell back, frightening the cat away as she did.

Tricia jumped, woke with a start.

'Oh 'arriet. Are you alright? Oh my 'ead. It feels just exactly the same as it did the last time we were in 'ere. I don't feel sick though 'arriet. It must 'ave been eatin' those sandwiches. 'ow about you? 'ow are you feelin'?'

'About the same as you, I think Tricia, thanks. Did you manage to sleep alright on there?'

'It won't let you turn over, will it 'arriet? I tried a couple of times and nearly took it all with me.'

'You're right Tricia. It's not the answer. But was I very glad I wasn't anywhere else last night.'

'Oh me too, 'arriet. To be truthful I'm not ready to go back 'ome. I've 'ad more than enough of Bob and the kids. What do you reckon? Where shall we go 'arriet?'

'Go Tricia? In there, I think. In spite of Mark, I don't think there is anywhere else *to* go.'

'Now that's were you might just be a teeny weeny bit wrong 'arriet. 'ow about if we disappear for a few days? It might do us both the world of good.'

'Gosh Trica! I'm not sure about that. Tempting though it is we've both got work on Monday.'

'Work 'arriet, wouldn't 'e let you 'ave a couple of days off? I thought you were supposed to be gettin' married 'arriet?'

'I didn't ask Tricia. Not with the day off for the house move on Wednesday. There wouldn't have been any point. We were going to leave going away until the summer holidays.'

'Oh of course 'arriet. I forgot about the 'ouse move. Anyway you 'aven't got that to worry about now, 'ave you? We can always phone in sick. 'e won't be wantin' to come round 'ere checkin' up on you. 'e'll know Mark will be comin' back 'ere. Oh let's get away 'arriet. We both need to get away from everythin', wouldn't you say? We need to give ourselves some thinkin' time.'

'You're right Tricia! Let's do it!'

'You're on 'arriet. Just let me call my mum. She can 'ang on to the kids for a few days. I'll tell 'er I'm very busy at work. She's got a spare key for the 'ouse.'

'What about Bob, Tricia? You'll have to go back to pack. What are you going to tell him?'

'Oh no `arriet. I won't be tellin' `im anythin`. I've got my suitcase in the car `arriet. I'm all ready to go. It's `ow you're goin` to get away without Mark knowin`. That's the question.'

'Gosh Tricia. You had it planned.'

'Oh yes I did `arriet. I'd decided I was goin` even if you weren't. I didn't mention it last night because you'd `ad enough to cope with yesterday.'

'Where to Tricia? Have you had any thoughts?'

'I think it might be best if we get ourselves to the airport `arriet. We'll check what's available and decide then.'

'Oh good thinking. I need to get in there. Get packing. A bit difficult if Mark's still in there.'

'Oh, I'll `ave a look now and see if `is car's there. We'll soon know if `e's gone or not. Ooh my `ead `arriet. It keeps comin` and goin`.'

'Touché Tricia. We could have eased off a bit if we'd known we were going to be doing this.'

'Rubbish `arriet! It's just what we both needed. We'll soon recover once we're on our way. Now `arriet, `ave you got somethin` I can stand on? I need to get out of this window.'

'Hang on Tricia. The small steps are here.'

'Right `arriet. Ooh that went a bit stiff again. `ere `arriet just `old on to them You might `ave to shove me through if I get stuck.'

With Harriet holding her, somehow she managed to poke her legs through then angle her body out of the small window, making sure her feet were firmly planted on the seat below before letting go of the frame. She jumped from the seat then crawled her way along to the side gate. Harriet, tense, could hear the bolt scratching back. In a flash Tricia was back at the window.

'No car `arriet. `e must `ave gone. Pass me that key and I'll open this padlock so you can get out.'

In a tick Tricia had the shed door open just as Harriet banged the window closed.

'Careful Tricia. He might be here yet. Oh get out of the way Pepper. Just let us get in.'

Cautiously she looked around. The place was exactly as she'd left it. No sign of Mark having been near.

'Oh `arriet it looks like `e's bein` really awkward. I `ad no idea your Mark could be awkward like that. We've been out there all night and we could `ave been all cosy in `ere. Men! What would you do with them `arriet?'

'Keep a wide berth, Tricia. Just as we've planned. Let me get packed before Mark decides to appear. Tricia would you mind filling the cat's bowl and a couple of extra saucers of food, please? Oh and if you can find the biggest bowl you can. Just fill it with water as well, please. Mark's bound to be back. He'll see to it while we're away.'

Tricia, barely finished, heard Harriet coming downstairs. With her jacket on she swung her packed case to rest against one of the cardboard boxes in the hall.

'That was quick 'arriet. 'ave you got your credit cards and passport and everythin'? It might be better if we go in your car 'arriet and I'll leave mine where it is. We can get my stuff on the way out, if that's alright?'

'That's fine Tricia. Come on let's go. Let's get off the drive whilst we still can.'

Quickly Harriet locked up. Grabbed her bag and case then closed the front door behind her. She hadn't noticed the green light flashing on the answer phone.

Chapter 10

They were lucky. Sunday morning airport. It wasn't too bad for parking space at the long stay car park.

'Ooh the last time I came `ere `arriet I was carryin` that big `eavy case for `im. `e `ad no right leavin` me with that. `e could `ave got me arrested.'

Harriet suddenly felt guilty. At the time nothing had pleased her more than him forsaking Tricia to be with her on the cruise. She spotted a parking space straight ahead on the end of the row. Drove straight in.

'Just let me get my notebook out of the case Tricia. It could save us a load of hassle.'

'Oh that's a notebook is it `arriet? I `aven't seen one like that. It looks like a very teeny weeny computer to me. What do you want it for `arriet?'

'We might just as well have a look on this Tricia. See what's left. Look there's room on that package holiday to Venice. Let's see. It leaves 10.07. Today? Yes, oh yes that's today. It is the 27th today, isn't it? Oh yes, that's the date down there. What do you think Tricia? The hotel's just by the station. At least we'd know where we'd be staying. Shall we go for this? Get away before they start tracking us down?'

'Oh I would say so `arriet. I've never been to Venice. Oh this is so excitin`. Go on `arriet book it now. I've got my credit card `ere.'

'That's OK Tricia. It's easier to put it all on mine. We'll sort it out again.'

'It's coming through now Tricia. The flight bookings. Have you got a pen in your bag?'

'Yes `arriet. I'll write them down shall I? Just read them off `arriet.'

'Ah that's good. The parking's gone through. Too bad if we should be somewhere else. At least it's paid for. Oh it looks like we can use the self-service check-in machines and print our own boarding cards off. Yes, right. That's it Tricia. The payment's been verified. Once we've checked in we'll need to go to Terminal 2.'

Harriet returned the notebook to her case, reached for Tricia's and stood them both alongside her as she locked the car. They half-ran struggling with their cases for fear of being spotted.

'This is silly `arriet. No one will `ave even missed us yet.'

Chapter 11

'Ooh am I glad to be sittin` in `ere `arriet. We are in the right place, aren't we?'

'Yes, that's it Tricia. Look up there. Departure lounge for Terminal 2.'

'I've never seen the like `arriet, `avin' to stand in one of those x-ray machines `avin' a photo taken right through my clothes. I felt most uncomfortable `arriet. We `aven't exactly `ad time to be `idin` anythin`, `ave we?'

'Well no, Tricia, but they don't know that, do they? Better safe than sorry.'

'Oh too right `arriet. Now where did those two go?'

'Which two Tricia?'

'Didn't you notice them `arriet. Right at the front. Two `unks of guys. One turned round. `e caught my eye `arriet. `e gave me such a lovely smile.'

'No, I can't say I did Tricia. I'm trying to avoid men just now. I can't be doing with any more.'

'Oh of course you can `arriet. It's like `avin` a drop the next mornin` to cure an `angover. That's funny, I can't feel my `ead now. This little trip's doin` me good already.'

Harriet fidgeted on her seat, wondering if this was such a good idea. She knew Mr. Sanderson would be wanting them to be in church together, hearing the banns read for the very first time. She looked at the doors. No going back. She opened her bag, touched at the phone. Couldn't decide whether or not to call him.

'`arriet there they are. Look those guys, over there. What do you think about us movin` a little bit nearer to them? I'd just like to get a better view.'

'If you want to Tricia. We might just as well sit by the window.'

'Right `arriet. Off we go.'

'There `arriet. Now you can see what I was talkin` about. Oh I *do* fancy `im `arriet. `e is somethin` else!'

'Which one Tricia?'

'The one with the dark `air down to `is shoulders. You can `ave the blonde one. You seem to go for them.'

'No Tricia, I don't want either of them thank you. Anyway I thought we were going to fix you up with Mark.'

'Oh of course we are `arriet. I'm only lookin` for an `oliday romance. We won't need to be tellin` `im. We've still got to get that frog of a woman out of `is life, remember?'

Harriet could hardly forget. She went over to the machine to fetch a couple of coffees, leaving Tricia to fantasise uninterrupted.

Chapter 12

Excited, they looked down to the land and the small remnants long since left to the sea. A cluster of tiny irregular shaped islands. Getting closer now, the lagoon sparkling in the sunlight as the plane steered its course to land.

'So this is Marco Polo airport. I'm very excited `arriet. We're actually in Italy. I'm so glad we're `ere at last. It was just a teeny, weeny bit too bumpy for me. I can't say I can be doin' with bumpy flights. You never know if we're all just goin' to drop to the ground. Now where are they `arriet? We've lost them again.'

Tricia looked behind.

'Oh no, I can't believe it. Look they've both at the back walkin' along with those two girls They're all laughin' and jokin'. Just my luck `arriet.'

'Come on Tricia, we're coming up to the customs hall. We'll need to get to the carousel. Find our cases. Come on Tricia, get your passport out. The sooner we pass through customs the better.'

'Ooh I didn't like the way `e looked at me `arriet. I thought `e was goin' to stop me for a minute. We were goin' through green and I went on amber then `arriet. I know just `ow you feel now and it's not very nice.'

'No, just at the moment it's not Tricia and neither is this. Let's find the rep and get out of here.'

They made their way through the arrivals lounge to the small group of people gathering round the dark haired young man holding his company board high above their heads.

'Ooh `e looks nice `arriet. `e can be my rep any day!'

Tricia edged alongside him. Anxious to establish her presence. Harriet, nervous, looked around. She could feel Tricia nudging her, trying to draw her into the conversation. She watched the last of their group filter through, fearful from somewhere behind Mr. Sanderson would suddenly appear. She turned around, vaguely aware the gathering cases to the side of them were being checked, being thrown onto a large trolley. She watched it being wheeled away. Another head count and the young man with dark hair was beckoning them all to follow, leaving them both at the back of the straggling group.

'Come on Tricia, the sooner we get away and on that coach the better.'

'No `arriet, look over there.' Tricia was pointing to her right. 'Look, that window over there. I think that's the money exchange window. We `aven't got our euros `arriet. We'd better do it now.'

Harriet wobbled for a moment in indecision. She wasn't sure about Venice. How easy it would be to exchange money anywhere else.

'Quick then Tricia. They've still got to load the cases. Let's get on with it.'

They watched the queue forming as they hurried over. Harriet edgy, decided this was the only choice they had. There was no way she fancied being stranded in Venice with only pounds sterling in her purse. It seemed like forever. She let Tricia go first. Then her turn. She nodded and smiled at the amiable face behind the glass, relieved to be able to zip it all into her purse as she hurried behind to get to the coach.

'Oh `arriet, we only just made it.' Tricia panted as the closed doors opened again to let them on.

'Sorry Josh. We `ad to get our euros while we could. I `ope you weren't about to go without us.'

'Totally irresponsible! I'm Violet Moss. Cedric and I don't care to be kept hanging around. Do we Cedric?'

'We `ad to get our euros.' Tricia declared. 'We didn't `ave time before we got `ere.'

'Totally irresponsible. There Cedric! What did I tell you about those two? I'm never wrong.'

The rep scratched his head. His dark curly hair wrapping itself round his fingers. His English perfect. 'Just a slight delay Mrs. Moss, we could not go without them.'

He stepped back directing them to the empty seats on the left, towards the back of the coach.

'Did you `ear that `arriet? `e certainly put `er in `er place. Did you see `is smile? Oh `arriet I think we're goin` to be in for a very good time.'

Tricia sat back to allow Harriet the window.

'I can see `im better if I'm on the aisle. I do `ope `e will be stayin` with us in the `otel.'

'I doubt it Tricia. We'll get dropped off then he'll be back this evening or tomorrow morning most probably to give us the lowdown.'

Tricia sighed, arranging her legs to sit sideways onto the passageway while Harriet looked out at the less than interesting strips of neatly laid agricultural land ahead.

Away from the airport now and on the road to Mestre. Hotels, apartments, shops, all of stark angular appearance. Flat windows against cement rendered walls. The odd window box struggling to impress. Small clusters of buildings rising in between short stretches of open land. Odd trees scattered carelessly. Rough land next to growing crops. Office blocks facing factories. The scene wasn't sufficient to distract Harriet from the dilemma she'd come away to escape.

She tried to concentrate on Josh and his potted history of Mestre.

"A town battled over for centuries." Josh had just said.

'Owing Venice no favours for tuning it into this,' Harriet thought.

"Taken over by Venice in the thirteen hundreds, but only centuries later brought into its administrative control to grow as it drew migrants in. Now home to most of those who work there." Josh again. He continued.

'Now Venice Mestre is well within walking distance of the hotel and well worth a visit. If you go only to sit and watch the world go by it will give you the true flavour of modern Italian life."

'No thank you,' Harriet decided to herself as she caught up with him. She switched off again, regretting she'd ever agreed to this irrational escape.

Chapter 13

'Ooh so this is the 'otel. It's right on the pavement, 'arriet. Still we were in a bit of an 'urry when we booked it. Oh look 'arriet, there's the railway line. I do 'ope we're not goin' to be kept awake by noisy trains!'

'At least we'll be handy for them. That's probably the station just up the road there.'

'Oh no, I don't think it's the station. Not looking up there 'arriet. Look up there just under that name, 'owever you pronounce it, "automeracato". I think auto might just be a teeny weeny clue. It might just mean car, don't you think so 'arriet? They most probably sell them.'

'I hope you're wrong Tricia. We need to be near a station. I don't fancy walking through these streets in daylight never mind after dark.'

'Nor me neither. We'll just 'ave to make sure we're back well before then 'arriet.'

'You two late comers at the back. Can I have your full attention, please?'

Tricia nudged Harriet. They hadn't realised Josh had started giving instructions.

'If you could all have your passports ready for collection so your details can be checked off. The hotel will retain them but they'll obviously be returned on request or departure.'

Harriet didn't like the sound of that. She looked at Tricia.

'Don't worry 'arriet. If we decide to go 'ome we'll just ask for them.'

Harriet smiled. Tricia always made her feel better.

They collected their cases from the back of the coach then followed their fellow passengers into the large square reception area of the hotel. Harriet looked around. It was modern, neat. Floor tiles under their feet, but other than that nothing about it exuding that Italian air they'd been expecting.

''ow are they all goin' to squeeze in that 'arriet?' Tricia said pointing to the small lift in the alcove opposite.

Harriet looked across. 'She'll never squeeze in Tricia.'

'She'll make sure she does 'arriet. She's got more plums in 'er gob than Belinda Oxfordshire, 'as Violet Moss. Oh she 'as got a loud voice 'arriet. I could 'ardly 'ear Josh for 'er chippin' in all the time. Oh look 'er dress is flappin' out between the doors. I 'ope she gets trapped and spends all 'er 'oliday goin' up and down in it 'arriet.'

Tricia turned to take the room key from Josh then struggled with her bag to hand him her passport.

''as 'e got yours 'arriet?'

Harriet nodded from the bottom stair.

'Come on Tricia. I think we're at the very top.'

'Ooh we should 'ave waited for the lift 'arriet,' puffed Tricia slipping the key card into the lock as Harriet leant on the door to keep it open.

'Stay there `arriet. Just let me bring yours through now.'

Harriet followed, the door springing back to bang closed before she'd hardly had chance to get in.

'Oh is that the best they could do for a window `arriet? We'll `ave to stand on a chair to see out,' said Tricia looking around the long, narrow room, dragging a chair across.

'We `aven't got much of a view `arriet. We're lookin` down at that `alf dead tree by the side of the `otel and that's an `orrible concrete wall right on top of us. It's the side of that funny narrow `ouse next to us. Did you notice those very long oblong windows and all those venetian blinds closed, `arriet? I don't fancy walkin` past there in the dark, either.'

'Me neither Tricia. I think we'll keep with the tours.'

'Oh yes, we `ave to join `im in an hour, don't we? We'll find out what's on offer `arriet and stick with the rest of them.'

'Good thinking Tricia. Now which bed do you want?'

'I may as well stay with this one `arriet, seein` as it's nearest to my case. Are you alright on that one? The ceilin` goes a bit low there. I don't want you bangin` your `ead.'

'No, I'll be fine thanks Tricia. After sleeping on that lounger last night, once my head's down I won't feel a thing.'

'Well just make sure you keep it down `arriet. Especially when you get up in the mornin`.'

Chapter 14

Harriet awoke the next morning, for a few seconds wondering where she was. They'd both crashed out after dining in the hotel. They'd been disappointed to learn that none of the excursions on offer were designed to take them into Venice.

"Just a ten minute train ride from here," Josh had told them. "Then I suggest you take the vaporetto. That's the water bus. Hop on and off just as you please. They work in exactly the same way as the London tourist buses. By all means try the gondola at least once before you leave, but I wouldn't advise using them to get around. You'll find it becomes very expensive. I wouldn't try haggling either. If you want to be sure of ending up at your desired destination then pay the price asked."

That was about it really, as far as Harriet and Tricia were concerned. Neither were up for a trip to anywhere further a field especially with Violet Moss on board.

She lay on her back for a moment, gazing at the curvature of the ceiling closing her in to the wall. She'd slept well from sheer exhaustion. Her mind clearer now. Feeling more entitled to the space she and Tricia had given themselves. After all Mr. Sanderson had completely taken over her life yesterday morning. She couldn't deny the initial euphoria but the constant wave of aftershocks she'd undergone had certainly taken their toll. All but stripped away the romantic bliss she'd been so steeped in for the last year or so. Of course she'd given her consent to marriage but she lay there wondering if she hadn't been just a bit railroaded. Maybe his mother was right after all.

'He can be very bossy. In fact he didn't know the wedding would fall through. He only asked me to marry him because it did! Why couldn't he have asked me on the boat in Falmouth? If he was that keen to marry me he'd have taken his opportunity before it was too late. Ah I know! He only asked me because he *thinks* I'm pregnant.' Then she suddenly realised. 'But no, he asked me before I told him that.'

Another Freudian slip. Harriet had managed to put it from her mind until now. She'd rationalised it away. After all in spite of all the signs she hadn't been pregnant last time. She'd heard about these tests sometimes misreading. Harriet couldn't believe how far her thoughts had swung. She took a deep breath, rolled carefully off the bed and followed the thin shaft of sunlight painting a path to the ensuite on the cold tiled floor.

Washed and dressed Harriet looked across to Tricia turning over.

'Morning Tricia, I hope I haven't disturbed you.'

'Oh no `arriet. I `eard you get up because I was already awake. Did you not `ear them in the night? Bangin` and clatterin` and shoutin` at the top of their voices. I'm afraid we've got some very noisy neighbours `arriet'

'Gosh Tricia, I went out like a light. Didn't hear a thing. I'm sorry you had such a disturbed night.'

'Oh it's alright `arriet. We'll get our own back tonight. In fact I'll bang around a bit in there and then start singin`.

'I'm sure that's a storeroom next door. I think we're the only ones up here Tricia.'

'Then it must `ave been comin` from outside `arriet all that bangin` and shoutin`. There's somethin` not quite right about that place next door. It makes me want to get out of `ere `arriet. If only we knew where we we're goin` that is. `ave a look at those on there `arriet. We might get a clue from them.'

'Ah, this one's all about Venice, Tricia. In English too. That's where we're going,' Harriet said as she sat on the bed browsing the various brochures. 'That's handy, there's a map at the back. That is a station Tricia. We'll take this one with us.'

'Oh that's good `arriet. I feel a bit better now. Is there a train timetable in there? We don't want to be walkin` past the `ouse next door in the dark.'

Chapter 15

'Ooh `arriet. This is the most excitin` thing I've ever done! Lookin` out there it feels like we're just ridin` on floatin` tracks.'

'I know Tricia. It's beautiful. I'm so glad we came now, I'm …' Harriet interrupted herself. 'Don't look now Tricia but it's those two guys again. They're just coming through now. Did you notice them looking our way last night when we were leaving the dining room?'

'Oh no I didn't `arriet. I was too busy rubbin` my ankle after that fussy Violet Moss woman decided to pull `er chair back just as I was walkin` past. You'd gone ahead `arriet. I was too tired even tell you.'

'That's a bit much Tricia. She might have looked behind her first.'

'That's just what I thought `arriet. She was too busy tellin` `er Cedric somethin` in that big loud voice of `ers. Tryin` to sound posh! She wouldn't be on this trip stayin` where we are if she was that posh `arriet.'

'Ah the last two seats. You don't mind if we join you?'

'Oh certainly not. We don't mind at all do we `arriet? Oh sorry, this is `arriet my friend and I'm Tricia.'

'I'm Barry, he's Andy.' They sat down stretching forward to shake hands.

'We noticed you two at the airport, didn't we `arriet?'

Harriet gave her a quick nudge.

'Oh we only noticed you because `arriet wanted to sit by the window to look at the planes, didn't you `arriet? That's why I'm by the window now because it's my turn. Just like you Andy, sittin` by the window now. I expect it's your turn, too. I was just sayin` to `arriet `ow much it feels like we're floatin` our way into Venice.'

'It's certainly different this place,' Andy agreed. 'Not the best time of year for doing it though as per train.' He looked around. 'We won't be able to move for tourists once we get there. It's better off-season.'

'Why Andy `ave you been `ere before?'

'We both have. It's just a bit too pretty for you though Barry. Isn't it?'

Barry laughed. Looked at Harriet. She could feel herself blushing. He'd met her eyes. She'd quickly glanced away. He was good looking. There was something about him that reminded her of Charles Ormerod, the steward who'd been so kind to her on the cruise. Taller though. Bigger build. Much bigger build, more Mr. Sanderson's size really.

His dark hair, resting on his shoulders, even longer at the back, gave Harriet the impression he was artistic, casual. Well suited to this place. Didn't quite fit with the comment Andy had just made.

'You two escaping from somewhere?' Barry laughed.

Harriet went bright red again, then panicked.

'Now why on earth would you be sayin` that to us?' Tricia piped up. 'We could just as easily be askin` you the very same question, couldn't we `arriet?

What are you doin` `ere anyway? You're not just `appenin` to be dodgin` those girlfriends of yours are you?'

'What's she going on about Andy? We haven't brought any girlfriends with us. We've come here to get away from them. We thought about the Foreign Legion didn't we Andy? But we've decided on being gondoliers instead. Look but don't touch. That's the way forward for us just now. We've come to suss it all out.'

'You're jokin` us, aren't you? You look a bit `eavy to me to be standin` up in the back of one of those singin` your `eads off while you're lookin` but not touchin`.'

The guys started laughing.

'No it's the chickas that can look but not touch. We'll have our big long oars to bat them all away if they dare step out of line.' Barry declared.

'She might just be the first Barry. Looks too much like trouble to me.' Andy replied.

'They're a bit full of themselves,' Harriet thought, relieved to see they were now crossing the small bridge over the lagoon that would bring them to Santa Lucia.

'Got your bag Tricia? Come on let's go.'

'Without a farewell?' Barry declared.

Harriet managed a weak smile as she made for the doors with Tricia close behind.

'Come on `arriet. That's where we go. All those boats lined up down there. That's what Josh was tellin` us about, the vaporettoes. Let's get away from them.'

'Hang on a minute Tricia. Where do we get our tickets? It's somewhere round here.'

'On the boat `arriet. We'll buy them on the boat.'

'No Tricia it's in the brochure. Look we have to turn right here, before that brick wall. I think we go down this alleyway. There's a ticket booth somewhere at the end.'

'It's this way girls. Keep going. We're right behind you.'

'Oh it's you again is it? I think we can find our own way thank you very much.'

'She's at it again. What's with this one Barry? We've left two just like her back home. Just our luck to pick up another one.'

'I beg your pardon! You most certainly `aven't picked me up. It's a shame you don't seem to `ave the good manners your friend `as got.' Tricia smiled across to Barry. '`ow come you got yourself such a very rude friend?'

Barry laughed. 'Take no notice of him Tricia. Let's just say he's had a very bad experience. She was a very pretty girl. Looked much like you. But not half so sweet.'

'Oh!' Tricia, taken aback by the compliment, continued. 'Oh I'm very sorry to `ear that Andy. I think we're all `ere recoverin` from bad experiences. May be that's makin` us all just a little bit too sensitive.' She looked up at Barry. 'As you can see we `aven't a clue where we are or what we're supposed to be doin`. `ow about we all do our sightseein` together?'

Barry nodded to Andy and then Harriet. She was uneasy. Wasn't sure this was the right thing to be doing.

Chapter 16

'All aboard. Now how far do you want to go?' Barry turned to Harriet, pointing to the map in her hand.

'Well, I don't know what you all think but it would be nice to follow the Grand Canal all the way down to there.' Her finger rested at Piazza San Marco. 'We could get off there at St. Mark's Square. Have a look round. A ride on a gondola even. Have lunch and on the way back stop off at anywhere that takes our fancy.'

'Good thinking Harriet.' Barry smiled. 'I'm up for it, what about you two?'

'Oh that sounds like a very good idea `arriet. If we keep lookin` at your map we won't be in any danger of gettin` lost.'

'What about you Andy?' Barry asked.

'Yeah. Fine with me. We've seen it all before. I reckon one place is going to be just as packed as another anyway.'

'Ooh `arriet. Isn't this excitin`? Isn't it funny `avin` all the roads made of water. Just look at that `arriet. Just look at the domes on that church.'

'It's just amazing. Gosh, look down there, and over there. Look at those narrow canals either side leading off from this. You can just see that tiny bridge down there.'

'It's quite something Harriet. I must admit for some reason I've never really fancied the place. Too touristy for me I suppose. Now South America excites me. I've done most of it. There's not a place like it in the whole world.'

'Really?' Harriet replied. 'Mark and I have done the usual places like France, Spain, Greece and Turkey, oh and Cyprus. We went there. Of course the girls were still quite young then so we were pretty much staying in places geared to kids. We didn't get to see too much of any of them.'

'Mark? He's the one you're betrothed to, I take it?'

'No actually.' Harriet wished she hadn't just said that. He was looking at the ring on her wedding finger.

'Oh I get it! Divorced! You're married to someone else now?'

'No actually.' She watched Barry's dark eyes crinkle at the corners as he smiled briefly.

'I've just come out of a horrific divorce me. She tried to take me for every single cent. I've given her the house. It was easier to let go of it and get her off my back.'

'Oh I'm very sorry to hear that Barry. I do hope things eventually work out OK for you.'

'Thanks Harriet. I'm not the age were I want to be starting again, though. I always wanted kids. She was never interested. We never could reconcile that difference.'

Harriet watched him take his camera from his pocket. His hands were long, nicely shaped not revealing they'd ever taken him through the rougher side of life. She liked him. He was well spoken and there was a certain sensitivity about him.

'Ooh `arriet. You're missin` all this. We've passed three beautiful palaces. The one we've just gone by was all arches right up to the water. I wonder `ow these places stay dry?'

'Good point Tricia,' Andy replied. 'There's a lot of decay in many of these very old buildings. Sometimes I wonder why there's not a greater sense of urgency with regard to restoration. They seem to be happy to just let it happen all around them. Of course it's sinking. That's the problem. It may be there's not too much they can do about it anyway.'

'Well I for one am very glad we've come now, before it `appens.'

Andy laughed. 'Oh I think it'll last a few weeks more yet.'

'Oh I `ope so Andy. This `as got to be saved. When I go `ome I'm makin` it my mission. I've just decided. I'm going to raise funds worldwide to save this beautiful place. It will give me somethin` useful to do while Bob's off out with `er.'

'It's like that is it?'

'I'm afraid it is Andy. Do you know I've `ad enough of `im. That's why I'm `ere, with `arriet of course. We couldn't `ave come to a more romantic place to `elp us forget our troubles.'

'Well I hope it works for you Tricia. You look like you need to unwind. Don't let it make you too defensive though. Not all men are the same.'

'No, you're most probably right. I think I owe you an apology for being a teeny bit rude to you on the train. `arriet and I are feelin` a bit raw just now. The last thing we thought would `appen would be to meet two guys in the same boat.'

'There you couldn't get better than that. One of those metathingies and we're actually sailing in it. That's Venice for you! It's doin` my brain the world of good.'

'We're just coming up to the Rialto Bridge now. This is the biggest of them all. Plenty of shops up there. We don't do shopping do we Barry? We'll leave them to it on the way back, shall we? Leave them to indulge their whims for expensive cheap tat.'

'`ow do you know that Andy? You must `ave been buyin` a bit of it yourself. That wasn't why she finished with you was it?'

Harriet nudged Tricia.

'Sorry Andy, only jokin`, but `arriet and I are not exactly stupid you know. We know rubbish when we see it.'

'Come off it you two,' Barry laughed. He looked at Harriet. 'Let's just see where the day takes us shall we?'

Harriet looked all around the busy bustling wide stretch of water. Boats of all kinds bobbing along. People standing, sitting. Tourists everywhere. The green water rippling to the activity. Boats coming and going, criss-crossing this watery heaven. A living page fit to stage the most magical of fairy tales.

'Oh just look at this. This is really something. The canal's widening out. Just look at those buildings.' Harriet could scarcely take it all in.

'Over there Harriet,' Andy pointed to his right. 'That's the palace where Lord Byron stayed in 1818. Palazzo Mocenigo.'

'Gosh, that must have been a source of inspiration, looking down from one of those windows up there.'

Andy smiled. 'Turn to your right. How about that one for elegance? That's the Palazzo Grassi. It was used for art exhibitions. I'm not sure it still is. It might be worth a look on the way back.'

'Gosh! It's absolutely amazing!' Harriet excited. Her senses on full alert. Lapping at every moment revealed by this meander. She felt any minute now she'd be sailing into the conglomerate of ancient buildings gracing the banks running to the water.

'We're crossing to the other side now. Look at that one over there just by the bridge. That's Accademia, they've named the bridge after it. Full of Venetian paintings. It houses the greatest collection in the world.'

Harriet was conscious of Barry behind her, clicking away. In their rush to get away neither she nor Tricia had even thought of taking their cameras. He could have been reading her thoughts.

'No camera Harriet? One day you might regret letting all of this go by.'

'No. This was a last minute booking. The thought never crossed my mind.'

'Pity! Still, you're online are you?'

Harriet smiled. Nodded.

'Then let me have your email address and I'll download them. Or your home address and I'll pop them on to CD to send you.'

'That's very kind of you Barry. I'll do that before we leave.'

'Ooh look `arriet. Look, you can see the sea out there. Oh it's even more turquoise than this. Look we're comin` to the end now. Which side is St. Mark's Square on then?'

'Pretty much opposite the end of this,' Andy answered. 'We'll be getting off over there.'

'San Marco, the end of the road. That's right isn't it Andy?'

Their eyes met. Harriet perceived an acknowledgement between them. Felt in inexplicable sense of unease.

'It most certainly is Barry!'

Chapter 17

'Oh wow! What a sight!' Harriet could hardly believe her eyes. So many people. A huge bubbling mix of people. Wealth and poverty and everything in between. This place was buzzing. With chatter, with music, with pigeons flying everywhere. Being fed the corn proffered from side stalls. Swooping, landing, pecking. A different kind of noise. An absence of everyday traffic. No revving, screeching, hooting, sirens. No cars, or busses, or vans, or lorries, or motorbikes going by. Just the gentle drone of the vaporettos from their comings and goings.

'Yes this is it. You've got the arcades on these three sides and that's St. Mark's church to the right.' Andy looked at his watch. 'We've got all day and night to do this. Let's find a table shall we before everyone moves at once? There's a place over there. We can watch the world go by and see the gondolas coming and going at the same time.'

The four of them wound their way through the crowds. Pulled the chairs away from an empty table to sit down. Harriet and Tricia just glad of the opportunity to take it all in.

'Pizzas all round is it?' Barry asked. Harriet fascinated listened to Andy's easy Italian as he spoke to the waiter.

He pulled back to the table. 'A glass of chilled Prosseco each? Well we'll start with *one* shall we?'

They laughed. It sounded good. It was hot, very hot. They had no trouble agreeing to that.

'The girls will have pizzas too, Andy,' Barry called.

'Oh look at that tower 'arriet. Do you think we could go right to the very top of that?'

'Some view from up there Tricia. I can't say I fancy all those steps though.'

'Oh 'ere they are now 'arriet. Let's ask them. We were just wonderin' about goin' up there. Is there a lift to get to the top?'

'Too right Tricia. That's over three hundred feet high. The views from the top are fantastic.' Andy replied.

''ow about we do that one first then?'

'We've no problems with that have we Barry?'

Barry nodded.

'So it's the Campanile de San Marco first, then; or to the uninitiated, the bell tower. Then the Doges Palace, that's that one over there. Behind that is the Basilica di San Marco, to you St. Mark's church. Both, I would say, the point of being here.'

They wined and dined, laughed and chatted. Harriet felt she'd just passed from one surreal world to another. Another glass of chilled Prosseco soon put paid to any sense of guilt for being where she was. She decided this was the right place at the right time for her. She'd let tomorrow take care of itself.

Chapter 18

Harriet found it difficult to absorb all before them. From the pink Veronese marble of the Doges' Palace with its vast hall and first floor loggia sporting beautiful views of the lagoon; to the Basilica with its statues of St. Mark and the angels crowning the central arch. They gasped at the fine alabaster columns supporting the alter canopy, beautifully painted with biblical scenes. The altar, resplendent, its panels decorated with rich and intricate patterns, depicted in gleaming gold.

Time. Moving on. Harriet had no idea the wealth of splendour all around could possibly have absorbed so many hours so quickly.

'We're not going to get to do much more than this today,' Andy said, looking at his watch. I suggest we have a wander through there. Just get a feel for the place. We can stop by for a bite or two on the way. One of those places, a bit like tapas bars. We can get enough to put us on before we get back to the hotel. We'll have another go at the sights tomorrow.'

Tricia nudged Harriet. They were both smiling. This had to be so much better than sitting on the coach listening to Violet Moss piping up every two minutes, spoiling any guided tour Josh might have offered.

They ate and then walked, crossing tiny bridges and on through alleyways to short, narrow streets. Still the searing heat. The sun just falling. Hitting every shade of pastel. Intensifying the contrasting variety of earthy hues. Buildings intermingling. Paradoxically hot and dry. The cool water tantalising the sun-soaked walls, playing with their reflections. The wind brushing the mix of colour along the rippling canals. Enchantment staging the night air. Musicians rising, artists painting, capturing the magic all around. The skyline, arches, domes, spires. A geometrical paradise set against the pink hue of the evening sky.

'Come on girls. This way. Tricia you look as though your feet have had it for today!'

'Oh, too right they `ave, Andy. What are you suggestin`?'

'A gondola all the way back to San Lucia.'

'Your jokin` me?'

'Nope! There's one ready and waiting.'

'Ooh I don't do boats very well do I `arriet?'

'Here, take my hand. It's no different from getting into a rowing boat.'

Tricia wobbled her way on, clinging to Andy.

'That's exactly what bothers me. Oh! Wooooh!'

For a few seconds Tricia sent the boat rolling.

'Just lower yourself down. You'll be OK,' Andy commanded sitting next to her. He spoke briefly to the gondolier then alighted to allow Harriet to take his place. Both guys on board now, sitting face to face. She looked across. Smiled. Sank back wallowing in the comfort of her ornate chair. Felt like a princess gliding to paradise as they made their way out towards the Grand Canal.

Cooler now. From her watery heaven she watched the sun setting, gradually drawing its veil of pink splendour away, changing the set. She looked up. Stars sparkling, shimmering silver dots into the cobalt blue sky. Young. Dancing their light. But some barely seen, tossed in like granules of sugar, scattered from the start of time. All playing their part in this dramatic final act. The skyline now magnificent, immersed in the light of the full moon. Atmospheric. Enchanting.

Spellbound, Harriet surrendered her soul to this exquisitely beautiful place. Ached to share it with Mr. Sanderson now. Wanted to marry him in the Basilica di San Marco. Wanted to take him to the end of the road.

Chapter 19

'That's it. We're here. Back to the start of the road and San Lucia.' It was Andy.

Harriet didn't want to hear that.

With great reluctance she stepped off the gondola behind Tricia. Glad to be following Andy and Barry making their way to the station. The light fading now. Harriet was pleased the guys were with them, especially having to walk down the back streets from the Venice Mestre station and past the house next door to the hotel.

The train virtually empty. Just a couple of men sitting the far end with their backs to them. Harriet turned to Andy and Barry.

'We'd never have done all this today without you two. We can't thank you enough can we Tricia?'

'Oh no! Do you know it's been the most wonderful day of my life. Thank you so very much. You were so good guidin` us all round Andy, I think you'd be wasted paddlin` one of those gondolas. You should definitely sign up to be a tour guide. Why don't you `ave a word with Josh?'

Andy was laughing.

'Because we've both got jobs of a sort, haven't we Barry?'

'Oh really?' Tricia was curious. 'And what do you both do then? If you don't mind me askin`?'

'We don't mind you asking,' Barry replied. 'We don't answer to that one though, do we Andy?'

Andy gestured a closed zip across his mouth. Harriet glanced at Tricia. It was time to drop it.

'Look,' said Harriet changing the subject. 'We must owe you a fortune. Can we settle with you now?'

'Forget it! Let's just say it's all in the course of duty,' Andy replied.

'Duty?' chimed in Tricia. 'You didn't `ave to do it you know? It was you who got behind us remember when we were gettin` our tickets.'

'There she goes. She's off again.' Andy laughed. 'I thought you said your brain had sucked in so much beauty as to improve its functioning?'

'No, I never said that, did I `arriet?'

'No Tricia. I think you were telling Andy we were all sitting in a real-life metaphor. You know "all in the same boat." Something like that anyway and it was "doing your brain a world of good." As far as I remember.'

'Oh I am sorry Andy. It's those metathingies trippin` me up again. I do wish people would stop usin` them. They get me into all kinds of trouble. You was replyin` to `arriet with one wasn't you? You didn't mean it was a duty at all. I do apologise. Anyway Andy we appreciate your very kind offer but we must pay our way, mustn't we `arrriet?'

'Oh yes, most definitely. It really is most kind of you both, but we're hoping to do the same tomorrow if you're still up for it? We must pay our way, though.'

'I thought we came here to get away from the chickas Barry?' Andy was laughing. 'What do you reckon?'

'Look don't touch, Andy. I'd rather be with them than have you all to myself any day.'

'Good point Barry. Tomorrow it is.'

'Brilliant!' Harriet declared. 'Now, what do we owe you?'

'Leave it for now. We'll settle up before we part company.' Barry insisted. Harriet smiled. She'd lost his attention. He was looking over her shoulder towards the two burly men sitting at the far end of the carriage.

Chapter 20

'I wonder where Barry and Andy went last night after they'd walked us back `ere `arriet?' Tricia looked around. 'They `aven't come down for breakfast yet. We're supposed to be sightseein` with them again today, aren't we?'

'Oh I expect they'll turn up Tricia. Look! There they are now. Just coming through.'

'Good mornin`,' Tricia chimed. 'We `ad such a lovely day yesterday, thank you. We `ope you don't mind doin` it all again today?'

'No, of course we don't do we Barry? Anyway we need to see more of the action if we're to become gondoliers.'

Barry laughed. Harriet wanted to move it on. There was something about the way he was looking at her.

'Well that would be good. It was wonderful you being able to tell us what's what Andy as we were going along. And speaking Italian, that's something else. I actually thought everyone would speak English.'

'No, not on the island,' Andy smiled. 'We've a few languages under our belts between us eh Barry?'

'Afraid so.' Barry looked at his watch.

'You're alright,' Tricia declared looking at hers. 'I was wonderin` where you were. I didn't want you to miss your breakfasts, but it's only just gone nine o'clock.'

Barry leant over to turn her wrist slightly towards him. Tricia looked up to smile.

'Look don't touch, that's the motto Barry!' Andy reminded him.

Barry smiled. Looked over to Harriet. 'Unfortunately!'

She blushed. 'Gosh we'd forgotten to do that.' He stretched across to lift her wrist.

'Yes yours needs to go forward an hour, too.'

'No Barry, you've forgotten about our clocks at `ome goin` forward in the summer. That's the hour.'

'They do exactly the same here. You don't want to be missing your flights home.' Barry replied.

'Oh I'm sure you wouldn't have let us do that,' Tricia returned, 'especially as we'll all be leavin` together.'

'No,' Barry corrected her. 'We're not part of this package.'

Harriet was expecting to hear the rest. Didn't expect him to stop right there.

'But you did come with us and you are stayin` `ere?' Tricia queried.

'It still doesn't make us part of this package.' Barry scratched his head. 'Give us half an hour or so and we'll catch up with you at San Lucia station.'

They watched them walk off to the far end of the room to help themselves to fruit juice.

Tricia suddenly swung forward on the two front legs of her chair to place her

61

elbows on the table and chin in both hands.

'Oh that's disappointin` `arriet. Did you notice `ow long `e `eld on to my wrist? Ooh `arriet `e was sendin` shivers of desire all down my spine. `e's got me tinglin` `arriet. Well `e was the one I most fancied in the first place, remember?'

Harriet laughed. 'You're welcome to both of them Tricia. I'm coasting at the moment, coasting away from complications and I couldn't be feeling better.'

Tricia smiled, 'Oh I am very pleased to `ear that `arriet.'

She swung back wobbling as she tried to sit the other leg of her chair down.

'Get it off my bloody foot will you!'

The voice was loud and posh. Tricia swung round with a start, left her seat to lift the chair leg sending the large woman over. The dining room silenced.

'Oh I'm most terribly sorry!' Tricia declared. '`ow did I know you were under my feet? I'll go and get `elp for you right now.'

Tricia flew out with Harriet on her heels. They didn't bother going back to their rooms. They ran, with streaming eyes, all the way down the back streets to the station as fast as their shaking legs and heaving bodies would let them.

They pushed their way onto the train, flopping on the two seats just vacated nearest the door, in giggling heaps. They didn't notice the side glances from fellow travellers, still standing. They didn't notice the two burly men watching them from the far end of the carriage, either.

Chapter 21

The train, hot and crowded rattled its way over the bridge to halt at San Lucia station. Every effort to stand to get off collapsed them both backwards as the crowds in their rush to get to work blocked the passageway. Clutching their bags they finally tagged on to the last of the stragglers walking along the platform. Still unaware of the two men watching them from the train window, in no hurry to get off.

They wandered down to the Grand Canal. Standing by the water bus landing stages, glad to be off the train and out of the station.

'Ooh it was `ot on that train `arriet. I thought we were never goin` to get off. I `ope no one noticed us laughin` arriet. I couldn't `elp it!'

She looked across to see the green water rippling, buzzing with boats, people waving, shouting, singing.

'It is a very special place `arriet, don't you think?' She started again. Her shoulders shaking. 'Ooh `arriet she reminded me of a grand piano lyin` there with the chair on top of `er.'

'Don't Tricia or you'll set me off again.'

'Well she did it to me yesterday mornin` without so much as an apology. Do you think she'll be alright though, `arriet? She did `ave plenty of cushionin` to land on.'

'She'll be alright.' They both jumped. Instinctively turned to the voice behind.

'She was up on her feet and walking away without any trouble as far as we could see. That right Barry?'

'I would say so. She managed to get to the reception desk anyway, with her old man shouting the odds. We went past to hear her filing a complaint in the name of Mr. and Mrs. Moss. She was wanting to know where you'd gone.' Barry finished.

Tricia's shoulders instantly stilled. 'Oh dear, I do `ope I'm not in trouble. Perhaps we'd better go `ome *now* `arriet?'

The guys laughed.

'I wouldn't worry about it. There's better things to be worrying about right now.' Andy was looking behind him to the two burly men just walking away from the ticket booth.

'I suggest we wend our way down on foot and head for San Polo. That'll take us right down to the Rialto Bridge. We'll need to lose you girls for a couple of hours though, but we'll meet you back there. Give you both chance to do some shopping. Come on. We'll lead the way. Keep walking while we're talking.'

'Oh we'd like that wouldn't we `arriet? I can't wait to buy one of those masks. Will they `ave any there Andy?'

'Stacks of them Tricia. They rely on people like you.'

'That's good. I `aven't seen any grass yet `arriet. Do you think there might be a bit when we get further along `ere?'

'Keep moving girls. We're going along here all the way to that foot bridge down there and then we'll be turning right.'

'Yes Andy. I was just askin` `arriet if she'd seen any grass. I keep seein` cats. It must be a bit `ot for them lyin` on flags and cobbles. I don't think your Pepper would like it would she `arriet?'

'You got a cat Harriet?'

'Yes Barry and she digs bigger holes for herself than I do!'

'Interesting Harriet. Of course cats have nine lives. How many have you got left do you think?' He fell back to walk along side. His arm round her as he waited for an answer.

'Too few Barry. I'm fast running out of them.'

'So you're always in trouble?'

'You could say that Barry. I'm trying not to think about it really.'

Annoyed with herself for letting that slip, she turned the corner dawdling a bit to let the guys get ahead again.

'I think we've left the Grand Canal be`ind now `arriet. I don't think me feet are goin` to be takin` much more of this. It's far too `ot to be walkin`.'

She wiped her forehead with the back of her hand.

'I just hope they're not walking us all the way to St. Mark's Square Tricia. I don't think I could do it.'

'Oh we've slowed right down `arriet. We'd better catch them up. We don't want to get lost round `ere. If we `urry up we'll see where they're goin`. They could be `eadin` for that bridge over there. Oh come on. We don't want to lose them `arriet.'

'It's OK Tricia, Barry's just turned round. They won't go ahead without us.'

'Oh won't they `arriet. Look they've started walkin` again.'

Panicked they panted their way forward and over the bridge rushing to see them turning right.

'Look there they are `arriet. Standin` lookin` at the water from that little bridge over there.'

'I `ope you're not tryin` to lose us you two. It's very `ot tryin` to run in this `eat isn't it `arriet?'

'Sorry we thought you'd both fallen into one of Harriet's big holes.' Barry laughed.

'It's far too `ot for metathingies today Barry, if you don't mind. We're not `avin` `alf such a nice time as we `ad yesterday, are we `arriet?'

'Oh it will get better Tricia. We just keep following the canal all the way down to there.'

'Bloody `ell Barry that's miles. This pavement's really `ot. I can feel the `eat burnin` me feet and just look at them midges comin` off the water. They could `ave planted some grass along `ere. Oh I most definitely wouldn't like to be a cat livin` `ere. `avin` to wear a fur coat all day.'

'That's it! Grab her feet Barry!'

Harriet gasped. Tricia swinging from side to side. Any minute now she'd be tossed into the canal.

'Put me down now. This minute! `arriet stop them will you!'

'Right Barry, one, two three. Ready to cool down?'

'No! `elp! What are you doin` now? Oh it's nice up `ere `arriet. I `aven't `ad a piggy-back for years. All the way to wherever Andy. That will just suit me fine!'

Tricia high on Andy's shoulders. Harriet, silent, following close behind. Dark narrow streets now, overpowered by steeply rising walls. Ancient buildings forced from their past, clutching each other, closing ranks as if desperate to defend every inch of hard won land beneath them.

Then a large space opening before them. Bustling with people. Walking. Eating. Chatting. Children playing, Laughing. Jumping from a low wall running neither square nor triangular. At its centre, a lone bedraggled tree sitting in unkempt grass.

'Now don't complain. What do you call this?' Andy stooped. Rolled her off.

'Oh I see they do `ave grass `ere, after all. That's better. This is much cooler `ere. Come and join me `arriet. It's lovely under this tree. Thanks for the piggy-back Andy.'

'Come on Tricia, you'll be sorry if you don't. It's second only to St. Mark's this.'

'Oh `ang on a minute Andy just let me cool off.'

He looked at his watch.

'Two minutes then.'

'A fair walk, that,' Barry said, looking around the tables. 'We'll lunch here if you like, but you're right Andy, it might be worth taking a look at this place first before we eat.'

'Yes, we've got see it while we're here.' Harriet said turning to Tricia. 'Are you coming?'

'I suppose so `arriet.'

'Oh Tricia. You've been lying in something. Look it's all over your back.'

'`arriet what is it?'

'It looks like cat dirt. Oh you've got it all over you.'

'I just don't know what they're doin` lettin` grass grow `ere `arriet. Stupid cats. The only bit of green for miles and they `ave to spoil it! I've `ad enough of this place. I think I want to go `ome. Look `arriet. Those two think it's funny. Laughin` their `eads off!'

'Come on don't let it grow under your feet.'

'Very funny Barry. I'm not in the mood for metathingies. I've already told you that. You're not thinkin` of goin` in there are you? That funny looking place. Look at all those round things. They look like towers don't they `arriet? A bit like those things they store gas in.'

'Not the most romantic of comparisons Tricia,' said Barry laughing. 'Come on Andy tell her what it is.'

'This is San Giacomo dell' Orio,' Andy explained. 'It's an interesting old place. An incredible mix of styles. It's amazing how well they blend. The ship's keel roof's fantastic! Just the height it gives. And the columns. There's a marble one. It's just a solid piece. They reckon it once belonged to a Roman temple before it was brought here during the fourth crusade. Come on in and have a look.'

'I do 'ope I don't smell.'

'Just as well the ceiling's high Tricia.'

'Oh you're not tryin` to make me feel any better, are you Andy?'

'Take it off then.'

'You've got to be jokin` me Andy. I might be covered in it, but I 'ave no intention of takin` my top off. I'd never do that. Not even to save Venice!'

They walked towards the main entrance opposite the canal, Harriet stepped in first. So light and airy. It took her by surprise. Still. Calm. But still the mustiness seeping up her nostrils. She followed Barry to the painting behind the high alter.

'That one's by Lorenzo Lotto, See the Madonna and the four saints. It's quite something, isn't it?'

She nodded her head.. She'd been drawn to it. Felt in awe of it.

For some time they walked around, almost in silence. The age old atmosphere exerting its pressure. Guarding tradition. Discouraging all words superfluous to its purpose.

Slowly they wandered back to the entrance.

'Thanks for bringing us here Andy. It's been absolutely fascinating.' She caught Andy's smile then looked across to Tricia standing next to him.

'I don't think this one needs savin` 'arriet. It looks alright to me.'

'Checking them out as we go along?'

'Oh I am Andy. I'll need to know the ones that will benefit most from my save Venice fund. Did I 'ear someone mention lunch?'

'That was the plan Tricia. It's off to the small ristorante then, on the corner overlooking the tree.'

'Oh I am glad to be sittin` down 'arriet. My feet are killin` me.'

'Me too Tricia. Still I wouldn't have missed that church for the world. Nor the walk. It's just so special getting that close to people's lives. Walking alongside washing on lines and seeing it hang high up from windows. It's a completely different way of life.'

'I don't know 'ow they put up with the pong. I didn't seem to notice it too much yesterday. Or is it me now 'arriet? Ouch and that's another bite I've just 'ad! I'll be buyin` somethin` to keep these mosquitoes away when we get to the Rialto Bridge.'

'Is she complaining again?' Barry from behind her chair, laughing.

'No, it's just that 'arriet and I are very 'ot 'avin` to keep up with you two. We've run all the way from San Lucia to 'ere!'

'Don't let him hear you say that Tricia. That'll be the last piggy-back he'll ever give you!'

'Oh I'm `opin` I won't need any more. I'm `opin` we'll be goin` back by boat.'

'We're in the heat of the midday sun now Tricia. It won't get any worse than this.'

'Oh I `ope not Barry.'

'This one's renowned for its spaghetti. Everyone OK with that? Oh and white or red today?'

'We'll leave it to you Andy; we don't mind do we Tricia?'

'No `arriet, just as long as it's wet.'

'Just as long as you let us pay.' Harriet said.

'Here Harriet. Write your address on this.' Barry laughed. 'I'll knock on your front door if I have to.'

Harriet blushed. She lifted the pen, then hesitated. Thought.

'Not 4 The Willows. No more big holes! I'll make sure we settle up before we go.'

'They've disappeared. I was about to give him this. Did you see where they went Tricia?'

'Well I just saw them noddin` at each other, `arriet and then they went shootin` off. I `aven't got a clue why.'

'There's something about them Tricia. I can't quite put my finger on it.'

'Yes `arriet I know what you mean. Oh look, they're only over there. They've stopped to talk to those street traders. Oh now they've disappeared again.'

'Yes, I'm sure there's something going on Tricia.'

'You wouldn't believe it. They've gone again. They've `ardly finished their lunch. I can't see either of them anywhere now. I don't know my way back from `ere `arriet. Do you?'

'No Tricia. but don't worry, they've ordered remember? They're not going to go without lunch.'

'Oh look `arriet. You're right. There's Andy again. Can you see `im over there? `e's standin` very close behind those two big men in `ats. They're probably `agglin` `arriet. They most probably all want to buy the same thing.'

'They're coming back now Tricia. Quick let's change the subject.'

'Where is it then? What `ave you bought? `arriet and I can't wait to find out.'

They both opened their hands to gesture nothing.

'Oh you were so close to those two men Andy, I thought you were `agglin` for sure.'

Harriet sensed a slight change in mood. She passed the slip of paper back to Barry.

'1 Haystack Close, Millington....' He began.

'It's time to move on,' interrupted Andy, his face serious now.

Chapter 22

'Right girls, by the looks of it I don't think either of you will make it to the Rialto Bridge. I suggest we hop on one of these,' said Barry pointing to the array of small boats lining the canal.

'Oh I can't think of anythin` better, can you `arriet? I'll `ave to wrap my `ankie round my nose though.'

'It's coming from you Tricia.' Barry laughed.

'Right it's the three of us then. We'll dunk this one, shall we? Get rid of the pong!' Andy laughing now.

'No! Get off! Put me down. I was only jokin`. I joke all the time don't I `arriet? Take no notice of me.'

The mood lightened. Harriet was glad.

'We'll sit `ere shall we `arriet? Oh it's wobblin` all over the place.'

'Gently Tricia. You'll have us all in.'

She let go of Barry's hand to flop next to Harriet. Barry sliding his way round to smile at them from the opposite side. Andy still standing. Chatting. The boatman laughing. The unmistakable lilt of fluent Italian passing between them.

'Look `arriet. Look! I think it's those two men Andy's just been squashin` into when they were `agglin`. Oh don't they look funny `arriet? I think they're runnin` to catch this. We don't want them sinkin` us into the canal do we? They're so `eavy they can `ardly run! Good `e's just started the engine. Are we movin` yet?'

'No he's waiting for them I think Tricia.' Harriet looked back to Barry tossing the barrel of the pen between his fingers. Instantly biting the end as the boat rolled sideways to their weight. A glance at Andy, then she watched him return the pen to the side pocket of his jeans. Touching their panama hats the two big men struggled into their seats. Heads down. Uncomfortable at facing forward from the back.

Harriet jumped. Suddenly Tricia stretching over, pointing towards the pavement by the side of the canal.

'Look out there `arriet, we're turnin` round, we're goin` to be goin` under that bridge I think.' Then whispering. '`arriet, those men. Don't turn round, keep lookin` out there. I'm sure they're the bruisers the PM `ad with `im at the openin` of our place. You know when they launched Starboard Marine North West.'

Harriet covered her hand with her mouth. Went weak at the thought.. Her stomach beginning to churn.

'Are you certain, Tricia?'

'I am `arriet. I know their faces.'

'You two OK over there?' It was Andy.

'Oh we're fine thank you. I was just remindin` `arriet of somethin` we `ave to do when we get back. Wasn't I `arriet?'

'Not paying us I hope?' Barry laughed. 'We've already taken care of that one Tricia.'

With all seats facing inwards, instinctively Harriet and Tricia kept their heads sideways, focussing intently on the maze of windows sunk into dark ancient walls. Buildings intent on blocking the sunlight from this narrow dingy canal. Harriet incapable of absorbing it all, could feel her anger rising. 'He must have had the airports checked. How could *he* put me through this after all *that*? How could Mr. Sanderson possibly have done the old school boy crony bit with the PM to get us both followed?'

It was only the canal widening out, allowing the sunlight to speckle the water, that jogged Harriet from her thoughts. A blast of hot, humid air hit them as the sun, escaped from its own shadows, finally got its way. The banks breaking in staggers now to loosely form crossroads either side, creating a small central lake.

'Unaccustomed silence,' Barry suddenly declared, nudging Tricia's toes with his feet.

'We're only restin` aren't we `arriet?' Barry smiled, turned to Andy.

'How much further Andy?'

'Not far now. From this bridge here we're about five minutes or so from the Grand Canal.'

Harriet glanced across. Managed it without drawing the men at the back into her sights. There'd been little conversation from them. A few minimal, low, unintelligible tones.

'A sharp contrast to Andy and the boatman,' she thought. 'Esoteric but bubbly and light at the bow. Almost sinister at the stern.'

'This one *is* going to San Marco, I hope?'

'It had better bloody be. I'm sure that's what he said. They usually do from here.'

Their voices low. Harriet just managed to make it out.

The small boat chugged its way. The widening water opening out now towards the Grand Canal. Harriet felt uneasy.

They swerved left, weaving their way through the myriad of bustling boats heading east towards the Rialto Bridge.

'Now there's a place to be staying if you ever decide to return,' Andy pointed out. 'We're just coming to it now. One of the most luxurious hotels in Venice.'

'Wow,' Tricia declared. 'That's what I would call posh.'

'Oh there's one posher than that,' Barry declared. 'The Cielo Misterioso, It looks straight across the lagoon to the Adriatic Sea.'

'What does that mean Barry? Mysterious something. "Cielo" Oh I know. Mysterious sky.'

'Well done Harriet!'

'So it's got to be down at the end somewhere. Whereabouts Barry?' Harriet wanted to know.

'San Marco, the end of the road.'

Suddenly the two men at the back jumped up to catch a stream of Italian expletives from the boatman.. Startled, Harriet and Tricia saw Andy reach across to him, still cursing.

'He's telling you to sit down if you don't want us all to end up in the canal.'

'We knew that much! Fucking changed his mind!'

The boat rocked violently again as they fell back in their seats.

'San Marco, the end of the bleeding road. That's where we're supposed to be fucking going! That's what he told us. What the hell are we doing going this way?'

The boat filled with another wave of gabbled, indignant Italian.

'He said he didn't change his mind. He was never going any further than the Rialto Bridge.' Andy passed the message along. 'He's stopping for an hour before he takes it back to San Lucia. He says you'll stand a better chance if you cross the bridge. There's plenty of boats there waiting to go to San Marco.'

Harriet and Tricia looked at each other. They knew just what each was thinking. The last thing they needed now was for Andy and Barry to desert them.

'San Marco, the end of the road,' Harriet thought. 'The end of the road. We might just have reached it Mr. Sanderson!'

She didn't know how she could ever forgive him for putting them both through this.

Chapter 23

The boat silenced a little to the slowing of the engine as it pulled into the side just before the Rialto Bridge. Harriet hurried off, shoved forward by Tricia anxious to be off and on the canal bank alongside. With backs turned they waited anxiously for Andy and Barry.

'OK girls. It's just down there and up the steps. You should be able to pass a couple of hours browsing without too much difficulty. We'll meet you back here, say,' Andy looked at his watch, 'at about four.'

They were gone! Harriet looked at Tricia.

'The very fat one with the big red face `arriet. `e's the one I told to fuck off. You remember? When we were gettin` pushed along towards the stage. Just before the PM tripped over your `andbag `arriet. Just before `e went flyin`.'

'Yes Tricia, I remember only too well. You're right, unfortunately. Absolutely right. There's no mistaking them.'

'Of course there isn't `arriet. I'm almost certain it was them I came across in Switzerland, too, remember?'

'Yes, I remember Tricia. Now, where did they go? Did you manage to see where they went?'

'Well no `arriet. We were both lookin` this way weren't we? Oh `arriet I `ope we don't get kidnapped!'

'Well they thought they were on their way to San Marco Tricia. We weren't going there.'

'No `arriet! That's just it! They thought we were all on our way to San Marco. They're after us `arriet. I bet there's plenty of dungeons under those churches to `ide us in.'

'But why would they want to do that Tricia? What's in it for them?'

'Ransome money `arriet. They only `ave to wire the PM, `e's loaded and most probably threaten `im with a bit of blackmail. Don't forget `e's got a few dodgy MP's there `arriet. They're bound to `ave somethin` on `im. All we've got to do is `ope `e pays up.'

'No Tricia, it's Mr. Sanderson. I'm livid with him. He's wired the PM to get those two out here. They've probably checked the airports. It wouldn't be too difficult to locate us Tricia. They're either here to keep an eye on us to report our whereabouts or they'll actually whip us off back home. I haven't worked out which way it'll go yet.'

'Oh `arriet. I `ope you're right. It would be better than being kidnapped. I think we'd just better find somewhere to `ide and `ope for the best.'

'Easier said than done Tricia.'

'`arriet, I've got the answer. We can't `ang round `ere just waitin` to get caught. Look `is boat's still `ere `arriet. It's wide open. Let's get back on and `ide on the floor. `e said `e would be back in an `our to take it back to San Lucia. I'm sure we'd be able to find our way back to the `otel once we'd got off the train.'

No sooner the word! The pair of them lying flat, side by side on the floor of the boat with a whole forty-five minutes to wait.

'What about Andy and Barry, Tricia?' Harriet whispered.

'Well they `ave left us `arriet. We don't know where they've gone, do we? I don't think they'll be `angin` around `ere too long waitin` for us, do you?'

'No Tricia,' Harriet whispered, longing to be sat upright on one of the seats. 'What do we say to them though when we see them at the hotel? They've been so good. Shall we just explain?'

'Oh no `arriet, I wouldn't. We don't know anythin` about them really do we? And we do think there's somethin` fishy about them `arriet.'

'Well I must say there is something that makes me uneasy, but maybe that's because we don't know them very well. Barry was telling me he's just come through a horrendous divorce. It could be they're doing exactly the same as us. Just grabbing some breathing space.'

'Well they could be `arriet but I've got a sneaky feelin` there's somethin` else goin` on with the pair of them. `ave you not noticed they side-glance each other? A bit too much for my likin`.'

'Everyone does that Tricia.'

'No `arriet they do it and then they move away from us. I'm convinced there's more to them than meets the eye.'

'Oh watch that midge `arriet.' The boat rocked. 'There I've just `it it with my bag. I was goin` to get somethin` to get rid of these little buggers `arriet. Up there on that bridge. Oh I've `ad enough of this place. I wish `e'd `urry up and come back. It's very `ot down `ere `arriet. Do you think we could risk lyin` across the seats? Oh look `arriet they've left their `ats and shades. It would be a lot more comfortable up there.'

'No Tricia. It's best to stay put.' Harriet looked at her watch.

'There's only twenty-five minutes to go.'

Chapter 24

'`arriet. It's not them `eavies back is it?'

'No Tricia. It's people talking as they're walking past. We'll know when he's back.'

'It *is* voices `arriet, and not just the boatman!'

'We're looking for our hats. Must have left them here.'

The deep voice startled them from the horizontal. Harriet and Tricia jumped up to send the returning boatman and the two heavies into a backwards roll before plunging straight between the boats into the syrup of green water below. From the corner of her eye Harriet could just see them struggling to cling to the gondola they'd grabbed and overturned on their way down.

'Run for it!' Tricia panicked. Snatching the hats and sunglasses she clutched at Harriet as they both leapt off the boat. Pushing between the crowds, their legs could hardly catch up with their feet as they disappeared down the nearest side street.

'Keep goin `arriet. I'm sure someone will `ave fished them out. `e's not goin` to leave `is boat to chase us is `e?'

'He won't Tricia, I wouldn't say the same for the other two.'

'Well I'd say those two were just a teeny bit too porky to be chasin` after us `arriet.'

Oh I don't know Tricia,' Harriet panted. 'Just keep going!'

They ran, turning heads in narrow side streets, crossing bridges. Keeping well into the shop windows under the continuous stream of overhanging canopies. They flew, darting from one street to the next until they came to the market.

'What now?' Harriet puffed. 'It's all open here.'

'`ere `arriet put this on your `ead and `ave these shades. We won't be so easy to recognise then.'

'It might be better if we just walk Tricia, once we turn the corner.'

Like spent joggers they half walked, half ran, their shades and panama hats affording little protection from the glancing crowds bustling around the stalls.

'Come on `arriet let's move into the thick of it. Let's get into the middle, over there.'

Eyes down, they broke from the impossibility of their intention. Out of the thick of it now and sprinting, Harriet looked sideways.

'Keep your elbows in. Watch this lot,' she panted, trying to steer Tricia away from a rack of long dresses racing towards them. Tricia stepped sideways and behind managing to get her foot caught, tripping the angry merchant to the ground. She glanced down to see this short tubby man, fists raging, roll over with his legs in the air as the crowds gathered around, not unaware he'd been deprived of one long couture gown.

Her newly acquired wings flapped behind.

'I'm not stoppin` `arriet!' Tricia could barely get the words out.

A rush of angry, loud Italian streamed to their ears.

'Oh gosh Tricia. I hope he doesn't catch up with us. He'll think you were trying to pinch it.' Harriet looked up as she spoke.

'Pinch what `arriet?'

'Tricia keep your elbows in again. Watch that lot!'

Too late. Flying strawberries! She'd whacked the top off a heap piled high on the corner of the last table in the market. Squelching them underfoot they raced ahead; turning left, splashing their way through the water from the overflowing canal as it sloshed back and forth over the empty side of the pavement.

With the market well behind them now they panted their way down side streets and alleys in as straight a line as they could manage. Harriet pulled Tricia to a halt on the corner at the end of the dark narrow alley. Almost collapsed. She pointed to the canal straight ahead.

'I can't go any more Tricia,' Harriet panted, straightening the panama hat on her head.

'Neither can I `arriet.' She grabbed at the thing hooked to her hat.

'What's this on my `at `arriet? I thought I `ad somethin` flappin` be`ind me. `ang on `arriet. I'm puttin` it on.'

'It'll trip you up Tricia.'

'Disguise `arriet. Disguise. Look `arriet,' Tricia could hardly get the words out. 'There's a boat comin` like the one we came on. Look `arriet. It's empty. `e could do with a few passengers. Let's flag it down.'

'As long as it's *not the one* we came on,' Harriet declared just as it drew up alongside them.

The boatman, soaking wet, spoke in broken English.

Harriet and Tricia all but died. They hoped against hope their hats and shades would work for them.

'You goa? Where you goa?'

Harriet's thinking, decisive.

'No choice! We're exhausted. Either way he'll chase us.'

'Santa Lucia, per favore,' she panted, taking her purse from her bag. Bringing out the notes in the hope he'd understand.

'Si Signora!'

Harriet passed them over refusing to take any change. Waving the notes at her he pointed to Tricia and then the notes again.

'Uno? Due?'

'Si,' Harriet said, touching Tricia's arm and then her own.

This poor wet creature smiled weakly as he split the bundle to push half of it back.

'No, no.' She shook her head pointing to him.

'Grazie!'

He smiled rolling them to the wedge he'd just taken from his pocket. They slid past him to perch on the bench across the back. He hadn't appeared to remember them.

'But for how long?' Harriet thought. She jumped as he turned round.

'I goa Granda Canala? Si!' He brushed down his wet clothes then opened his hands.

'No, no,' Harriet panicked. No this way, per favore.'

'No! I goa Granda Canala. Rialto bridge, due uomini Si? Ragazze? Si? Girls? Si? Scomparso alla vista!' He held his nose and swam his arms around, before bending down. Aqua! Si!'

Harriet panicked, although his words meant nothing his rantings said it all.

'Santa Lucia grazie.' She pointed straight ahead, then stood to look at her watch before pointing down the canal again.

'Ah! Fai presto! I no goa back Granda Canala! Si?'

She breathed a sigh of relief.

'San Lucia?' was all she could say.

'Si! San Lucia.'

Harriet sat down again. Relieved to feel the boat moving along at last.

'San Lucia! Fai presto! Polizia!'

Horror drained away all attempts at further communication. Harriet and Tricia steeped in each other's expression remained silent. Between them they knew exactly what he meant. The boat hummed its way along the small criss-crossing ribbons of water to finally join the canal they'd first walked along on their way to the church. Relief surged through Harriet as she tried to signal recognition into Tricia's white expressionless face. Now almost frozen to her seat, it took the final left turn into the Grand Canal before she nudged Harriet. Just a faint smile. She knew where she was now. She pulled her hat further down her face. Pushed the sun glasses further up her nose. Harriet took a very deep breath. These last few metres seemed endless.

Under the bridge now, Harriet looked across to check her bearings by the road they'd first taken. They motored on down, both watching the canal sweeping back on itself, at last the final turn to the station.

Almost there. Harriet held her breath as he steered them into the landing stage, tossing a rope at the bollard. The tension setting his face as he pulled hard to secure the bow to the side, leaving the stern adrift. Alarmed. Desperate to escape. They watched him jump off as they both struggled to stand.

He walked in one small circle then scratched his head before kneeling to pull the swinging boat in.

'Grazi,' Harriet managed, pushing Tricia forward first.

Without waiting for a reply they quick marched forward to the main entrance of the railway station stumbling up the steps to get through.

Only when the wheels moved from under them as the train rolled away to leave the platform did they manage to control their shaking.

'Oh `arriet. At least it's still light. I'm glad we `aven't got to walk to the `otel through those back streets in the dark. I think we've `ad enough for one day.'

'I think we have Tricia. Is it safe to take these off yet?'

'Oh no `arriet. I think we'd be better leavin` them on. You never know who we might meet!' Cautiously she looked around.

'Do you think he suspected us Tricia? I thought for one moment he was going to leave us like that.'

'No `arriet, `e wouldn't `ave done. I'm sure if `e thought `e `ad us `e'd `ave been phonin` the police there and then on `is moby. I don't think `e would `ave allowed us to escape `arriet.'

'Oh Tricia. We can't do tomorrow. I don't think we can risk it. I just want to get away from this place as soon as we can. We're being followed Tricia. I'm absolutely furious with *him*. Involving the PM. Getting those two heavies to find us. After making great play of being so understanding as well.'

'No. You're absolutely right. You've been through a great deal of trauma `arriet `avin` Mark dump you like that. `e `asn't. `e doesn't care! It was like `im leavin` me at the airport with that case of `is. `e didn't care about gettin` me into trouble then, did `e? It could `ave `ad anythin` in it. I could `ave been accused of takin` through stolen goods `arriet for all `e cared.'

'I know Tricia.' Harriet went quiet. She'd been so pleased at the time he'd left Tricia to it.

Barely aware of crossing the lagoon, they silenced, anxious to get to Venice Mestre station and off the train for good.

'We've got to get back to the hotel as quickly as we can now Tricia. Let's see if we can't book a flight from our room and be away from here before the day's done.'

'You're right `arriet. Let's just `ope we can remember the way.'

Chapter 25

'Gosh Tricia I thought I knew the way back.'

'No `arriet. I think we should `ave turned left there. That's the one before the `otel road.'

'OK Tricia,' Harriet puffed. 'Let's go back.'

'This is right now `arriet. We are in the right road now. Look there's a car showroom over there. The `otel is just a bit further down on the other side.'

Harriet, relieved, slackened her pace.

'Tricia. I'm wondering if that place does taxis? We're never going to be able to book one over the phone.'

'Oh let's `ope so `arriet. It looks like it sells cars to me, but we'll `ave a look on our way past.'

They hurried towards it. Harriet's heart sank.

'You're right Tricia, it is a car showroom. I was mixing it up with the station.'

'I told you it was `arriet. We might be able to get the `otel to order one.'

'Come on Tricia. Keep going, let's find out.'

'Look `arriet. Just look. Let's go back. I'm sure I spotted a sign by that little place tucked in next door.'

'Tricia we don't speak Italian!'

'No `arriet I'm sure I saw the word taxi just out of the corner of my eye.'

"Autopubblica - aeroporto -Posteggio taxi." There `arriet I was right.'

Harriet looked at her watch. 'It's half past four Tricia, come on let's book it.'

'We `aven't even booked our flights yet `arriet.'

'I don't care Tricia. I'd rather spend the night in the airport than here. We'll do it while we're packing. You can throw my stuff into the case while I'm online.'

'Can you use your computer from `ere `arriet?'

'Yes Tricia just as long as the wifi works.'

They pushed the old wooden door open. Harriet beckoned the man at the counter to come outside. She raised her hand to the notice on the wall and pointed to the number five on the dial of her watch.

'Aeroporto Marco Polo, per favore.'

'Si!' The young man replied. They watched him write it down on the pad while Tricia cleaned her purse of notes. He took them, counting them out on the dark wooden counter beside him.

'Grazie!' He counted them out. Returned ten as he ticked the booking off. Harriet showed him the dial on her watch again leaving him smiling as they rushed away.

'Oh `arriet, slow down a bit. Let's cross over. I'm sure I saw a car stop outside that `ouse next door to the `otel. Well I did see one `arriet. Look it's just turnin` round.'

'It's probably a taxi dropping people off Tricia. I wouldn't worry about it.'

77

Tricia was already crossing the road.

'I don't know 'arriet. I've just got a funny feelin'. Oh I will be glad when we're both out of 'ere.'

The tall thin house looked back at them as they glanced at the venetian blinds still closed at the long narrow windows.

'There's somethin' goin' in there 'arriet. I'm sure of it. Oh I do 'ope we don't end up as 'ostages in there!'

'Hurry up Tricia. Let's make sure we don't!'

With all quiet in the hotel foyer they crept upstairs. Harriet slid the key card into the lock gently closing the door behind them. She opened the carry case, scrambling through the accessories to locate the adapter that would enable her to use her notebook. She plugged both ends in. No signal! She panicked.

'Bloody hell Tricia there's no signal!'

'Oh unplug it all and try again 'arriet. Just keep tryin' while I'm packin'.'

With stomach churning she breathed a sigh of relief as the first flickers of cooperation lit the screen.

'Flights Marco Polo to Manchester or Liverpool John Lennon Airport.' She watched the little line whiz the words away as she took it all out, suddenly remembering where she'd left the car. She tried again.

'Ah I've got it now Tricia.' She scrolled down to "Last Minute Flights".

'Right I'm booking this Tricia. There's one out to Manchester leaving at 19.32. Pass my bag please. Quick Tricia. Oh my credit card. It never wants to come out when I'm in a hurry.'

''ere 'arriet give me your purse. 'ere it is. I'll read it out. Go on start puttin' it in. Quick!'

'Gosh my hands are trembling. What was the code on the back again?'

'525 'arriet. And it nearly is. Ooh we'd better 'urry up.'

'Come on, come on. Don't give up now.'

At last the secure payment page. She entered her password. Her stomach in shreds.

'Oh thank goodness. It's the payment successful bit! Write this down Tricia, quick while I read it out. It's the booking reference number.'

'All done 'arriet. Let's go!'

'Oh thanks Tricia. Oh I got a fright then. Gosh packed already. You've done well with that.'

'Oh I don't know who's things went in where 'arriet. We can sort it all out when we get 'ome. I'm keepin' the dress 'arriet. Do you know it's one of the most expensive designer gowns you can get?'

'We're off Tricia. Have we got everything?'

'Oh bugger 'arriet! I've just remembered. We gave our passports in. We 'aven't got them 'ave we?'

'Oh no! There's no one around to ask Tricia. Bloody hell Tricia what *are* we going to do now?'

'We're going to 'ave to look for them 'arriet. They might be under the counter down there.'

'But they won't be out Tricia. They'll be locked away somewhere.'

'`arriet, come on we're goin` to `ave to find them.'

Chapter 26

Harriet, with both cases at her feet propped her jellied legs up against the counter in the foyer while Tricia struggled underneath searching in vain.

'No 'arriet they 'aven't left any under 'ere. Oh just a minute 'arriet, there's a filing cabinet over there.'

'Locked Tricia!' She looked at her watch. 'The taxi will be waiting now Tricia. We'll have to go.'

'We can't go anywhere without them 'arriet. Just a minute 'arriet. Pass me your keys. Quick!'

'You can try them all Tricia but you won't find anything there to open that.'

'Don't you be so sure 'arriet! What 'ave you been usin' this little bit of wire 'angin' on the end 'ere for?'

'Oh Tricia. Mr. Sanderson gave it me to open the filing cabinet at home. Try it Tricia! Try it!'

'Oh no 'arriet. It's not doin' anythin' I'm afraid.'

'Come here Tricia. He said it never fails. Let me try. Let's just see if I can manage it.'

'Ooh 'arriet. 'ad I better be runnin' down to tell the taxi man to wait?'

'No! I've done it Tricia. Look they're here. All the passports. Alphabetical order. G and H. At least they're together. I've got them.'

'Just bang it closed 'arriet and let's get out of 'ere before we're spotted.'

'It won't close Tricia!'

'Oh 'arriet,' Tricia insisted from the doorway. 'Leave it then. Come on let's go!'

''ang on a minute one of those bouncers soakin' wet 'as just come out of that 'ouse next door and gone back in again. 'ow could they 'ave got back before us? At least 'e's alive 'arriet. Now! Quick 'arriet. No! I've just seen those venetian blinds move. Oh they've closed them again. NOW 'arriet run as fast as you can!'

Flying now. Veering towards the taxi Harriet looked back. Already three minutes past five.

'Get in Tricia! They're after us!'

They scrambled into the back, hurling their cases at the driver.

''urry up with that boot lid will you,' Tricia muttered pulling Harriet right down.

In a tick he was back. At the wheel. The gross men. Their wet sleeves against the windows just jumping clear of the cab as it moved away to the blast of the horn.

'Second time today 'arriet. They'll be thinkin' their number's up. Let's 'ope it's third time lucky. Get rid of them once and for all.'

'Ooh we can't wish that on them Tricia. Prison will do.'

'Oh yes we can 'arriet. They wouldn't think twice if it was the other way round.'

'The driver, `e's cursing non-stop Italian at them. Look `is `ead's out the window. I `ope `e remembers `e's got our lives in `is `ands. Look! They're tryin` to run. They're leggin` it back to the `ouse. I do `ope they're not goin` to follow us `arriet.'

Harriet, shaking, refused to look.

'They `*ave* been spyin` on us and that's where they've been stayin`! Oh `arriet I've gone all creepy.'

Chapter 27

'Ooh `arriet, we only just made it. I can't say I enjoyed going through security though. I'm sure this panic was showin` all over my face.'

'Me too Tricia. Sitting in the departure lounge for two hours was a complete nightmare. I was convinced they'd be flying back with us.'

They were climbing. Looking down to the airport, scaling down now as the plane gathered speed. Below them the land. A tapestry of tiny coloured blocks set in differing shapes and patterns against the backcloth of green.

'We're still `oldin` these.' Tricia looked down to the panama hat on her lap. 'Maybe they wanted them back `arriet. Ooh, I do `ope we don't get done for pinchin` them.'

'We've got a lot more to worry about than that Tricia when we get home.'

'Oh we `ave `aven't we `arriet. What day is it? Oh it's Wednesday `arriet and we've both missed two days work. Your Joris isn't going to be too pleased about that.'

'That's the least of it Tricia. I was supposed to be in church with him on Sunday to hear the banns. Not to mention just disappearing. He'll be furious.'

'Oh `arriet we `ave been a teeny bit irresponsible `aven't we?'

'I'd say so Tricia. There's Josh, too. He'll be doing a head count tomorrow morning and he won't have a clue where we are.'

'Oh no `arriet and I do `ope Andy and Barry aren't still waitin` for us by the Rialto Bridge. And `im `arriet, the boatman. I `ope `e `asn't come to `is senses and realised it was us `e brought back to San Lucia this afternoon.'

Harriet sneezed. Brought the hotel key card out with her hanky.

'Oh bless you `arriet. You're not catchin` a cold I `ope?'

'We should have left this somewhere Tricia.'

'Oh arriet, we broke into the safe as well. I do `ope we don't get arrested when we get off the plane.'

Chapter 28

'At least we got through customs,' Harriet panted.

'Oh I know `arriet. I'll feel a lot better once we get to the car though.'

'Same here. I don't care if Mark's there or not. I just want to get back home. Oh we go over there. Long stay car park, it's pointing that way.'

'There's yours right on the end. Oh I'm glad it's still `ere arriet.' Tricia struggled the words out.

Both in. Less than a tick! Harriet reversed, then forward. They were on their way.

'At least we didn't get arrested. Well not yet `arriet. We've got to be very thankful for that.'

'Oh I am Tricia. Believe you me I am.'

'What will we do `arriet? Bob will be furious. I've `ad four secret nights away and `e won't `ave taken the kids. My mum will be gettin` very fed up with them by now. Not that I'm bothered about `im. `e's lucky I'm comin` back at all. And it will only be until I marry your Mark `arriet. That's if you've really `ad enough of `im?'

'Too right Tricia. I've had enough of him and I've had more than enough of Mr. Sanderson. I'm absolutely furious with him Tricia. I can't believe he got in touch with the PM to arrange for those heavies to be sent out like that.'

'Will you still be marryin` `im `arriet?'

'That remains to be seen. Actually no! That's the way I'm feeling right now.'

'What will you do then `arriet? `ow are you goin` to cope with Mark livin` at your `ouse?'

Harriet paused for a moment to allow herself time to get round the roundabout and on to the motorway.

'I think it's unlikely Tricia. He didn't turn up on Saturday night, did he? If he'd meant what he'd said he'd have staked his claim then.'

'Ooh I do `ope you're right `arriet. I don't think I'd like to be in your shoes.'

Harriet went very quiet. Almost in denial, she'd convinced herself it would all be the same as last time. No pregnancy then so not pregnant now.

'I'll tell Tricia. No I won't. I won't just in case.' She let the thought trail away as fast as the motorway behind them.

'It won't be long now `arriet. I do `ope we don't find the police on our doorstep. I `ope we `aven't been reported as missin` persons. Missin` wanted persons `arriet.'

'I know. It's really scary Tricia. At least the boatman didn't drown, so we can't be done for manslaughter.'

'Oh don't `arriet. You're really frightenin` me now. What about that gown `arriet? Will I be accused of stealin` it? And these `ats `arriet and the shades. I `ope those `eavies don't want them back.'

'Not to mention breaking into the filing cabinet Tricia and I've still got the hotel key card.'

'Oh 'arriet and that market trader I tripped up. I 'ope 'e's still alive. Oh I 'ope 'e didn't bang 'is 'ead and die. Oh 'arriet I don't want to be servin' a life sentence. Do you think it might be better if we spend the night in your shed again 'arriet? It would give us chance to get our 'eads together.'

'Good thinking Tricia. At least we'll be safe for tonight.'

Chapter 29

'Ooh I'm glad we're nearly 'ome. That's good 'arriet I've just looked back down your road and I didn't see any cars on your drive. I think it'll be safe for you to park on yours.'

'You're joking Tricia. We're going to have to walk back. I'll leave this alongside yours for tonight.'

'Good thinkin' 'arriet. Your car on the drive might just be a giveaway.'

'You'll have to point me in the right direction Tricia. Will there be room for this alongside?'

'Oh yes 'arriet. You know that short road with the bungalows in. 'ere 'arriet, it's the turn off at the bottom of this one. It's a cul-de-sac with a bit of waste ground at the end before you get to the football field.'

'Oh yes I know where you are now Tricia,' said Harriet, taking a left turn. 'It's left again at the bottom, isn't it?'

'That's right 'arriet. Just keep goin' left.'

'That's it. Oh no Tricia, where's your car?'

'Bloody 'ell 'arriet it's not there! It's gone missin'. I left it just there, parked alongside this bush 'ere. Oh no 'arriet. That's all I need. I wonder if it's been pinched? Or 'as Bob found it and taken it 'ome?'

'It could have been Bob. They're bound to have been looking for us. After all we did go missing.'

'I need it for work 'arriet. That's if I've still got my job. 'ow am I goin' to get there now?'

'I'll give you a lift Tricia. Don't panic. Let's go and see if it's on your drive.'

'Oh 'arriet I don't want to be seein' Bob.'

'We won't stop we'll just drive past.'

'What 'ave we done? I do 'ope you're right. I do 'ope it's there.'

'We'll soon find out Tricia. Just a couple more minutes.'

Harriet tried to keep calm as they turned into Tricia's road. She pulled to a halt.

'We'll 'ave to go right down 'arriet. It's not like yours. You can't see over the 'edge from 'ere.'

'OK Tricia. Do you want me to wait here while you go and look or shall we just drive past?'

'That's a good idea 'arriet. You wait 'ere while I duck down. We won't be drawin' attention to ourselves then. 'e's always lookin' out of the window, the minute 'e 'ears a car. I'm sure 'e thinks 'e'll see 'er, all love-sick dyin' for a glimpse of 'is 'ouse.'

Harriet smiled. With the engine ticking over she watched Tricia's walk stoop to a crawl as she neared the house. She glanced in her mirror. A car revving behind. Someone turning in. Driving past now. Tricia's car! Bob at the wheel! Tricia on hands and knees still, peering round the gate post. Bob screeching to a halt. In a flash! Out! Marching Tricia in.

For a moment Harriet sat there dazed. Frozen. Then she panicked. She had Tricia's case in the car. It suddenly gained unprecedented importance as she decided to drop it in. Then decided not to. Then decided they should face the inevitable anger together. Switching now from one state to the other. In a complete pelt. Her stomach churning. Energy draining fast. With hands limp at the steering wheel and several attempts at a three point turn she drove back, trembling at the thought of facing the onslaught of wrath from all sides. Not least from Mr. Sanderson. Then horror of horrors. She turned into The Willows to spot Mark's car on the drive.

'Oh no Tricia you got the wrong house. You've just told me it wasn't there!'

Her thoughts came crashing in. She took a very deep breath. Didn't know how she'd deal with it.

Chapter 30

'Like old times Harriet!'

'No. Not like old times Mark! I wasn't expecting to meet *you* on the drive. Popping up from under the bonnet. Like that.'

'I live here Harriet. Remember?'

'Not on Saturday night you didn't Mark. You didn't come back then.'

'That doesn't forfeit my right to return. I can come and go exactly as I please. Just as you can. And do. Here, let me give you a hand with that case. So you saw common sense after reading my note and took yourself off, right out of his life.'

Another shock. She felt sick, almost as bad as Saturday morning.

'You're not looking too good at all Harriet. Where the devil have you both been, anyway? Bob and the kids have been going up the wall with worry. The pair of you totally irresponsible! I've had nothing but lard ball and your sodding mother on the phone for the last four days. It was *him* that got you back wasn't it? He said he'd put the feelers out.'

'Oh he did that alright. We've only been followed by a couple of the PM's heavies since we got there.'

'Serves you right Harriet. You've been playing with fire. I said you didn't know what you'd be getting yourself into with him. Perhaps you've finally got it through your thick head you're completely out of your depths. I was right. You were never the one to take any notice of me though Harriet.'

She followed him into the house. No packing boxes around. Everything back in its place. Almost surreal as if none of it had ever happened. Her head spinning like a treadless tyre squealing against ice.

'I've got to sit down Mark. I think I'm going to pass out.'

He ushered her to the kitchen. Pulled the chair away from the table. Placed her head well down between her knees.

Consciousness returning. Cold water smashing into the kettle. Mark clicking the switch. She went to move.

'Come up slowly Harriet.'

Same words. Same advice. Saturday morning flooding back. In *his* car. Her head down. Buried in the silk of her long blue dress.

'There Harriet. There's plenty of sugar in it. Just take a couple of sips and let me get you to bed. Then I'll bring it up.'

'Thanks Mark.' She reached for his hand.

'Loosen everything and lie down.' He grabbed his pillows. Propped them behind her.

'I'll get your tea. Just lie still for a moment.'

Just him going downstairs. Harriet trying to fight this overwhelming sense of comfort. She didn't want this. She wanted to think things through. He'd ditched her. She needed to ask.

'Thanks Mark. Oh the best cup of tea for days, but why are you doing this?'

'Because you've come to your senses Harriet. And so have I. I've been worried sick.'

'But what about Melissa, Mark? You turned me down for Melissa! Why would you want to be worried sick about me?'

'This isn't the time for setting the record straight. I'm not taking any more calls today either. Let them wonder. The lot of them. The best thing you can do now is sleep. You look exhausted. We'll talk tomorrow.'

Harriet, propped against four pillows lay staring out of the window searching her mind for the rationale behind Mark's kindness. She sipped her tea Then realisation. 'He thinks I've finished with *him*!'

Anger rising now.

'How could *he* have had us followed like that? Trying to frighten us back. We could have ended up hostages tied up in that spooky house next to the hotel. He couldn't legislate for the way they chose to handle it. Mark's right. I *have* finished with *him*!'

She looked down. A little black face jumping towards her. She breathed a sigh of relief as it curled itself into a purring ball alongside. Grateful to be in bed at 4 The Willows. Grateful Mark had refused to complete the house deal. Grateful she'd been spared marriage to Mr. Sanderson. Wondering what else she didn't know about him. Wondering what Belinda Oxfordshire had told Mark. Wondering what Mark had written in the note.

She placed her empty cup on the side. Wriggled out of her jeans. From under her blouse she slipped the hooks undone on her white lace bra. Nudged the top two pillows back to Mark's side of the bed. Closed her eyes and drifted into a deep, deep sleep. Tomorrow wasn't on the agenda.

Chapter 31

Harriet awoke. The other end of the duvet flung towards her. The pillows at her side sunken to the middle. She yawned and stretched to Mark thudding himself and the tray up the stairs.

'Tea Harriet. You didn't have any trouble sleeping last night, unlike me. I've been awake all bloody night! You were certainly doing the rounds with someone. It's a wonder you didn't wake yourself up.'

'Oh, thanks Mark. I don't remember a thing. And certainly not sleeping with you. I don't believe you're being this horrible after being so nice to me last night. Anyway, it's my bed. You could always have gone next door. I didn't ask you to get in.'

'Oh so could you have gone next door Harriet. It's my bed too, remember? You didn't exactly have any problems last night, I noticed.'

'I was exhausted Mark. I'd have slept wherever you'd put me.'

'Quite Harriet! Oh don't worry. I wasn't of a mind to ravish you in the night. Not after you've been with *him*. That will certainly take some coming to terms with.'

'Oh would it now? And what about you Mark? You and Melissa. Just how do you think that makes me feel? And ditching me on our wedding day! You couldn't have left me in a worse state.'

'I did the honest thing Harriet. I wasn't about to marry you. But even if I was you'd have gone ahead and married me. Kept it all to yourself having it off with him. Moved to Millington in the hope I'd never have found out.'

'No Mark! I was …' Harriet stopped herself. Lifted the mug of hot tea to her lips. She mustn't tell him about wanting to take him to the vestry.

She silenced. A tsunamic realisation crashing through her mind.

'You were what Harriet?' He refused to let go.

'I was going to give you the chance to pull out. That's all.'

'You could have done that over the phone Harriet.'

'No it was a last minute thing. I didn't want to push you over the top. And as it happened I was right.'

The best she could do. At least it was half true. She felt vulnerable. Reached round her back, struggling with her bra. Trying to catch the hooks to the eyes. Finally managed it.

'The note you left Mark?'

'Yes Harriet. The reason you came back. At the time I didn't want to let you go. I was only asking for the chance to stay just as we were. No bit of paper. None of this legal stuff. We'd managed for long enough. Until lard ball slid in from under. Before I knew he'd fucking had it off with you! Now it's different Harriet. You've come back to me but now I'm not so sure. We'll just have to see how and if it works out.'

She gasped! Absolutely speechless. She'd walked straight into it. Hadn't read the note. Hadn't wanted to. Never in a million years could she have guessed that's what was in it. She couldn't bring herself to tell him she hadn't read it. Didn't know how. Didn't know where to start. Thought he'd misunderstand.

'How and if it works out Mark. That's good coming from you. You who've been with Melissa.'

'You already knew about that when you decided to come back to me Harriet.'

'Well maybe I haven't quite decided on that yet Mark. Maybe I'll just go off with someone else and let you all get on with it.'

Barry. She could see him standing back, smiling at her. Tall, artistic, quietly spoken. She owed him money. She'd given him Melissa Scott's address. Wished she hadn't now.

'So you were planning on leaving lard ball standing at the church then in three weeks time? That's good Harriet. I like that, except he wouldn't be there.'

'What are you talking about Mark, he wouldn't be there?'

'I decided to make one call after all last night Harriet. Just one to tell him you've come back to me.'

'Bloody hell Mark. You had absolutely no right whatsoever to do that. That was up to me. What did he say?'

'He said he'd speak to you in school on Friday morning.'

'What about today, why leave it until then?'

'Because I told him that would be the earliest you'd be in.'

'Well thanks for that, at least. What else did he say?'

'Nothing else. That was it Harriet.'

Harriet went quiet. Lay back on the pillows just staring at the ceiling. She rested her hand on her stomach trying to stop it from churning. The foetus inside her nearly three weeks old now. Mr. Sanderson's baby growing inside her. Mark knowing nothing of it! Asked herself, 'Just how deep can this hole get?' Turned to Mark.

'Just what was it Belinda Oxfordshire told you about *him*, Mr. Sanderson? What did he do to her that was so terrible she wanted him back?'

'I promised to keep it confidential Harriet. You don't need to know that.'

'Yes I do Mark. I want to know that. After dumping me the least you can do is tell me. I'm not going to be telling anyone, I give you my word.'

Mark fixed his eyes to hers. His face serious.

'I'll tell you Harriet but DON'T mention it to Tricia or anyone else. It's deeply personal to Belinda Oxfordshire. She only told me in a fit of pique because of lard ball announcing his marriage to you.'

'Get on with it Mark. I'm not going to tell anybody.'

'Apparently she was pregnant. She wanted the baby. He didn't. He offered to marry her if she agreed to an abortion, by him, Harriet. That's how they got engaged.'

Harriet gasped.

'But he broke it off Mark.'

'Yes no doubt because of you. After putting her through all that he broke it off. Obviously didn't want the remorse bit from her backfiring on him. It shows him for the low life he is. And the stupid woman still wanted him back. That's why she's had it in for you all along. She knew you'd chase him all the way to the alter.'

Harriet wriggled herself down the bed, pulling the sheet up to her nose. Crimson. Anxious to speak.

'That is just absolutely unbelievable! I would never have put him down for doing that. He's a doctor Mark. That would have been unethical. Oh no, I really don't see it. She's got to be making it up.'

'I don't think so Harriet. You think about it. In my opinion lard ball suits himself. The number of times you've told me he's never been in school. Leaves it all to his deputy no doubt. Doesn't give a damn about anyone. I wouldn't put it past him to play just that kind of trick on you Harriet.'

'He's already offered me marriage Mark. We were supposed to be getting married three weeks tomorrow.'

'Oh he might have married you Harriet. But that baby you've been desperate for. Even if he'd relented to please you and you'd managed it with him, how long would you have been allowed to stay pregnant living here? No Harriet. He wouldn't have wanted his first born sculling round this place. Not here. Not in 4 The Willows. Being brought up in this old semi. You've got to be joking. What's the betting if you'd got pregnant and refused to move into his gingerbread house an abortion wouldn't have been on the cards for you, too.'

Harriet felt sick. "Save that for me." That's what he'd said. Her baby OK then. But not Belinda Oxfordshire's. He didn't need to get her pregnant. A doctor. With a fetish for abortions? Her world turned black. Never ending nothingness. No way in. No way out. Then a torrent of nerves, spewing like hot volcanic ash lighting the void. Burning her mind. Hell! Like she was tumbling to the centre of the earth.

She turned over. Tried in her mind to work it out. He'd disappeared for ages last summer.

'Was that it? Was that why? But it doesn't make sense. He couldn't do that. Suppose I don't really know him. Suppose it's true? I'm better out of it. But I'm pregnant. Why oh why did I let him do that? I might not be. It's early days. These testing kits are not always right.'

Of all the holes she'd ever dug herself she knew this had to be the deepest. She needed a solution. Thought about Barry. Felt if she could just talk it all through he'd come up with the answer.

'I've got to go into work today Harriet. I've taken too much time off already on your account. Oh and I won't be hanging around when I get back. I'm straight off to the club tonight.'

'Not at my request Mark. I didn't ask you to take time off work. OK so I'm back. You're back. We live under the same roof, for the time being at least. It means no more than that. Between us we've managed to screw the whole thing up. Goodness knows what Clare and Rachael will make of it all. There's my parents, your parents, his parents.'

'It's got sod all to do with any of them Harriet. We'll take this a step at a time. In our own time.'

'And what about Melissa Scott Mark? At least I thought you were up for her lovely mummy-in-law.'

'Marriage isn't on the cards with anyone Harriet. If you hadn't spent so much of our lives pushing for it we wouldn't be in this mess now.'

'So it's all my fault? I don't think so Mark. Not for one minute is it all my fault.'

'Oh it is Harriet. Lard ball's been a challenge you couldn't resist regardless of your feelings for me. Well let's hope you've learnt your lesson now you've had your fingers well and truly burnt. Just steer clear of him!'

'And will you steer clear of Melissa Scott. Mark?'

'I might. I might not.'

'And I might or might not then. It's just as it's always been. We're both free to please ourselves.'

Chapter 32

Friday morning. Even with Mark at work Harriet hadn't enjoyed the last couple of days. Mark sanctimonious. A different atmosphere now. Their proximity intense. Unsatisfactory. Harriet vulnerable. Angry. Scared. Frustrated at drawing comfort from a disagreeable familiarity. Hating the paradox. It did little for her anger towards Mr. Sanderson. Now dreading seeing him. Just the first in a long line of people. She looked at her watch. Time to go. She didn't know how she'd have the energy, either, to face a class of children all day.

Pushing the cat away from her legs she threw her bags into the back of the car.

'See you later Pepper.' She waited. Watched it jump up and over the side gate. Safely out of the way. This was one confidante she couldn't afford to lose. Backing off the drive she thought about Tricia. Wondered if she'd already returned to work to face the music.

She stopped at the lights as they changed to red outside Starboard Marine North West. Glanced across. Saw her car.

'At least she survived Bob to tell the tale.' She wondered how she'd dealt with it. She needed to talk to her. Decided to phone just as soon as she got in from school.

The school entrance. All too soon. Harriet groaned. Thought.

'Oh no! Mr. Brown. Why do you insist on caretaking round the front. Every time I drive in you're there. Get lost!'

No chance. Harriet and Mr. Brown. Antagonists! No one could persuade him she didn't have it in for him. She'd inadvertently attacked the poor man so many times for long enough he'd taken to fleeing at first sight. Not any more though. Lately he'd been standing his ground. Now in the doorway. A smirk on his face. She drove past. Parked as far away from Mr. Sanderson's car as space would allow. Grabbed her bags. Locked the car and headed towards him.

'So you managed to pull it off then?' He sniggered.

'Excuse me Mr. Brown I'd rather like to get in please.'

'I expect it'll take a bit of time to repair the damage 'arriet Glover.'

'It's absolutely none of your business Mr.Brown. It's about time you stopped lurking in doorways and got on with your job for a change. The last thing I need this morning is being met by you.' Her head well down now 'You miserable old devil!'

Harriet, furious, pushed past him to go straight to her classroom. Decided she'd take no nonsense from anyone. Not him. Not the kids. And certainly not Mr. Sanderson.

'If he wants me, he can find me!' She decided.

She tucked her blouse back into her skirt, expecting the worst. Sensed gossip rushing towards her as she hurried along the corridors. 'Dumped at the church to be bailed out by *him*! If Mr. Brown knows, so will the whole school,' she thought. 'It's nothing to do with anyone. Be brisk. Just refuse to be drawn in Harriet.'

She'd hardly finished thinking the sentence when the door flew open. *Him?* She jumped. 'Not now, surely? Not when the whole class are about to arrive.'

'Oh `ello Miss.'

'Hello Mrs. Bustard. Danny. Everything alright?'

'Now you're back it is. We were sorry to `ear you've not been well. Are you feelin` better now? Our Danny's really missed you. `e `as. I'm not kiddin` you. `e said `e wouldn't be comin` back to this rubbish school if you weren't comin` back.'

Harriet smiled.

'Yes, I'm fine thank you Mrs Bustard. Everything OK now with you and Mr. Bustard?'

'It is thanks to you Miss Glover. It's just like you said. `e can't wait to go on that `oliday to Butlins. Oh and `e's gone right off onions. I don't `ave to be frizzlin` and fryin` them anymore. And the best thing Miss is `e's never late `ome from work now. `e's seen that Mrs. Atkins for the little tart she is. I don't think the `ead's very keen on `er either. It didn't look that way to me on `is boat Miss Glover. But you've been away, `aven't you? You won't `ave `eard the news. Well we all thought

Mr. Sanderson `ad is eye on Miss Lawton `is new deputy and now we know. It's all over the school. She `asn't been in all week either. Rumour `as it `e proposed to `er and they'll be gettin` married in three weeks time. Fast worker that `eadmaster Miss Glover. Anyway it's nice to `ave you back. Keep an eye on our Dannybabes will you, `e's turned into a right little bugger since you've been away.'

'Bloody Lucinda Lawton! Someone's got their wires crossed but then there's no smoke without fire.' Harriet raged at the prospect all day. And what a day she'd had of it. What a day with Danny. Mrs. Bustard had never spoken a truer word. Harriet on edge. No sight of Mr. Sanderson. Spent all day prising Danny from clusters of fighting kids. His banana sitting on the shelf behind her desk. Confiscated. He'd given it away and grabbed it back so many times Harriet had lost count. She passed it over to Mrs. Bustard at 3.30 glad to be closing the door on them all.

'Not the best start to the day Miss Glover!'

She jumped. Him against the door. Pushing his way into her room. Banging it shut. Striding towards her. Startled. Bright red. She put her hands to her face.

'Sit down Miss Glover.'

He moved to the other side. Sat himself full square in front. Angry. His hair settling in the broad slips his fingers were making as he ran them sharply through.

'Brown Miss Glover. Another complaint. Didn't take to being called a miserable old devil! Such rudeness totally uncalled for.'

Harriet gasped.

'His words to me were anything but polite Mr. Sanderson. "So you managed to pull it off then. It will take some time to repair the damage." It's actually got absolutely nothing to do with him.'

She watched the layers of thick blonde hair settle again as he shook his head, impatient to move on.

'I would say it has Miss Glover. It's not inconceivable he should think you were responsible for backing into his wire-mesh cone store, pulling out the metal stays and half the wall with it. Yours was the last car parked there last Friday and as you haven't appeared since he's naturally assuming you were responsible. Were you Miss Glover?'

'No I most definitely was not. I parked round the back only because it was full out there at the front. Haven't asked around? Why assume it's me?'

'Damage done Miss Glover. It will get repaired. It's hardly here nor there in the face of your current performance. Just make sure you catch Brown and apologise will you?'

Harriet took a deep breath. He certainly wasn't on her side.

'Now! Where in fucking hell have you two been exactly?'

'I think you already know that Mr. Sanderson.'

'I don't ask superfluous questions Miss Glover. Do you realise just what you've put me through over these last few days?'

Harriet hung her head. Looked down at her skirt.

'Your family. My family. And presumably the rest of the world by now know the pair of you did a runner. Utterly and totally irresponsible behaviour Miss Glover! I can't believe my own folly in getting embroiled with you. OK so even if we put it all down to stress; your decision to stay with Mark, and have him inform me of it! Well! I'm lost for words Miss Glover! Didn't you feel I deserved a little more courtesy than that?'

He moved on giving her no chance to reply.

'Of course it goes without saying there will be no wedding in three weeks time. Not only do you dig yourself into the deepest of holes you have the gall to take others down with you. No! It's the end of the road Miss Glover!'

'No Mr. Sanderson, San Marco that was the end of the road for us.'

'San Marco? So you've been to Venice. That's where you decided it was all off indeed. Well let me remind you Miss Glover you're carrying my baby. You still are, aren't you?'

Harriet looked up. Didn't answer.

'Miss Glover I have a right to know. Are you or are you not still pregnant?'

'I think I must still be.'

'This is something we're going to have to sort out Miss Glover!'

He hit the table-top hard as he banged his hand down to stand, sending the few loose papers flying. She turned. Watched him stride off. Furious, she gathered her bags cutting through the fire exit to her car. Needed to get out and away before him. She screeched out of the gateway without a glance in her rear mirror. All she wanted was to get back to 4 the Willows.

Chapter 33

'Oh, out of the way Pepper. Just let me get in. Thank goodness it's the weekend.'

She opened the door to the answer machine furiously winking at her. She pressed it. Glad of the distraction. Livid with him. About to try the same thing on her as Belinda Oxfordshire. Wanting to get rid of her baby himself.

'No chance Pepper. Absolutely no chance!'

'Harriet! Daddy and I are hoping you are back. We've had no word from anyone. We can't hide our fury Harriet you have behaved atrociously with that common girl. Well that's exactly what you did to that poor man. Isn't it? Went off with her, leaving him worried sick. I don't know how many times he's been on to James trying to get news of you. After that beautiful speech in the church as well Harriet. James and Geraldine and your daddy and I can't believe it. What is the matter with you Harriet? It was the one sensible thing you'd ever done in the whole of your life and you decide to turn him down in the most despicable of ways. It wouldn't have been half so bad if I hadn't phoned all my WI friends with the good news on Saturday afternoon. You've made me look a fool Harriet. A complete and utter fool. Goodness knows what kind of a fool you've made Sir Joris Sanderson look. A Sir! You had the chance to become one of the titled Harriet and you threw it all away. Goodness knows what his mother thinks. Olivia and I were getting on so well, too. I do hope you haven't taken a fancy to that common girl Harriet. It happens you know. You seem to think more of her than all of us put together. I shouldn't think even Mark would want you back now. Though even that would be better than you spending the rest of your life behaving like some silly school girl with that one. Now you give me a call Harriet just as soon as you can. Daddy and I are out of our minds with worry. The best we can hope is it's all due to the menopause. Though never in all my life have I heard it taking anyone the way it's taken you. Alright Daddy I'm coming. I'll save the rest for when she phones back. That's if she ever does.'

Harriet took a deep breath. 'Oh Pepper! Why does she always get the wrong end of the stick? That would be just as daft as me telling her she fancies all her friends in the WI. She won't be saying that in a few months time Pepper. Not when it starts to show. Oh gosh Pepper how could he want to get rid of it? Gosh have I seen a side to that man I could never have dreamed existed.'

She lifted the cat. It's soft fur comforting against her arms. Pressed the button for the next message.

'Good morning. This is Suzie from Hotonyourheelstravel.com. A message for Harriet Glover. You booked a package holiday to Venice with us last Sunday 27 June and made an independent return with Mrs. Harrington I understand. Now there are some outstanding issues which we need to discuss with you. Could you please return this call on our Head Office number. Thank you.'

'At least it's not the police Pepper.' She clung to the cat feeling her stomach sink. She wondered how long her tiny baby could survive the onslaught of stress hormones threatening her body.

'I've got to phone Tricia, Pepper. No, hang on. Let me feed you first.'

'Hi Tricia. It's you! Thank goodness you're there. How did you get on with Bob? Talk about bad timing! He drove past me just as you were getting in, didn't he? Were you OK?'

'Oh `arriet. No. No and I'm still not OK. I've `ad `im round my feet watchin` me all the time. When `e decides to come back from bein` with `er that is. I'm sorry I `aven't been able to get back to you what with `im and my mum and the kids. Do you know `e marched me in and wiped the floor with me `arriet. `*im* wipin` the floor with *me* after the way `e's been be`avin`. We only went on a little `oliday `arriet there was nothin` wrong with that. Anyway I threatened to walk out on `im and then I said on second thoughts `e could go. Go and live with `er if she'd `ave `im. So do you know `arriet `e said `e'd go in `is own good time and I was quite at liberty to take the kids to my mum's and stay there forever. Well that would just `ave suited `im down to the ground `arriet. The `ouse all to `imself and no kids to bother `im so `e could spend all `is time smellin` `is designer aftershave and smilin` at `imself in the mirror. "You've got to be bloody jokin`" I told `im. I said I now `ad other fish to fry and from now on I'd be sleepin` in the back bedroom.'

'Gosh Tricia, we're almost in the same boat.'

'Now `arriet I don't want you to get me wrong but can we leave those metathingies out of it. Especially the ones that sound like boats. I `aven't forgiven `im either for wipin` the floor with me. I've `ad enough of Starboard Marine North West `arriet and that big posh lump rantin` and ravin` at me. My `ead's splittin`. I `aven't got enough room in it to take not one more metathingy on board. Oh you've got me doin` it now `arriet. The only way I can put `im out of my mind is to leave `arriet but I can't. I need my job for when I leave Bob. Which will be any day now, I can tell you!'

'What happened with Mr. Sanderson Tricia? He's just given me a pasting. I'll tell you something. The wedding's definitely off. Who'd want to marry *him*?'

'Not Belinda Oxfordshire `arriet. She's `ell bent on Bob. Do you know `e didn't touch a bit of washin` while we were away. I `ad to do it all. I was empyin` `is pockets and didn't I just find a note in the back pocket of `is jeans. "To my sweetest Chirpy Cheeks, What a Monday!" it started `arriet. I don't know whether she meant `is bum or `is face. Anyway it went on "Mr Passion Pants, You're as hot as a cinder. Come back tonight and light up Belinda." She's probably `ad a few poems off Guy `ammer like you did `arriet. Gave `er the idea. Bloody `ell `arriet we were only away for a few days it didn't take `im long did it? `e must `ave stayed off work then. It's finished `arriet. It's the end of the road with `im. What was it Andy or was it Barry said in Venice about the end of the road?'

'I think it was Barry, Tricia, on our way down the Grand Canal to St. Mark's Square. He said "San Marco the end of the road." '

'Yes that was it 'arriet and it most certainly is for 'im. I reckon 'e was probably 'avin' it off with 'er at the very same time as we got there. That was Monday too, wasn't it 'arriet?'

'It was Tricia and I've just listened to a message the travel agent left. I've got to phone them back. I'm not looking forward to it.'

'Oh no 'arriet. You've still got the 'otel key 'aven't you? And we opened the filin' cabinet ourselves to get the passports. Oh 'arriet I've been so furious with Bob I 'aven't 'ad room in my brain for anythin' else.'

'When did you go back to work Tricia?'

'Only today 'arriet. I 'aven't seen our friend Joris though, not today. Do you know 'e 'ad the cheek to come round 'ere yesterday mornin'. It was a good job I was on my own. The kids were in school and we both know where Bob 'ad spent the night, don't we?'

'Oh gosh Tricia. I'm so sorry it's all piled up on you like this.'

'I could see it comin' 'arriet. That's why I wanted to get away in the first place. Anyway as I was sayin', he invited 'imself in, then accused me of leadin' you astray!'

'Oh Tricia! He never did that, surely?'

'Oh yes 'e did 'arriet. Then 'e 'ad the bloody cheek to suggest we'd gone off for a good time and that's all I was fit for. Then he said that my be'aviour towards him regularly suggested just a little more than flirtin', 'arriet. I couldn't believe my ears. 'ow conceited can you get? I said "Oh no Mr. Sanderson I think you've mistaken my very friendly nature for something else." I 'ave to say 'arriet 'e did clear 'is throat very quickly and apologise. 'e said 'e had been demented with worry about you 'arriet. Not me 'arriet. Just you! You wouldn't think I was employed by 'im at all. You wouldn't think how 'ard I've worked to get 'is soddin' coffee shop off the ground! It all counts for nothin' 'arriet. Men like 'im they pick you up and put you down. Oh 'e'll never admit givin' me those looks 'arriet. I know 'e fancied me. Not like 'e fell for you though 'arriet. I still think the speech 'e made in church was beautiful. No! 'e probably saw me as some little bit of stuff to keep 'im entertained during 'is visits to Starboard Marine North West. I'll get 'im back 'arriet. Don't you worry. 'e won't find things runnin' quite as smoothly as they 'ave been doin'. I'm goin' to be doin' a bit of my own fund raisin' down there. I've decided I'm definitely goin' to save Venice!'

'Gosh Tricia. That's a noble cause.'

'Well I've fallen in love with it 'arriet. It's given me somethin' else to think about these last few days. It's the only thing that stops me from changin' the locks on 'im, chirpy cheeks. I'm seethin' 'arriet. After twelve years of marriage 'e decides to go with 'er. I 'aven't quite worked out 'ow to get my own back on 'er yet, but I will 'arriet. It's worth stayin' there just for that.'

'Oh Tricia, we have taken a tumble the pair of us. I can't believe he said that to you. He never mentioned you tonight, well only to say that the whole world would know the pair of us did a runner. He came to my room at half three and laid into me something awful.'

'No 'arriet. You didn't deserve that. Couldn't 'e understand the trauma you've 'ad to go through since Mark stood you up?'

'It's complicated Tricia.' Harriet paused. Thought. Decided to tell. 'I never could have married Mark. I'm pregnant Tricia. I'm expecting Mr. Sanderson's baby!'

'Oh 'arriet! I don't know what to say. Oh you poor thing. You 'ave been through it. You still are going through it 'arriet. What about Mark. Does 'e know? Is 'e wantin' you to go back to 'im?'

'Oh Tricia what a mess. It's all such a mess. Mark gave me a note outside the church. I couldn't bring myself to read it though. He thinks I have. He thought I'd gone away to think and decided to come back to him. Yes that's what he wanted Tricia. It must have been in the note. Do you know he phoned Mr. Sanderson to tell him I'd come back to him. It was when I'd crashed out the afternoon we got back.'

'Oh so 'e knows then?'

'Certainly does Tricia! Mark had no right to do that. But at least I got out of him what Belinda Oxfordshire told him at the reception. You know when she rushed him back outside.'

'Ooh 'arriet maybe you should 'ave read it. Anyway what did she tell 'im then?'

'Please, please Tricia promise me faithfully you'll not tell anyone at all about this?'

'I promise 'arriet. I do promise.'

'It looks like he got her pregnant. She wanted it. He didn't. He said he'd marry her if she had an abortion. By him. He did it Tricia. He's a doctor and he did it. That's when they got engaged and as we know he broke it off. She still wanted him. That's why she threatened to sue me over the hat Tricia. Remember me telling you I'd squashed that bag of cat's mess on top of her head at Clarissa's wedding?'

'Ooh yes I remember 'arriet. That was so funny that.'

'Well obviously she wanted me out of his life. I can't believe she wanted him back after the way he treated her, but she did Tricia. She certainly did.'

'Yes 'arriet. It was 'im she really wanted. Bob only got 'is way with 'er because she knew Mr. Sanderson would marry you, 'im 'avin' declared it like that in the church.'

'You could be right Tricia. It wouldn't do a lot for Bob's ego if he knew that though.'

'It's so big 'arriet now. He thinks that much of 'imself 'e'd never believe it. Not that I'll be tellin' 'im anythin', of course. You can trust me 'arriet. You need a friend you can trust just now.'

'Ah, thanks Tricia. Do you know what he said? Do you know what Mr. Sanderson said about the baby. His parting shot. "That's something we're going to have to sort out Miss Glover." Then he banged his hand down on the table and marched out.'

'Oh `arriet, `e `asn't got designs on gettin` rid of your baby `as `e?'

'He won't get chance Tricia. There's no way I'll let him near.'

'What about Mark `arriet? Does `e know about all this?'

'No Tricia. He admitted going with Melissa Scott so there's no moral high ground he could grab there, but no. No, he doesn't know about the baby. Anyway he's biding his time to see how things go. He didn't expect Mr. Sanderson to jump in when he wrote that. He's not wanting me back just yet. He'll decide as and when. I told him not to bother Tricia. I said it was merely a matter of convenience to us both to live in the same house. Do you know Tricia I couldn't believe he'd climbed into bed next to me. He won't budge. He says it's as much his bed as mine so I've been like you Tricia sleeping in the back room until he clears off.'

'Do you think `e'll go back to that new `ouse you were goin` to buy `arriet and live with `er?'

'No I don't think he will Tricia. I think he's out to make life as awkward as he can. You'd never believe it was him who ditched me!'

'Oh `arriet. I do think you `ave to still bear in mind you were pregnant by another man on your weddin` day. You were just unlucky though `arriet. After all you were single when you did it. You were free to sow a last wild oat `arriet. Oh not another metathingy. Or is it `arriet? At least it's a dry land one. I'm so glad you've escaped from our seedy friend Joris Sanderson. We'll get through our problems together. Now don't you worry `arriet.'

'Nor you Tricia. You're a good pal Tricia. The best. Better go now. I'll keep you posted.'

'Bye `arriet. Me too. I'll let you know as soon as there's any more `appenin`.'

Chapter 34

Harriet looked at her watch. Then at the flashing green light on the answer machine. She felt better, so very much better for being able to offload onto Tricia. Tricia understood. Harriet felt for her. Even in her own lapse the hurt of Mark sleeping with Melissa Scott seared through her like the sharpest carving knife in the kitchen drawer. But Tricia, as far as she knew, had never played away. Just flirted. She knew for her, it would be like trying to swallow a bunch of stinging nettles after twelve years of marriage.

She hovered. Felt irritated by the discomfort of indecision.

'Now Pepper. What is it now? Oh I can't phone the travel agent back at the moment. Tomorrow. I'll do it tomorrow. Anyway I want to get the evening meal started. Mark's off early to the sailing club tonight.'

She felt the cat's soft black fur against her legs.

'Oh sorry! It's milk you want Pepper. At least that'll be you sorted.'

She lifted the blue plastic bowl from the floor. Hot from the day's sun. The warm water splattering her fingers as she tipped it down the sink. Reached for the milk. Felt the bottle slide through her hand. Slow motion. Then the crash of glass. In an instant. The cat vanished. A key in the front door. Mark shouting from the hall.

'Bloody hell Harriet what are you doing now?'

'Didn't do it on purpose. It just slid out of my hand.'

'Like so many other things Harriet.'

'Thanks Mark. An offer of help wouldn't go amiss.'

'Oh no. You're job Harriet. You make the mess. You get yourself out of it.'

'OK Mark, I've got the message.'

'Speaking of which there's a couple out there. Have you bothered to play them?'

'Just the first two and they're both for me. I prefer you didn't listen to them.'

'Suits me Harriet. Why didn't you delete them?'

'To remind me to answer them that's why. I'm not in the mood at the moment.'

'What happened to the cat? Still alive?'

'Of course it is. Nine lives Mark.'

'I bet she's got more left than you. Lard ball knocked another one off today then, did he?'

'Yes and it wasn't your place to do that Mark!'

'It was the best call I've ever made in my life Harriet. It wasn't his sodding place to jump in and swipe my bride!'

'Swipe your bride? I just don't get you Mark.'

'So what did that lard ball of a loser have to say for himself then?'

'I don't wish to talk about it. It's all over. Finished. Now can we leave it right there?'

'We certainly can Harriet. It should have been left right there the day he offered you the job.'

'I told you Mark, I'm not prepared to talk about it. How would you like it if I asked you what Melissa Scott thinks about you living back here with me in this house? So what does she think about it anyway?'

'She doesn't know Harriet. I haven't told her because it's nothing to do with her where I live and who I live with.'

'Oh, I see. So she thinks you're here on your own, does she? What if she decides to pay you a visit and I open the door. What then Mark? She might be sorry she came.'

'Pots and kettles Harriet. Just as long as you keep lard ball away from here, I'll do the same with her.'

'Suits me. There's some stroganoff left if you want it.'

'No thanks Harriet. You get yours. I'll get something down there. I want to catch Bob anyway before the race starts.'

'That's two of you then.'

What are you talking about now Harriet?'

'You and Belinda Oxfordshire. Both want to catch him. Poor Tricia. I think he's behaved despicably. They're finished. It's all over between them. Just like us. Under the same roof for convenience and that's about it.'

'What *are* you talking about Harriet?'

'Oh he hasn't told you? I can't believe that.'

'Told me what Harriet? I've been sorting this place out don't forget while you've been swanning around. I've hardly seen him, apart from last Sunday when you both went missing. We didn't talk about anything else.'

'Oh well he'll swank about it later. You'll soon get to know.'

Harriet turned sharply. Kicked the cat's bowl to send it spinning, clattering across the floor. Her foot skidding as the rubber sole on her sandal hit the milky wet tiles from under. In a split second. In Mark's arms. Held firm. Safely pressing into the gap between the lapels of his jacket. Saved from a nasty crack on the glass splintered floor.

'Steady on Harriet! Are you alright?'

First thought. Her baby.

'I'm OK thanks Mark. My fault. I should have cleaned it up straight away.'

'Are you sure you're alright Harriet? I don't want to go out leaving you like this.'

'No Mark. I'll be fine. You go.'

'I'll leave the phone on Harriet. If you need me.'

'OK Mark. Thanks for that. Good luck with the race.'

Mark. Changed and away. Harriet set to work on the floor. Finished. Went out. Sensed a slight cramping as she stretched to lift the bin lid. The carrier bag hitting the bottom. The sound of crashing glass jarring her ears. Concerned now, her hand on her stomach. Her baby. She didn't want it to slide and crash. Like the bottle from her wet hand.

She tried to settle the thought. The rice bubbling away. She drained it. Heaped it onto a plate, filling the hole she'd made in the middle with last night's stroganoff, conscious all the while of her baby. Wondering if it could take any more. Wondering if her body would give up on nurturing this tiny mass of multiplying cells into a new life.

'Gone now!' She breathed a sigh of relief as she finished eating. Tried to stand. Instantly feeling her stomach fold to the crease of dragging pain. She moved to the lounge. Stretched across the sofa. Convinced this was the beginning of the end.

'Just like last time,' she thought. 'Worse than last time. It will be worse than that. This time I know I'm pregnant.'

She lay still. Like being in labour now. She tried to go with the pain.

'Not contractions Pepper. I don't want them to be.'

Subsiding now. Easing. She curled her knees towards her stomach gearing for the next one.

Waiting. Watching the evening sun lining itself up with the cowl on the chimney pot over the road. Cautiously she lifted her head. Sat up to an eager little visitor returned to meow its intentions at her feet. Leaping now. Settling into a ball of black fur on her lap.

'No glass in your fur Pepper. Quicker than me. That's how you hang on to all those lives.'

Her hand against fur. Each stroke rising and falling, catching the gentle vibrations as it purred towards sleep.

'It would be convenient Pepper. So very convenient for everyone if I lost it. Especially *him* Pepper. But I've been jolted out of denial. I don't want to lose it. I don't want to lose it. I've waited a long, long time for this one Pepper. Oh of course Mark will find out. Everyone will find out. It's not something you can hide Pepper. Not exactly. So what's our plan Pepper? You and me. How are we going to deal with this?'

She watched the cat gently close its eyes. The distinct, satisfied rhythm intensifying almost to a snore as it drifted away to better things.

'Of course when Mark does find out he'll be off like a shot to Millington and Melissa Scott. Somehow I'll have to buy his half of this back. I couldn't do with selling again. I can't be bringing my baby up in an apartment Pepper. At least I've still got my job. Let's see now. I'll be able to work until December and then I'll take maternity leave. Of course I'll have to go back to school and get childcare. I don't see Mummy and Daddy helping out. Gosh no, especially as they're doing so much for Paul and Susan's baby. It's getting harder for them anyway now she's ten months old. In any case Pepper I've probably been ostracized from the family by now. Mummy's message was hardly sympathetic. And I don't want a penny from *him*! No Pepper, Mr. Sanderson wants to get rid of my baby just like he did Belinda Oxfordshire's. No! He's forfeited all rights now. And he's most certainly not having access. Do you know Pepper he's done me the biggest favour he could. Oh yes he's handsome, gorgeous to the point of distraction. Charming, intelligent, well connected. Very well connected. Fancy turning to the PM borrowing his heavies to set on us Pepper. No thought. No understanding. No concept of how scary it all is. And he's supposed to have been a doctor Pepper. Pity his poor patients. Probably wanted to abort their entire nervous systems. I expect that's the real reason he left the profession. He probably got kicked out Pepper. No Pepper. He's done me the biggest favour of all. He's moved me from amber to green. I want neither him nor Mark. They've both driven me to the end of the road.'

Chapter 35

Saturday morning. In her own bed in the back room Harriet awoke. Drew the curtains back on all those sights and sounds hallmarking a beautiful summer's day. She could hear Mark in the kitchen. Worried about the messages. She didn't like him being up before her. Quickly she hurried to the bathroom. Showered and dressed. Caught him on the stairs.

'No calls or messages last night Harriet. I presume you were alright?'

'No. No need to call, Mark. I was fine thank you. Did you win?'

'No, thanks to that arse of a lard ball. We're damned sure he jibed unexpectedly on purpose. Sent Bob and I heeling. Straight over. Bloody soaked! It's a good job we had a change of clothes down there.'

'What! Was *he* racing? Not in his boat surely?'

'No not in his boat Harriet. Way out of class. No he was racing with that girl Lucinda something. She'd been showing Bob her boat earlier. Very nice. A brand new Laser. Lard ball talked her into letting him take it down there so they could race it together, or so she said. Apparently she's not long taken over the deputy's job at your place so you'll know all about it.'

'How would I know all about it? She doesn't sail to school.'

'I'll ignore that one Harriet. It didn't take him long to get over you then?'

'Well it's like you've just said Mark. His boat's down at the Tideside club and in any case it's far too big to race down there. So he would, wouldn't he? He's an opportunist so if he wanted to race that's just what he'd do. Find someone to do it with.' Harriet seethed. This rash of jealousy threatened to throw all her calm deliberations of last night to the wind. Her thoughts whizzed away.

'So there is no smoke without fire. Mrs. Bustard was right. No wonder Lucinda Lawton got drawn into the story. How long had he been befriending her before he made love to me on the sand? Mark was right. He'd have had me living here. Out of the way. A convenience for his desires. Nothing more. If he'd really wanted to marry me he'd have asked me then, on the sand, before my supposed marriage to Mark. He only asked me because he wanted to do the grand thing. He hasn't exactly made much of an effort to get me back.'

With logic skewed by fury she took herself back upstairs. Mark had just squeezed an ocean of raw lemon juice all over this beautiful summer's day. The taste was sour and bitter in her mouth.

'I'm off to Millington this morning Harriet. I'll be back later.'

'Off to Melissa Scott, Mark?'

'My business Harriet. Separate lives Harriet don't forget. You dug your own big hole, remember?'

'Bloody cheek Mark. You ditched me, or have you forgotten?'

'And you were going to let me off the hook anyway Harriet. Or have you forgotten that?'

Harriet didn't answer. Could feel the tears seeping. She swallowed hard. Her tiny baby growing, and the cat. All she had left now.

'Out of the way Pepper, please. Let me get to the phone. Go away. You can hear it's ringing.'

'Oh Molly, it's you. It's lovely to hear from you. How are you and Percy?'

Harriet's stomach churned. She'd hit the interface. The first of the wedding guests. Now having to explain.

'We're very well thank you Harriet. But I'm phoning to see how *you* are dear. We had a call from our friend Joris. Well I hope he's still our friend Harriet. Yours as well I mean. I've been hoping nothing's gone wrong between the two of you. No, of course not. I'm being silly Harriet because he's already called to say that unfortunately you're not well and the wedding was having to be postponed. Oh Harriet dear, Percy and I are most concerned about you. We do hope it's nothing serious.'

Harriet took a very deep breath. 'Gosh he must still want me.' Tried to sink the thought. Molly with her comfort had done it again. Just as she did on the ship. She tried to fight against it. 'NO, NO, NO, NO! So he's playing about with Lucinda Lawton and still wants to marry me. He can just sod off!' Then a thought. 'No he's just stalling Molly to save his own face.'

'No Molly, thank you. I'm feeling a little better now. They're trying to get to the bottom of it. It's probably some debilitating viral thing, or so they think.' Couldn't believe she was now lying for him.

'Oh thank goodness for that Harriet. You've been through so much, I think the sooner you marry our friend Joris and get settled, the better you'll be. Now Harriet we're moving into our house in Lower Tideside in two weeks time. I'd like you and Joris to be our very first dinner guests. Of course I mentioned it to Joris when he phoned and naturally he's already accepted for you both. He hasn't mentioned it yet?'

Harriet could hardly believe it.

'Er no Molly. He's probably been too busy phoning everyone. He's had a lot of things to sort out.'

'Oh of course Harriet. Silly of me. Do you know I'm so excited about moving in I'm all of a flutter. I'm not thinking straight at the moment. Anyway Harriet you hurry up and get yourself well again. Percy and I want to see you both two weeks today.'

'I'll do that Molly and thank you so much for phoning. If you need any help with the move I'm sure Mr. Sanderson will be only to pleased. He likes moving things for people.'

'Oh does he Harriet? Yes, you're right. He's just that kind of man. He can't do enough to help people. I'll mention it to Percy. Now you look after yourself dear and we'll see you both very soon.'

Harriet replaced the receiver wondering why on earth she'd gone along with his little charade.

'I can't make it out Pepper. I can't make out where he's coming from. He definitely told me it was the end of the road. I don't know which road he's talking about but mine ended at San Marco. He needn't think he's marrying me.'

She stood for a moment. His strong tall masculine frame almost there, in front of her. His smile. She could see that slight imperfection enhancing those white even teeth. The dimples in his cheeks elongating sparking the broadest of smiles. His eyes, deep deep blue, twinkling, sparkling like the sun on the surface of the sea. Speaking silent depth. Fathoms of raw masculinity. She pressed her hand hard against her baby. Felt that same intense physical pang of need. That man. How could she still feel like this for him? Feel like this again knowing all she did.

'No Pepper. I'm having an irrational moment. I'm not doing a Belinda Oxfordshire. No way am I going there again.'

She opened the back door. Left it that way. Let the cat jump ahead. The summer sky in devious mood drawing her senses to the wild flower meadow. Her field of flowers. Buttercups, daisies in the grass. She lay down. Stared high. Crystal blue infinity. His eyes. She could see his eyes serious now. That expression. That look. She returned her hand to sit hard against her stomach. His baby. Her body opening, twisting against the soft green grass, hopelessly drawing him in. Just the buttercups kissing her cheeks. What had she done?

Chapter 36

Just faintly. The phone ringing, breaking into her dreams. Whoever, wasn't letting go.

'Oh `arriet. I just `ad to phone you. Is it alright to talk now?'

'Yes of course it is Tricia. Mark's out all day exercising his right to be where he wants when he wants with whom he wants.'

'Oh so where will that be then `arriet?'

'Millington Tricia. 1 Haystack Close to be precise.'

'Oh so `e's back on Melissa is `e?'

'I'm not sure he was ever off her Tricia. All I know is he's not going to marry her.'

'Well that's somethin` `arriet. `ave you managed to put a word in for me yet?'

'No Tricia. He's completely off me and by association you as well. He thinks we behave like a pair of school girls. He's too much on Bob's side at the moment.'

'Well we'll just `ave to see what we can do to change that, won't we `arriet? Anyway I'm phonin` to tell you our friend `as been round `ere this mornin`. `e's only just gone. Bloody cheek `arriet. `e thinks `e can just come and go as `e pleases.'

Harriet switched to full alert.

'You mean Mr. Sanderson Tricia? What did he want?'

'`e only wanted to know all about our trip to Venice `arriet. I told `im I didn't know why `e was askin` seein` as `e knew already. Well `e did `arriet. Those minders `ad to be fillin` `im in. That's what `e would `ave been payin` them to do!'

'No that would have been favours Tricia. Just a word from the PM. They're all as thick as thieves.'

'Yes you're most probably right, now where was I? Oh yes. Now wait `til you `ear this `arriet. `e said `e'd `eard on the grapevine a complaint had been filed with the authorities. That's the Italian authorities `arriet. We won't say the word in case this call is bein` listened to. You never know `arriet, do you?'

'No Tricia. Go on. Don't keep me in suspense.'

'It was `im `arriet. It's that boatman we sent flyin` into the canal. But `e twisted the story `arriet. We're now bein` accused of pushin` `im in and `e was only saved from drownin` because `e managed to `aul `imself out, but `e `urt `is back so badly as a result `e's after compensation!'

'Oh no Tricia. There didn't look much wrong with him when he took us back to San Lucia. He's making it up. You didn't say anything did you?'

'Of course not `arriet. I kept mum after I told `im it was such a flyin` visit I could `ardly remember anythin`. But you're right. Remember `ow `e pulled that boat round when we got there? If `e'd `urt `is back `e most probably did it then, I would say.'

'Yes you're right Tricia. We're not getting done for that!'

'Anyway `e said the authorities are making their investigations `arriet. Then `e said they were cooperatin` with the British authorities, I won't say that word again but you know what I mean, as `e was almost certain the culprits were two English girls.'

'Oh no Tricia.' Harriet's aching desire for him drained away. Just the pangs of sickly nerves across her stomach now.

'Oh yes `arriet. It `asn't taken long for them to catch up with us as it? But there's worse to come. They're linkin` it to a break-in of an `otel filin` cabinet `arriet. `e said two men stood in the doorway of the `ouse next door watchin` two girls of the same description runnin` out of the `otel to a waiting taxi.'

'Bloody hell Tricia. The game's up!'

'No it's not `arriet. We'll deny all knowledge. No one can prove it was us. Anyway it incriminates our friend Joris `arriet. It's `is two spies that `ave blown the cover!'

'Gosh Tricia you're right. He's going to have to do some swift old boy networking to get out of that one. What else did he say Tricia?'

'Well he said it was in our interests to tell him as much as I could. So I said "What about `arriet? `ave you been askin` `er about it?" So `e said in `is very posh voice. "I doubt if Miss Glover can even remember her name never mind what went on in Venice. She appears to have lost it completely Mrs. Harrington." Oh `arriet and then `e smiled me that smile. Are you sure you're doin` the right thing? Oh if I `ad `alf a chance to marry `im I'd grab it. That man's off the planet gorgeous. I don't think I'll ever be able to stop wantin` `im `arriet. Belinda Oxfordshire's makin` do with a very poor second with four-cheeks Bob. `is firelighter `ardly gets goin` arriet before the flame goes out. Oh `arriet I think that's the best metathingy I've ever come up with. Do you know I think I'll make more of an effort with them now I've truly got the `ang of them. Maybe I'll think of a few to `elp me save Venice.'

Harriet hardly heard. She was seething.

'Oh and then `is phone went `arriet. `e said "I'll call you back Lucinda." Isn't that the one who got the job you wanted at your school `arriet?'

'Oh don't remind me Tricia. Go on. What did he say next?'

'`e said inevitably the press would get `old of it and there was no way `e wanted it linkin` back to `im. `e said `e'd `ad quite enough of our be`aviour as things were only just startin` to settle down after the Rappin` `ammer affair. So I told `im `arriet `is coffee shop wouldn't be doin` `alf as well as it is if we `adn't got all that publicity for `im. So `e said lookin` down `is nose. "Too higher price to pay Mrs. Harrington. Such antics don't sit well with the ethos of the school." Then `e said "Should your short term memory take a turn for the better I'd appreciate a detailed account of all your activities whilst you were away. This is a concern I can simply do without." Then `e moved on `arriet `e said `im and Lucinda were organisin` a campin` trip in the summer `olidays and `e wants us to go `arriet as well as the summer fete which the Parents Association `ave taken charge of.'

'Gosh Tricia, he doesn't want much does he? Well I think there's no end to his cheek. I suppose I'll be roped in for that lot too!'

'Oh yes `arriet `e did say somethin` about Belinda Oxfordshire keepin` a close eye on us both just to make sure we add nothin` more to the mess we already appear to be in.'

'Cheeky sod! And what did you say to that Tricia?'

'I said "I don't know what you're talkin` about Mr. Sanderson. `arriet and I were very stressed with our marital problems. We just `ad to take a little break away that's all. We just forgot to mention it before `and. It's very easily done when you're in a hurry." Ooh `arriet then `e said, "The pair of you were in too much of a damned hurry. You couldn't wait to go. You couldn't wait to get back it seems. Unless you refresh your memory rather more quickly Mrs. Harrington you could both be landing yourselves in more trouble than you could ever have dreamed of. Good day to you." `e's not been long gone `arriet. I just `ad to phone you.'

'Oh I'm glad you did Tricia. We're going to have to decide which is the best way to play it. It sounds like he wants to make sure it *was* us before he wires the stop via the PM.'

'Let's see `ow it goes `arriet. This is the first we've `eard of any of it. It's summer `arriet and don't forget we were wearin` those shades most of the time. There would `ave been `undreds of girls like us in Venice then. Remember the trains `arriet? Some of them girls goin` to Venice must `ave been English. `ow would they ever know it was us?'

Harriet looked down at the messages still flashing on the answer machine.

'I've got a message here to phone the travel agent back. After all it was our own passports we took Tricia. Clear evidence of our intention to do a runner. I don't think we've got much choice but to come clean with him.'

'Ooh `arriet. Maybe you're right after all. I think we might just need is `elp with this one. Let me know what the travel agents say `arriet. I'll stay `ere by the phone. I've gone all nervous again.'

Chapter 37

Harriet promised. Couldn't face the call without a strong coffee and more than a splash of brandy. She sat at the kitchen table. The kettle taking for ever.

Couldn't believe the momentarily relapse she'd had for Mr. Sanderson. Furious; the last thing she wanted was for him "to have a word". For him to exert his influence to get them off the hook. She watched the brown crumbs of synthetic coffee crumble under the boiling water. Breathed in the aroma. Like life. A promise of more it was able to deliver. She plonked it down on the kitchen table, staring into the central swirl drawn by the teaspoon on the surface. She took a deep breath. Then a brainwave. Josh. If she could just get to speak to him. He'd taken their passports away. He'd said they would be returned if requested.

Mesmerized by the small sway of circling bubbles gradually drawing to a halt, suddenly she jumped up, played the message and then pressed 3. She waited for the connection. Tucking her chin well down to her neck she knew she had one chance and one chance only to make this work.

'Ah good morning.' Her voice was as deep and as posh as she could make it. 'This is Violet Moss speaking. My husband and I joined your package tour to Venice Mestre on Sunday 27th June.'

'Ah, yes Mrs. Moss. I remember now. We are investigating the complaint you made against two of our clients. In fact I've left a message. I'm hoping we'll be able to get back to you shortly.'

Harriet nearly died. She had to keep her nerve. Thought fast on her feet.

'Well Cedric and I wish to drop the complaint. Now if you could transfer me to Josh your rep there are just one or two things I'd like to tie up with him.'

'Certainly Mrs. Moss. Now are you sure about dropping this complaint. You won't be able to claim compensation you know?'

'Over and done with! Now put me through if you would be so kind.'

Harriet didn't know how she'd managed it. Her legs were trembling. She was sorry she'd started. Didn't know whether to remain as Mrs. Moss or go back to being herself.

'You're through now.'

'Ah good morning Mrs. Moss. How may I help you?' She heard the click. At least it was just the two of them.

'Ah Josh.' He intervened before she could speak further.

'Right Mrs. Moss. Just bear with me. I'll need to get to the files in my office.'

'Oh thank goodness for that.' Harriet thought breathing a sigh of relief.

'Now how may I help you Mrs. Moss?'

'No Josh,' returned Harriet. 'It's me, Harriet!'

'What's all this about Harriet, feigning Mrs. Moss?'

'I don't know what you mean Josh.'

'Oh forget it for the minute. Look, I did a head count on Thursday morning and no sign of you or your friend. Of course the filing cabinet was open so I had to pretend I'd given you your passports and forgotten to lock it. I'm supposed to be responsible for my clients Harriet. I wasn't prepared to get myself or the company into trouble with the hotel. How did you get in there anyway?'

'Oh it was just a wiry thing we used for ours when I lost the key.'

'Why didn't you contact me Harriet. You were given all the instructions. I was only a phone call away. I could have lost my job over that!'

'Look Josh I really am sorry. One day I'll be able to explain it to you but not now. Please just believe me we had to do it.'

'Hell's bells you're not the two they're after are you?'

'Two they're after Josh? What do you mean?'

'It's been coming through. We've been asked to give details of all clients travelling to Venice at that time. Oh it's not just us. All the travel agents have been requested to cooperate. For some reason they're trying to keep it quiet. They want to stitch it up before the press get hold of it.'

'Stitch what up Josh?'

'Well from what we can gather these two have managed to blow a world wide under cover investigation just on the verge of it getting underway. Apparently it started in Venice.'

Harriet's relief was tangible.

'No not us Josh. That's certainly nothing to do with us. No it was personal reasons that forced us to get home quickly like that. I can't tell you now, but if I ever travel again with Hotonyourheels.com and you happen to be our rep I'll explain all.'

'Hell's bells Harriet. Please don't. There's plenty of others to inflict yourself on. I'm treading a fine line here. You do realise the rest of the passports could have been stolen?'

'Golly, gosh Josh!' She coughed as the words sloshed around her mouth. 'I'm so sorry. Honestly it was an emergency. Life or death Josh. We'd never have done it otherwise.'

'So now tell me why did Suzie put you through as Violet Moss? How am I to know who was on the other end?'

'I don't know Josh. I wondered why you called me Violet Moss. I hope I don't sound like her.'

'Has Suzie got her wires crossed again? She gets so many calls that girl, she's always switching the wrong people. I've had enough of this half-baked company. What with bum-stickers refusing to get off coaches, loony clients and you and her dropping me right in it, I think I'll be looking for another job. On second thoughts I wouldn't want you messing up again. I'm better staying put. Just don't touch Hotonyourheels.com ever again. You and your friend. That's the least you can do!'

'Promise Josh. You're a life-saver. You'll never know how grateful I am. Thanks Josh.'

'OK Harriet.'

Harriet replaced the receiver. Josh had saved their lives. She wanted to get the good news back to Tricia straight away once she'd called the travel agent. No! On second thoughts it would be better to wait. There was no panic now. Violet Moss had dropped the case!

She picked up the phone.

'Tricia. Good news at last! Oh hang on a minute there's the doorbell. Look I'll phone you back. I won't be two ticks.'

'Just a quick word Miss Glover.' Mr. Sanderson stepped in. 'If I may?'

Harriet glued her eyes to her feet as he followed her into the lounge. 'Get this damned cat out of the way will you?'

She lifted it up. Kissed the smooth shiny black fur flat between its ears and shoved it into the kitchen.

'Right Miss Glover. Take a seat This won't take long.' He glanced at his watch. 'Even so I'll have a quick coffee if you're making one. Leave the brandy off will you!'

Without a word she returned to the kitchen, wondering how he knew but grateful for the couple of minutes space he'd just given her.

'It's the wedding,' she convinced herself. 'He wants to fix a new date.'

Chapter 38

Both mugs in hand she backed herself into the lounge trying desperately not to catch his eye.

'Just on my way back from Mrs. Harrington, Miss Glover.'

She sat down, sipping away at her second cup of brandy laced with coffee in less than fifteen minutes. So grateful for something to hold on to.

'Now Miss Glover. It's a question of "mens san in corpore sano" as far as you're concerned. That's why I hesitated to come here.'

'Meaning?' Harriet wasn't taking to being patronised.

'Meaning a sound mind in a healthy body Miss Glover and I'm not so sure you are possessed of either!'

'I can assure you there's nothing wrong with my mind or my body Mr. Sanderson. In fact I've never felt better.' She coloured to the pink of the roses sitting in the glass vase on the window sill.

' "Nullum mendacious",' Miss Glover.

'Meaning?'

'No lies! I want to know just exactly what you both got up to over there.'

'Sight seeing Mr. Sanderson. That's all it was. We needed to clear our heads.'

'Yes, yes. I've already had that side of it from you Miss Glover. Now unless you're prepared to come clean you could both land yourselves in very serious trouble. There's been a number of things going on over there, I must say suspiciously coincidental with your arrival.'

'What do you mean Mr. Sanderson? I think you've got hold of the wrong end of the stick.'

'I beg your pardon Miss Glover! I have it on very good authority complaints have been coming into the Italian authorities regarding two British females causing meyhem over there. Of course that's not the least of it. There are wider, deeper implications to their behaviour.'

'Oh I know what you are talking about now Mr. Sanderson, I've just been speaking to the travel agent and that's definitely not us. It's got nothing at all to do with us. No I was starting to feel a bit unwell so we decided to come home early. That's all.'

'Unwell Miss Glover? In exactly what respect may I ask?'

'Probably the heat and the smells. That's all.'

'You've paid no heed to the fact you're pregnant Miss Glover. No heed whatsoever. We're going to have to look at this. It requires some action. Sooner rather than later I would say.'

Harriet glowered. Living proof. Exactly the same words to Belinda Oxfordshire. It might just as well have been her sitting there.

'I don't think so Mr. Sanderson. That would be totally unethical.'

'Unethical Miss Glover? Indeed quite the opposite! And just how ethical was it of you to walk out on me after my proposing marriage to you?'

Harriet didn't answer.

'Anyhow we're looking at a school camping trip in the summer holidays. Lucinda will give you the low-down on it. Oh and a week on Saturday Miss Glover. Keep it clear for the summer fete will you? Oh and that reminds me. We've been invited to dinner that same evening. Molly and Percy. Now my nearest neighbours. Common courtesy to attend Miss Glover. As far as they're concerned the wedding has been postponed. That should tide us over for the evening. The news it's off will filter through of its own accord. I'm not particularly anxious to help it on its way.'

Harriet furious he should want to abort her baby couldn't believe herself struggling to sink her involuntary wave of disappointment at his words.

'Ah that's your doorbell Miss Glover. I'm on my way out.'

She followed him through the hall, standing back to allow him to open the door. He brushed straight past without even turning his head.

'Barry! How on earth did you get here?'

'Aren't you going to ask me in Harriet?'

Chapter 39

'Thanks for that Harriet.'

She lifted her third cup of coffee in unison with him. Not sure about draining the last from the brandy bottle, though.

'How did you get here Barry? I'm sorry I gave you our new address. Expected to be moving in. Things moved along unfortunately. You must have gone to Haystack Close.'

'That's about the measure of it Harriet.'

His dark hair just touching his shoulders. His face longish, high cheek-bones. Artistic. His eyes, deep brown, soft, intelligent. His eyebrows, very dark, as good as straight, almost touching across the top of the narrow bridge of his nose.

'Good looking,' Harriet thought. 'Couldn't be more different from *him*!'

'Was that guy Mark then?'

'Oh no definitely not Mark. No he's my boss, just popped in to sort something out.'

'You talking about the blonde guy Harriet? Just left. His face looks familiar. I just can't place it.'

'Oh I thought you meant him.'

'No. No. The guy at the place you sent me to Harriet. The one who gave me this address.'

'Oh sorry Barry. Yes it would have been. That's where he was spending the day.'

'And the girl with him?'

'Let's just call her a very close friend. She works with him.'

'Right. I see. You two split then? I remember Tricia saying something about you both getting away from problems, the same as us.'

Harriet shifted on her seat. Didn't want the reality of getting into this relationship thing with him just now.

'You've come for your money Barry. I'll just get my cheque book.'

'No Harriet. I wouldn't dream of it. I promised you these.'

He passed her the CD of photographs. Harriet smiled. Thanked him.

'No, more to the point, I've come to find out what happened to you both. Why you absconded.'

She went quiet. Wasn't too sure it had anything to do with him. He sensed her unease.

'Oh not that it matters a great deal Harriet. We were very concerned for your safety that's all.'

'Well, yes Barry. That's very kind. I know we were supposed to wait for you to come back from San Marco but I wasn't that well. We decided to go home. I'm sorry we couldn't let you know.'

'*You* were sorry Harriet? I don't know how many times we were up and down those steps, combing the Rialto Bridge looking for you both. We couldn't

116

believe it when we heard you'd left without informing anybody. Strange behaviour!'

He stopped to study her expression. Guilty! Harriet was well out-doing the vase of roses now on the window sill. She knew. She could feel her face burning.

'You see Harriet that particular hotel isn't well sited for tourists. Well you could see the area for yourselves. We were concerned you'd become embroiled in er, shall we say, things outside your control.'

'What do you mean Barry?'

'Just a hunch Harriet. What exactly happened to the two of you between leaving the Rialto Bridge and getting back to the hotel?'

She was tempted to come clean. But contrary to his relaxed air there was something almost official about his manner. His questioning. As if he knew more but was not about to tell.

'Not a lot really. We just got ourselves back to the hotel, then the airport and home.'

'How did you get hold of your passports Harriet? According to the hotel manager that filing cabinet was locked. How did you open it? Who helped you? Why were you both in such a hurry? It looks like the pair of you have well and truly screwed it. San Marco was supposed to be the end of the road.'

'Just a minute Barry. Are you working for MI5 or something?'

He stood up.

'Here's my number Harriet. If things get sticky give me a shout.'

Chapter 40

Harriet closed the door on him wondering what else this day would bring. Decided against staying around to find out. Slamming the car door shut, she backed off the drive. Tricia's was the only place to be, just now.

'Oh `arriet. You've come just in time to join me for lunch. I've made Bob take the kids out all day so there's no danger of bein` interrupted. `e's been round to you `asn't `e `arriet? I can tell by your face somethin` isn't right.'

'Oh thanks Tricia. No coffee though I've just had three.'

'Three `arriet! I `ope you `aven't become a caffeine junkie'

'If that's where it stops then I'll be alright Tricia. Just don't mention the brandy.'

'Ooh `arriet I do `ope you're alright to drive?'

'Probably better for it Tricia. Gosh! Yes! I've had him round but on his way out he goes and walks straight into Barry on the doorstep.'

'You what `arriet? You `aven't `ad `im round as well? No wonder you `ad the brandy! I'm not sure you should be drivin` though. Anyway `however did `e find you `arriet?'

'Oh he's been to Millington. He would choose today. Caught them both in. Mark sent him over.'

'Oh gosh `arriet. You didn't want `im to know your address did you?'

'No I certainly did not Tricia and definitely not now.'

'Ooh why `arriet? What's `appened? What did `e want? Apart from `is money of course.'

'No Tricia he wasn't interested in that. He wanted to know why we left Venice in such a hurry and how we opened the filing cabinet and what we did between leaving the Rialto Bridge and getting back to the hotel. He said they'd been concerned for our safety.'

'Bloody `ell `arriet `ow many more of them are goin` to be givin` us the Spanish inquisition? What did you tell `im, anyway?'

'Only that I felt unwell and so we decided to go back home Tricia.'

'Good `arriet and that's all we're ever goin` to say to anyone. We `aven't done anythin` wrong. Well not seriously wrong. Not deliberately `arriet.'

'No you're right Tricia. In fact I've got some really good news.'

'Oh I will be glad to `ear that `arriet!'

'Well I had a brilliant idea over my first cup of coffee Tricia. I decided to phone Josh before getting embroiled in returning the travel agent's call. I thought it would be better to try and find out what happened about the filing cabinet.'

'That was a good idea `arriet but `ow did you manage to get `old of `im without gettin` them all suspicious?'

'I pretended to be Violet Moss. Just wait until I tell you this. That Suzie receptionist girl jumped the gun. She said straight away they were dealing with the complaint Mrs. Moss and her husband had filed against us Tricia! So I told her Cedric and I had decided to drop it and would she be kind enough to put me through to Josh as there were a couple of outstanding matters I needed to consult him on.'

'Gosh 'arriet that's brilliant! But 'ow did you make yourself sound like Violet Moss? She's got such a loud, deep posh voice.'

'I don't know but I must have managed it. Josh wasn't too pleased. The hotel had obviously given him a key to that filing cabinet Tricia because fortunately he came back to find it open before anyone had noticed. He locked it straight away. He only realised our passports had gone when he did a headcount on Thursday morning. I don't think anyone in the hotel could have missed us Tricia.'

'Bloody 'ell 'arriet that was a stroke of good fortune. Why did 'e take the blame 'arriet?'

'Well he didn't want to lose his job over it. As he said, all the passports could have been stolen. He's told me never to book with Hotonyourheels.com again.'

'Well we wouldn't want to would we 'arriet? And to think I twisted my back round to sit with my legs in the aisle of 'is coach just to get a better look at 'im. I wouldn't 'ave bothered if I'd 'ave known. Anyway 'e wasn't much of a rep. 'ow many times did we see 'im exactly? Twice at the most I'd say. If 'e'd been around a bit more we might 'ave been able to ask 'im for our passports. No 'arriet. I think 'e deserved the fright 'e got.'

Harriet smiled. Sat down to the table.

'No 'arriet. We'll go in there where it's more comfortable. We'll 'ave it on our knees. Are you sure you don't want a tea or a coffee?

'No thanks Tricia. Just a sandwich is fine.'

'So 'ow did you get on with our friend Joris, 'arriet? Did 'e tell you about the campin' trip and the summer fete?'

'He did. He told me Lucinda would give me all the details. Bloody Lucinda Lawton, Tricia. That's all I needed!'

'Oh I know exactly what you mean 'arriet. I've never even met 'er and I can't stand 'er. I've 'ad Bob takin' great delight in tellin' me 'ow our friend Joris talked 'er into gettin' 'er boat down to the club and 'ow it wouldn't be a problem for 'im to race it with 'er. I said to 'im "So why are you so interested in Lucinda Lawton all of a sudden Bob? 'as Belinda Oxfordshire managed to blow your birthday candle out?" '

Harriet laughed.

'Oh 'e didn't like that one 'arriet. 'e marched straight out and banged the door be'ind 'im. Anyway 'arriet I do 'ope you'll be up for campin'. I don't fancy goin' if you're not goin' to be there.'

'Oh I'll be there alright Tricia. I couldn't leave you to the mercy of them all. *He's* not concerned about me being pregnant. Anything but! Anyway how far off is it? Let's see. Did he say when it was?'

'The last week in July 'arriet. Just as soon as they break up.'

'Well that's only three weeks away. It won't be a problem for me. He doesn't believe in giving much notice though, does he?'

'That's typical of 'im 'arriet, although 'e did say the summer fete would be the week before that. So at least we know about that one in good time. Why don't we organise 'im a little surprise to make it go with a swing 'arriet? 'ow about we try to get 'old of Rappin' 'ammer again. Yes 'arriet I've decided I'm goin' to do it. I'm goin' to 'ave 'im back to 'elp me raise funds for savin' Venice. You know that strip of land next to the playin' field adjoinin' your school? You know sometimes they 'ave events there? Well I'll see if I can't get Rappin' 'ammer to run a charity gig right at the same time 'arriet. It won't 'ave anythin' to do with our friend Joris. I'm sure 'e won't notice me slippin' through the gate with me charity bucket.'

'Gosh Tricia. After what you did to him? You left him pretty exposed to say the least. And how are you going to pay for it? We didn't exactly leave him in the right frame of mind for that kind of thing.'

'Don't worry. 'e probably enjoyed 'avin' 'is black leathers pulled down. 'e's an exhibitionist 'arriet. 'e might be 'avin' girls doin' it to 'im all the time!'

'He didn't look as though he was enjoying it Tricia. Can't you think of asking someone else?'

'No 'arriet. You do remember don't you, 'ow much trouble I 'ad tryin' to get 'old of the royal family last time? No 'e's on the 'ook 'arriet. You know 'ow much 'e sucked up to our friend Joris over the Fastnet thing. I'll tell 'im if 'e does it for free Mr. Sanderson will take 'im on as crew in the next race. That'll do it 'arriet.'

'Oh Tricia. Don't you think we're in enough trouble aleady?'

'Not compared to the trouble Venice is in 'arriet. It's the most magical place on earth and I would be failin' in my duty as a citizen of this planet 'arriet if I didn't risk all to save it. Anyway I've got nothing else now. I've lost Bob to 'er and I've certainly 'ad enough of the kids. Your Mark can't keep away from that funny woman 'e works with. So what else 'ave I got? Only to save Venice. And I will 'arriet. I will you'll see. Will you 'elp me 'arriet?'

'Of course I will Tricia. I know what you mean. It was heart breaking to see some of those buildings, decaying, just crumbling away.'

'Good 'arriet. I knew you would. Now which part shall we concentrate on first?'

'Maybe San Marco Tricia. There was some restoration work going on there, remember? If we could make a substantial donation while the scaffolding's still up it might mean they could really progress the work.'

'Oh yes 'arriet, we'll 'ave to 'urry up as well because it is sinkin' fast. No time to waste. I'll go to the garden centre this afternoon and see if I can get Guy 'ammer to 'ave a word with 'is cousin.'

'I'm not sure about Wayne Hammer and this Fastnet thing, though Tricia. I think we're going to have to tread carefully with Mr. Sanderson. We might end up needing his help.'

'Oh and why do you say that 'arriet? I thought that was the last thing we needed.'

'It was Barry Tricia. The way he was questioning me. He said we could well and truly have screwed it. He said that San Marco was supposed to be the end of the road.'

'Oh and what did he mean by that `arriet?'

'I haven't any idea Tricia, but we'll have to mind San Marco doesn't turn into the end of the road for us, too!'

'No `arriet. I can't go with that. We `aven't a clue what Barry was talkin` about, `ave we? So I refuse to be deflected from my mission. It won't `urt our rich friend Joris to share `is great big boat. After all `e `as got two. Don't worry `arriet they'll sort it out between them.'

'Just at the moment we've got much more than that to worry about Tricia.'

'What do you mean `arriet?'

'Barry and Andy. Do you remember how we couldn't quite make the pair of them out?'

'Oh I do `arriet. Yes I do.'

'Barry. His questions. I side-tracked them Tricia. I asked him if he belonged to MI5 or something.'

Tricia paled. 'What did `e say `arriet?'

'He didn't Tricia. He immediately stood up. Gave me his phone number on a piece of paper. Told me to phone him if things started to get too sticky. Then went.'

'Oh gosh `arriet. You don't think they were spyin` on us as well do you?'

'I don't know what to think Tricia. That's exactly why I came round to see you.'

'Ooh I don't think I want to know where all this might end up `arriet.'

'No Tricia, nor I. It's unlikely they'd deploy MI5 just to find us. That's if I'm right. But you know there was certainly something going on between them. And what about when they both went chasing off while we were lunching outside that church. You know the one with roof like an upside down boat.'

'Oh yes `arriet and those two `eavies got on that boat from there back to the Rialto Bridge with us, but they thought it was goin` to San Marco. And, don't forget, Barry and Andy left us to go to San Marco. Ooh it's not lookin` good is it `arriet?'

'No Tricia, it certainly isn't. We do know for sure those heavies were after us but it could be there's something else going on and we've walked straight into it.'

'Well that fits in doesn't it `arriet. It fits in with what Josh said and our friend Joris. Ooh `arriet we're up to our eyes in it. What's the best thing to do?'

'But we don't know what we're up to our eyes in, do we Tricia? Therefore we can't be guilty. The worst thing we did was open the filing cabinet and Josh has sorted that one. Thank goodness.'

'Well it was the worst thing you did `arriet. I knocked that fella flyin` and ran off with `is designer gown. `e wouldn't know. `e might `ave thought I was tryin` to pinch it. It's still in my case. I'm not gettin` rid of the evidence though, `arriet.

It really suits me. I was meant to 'ave it. It's beautiful just like Venice. In any case 'e wouldn't know anythin' if 'e's dead. 'e wouldn't want 'is gown back then. Oh no, I might just 'ave killed 'im 'arriet.'

'Oh I think if that was the case we'd have been pulled in long since.'

'Oh 'arriet. I do 'ope you're right.'

'Tell you what Tricia, I think it might be best if we give ourselves the rest of the day. We'll just wait to see if anything else turns up. We don't want to be crawling to Mr. Sanderson just yet. Not in the face of him taking up with Lucinda Lawton. I'd turn to Barry before I'd turn to him anyway. No I'll give you a call tomorrow and we'll decide what to do then.'

'Yes 'arriet. I think you're most probably right. I'll get myself down to the garden centre this afternoon and see if I can 'ave a word with Guy 'ammer. 'e'll be lookin' for a distraction now Belinda Oxfordshire's switched 'er attentions to bunion Bob. Do you know 'arriet 'e's bought 'imself some of those designer trainers to impress 'er. I know they're killin' 'im but 'e keeps wearin' them. I said "It will serve you right if you get bunions." 'e's got fish feet 'arriet. I said "Oh go on then get bunions on your flat feet. It'll give them a bit of shape. She'll be very attracted to them lookin' like two big plaice suckin' gob-stoppers."

Harriet laughed as she stood to go.

'Are you sure about Rapping Hammer Tricia?'

'Ooh I am 'arriet. I've already told you all I want to do is save Venice and I'm startin' this afternoon.'

Chapter 41

With her brandied head whirling, Harriet drove home hoping Tricia wasn't about to make everything a whole lot worse.

'Oh do let me get in Pepper. One of these days we'll have a nasty accident between us. OK, OK I'll feed you first and then I must phone the travel agent. I'll feel better once that's out of the way.'

'Ah, good afternoon. Suzie left a message yesterday and this is the first chance I've had to get back to her.'

'Sorry she's not in this afternoon.'

Harriet couldn't have been more pleased.

'Oh that's alright. I'm Harriet Glover. Unfortunately for personal reasons I had to return home urgently and Mrs. Harrington kindly came back with me.'

'What was your booking reference number?'

'Oh sorry I haven't just got that to hand. We flew out last Sunday 27th June. It was your four night package tour to Venice…'

'Er just a minute. I seem to remember something coming in about that one. I'll go and check.'

Harriet went from one foot to the other waiting endless anxious moments for his return.

'Oh yes. Suzie's left a note here. Oh and what's this she's crossed out? Ah right! There was an issue over a fall here concerning a Mrs. Violet Moss. Ah right, I see. She withdrew the complaint this morning apparently.'

'Oh I wasn't even aware of it.' Harriet declared, dealing in less than half-truths.

'So that will be it then, or is there anything else I can do for you Harriet?'

'Well not that I know of. I've explained why we left early. Oh yes. The other thing is the hotel key card. There was no one around to give it to. Will it be alright if I send it back to the hotel?'

'Just return it to us at the contact address on the website Harriet. We'll forward it with the explanation. They do get this happen from time to time. Make sure you send it recorded delivery.'

'Right I'll do just that. Thank you very much for your help.'

'My pleasure Harriet. We look forward to dealing with you again in the future, maybe?'

'Certainly. Yes most certainly.' Harriet replaced the receiver. 'Most certainly not Pepper! Once I've got the address from that Hotonyourheels.com website that will be it. Let's hope there's no more of it. Talk about living up to their name!'

She tried to sit on the nervous pangs beginning to haunt this inconclusive conclusion. She wondered how long it would be before Violet Moss twigged she'd been impersonated. She didn't like the growing web of lies, so easily told in desperation to get her and Tricia off the hook. She thought about Barry.

Hoped she wouldn't need him. She thought about Mr. Sanderson. Couldn't make out why he should want to keep up the charade for Molly's benefit. She wasn't looking forward to that either but she'd already decided she was in too much of a mess to infuriate him further by refusing. He might just be needed to bail them both out.

'That's if Tricia doesn't blow it completely with him Pepper. Rapping Hammer will never agree to that. Not after all that being broadcast on television on Christmas night. I'd be surprised if he had any fans left. I think I'll go down to the garden centre, too, Pepper. I need some tomatoes and I'll see if I can get Mummy another planter of autumn bulbs to make up for scattering all her spring ones on *his* drive at Christmas. I'll get her something to fill that planter too. Those tomato plants will soon be coming to an end.'

Harriet closed the back door on the cat, grabbed her bag and went in the hope of catching Tricia to talk her out of it. It was busy. The half-price bedding plants always drew the less than keen gardeners. She squeezed herself into the only parking spot available. Right opposite the sheds. She thought of Belinda Oxfordshire banging the door closed on them. Of how she'd managed to poke a thick twig down through the metal loop where the lock goes, trapping her and Mark inside. They'd had to buy it. Mark had kicked hard at the door. Guy Hammer had spotted the damage. She shuddered as she walked past them. Hoping not to meet with her. Belinda Oxfordshire was the last thing she needed just now.

'Oh Harriet. I thought it was you. It's so busy in here. I just caught sight of you behind that boy wheeling his barrow across. What a time to be restocking shelves. Especially with big bags of compost. He could hardly keep his barrow straight. Do you know Daddy and I... He's just over there Harriet. I left him by the weed-killer. Come on Harriet he'll catch us up outside. Let's start walking to the car. Now where was I? Oh yes, on our way in Daddy and I met with Mr. and Mrs. Moss. She's only recently joined the WI Harriet. She's ever such a nice woman. They've just come back from a trip to Venice apparently. Oh you wouldn't believe what that poor woman went through Harriet. Anyway they've filed a complaint, I won't go into it now. Now where was I? What was I going to say? Oh yes that rude lad almost turned his wheelbarrow right over. Running straight at her he was. She only managed to jump out of the way just in time. Landed on Cedric's feet Harriet. That's her poor husband. He was positively hobbling behind her. That's why they were going Harriet. So soon. Only just got here! She was going to have to drive home. Poor woman hasn't got behind a steering wheel for the last ten years. Apparently. I do hope she gets them home in one piece Harriet. It's his fault. Young lout!'

Harriet was about to open her mouth to speak.

'I left you a message Harriet. Do you know Daddy and I have been worried sick about you? And poor Mr. Sanderson, Harriet. I hope you've come to your senses and apologised to him. I'm just hoping he'll understand it's all to do with your age Harriet. After all he is a doctor though I don't expect he ever came across anyone quite like you Harriet while he was in practice. Poor man having to postpone the wedding like that. You're most fortunate he's prepared to give you a second chance.'

'Postpone it Mummy? Where exactly did you get that from? According to him it's off!'

'Well there you go Harriet. My worst fears come true! So what will you do now? Not go back to that Bohemian boyfriend I hope? Not after letting you down like that at the church. Really Harriet don't you think you've put Daddy and I through enough?'

'Not intentionally Mummy. It's just the way things went. You wouldn't be saying all this if Mr. Sanderson hadn't stepped in. Don't forget I didn't ask for any of it!'

'Of course she didn't Frances. Now don't be so hard on her.'

Harriet felt her father's arm around her shoulder.

'Oh Daddy. I'm sorry. I'm really *so* sorry.'

'There Frances now look what you done. You've made her cry.'

'No, I'll be alright Daddy. Mummy's right. I don't think I've ever really grown up.'

'Of course you have Harriet! Now best foot forward. You know Daddy and I love you. You know we only want the best for you. Now are you coming back to us for a nice cup of tea? Maybe we could invite Violet and Cedric in as well Daddy. Help her to get over that nasty experience. Rude boy! Introduce them to Harriet. You know I've been wanting to do that. Ask them in ever since they moved in next door.'

The tear about to roll down Harriet's cheek almost froze. Instantly recovered she made her excuses.

'Sorry Mummy I've got too much to do. Don't forget it's back to school again on Monday.'

'Oh of course it is Harriet. The weekend doesn't give you much time. Now if there's anything at all Daddy and I can help you with you only have to ask.'

'I know that Mummy. I promise to call round before long.'

'Now do that Harriet. While you're in there would you mind picking up a hanging basket for me? Daddy wouldn't let me buy one. You said it would make too much mess in the car, didn't you George?'

'Aye and she's not going to be wanting to mess hers up, either!'

'Oh it's alright Daddy. Mine's a battered old thing anyway. No, I'll get you one Mummy.'

'That's good of you Harriet, now don't be too long getting it back to me. Violet was saying how lovely Mrs. Jones' front looks. Of course I never did get a show of spring bulbs Harriet. I expect Mark's mother's planter was overflowing with them. Hippy, Harriet. No manners, giving me the one that had spilled out. Now don't you be getting tucked up with him again. Oh we know you're not moving Harriet. Mrs. Moss had shown interest in your house before deciding on the one next door to us. Apparently she wanted to know why it was back on the market. Spotted it when she picked up the keys on moving in day. She was told the sale had fallen through.'

'No Mummy, they just haven't caught up with it yet. We're still waiting for them to take the board down.'

'Oh I'll tell her. It was her daughter who wanted to know. Apparently she's another one. Living together! Violet's very upset Avril couldn't have found someone of the same class. Pregnant she is and they haven't got two pennies to rub together. So Violet and Cedric are helping them find somewhere. Of course they're entitled Harriet as they'll be all but financing it. She knows they won't end up with much, but at least yours would have given them that extra room for the baby. That's why they've moved here Harriet. You know they're from Hamesforth Harriet. Plenty of money there! Downsizing to help them out. What a good woman Harriet. She'll be so disappointed.'

'Come on Frances. We're blocking the way. Harriet wants to get on, don't you love?'

'Oh that's alright Daddy. But yes, I suppose I'd better go. Get Mummy's hanging basket.'

'Oh do hurry up Harriet. There was only two left when I last looked.'

Harriet stepped sideways to let people get through, pecked their cheeks and watched them walk away, waiting until they'd reached their car. With a quick wave she continued on her way. Desperate to find Tricia to impart the unbelievably bad news of Violet Moss's whereabouts.

Chapter 42

'Ah Harriet my dear. It's good to see you back. Now what's this I've been hearing about our friend Joris and his new young lady? Fill me in Harriet my dear. You'll know who she is her working in the school and all that.'

'Oh hello Mr. Bridgewater. Gosh I'm bumping into everybody today. Just seen Mummy and Daddy, too.'

'Well it's the sunshine, always brings them out! Now what about those tomatoes I gave you dear, did you enjoy them?'

'Oh yes thank you Mr. Bridgewater. Of course I left them in Mr. Sanderson's car by mistake so it was a couple of days before I got them back. I've been meaning to thank you again, though. Certainly prize tomatoes those!'

'Oh don't you worry your pretty little head about that Harriet. I've been away you know. Just come back to catch the tail end of the gossip. Then off again.'

'Not Lucinda Lawton again,' Harriet thought. She certainly wasn't about to fill him in.

'The tomatoes Mr. Bridgewater. How did you manage to get them to taste so good?'

'Well it's all down to Mr. Swift, Sanderson's gardener you know Harriet. He's quite an expert with the old propagation. How he managed the heart shape as well dear, I'll never know. But there you are! I'll see if I can get some more to you sweetheart. Now I've promised Mr. Swift a couple of trays of plants I've been growing from seed. You'll be in school on Monday Harriet, will you?'

'Yes Mr. Bridgewater.'

'Well now Harriet I wonder if you could help me out dear?' He looked at his watch. 'I'm meeting Iris at the sailing club now. We're going through the accounts together Harriet before we go. Yes, I'm away again but not on my own this time dear. Iris and I have become very good friends.'

He winked.

'We're off for a couple of weeks. Old Joris is looking after the sailing club for me. No, she's a wonderful woman Harriet. She's got it all up there. Does more than make a mean cup of tea. No I've never looked back since she's been appointed treasurer. Anyway It'll save me popping back. I've a good neighbour who'll be looking after the place while I'm away so don't worry about closing up. Now if you'd like to pop in there on the way back from here, the side gate is open Harriet. There's a few bags of tomatoes sitting alongside the trays of plants in the greenhouse. Just by the door as you go in. Take all you want Harriet and if you wouldn't mind taking the plants to school on Monday and passing them over to Joris. Take him some for the school as well Harriet and keep the rest for yourself. They're very nice flowers are those. Late flowering of course. A mix of colours. Can't just remember the name. Anyway if you can clear that side Harriet then I can get the seedlings up off the floor.'

'Oh would you like me to put those on the top for you?'

'Now that's very kind Harriet. It'll save Gordon a job. He'll be in to water them.'

'Oh that's no trouble at all Mr. Bridgewater and thank you very much for the tomatoes, too. I was going to get some from here anyway.'

'Now Harriet, just before I go, can you throw any light at all on what Joris is up to? Rumour has it this young lady's already turned him down once, but he's not giving up. He's determined to marry her. Now what did they say her name was dear? L.., Lavenda. I think it was Lavenda, just like the flowers. So pretty they are when you look into them Harriet. I doubt if she'd be as pretty as them, or as you, dear.'

'It's Lucinda, Mr. Bridgewater. It's Lucinda Lawton and she's much prettier than me!'

'Never mind dear, we all have to go with what we're given. Beauty is in the eye of the beholder Harriet. That's what they say. And for what it's worth I've always found you very attractive my dear.'

He paused to stroke his chin.

'Now there's a good looking young woman. Belinda Oxfordshire,' he continued. 'As you know I had the pleasure of driving that young lady all the way back from the Palace. She was very put out no one could see their way to recommending her for a damehood. I told her to bide her time. I said it wouldn't be long before Joris swung it for her. All she needed to do was get him back. But there you go Harriet. I was wrong. I was convinced their engagement would be back on by the time we all got to the Palace. Not to be. Looks like he already had this other young lady in tow.'

'Quite Mr. Bridgewater. That's exactly what it looks like. I must get on if I'm to be collecting those plants from your house on my way back.'

'Yes of course. Goodbye my dear. Give my best to Mark.'

Harriet seethed her way past the row of bushes lining the walk to the side entrance. Glaring at the newly stacked bags of compost, she made her way through to the crafts department, just stopping short of the knitting patterns. There it was. Identical to the one she had in her knitting bag at home.

'Well it's not going to be for Mark and definitely not for *him* now. It looks like his mother's beaten me to it anyway! I'll finish it. Oh I'll finish it alright. And I'll finish it for Barry!'

Still fuming she felt better for having the thought as she continued to the outside. Then she didn't. She suddenly remembered MI5.

Chapter 43

'Oh 'ello love, I 'aven't seen you down 'ere for ages. Where 'ave you been 'idin'? In that shed? Or 'asn't that funny bugger of yours put it up yet? I'll do it you know. Just let me know when 'e's out. I'll 'ave it up in a tick.'

'Oh no thank you Guy. That's very kind of you but it's already up. Daddy came round to do it.'

'So you've been 'idin' in it then?'

'No, no. Not that one at least Guy. Sorry. Just a joke! You haven't joined your Wayne then and gone off rocking?'

'No 'arriet and it's not for the want of droppin' 'ints. I'm better than 'im with a plectrum any day. I'm better than 'im without one too, if you know what I mean? I've always been good with my 'ands.'

'Oh I'm sure you have Guy. Anyway I must get on.'

''ang on a minute love. I've just been talkin' to that friend of yours. She's 'ad me on the phone to our Wayne wantin' 'im to do another gig in aid of saving Venice. I didn't think our Wayne would go for it after what she did to 'im, 'e 'ad to go into therapy after that. Of course our Wayne, just 'is luck, ended up gettin' 'is leg over the therapist didn't 'e! 'e's still seein' 'er, not for therapy though, if you know what I mean?' He grinned then continued.

'Apparently she detraumatised 'im by showin' 'im 'ow Leonardo da Vinci got to work on the human body.'ow 'e stole dead bodies to study them so 'e could sculpt the male form in all its glory, if you know what I mean? She told 'im 'e'd advanced mankind not only by being the first to show 'ow the body worked, but also by makin' the naked form public. You know, carved in stone, statues like. Drawings. Everyone could see 'ow little some of 'em 'ad. If you know what I mean?'

Harriet, uncomfortable, shuffled from one foot to the other as he began again.

'She said our Wayne 'ad done the nation a favour. 'im bein' a sex rocker and all that. Hyped up to make the girls think there was plenty be'ind that black leather in the front, if you know what I mean? She told 'im by revealin' all 'e'd given a realistic insight into pop idol's… Err if you know what I'm sayin'? Calmed the expectation for millions of girls while their boyfriends would be breathin' one big sigh of relief.

By the time she'd finished she 'ad 'im convinced 'e'd made a very valuable contribution to both art and science 'imself by being exposed on national TV. Of course it was really only when our Wayne got 'is leg over was 'e truly convinced 'e 'ad enough for 'er needs anyway.'

Harriet wanted to go. This was so embarrassing. She opened her mouth. Closed it again. He wasn't quite finished.

'I wouldn't be 'avin' that problem myself. I've known 'im put a small cucumber down there so 'is leathers zipped that tight 'e could 'ardly move. That was when `e really wanted to work the crowd though. `e'd always do that for live TV. `e wasn't expectin` to be endin` up on telly after dressin` up as Father Christmas. Good job `e wasn't. `e'd `ave looked a right fool if `is cucumber `ad dropped out! Anyway `e's so glad to be rid of it `e said `e owes a lot to Leonardo da Vinci. `e's opin` to get over there `imself with the tape measure just to make sure. `e wants to get measurin` a few before they crumble away! Yeah, so yeah! `e's goin` to do it for a good cause.'

'Oh I see. Er no mention of Fastnet then?'

'Well yeah it would take more than that to get `im back. That's what made `im say `e'd push the Venice thing to the lads. They've always wanted to do a gig there. `e reckons this charity thing'll give them a publicity boost in advance of their concert. So `e said `e won't be chargin` Chick-Lips.'

'Something in it for everyone then.'

'Eh don't go tellin` `er I've told you all that. We don't want to send `im back into therapy do we, if you know what I mean?'

'No, certainly not Guy. You can trust me!'

'Well I wish I could trust Paula the same. I'm not tellin` `er anythin` again. You don't fancy a night out to the Arena Central do you? See `ow `e's gettin` on without `is cucumber!'

'No thank you Guy. You take Paula.'

'Ah eh. That happened last time!'

Harriet bustled past him to try to find Tricia. No sign. She threw her bag into an abandoned trolley and headed for the hanging baskets, grabbed one together with four half-price trays of French marigolds. Arrived at the checkout. Thought. 'Flipping heck. Him! With them both!' She could see Belinda Oxfordshire on one side and Lucinda Lawton on the other. The pair of them with one hand each stretched back to the trolley handle and him standing in the middle. A swift reverse took her back towards Guy Hammer's shed.

'Do you want me to run them through the swipe `arriet? It's busy through there.'

'Oh thanks Guy. That's brilliant.'

'Don't forget, if you change your mind it's two weeks on Saturday our Wayne'll be at the Arena. Straight there after doing your friend's gig. I don't know `ow `e keeps goin`.'

'No, busy life. Anyway, terribly sorry Guy. Can't make it. Actually I've got something else on then. Sorry!'

She urged her trolley through the bark chippings and out on the side path back to her car.

'Yes I've most certainly got something on two weeks on Saturday,' she thought. 'Two weeks on Saturday I've got to go to Molly's with *him*.'

Driving along. Almost at 4 The Willows now, she suddenly remembered Tarquin Bridgewater's plants. A sharp turn right instead of left brought the traffic screeching to a halt both forward and behind. She carried on, horns beeping in all their noisy variety blasting her ear drums until she was well on her way to his front drive.

She pushed the side gate open, not sure she wanted his tomatoes now, after him completely sinking her self-esteem.

'Gosh the size of his greenhouse!' She couldn't believe her eyes. 'I'll never get all these in the car,' she said to herself, sliding the door across. Both sides, tomatoes everywhere. Some sitting in bags, some sitting on bags, spilling over to the trays of plants lined edge to edge either side, running their length, all the way to the back. Not yet in flower. All looking the same.

She looked at both sides. Counted twenty eight trays to her right. Couldn't distinguish one side from the other only that there was probably more tied off bags at the end where the door didn't slide back so she went for those.

'Bloody cheek. I need a van for this lot!' Fuming she backed the car onto the drive. Opened all the doors and the boot. Trecked back and forth until the whole side was cleared of trays.

'And where am I supposed to put this now?' She said out loud, lifting the hanging basket off the ground. 'I suppose it will just have to hang from the grab handle above one of the doors.

She struggled trying to hold the basket up. The plants trailing her arms as she looped the double chain through the handle, twisting it through and back on itself to make a knot. Barely able to see her way off the drive from her rear mirror, she backed off heading straight for home.

'Oh Pepper, I'm sorry I bothered. Look I've been lumbered with this lot. I don't want to be seeing *him,* having to give him plants. It's bad enough having to go to school with him there, never mind this. Oh come on Pepper let's get them out of the car and take them all round the back. I can't remember which ones I bought for Mummy now. They all look the same. Just a minute Pepper. That sounds like someone coming up the side.'

'Oh there you are `arriet. I thought I saw your car ahead of me, but I got stuck with the lights. You've got plants all over the place! Are you thinkin` of openin` your own garden centre `arriet?'

'No I most certainly am not Tricia! I went down there to see if I might catch you. Didn't I just see everybody else? Oh come on in Tricia. Let's make a cup of tea, these can wait until later.'

'Now that's a good idea `arriet. I didn't see any sign of you either, though of course I wasn't exactly lookin` seein` as I wasn't expectin` you to be there. Still I did see our friend though `arriet. Puttin` `is arm round Lucinda Lanky. Oh you should `ave seen the look on Belinda Oxfordshire's face and she's supposed to `ave the `ots for fish-feet-four-cheeks! That's what I call `im now `arriet. I don't know `ow long it's goin` to last livin` under the same roof as `im.'

'Ah sit down Tricia. Let's put the kettle on. I believe you've got some good news to tell me.'

'Oh you've seen Guy `ammer aven't you `arriet?'

'I did Tricia and I'm pleased Rapping Hammer's agreed to it. A stroke of good fortune him also interested in saving Venice.'

'Yes `arriet. I couldn't believe my luck. Apparently `e's been after doin` a concert there for ages and `is agent's never been able to swing it for `im. `e thinks it'll `elp if `e's seen supportin` my charity.'

'Oh Tricia. There's something else as well. Here Tricia, open these while I make the tea.'

'Thanks `arriet. Oh chocolate chips. I love these `arriet. Now don't keep me guessin` any longer.'

Harriet plonked the mugs on the table to watch Tricia dunking her biscuit.

'I've been sworn to secrecy Tricia so don't let on, promise?'

'I promise `arriet. Now what is it you `ave to tell me?'

'It's Rapping Hammer Tricia. He had to have therapy after that do at Starboard Marine North West.'

'Ooh `e didn't did `e `arriet?'

Harriet could feel her shoulders starting to shake.

'Oh Tricia, he….' She took a deep breath, trying to control herself.

'Go on `arriet what did `e do?'

'He was so traumatised at the zip going on his leathers and you pulling off his nylon scarf and then it all being shown on TV, he lost it Tricia.'

Tricia started giggling.

'Where did `e go for therapy `arriet?'

'Well I don't know where but it was some woman using Leonardo da Vinci's desire to get the male anatomy right for his drawings and sculpture, by pinching dead bodies, Tricia.'

'Pinchin` dead bodies `arriet? That's revoltin`!'

'Too right it is Tricia, but wait until I tell you this.' Harriet started shaking. 'She convinced him that by exposing his little one to the whole world he was destroying the macho rock star image for good!'

'Oh `arriet. Am I really `earin` this?' Tricia now creased in two.

'I haven't finish… I haven…. I hav… I…' Harriet was tearing at the kitchen roll wiping her cheeks.

'Not more `arrie… Not more `ar…' With her legs buckling Tricia leant against the glass in the back door struggling to keep from sliding.

'Ooooh she's persuaded him to take the cucumber out of the front of his black leathers. She said he had enough sex appeal just as he was. Then Guy Hammer said his Wayne had got his leg over, Tricia, and that's what had convinced him!'

'Oooh `arriet. Don't tell me any more. I can't take any more. I'm goin` to die `arriet!'

'Then he said … Then he… Then…' With her hand on her stomach Harriet finally screeched it out.

'He wants to go to Venice to find some male statues to measure them all Tricia before they all crumble away, just to make sure she's not having him on!'

The pair of them screeched from one worktop to the other, rolling round the kitchen in severe physical pain. They didn't hear the knock on the back door.

Just looked up to see the face at the window.

Chapter 44

He was there. Had opened the back door and was standing full in the doorway. His expression. Looked like he'd just walked into the Hadron Collider. His face cold as steel.

'Lucinda's out there Miss Glover. Just tripped over one of those damned trays of plants you've left lying around. Quite a nasty fall. Rolled backwards, startled the cat. Ended up scratched all the way down her right arm. Belinda's out there now seeing to her. Have you got anything antiseptic? Quick Miss Glover. Cat's get their claws everywhere!'

Instinctively Harriet flew to the bathroom. Came down to him drumming his fingertips on the end of the banister at the bottom of the stairs. She passed him a flattened tube.

'I doubt if there's anything left in this Miss Glover.'

He opened the front door while the back door banged shut. Marched out.

'Bloody hell Tricia he's got no right bringing them all round here. It wasn't my fault!'

Tricia nudged her with her elbow.

In again. His foot on the pedal at the bottom of the bin.

'Barely sufficient Miss Glover. Belinda's taking her home. Damned nuisance. We called in to collect the plants from Bridgewater. I've just seen him at the sailing club. He told me he'd asked you to bring them to school on Monday. Anyhow as we had the two cars between us I thought it a good opportunity to get them distributed along with the rest. It looks like you two had better give me a hand instead.'

Harriet looked at Tricia. It was Saturday afternoon. They were reading each other's fury.

'Right Mrs. Harrington if you'd like to take half down to Starboard Marine North West, Miss Glover and I will take the rest to the school. My boot's already full to overflowing with those we picked up at the garden centre.'

'Err Mr. Sanderson, Mr. Bridgewater said two trays were to go to Mr. Swift...'

'Right, right. Not a problem. I'll empty my boot of two now and we'll pop those in their place.'

'But Mr. Sanderson I bought four trays for Mummy this afternoon from the garden centre as well as a hanging basket.'

'There's four out there Miss Glover. I nearly broke my neck on them. I can't think why you should leave them right across the path behind the gate. No sense of order whatsoever.'

Tricia glanced at Harriet.

'Right it's the rest of them then. Come along. We're all having to give up a couple of hours of our spare time today. Let's get this over and done with as quickly as we can.'

Harriet grabbed her bag and locked the back door. Their tea left to go cold on the kitchen table. His silver Mercedes. Outside. Boot lid up. Switching plants. Tricia loading hers. Waving to Harriet. On her way now to Starboard Marine North West.

'Right Miss Glover. I'll follow you. We can't be having you stopping off at Starboard Marine North West first, the damned things will never get delivered!'

'Bloody cheek,' Harriet thought as she backed the car off the drive to go on ahead of him. 'What a bloody cheek that man's got!'

She stopped at the lights outside Starboard Marine North West. Looked across to see the boot of Tricia's car open. Strained her neck to see if she could see her. Then jumped as Mr. Sanderson beeped loudly on the horn to move her along. She fumed her way to school, determined to let her feelings be known.

Once through the gateway she pulled to a halt outside the main entrance. He stopped behind. Got out.

'Round the back Miss Glover. Let's leave them somewhere sensible for Brown. We're hardly going to be leaving them on the front step now, are we?'

Furious she drove round the back. Got out and opened the boot lid. He parked alongside her.

'I see you've now recovered your equilibrium sufficiently Miss Glover to see fit to indulge in unseemly giggling school-girl behaviour with Mrs. Harrington. It's high time you acted your age.'

'No law against laughing Mr. Sanderson.'

'You're still employed and therefore under my authority Miss Glover. Just remember to whom you are speaking! You seem to have forgotten the trail of devastation the pair of you have left behind on your return from Venice. Maybe you are right Miss Glover. There's certainly no law against laughing. There is however a law against criminality and feedback suggests you two are flying very close to the wind. Oh they've pinned it down. Have no fear of that. It's only my intervention that's stopping you both from being arrested. Indeed the PM is now anxious to speak with you both. There's only so much he can do Miss Glover. Once it becomes expedient for MI6 to throw it all open they will. And believe you me they will Miss Glover. You do realise that between the pair of you you've blown the cover on an opertion that's taken three years to pull together. They were just on the point of arrest and then you two come on the scene. Yes indeed, Miss Glover. You who chose to abscond with Mrs. Harrington. You both, who seemingly are able to toss all sense of responsibility to the wind, leaving me with far more than pieces to pick up Miss Glover. Believe you me!'

Harriet paled. He meant it.

'Now Miss Glover. Has there been any sign of miscarriage? No period type symptoms at all?'

She looked down, the colour flooding her cheeks.

'Come, come Miss Glover. No need for embarrassment. We've been here before. I have a right to an answer.'

'No sign Mr. Sanderson.'

'We can't delay discussing this any further Miss Glover. I want you in my office sharp at 3.30 Monday.'

Chapter 45

Harriet returned home to the phone ringing. She let the answer machine click in. She didn't feel like talking. He'd just hit her from both sides.

'Mum it's Clare. Do answer Mummy we're phoning from the Seychelles. We want to know how you and Daddy are. How does it feel to be married? We love it!'

Harriet took a very deep breath as she lifted the receiver. She couldn't not. They were her babies still. They knew nothing of any of it. What to say? She hardly knew where to start.

'Clare it's lovely to hear from you. How did it go?'

'We emailed the photographs Mum. Didn't you get them? Watch out for them in case they've got caught up somewhere.'

'Thank you Clare we'll certainly do that.'

'Now how did your wedding go Mum? Does it feel any different being married?'

Harriet dithered. Decided there was nothing else for it but to come clean.

'We didn't actually get married Clare. In the end we both had our reservations.'

'Oh well done Mum. Rachael and I didn't want anything to change. What about the house? When are you moving to Millington?'

'We're not moving Clare. We decided to stay put.'

'That's even better Mum. Wait until I tell Rachael we've still got the family home. What about the people though? You'd exchanged contracts. What happened about that?'

'Oh, thankfully it all worked out. Someone from Dad's work, just got divorced, needed a place. She stepped in. Her parents put the money up so it wasn't a problem.'

'Whoosh Mum that was lucky. We'll see you soon. We're all planning a trip up in a few weeks time. Probably at the end of the month or early August. Something like that.'

'That's lovely Clare. Can't wait to see you all. Oh you might like to time it to coincide with Rapping Hammer, he's doing a gig for Tricia's new charity on the same day as the school fair.'

'Oh yes we'll certainly do that then. Wait until I tell Rachael. We'll definitely be up for that. Anyway I must go. Rachael sends her love. They're snorkelling at the moment. Not quite my thing so I've been lying on the beach. Just come back in to make this call.'

'Well I appreciate it Clare. You enjoy this next week and we'll speak again once you all get back.'

'If we get back Mum. If that Icelandic volcano stops hurling clouds of ash into the sky. What's it like now? Any signs of things getting back to normal?'

'Just starting to Clare. I'm sure by next weekend there won't be any problems at all.'

'That's good Mum. Clare and I can't wait to get back to play married housewives. We're going to look for houses nearby so we can be close together.'

'That's lovely Clare. I'll look forward to hearing all about it.'

'Bye Mum. Give Dad our love.'

Harriet put the phone down. There was no way she would have spoilt their honeymoons by trying to explain. At least she'd been able to offer them Rapping Hammer, thanks to Tricia. At least it was something she'd been able to mention. She looked at her watch. Wondered what time Mark would appear. Unwittingly Clare had thrown her right back to amber. For the first time she focussed her mind on the havoc she'd wreaked on the family. She knew it wouldn't be easy trying to explain. Especially from prison!

She looked at the phone. Picked it up. Put it down. Couldn't decide whether to phone Barry. It was all starting to feel very sticky. Couldn't decide what to do. She needed to tell Tricia about the PM. The PM wanting to talk to them. Yes she needed to tell Tricia they'd been identified. They'd blown it. She lifted the receiver.

'Ooh `arriet, I've only just got back in. You wouldn't believe it `arriet. I `ad that toffee-nosed Lucinda woman limpin` all over the place and Belinda Oxfordshire gettin` under my feet unloadin` more plants from the boot of `er car. She would never `ave `ad room to take your lot `arriet, so we'd `ave got roped in anyway. Anyway `arriet I `ope you don't mind but I pinched one of your trays for myself. `e's goin` to `ave far too many plants `ere.'

'Of course not Tricia. It'll give you something to take your mind off this.'

'Off what `arriet? What do you mean?'

'Mr. Sanderson, Tricia. They know it's us. They've traced it back to us!'

'Ooh `arriet. Just a minute let me pull a chair up. I don't think I like the sound of what I'm `earin`.'

'No Tricia. I'm wondering whether or not to go back to Barry. The PM wants to see us both Tricia. He wants to talk to us.'

'Whatever for `arriet? What's it got to do with `im?'

'I'm not sure Tricia. All I know is it proves we were right about Mr. Sanderson using the PM's heavies to track us down. They've probably given him a blow by blow account by now. I can't think what it's got to do with the PM unless those bruisers were out there already investigating something else and somehow we've blown it for them. Mr. Sanderson seemed to be suggesting something like that.'

'Oh `arriet. You mean because we jumped up just a bit too quick and shot them off the boat into the water before they'd `ardly `ad chance to get onboard?'

'Yes Tricia that's exactly it. When you think about it Mr. Sanderson's obviously mentioned our disappearance to the PM. He's had us traced via the airports Tricia. Told him we'd flown to Venice. He'd have got all the details Tricia. Known the hotel and everything. The PM then tells Mr. Sanderson his bodyguards are out there on a case, whatever that would be about I don't know.

Anyway they're instructed to keep an eye on us at the same time. And of course we've blown it. They'd probably had enough by the time they'd nearly drowned Tricia. Lost all thread and came back.'

'Ooh `arriet. I think you're right. But then they were supposed to be going to San Marco weren't they `arriet? They were supposed to be takin` a boat from over the other side of the bridge to finish the rest of their journey, so why would they come back `arriet? We didn't stop them goin` there if San Marco was where it was all `appenin`.'

'No you are absolutely right Tricia. Why did they come back?'

'Unless they came back for their `ats and shades `ariet. Those bald `eads would most probably be gettin` a bit sensitive in that very `ot sun.'

'No Tricia. They could have picked any amount of straw hats up between the Rialto Bridge and San Marco. I'm sure I saw them stacked on some of the boats. No Tricia that doesn't make sense. If it was all happening in San Marco and they were on the case that's just where they would have gone.'

'Ooh maybe your right `arriet. But I still think it's got somethin` to do with us tippin` them in the water.'

'Unless they had cameras on them Tricia and the evidence for whatever was ruined. Do you think it might be something like that?'

'It could be `arriet but it still doesn't explain why they came back.'

'No and none of it explains what Andy and Barry have got to do with it all. They must have something to do with it Tricia. Barry wouldn't have given me his phone number to contact him if things got too sticky.'

'`is that what `e said `arriet? Oh yes of course `e did. I remember you tellin` me now. Well if those two `eavies were on the case why would Andy and Barry be `elpin` them out? We never saw them talkin` to them did we? No `arriet I think we've got it all wrong. I think those two were just `avin` an `oliday. An `oliday watchin` the girls. They said somethin` about lookin` but not touchin` didn't they? That's why they were divin` off all the time. Nudgin` each other when they spotted one. No that would be it `arriet. That would most definitely be it.'

'Do you think so Tricia? Well why would Barry be offering to help out like that? You know he definitely said he was frightened we'd become embroiled in things outside of our control. He also said San Marco was supposed to be the end of the road, but we screwed it up.'

'Well we don't know why they were goin` there do we `arriet? Maybe they'd gone on ahead to arrange a nice surprise for us. They could have booked us all another romantic evenin` on the gondola, followin` dinner, of course. They might just `ave wanted to give us a lovely surprise. After all they were only talkin` about bein` away for a couple of hours. We don't know what nice things they `ad in mind for us do we?'

'Well no Tricia. I've probably read too much into what he was saying. We'd already had them up for being part of MI5. I suppose that was a bit far fetched. Perhaps it was just that they were concerned about the area around the hotel.

There's probably all kinds of things go on there. No, that was more like it Tricia. I think you could be right. But then Mr. Sanderson said something about MI6. He said something like "Once it becomes expedient for them to throw it all open, they will." '

'Whatever that means `arriet? It doesn't mean that Andy and Barry `ave got anythin` to do with it. That's just the construction *we've* put on it `arriet.'

'Do you know Tricia, you're right. It still doesn't answer the question though of why Barry offered to help out.'

'Well that would be in case we get into trouble for abscondin` `arriet. That would all be about the `otel and breakin` into the filin` cabinet. Oh and Violet Moss. That's what it would all be about. Barry probably wants to stick up for us if it gets too sticky. That's all `arriet.'

'So what do you think Tricia? Fingers crossed. Do you think it's pretty much sorted out with regard to the hotel? Shall I give Barry a call? We could bounce a few things off him and Andy without giving the game away. At least it would give us the chance to see if we are right about them.'

'Yes I think that would be a good idea `arriet. We don't want to be `avin` to go crawlin` to our friend Joris. Just tell `im we `aven't done anythin` wrong and we won't be seein` the PM under any circumstances `arriet.'

'Right Tricia. Easier said than done.'

'Oh give `im a kiss `arriet. That'll work wonders for `is bad temper on Monday.'

Chapter 46

Harriet closed the classroom door on the 3.30 stampede. Always louder, always faster on a Monday. She'd spent the day wondering. Wondering how she was going to deal with Mr. Sanderson. Wondering why Mark hadn't come back from Millington. Wondering why he should want to spend all his weekend with Melissa Scott when he'd told her she was not on. Not on for marrying her, at least. Harriet felt sure that wouldn't please Melissa's lovely mummy one bit. She'd come to the conclusion Mark was only back at 4 The Willows to dodge her, having accomplished his mission to squash Mr. Sanderson once and for all. She looked at her watch. Smoothed her hair and pulled her top down over her skirt. Thought about her baby. She'd fight her corner to keep it!

'In Miss Glover! Take a seat will you.'

Harriet stepped forward. He closed the door behind her. She sat down, carefully placing her bag under her chair. She didn't want the long strap tripping anyone up this time. She looked away to the bench by the wall. Spotted a plastic bowl sitting on a folded white towel A pair of transparent surgical gloves alongside.

'Now Miss Glover.' He looked at his watch. 'I trust you're not in a hurry as I've got quite a lot to get through.'

In a panic Harriet reached for the strap on her bag. Thought. 'Oh no! He needn't think he's doing it now. Here. Right here.'

'Relax Miss Glover, will you. It's not going to take all that long. You were never that averse to spending time in my company as I recall.'

She dropped the strap. Thought. 'Don't be so stupid Harriet. There's no way he could do it here. Anyway I'll go. I'll just walk out. I'm the right side of the desk. I'll get out before he can stop me.'

She managed to calm herself down. Looked at him. Tried to sit on that feeling again. His hair thick. Blonde. His deep blue eyes searching. Serious. Scanning her face. Moving down. Resting on her breasts for a brief moment. Then down settling his gaze around and below her waist. Through the window. Red brick all the way to the sky. The buildings offering a narrow gap to the afternoon sun cutting like a sword straight into her eyes. Outlining him. His shoulders. Broad. Strong. Both his hands on the table now. Open. Flat. Palms set hard against the old grained wood.

'In your eyes Miss Glover? Here let me pull this down.'

She panicked. Thought. 'He's going to! No one can see in!' She reached for her bag. He stopped. Only half way down. She felt silly. Pulled out a tissue. Blew her nose.

'Now Miss Glover. First things first. A difficult one that. You're in such an atrocious mess it's virtually impossible to prioritise. Maybe you'd like to suggest just where we might start?'

'I've spoken with Mrs. Harrington, Mr. Sanderson. We've been through everything we did in Venice over and over again and apart from cutting the trip a bit short, we're quite certain we didn't do anything at all wrong and in which case we have decided we are not going to meet with the Prime Minister.' Her trembled-out words resonated between them as she tried to stop from shaking.

'Most unwise Miss Glover. I don't think you have any choice whatsoever in the matter. We've already put the kindest construction we can on your behaviour. Based of course on the fact that this trip couldn't have been anything other than impromptu given the circumstances you, err, we were in. But it needs verifying Miss Glover. Even that could suggest involvement. Those kind of people operate on the edge. Call in accomplices, decoys at a moment's notice. They know every trick in the book and they use every trick in the book to keep their outfits operating.'

'But whatever's been going on has nothing whatsoever to do with Mrs. Harrington and I, Mr. Sanderson. Please tell the Prime Minister we'd be wasting his valuable time. We were just a couple of tourists like millions of others. Perhaps they'd better get looking. It's nothing to do with us. Nothing whatsoever.'

He stood up. Ran his fingers through his hair. Sat down again.

'I can see I'm wasting my time Miss Glover. Complete and utter waste of time. You're missing the point completely.'

He stood again. Walked over to the long table on the other side of the room. Picked up the bowl. Put it down. She could feel the gap in her chest as her heart missed to throw the beat into her throat. It stuck. The panic cutting in as her fingers reached for the pulse in her neck to check if her heart was still beating.

'Err if that's all Mr. Sanderson, I'll be off then.'

'Indeed it most certainly is not all Miss Glover. Resume your seat!'

She watched him put the bowl down. Drum his index finger against his upper lip. Then put his hands in the side pockets of his trousers, trapping his jacket behind him. His movement sharp. Instantly splitting the ends of his shades of aqua silk tie apart to reveal the expensive double fold covering the buttons down the centre of his pristine white shirt.

'To use a euphemism Miss Glover. Period. Any signs?'

Harriet felt sick. She looked across to the bowl on top of the towel.

'Yes Mr. Sanderson. This morning actually!'

'Priorities Miss Glover. That's the first thing you should have told me. Obviously not taken you as badly as last time. You most certainly shouldn't have come in here today. You should have been lying down. You could well be miscarrying. Did you not give one thought to the baby. One thought to saving it?'

Harriet now indistinguishable from a beetroot slipped another lie to fend him off. She'd never seen him so beside himself with fury.

'The guy you let in as I departed the other day, Miss Glover. Who is he?'

'With respect Mr. Sanderson I'm not sure it has anything to do with you.'

'That's were you are wrong again Miss Glover. It does indeed have everything to do with me. Regardless of your flippancy towards this pregnancy there's still an outside chance what you're experiencing is a consequence of hormonal changes, Miss Glover. I don't want you sleeping around. With anybody! Understand?'

Furious, Harriet could scarcely find the words.

'I beg ....' She stopped. A quick tap. The door opened.

'Sorry Joris I thought you'd left. Just want to return those to the first first aid cupboard before I go, if I may?'

Harriet couldn't help but notice the long scratch on her arm as she limped across the room. Praised the cat in her mind.

'Yes, yes, take them Lucinda. We're finished here. Come back when you've done that will you, I want a word.'

Chapter 47

Trembling with rage Harriet could hardly get the car home fast enough. He'd just implied she was a tart. A little tart. How could he, when even though not married she'd only ever stayed faithful to Mark. Just once. Just that once with him and he was speaking to her like that. Like that after him aborting Belinda Oxfordshire's baby. Fizzing with rage she stopped the car abruptly on the drive. Grabbed her bags and slammed the doors, sending the hanging basket swinging against the back window.

'That arrogant swine of a man Pepper. How dare he talk like that to me! How dare he! He wants "a word" Pepper. He wants a word with her. With Lucinda Lawton. He's always wanting "a word" with someone. Stupid place to leave all that first aid stuff. It frightened the life out of me Pepper. '

The cat offering no more than a nonchalant meow rubbed its head against her legs as she let herself in. Still no Mark.

'No of course not Pepper. He wouldn't be in from work yet. If that's where he's been. Obviously hasn't been back to feed you. Come on then, let's sort you out.'

She threw her bags down on the bottom stair, glancing the green light flashing its messages on the answer machine.

'They can wait Pepper. I'm not in the mood for pleasantries or otherwise with anyone. Do you know I can't believe that toad of a man has just spoken to me like that. That's why he wants to get rid of my baby Pepper. He can't be doing with his child having a mother like me!'

She pressed the teabag hard against the sides of the mug, threw it in the sink then stirred the milk round and round and round. Almost in a trance now, wondering, as she sat herself and the mug down at the kitchen table.

'Or have I got that wrong Pepper? He was telling me to rest. He was surmising. Thought it could be due to hormonal changes. Oh gosh Pepper I was so frightened he was going to do the deed there and then, I wasn't really thinking straight. I think I *have* got him wrong Pepper, now I come to think about it. But I'm not telling him I am still pregnant Pepper. Let *him* wonder! I'm not answering any more of his personal questions. Why should I? He dumped Belinda Oxfordshire after putting her through all that. He's moved on just a bit too swiftly to Lucinda Lawton. He's a doctor Pepper. You'd have thought he'd make a few allowances for the state of shock I was in.'

'That's not the way he operates Harriet. How many times have I told you that?'

'Mark!'

Harriet jumped. What with the kettle boiling and feeding the cat, she hadn't heard him come in. Hadn't a clue if and when he'd be back. She wondered just how much he'd heard. She wasn't ready to enlighten him just yet.

'Had a good weekend with Melissa Scott then Mark? You've obviously left a shirt and suit round there to get yourself to work without coming back here.'

'Free agent Harriet. That's a right mess out there. Soil all over the place. You haven't been driving round with that thing hanging in your back window, have you?'

'Not your concern Mark.' She breathed an inward sigh of relief. Thought. 'I'm glad that's all he's bothered about.'

'I had a call from Clare. They all send their love,' she flustered.

'Oh yes and how did it go for them? They having a good time?'

'Certainly are. They'll be up shortly. The weekend after next. I told her Tricia's roped Rapping Hammer in to do a gig for the school fair. She was so excited. Wants to be up for that.'

'Not exactly for the school fair, is it Harriet?'

'What do you mean Mark?'

'Oh word gets round Harriet. Bob found out where you both went. Venice no less! And now she's got some crackpot idea of trying to save it. Can you wonder at Bob taking up with Belinda Oxfordshire?'

'No. She's obviously a prime source of information. Guy Hammer pass that one along, did he? I saw her at the garden centre on Saturday. No doubt she's still chatting him up. Whispered it all to Bob between the sheets. He blabs it all to you.'

'More likely lard ball Harriet. It looks like he's known all along.'

'Whoever it was it's still her passing it along to Bob. What else did he tell you about her Mark? Has he rated her performance in bed yet? None of it's very nice for Tricia.'

'Oh Tricia's more than capable of standing on her own two feet. Not short of lying between someone else's sheets either, according to Bob. Their marriage hasn't exactly been a bed of roses Harriet.'

'He's making it up Mark. Tricia would never do a thing like that.'

'You did! Why shouldn't she?'

'Because I'm not married Mark. At least Bob had the guts to marry her.'

'He had the guts to stay with her you mean. Their Adam isn't Bob's you know Harriet.'

'Of course he is Mark. They're two peas in a pod Adam and his dad.'

'Not his dad Harriet. Bob married her in the full knowledge she was pregnant by somebody else. So it's his turn now.'

'Never! Tricia's never said. She would have told me. I know she would.'

'Why would she Harriet? For all we know they might have kept it from Adam.'

'Then it's contemptible Belinda Oxfordshire should have come between them.'

'She wouldn't know that Harriet. Bob's not that daft as to tell her.'

'Well I certainly hope so. He must have thought an awful lot of Tricia to marry her in those circumstances. No wonder she's throwing herself into saving Venice. I wish that flipping woman would just get out of everyone's lives.'

'Well she's not about to get out of Bob's life Harriet. To answer your question. She's right off the scale in bed. I can't think why lard ball chucked her.'

'Because she's not particularly nice Mark. That's why he got rid of her baby. He didn't deem her a suitable mother for his child because she's not nice. He promised her marriage because that's the only way she'd agree to letting him do it. He never had any intention of going through with marrying her. Oh no it had all gone too far once he'd got her pregnant.'

'So there you have it Harriet. By your own admission. Just look at the slime ball you've been chasing.'

'I know Mark. I know.'

'Anyway, I'm home early because I need to get down to the club. I promised Tarquin Bridgewater I'd keep an eye on things while he's away. Don't worry about dinner. I'll get Iris to rustle something up.'

'No you won't Mark. Iris has gone with him.'

'I didn't know that. Who's doing the catering down there then?'

'I don't know. Can't say I care. Anyway Tarquin Bridgewater told me Mr. Sanderson's doing the honours.'

'Bloody Bridgewater. He wants to stop bumbling around and messing people about. So that means I'm likely to bump into *him* now. Phone him up Harriet and find out what the arrangement is.'

'No Mark. I'm not phoning him up. It's nothing at all to do with me. You phone him. Or don't. He's busy. The chances are you won't see him there anyway.'

'I won't be responsible for my actions if I do Harriet. I'll more than likely land him one!'

'Better that you don't Mark. Someone might just get into bother on the water, especially if there are kids from school down there. You'd hardly come out of it very well if someone drowned while you were fighting!'

'No you're probably right Harriet. If I see him down there I'll tell him it's either him or me. He stays, I go. I'd better get down there before the kids then.'

'What will you do about something to eat?'

'Oh if the worst comes to the worst I'll get someone to pick me up some fish and chips. I doubt it though Harriet. I'm sure Tarquin Bridgewater will have organised a stand-in for Iris.'

Harriet watched him go upstairs. Heard him get changed. Then off out. She sank her mug into the bowl of soapy water unable to come to terms with Mark's revelation. Thoughts coming fast. 'Adam must have grown up believing Bob to be his natural father, otherwise I'm sure Tricia would have told me.'

She went back into the hall. Pressed play. The first message sprang to life.

'Oh 'ello 'arriet. It's only me. Only I just 'ad to tell you my news 'arriet. I 'aven't 'ad chance to tell you before. There was a message on my desk when I got in this mornin'. For the next two weeks I'm workin' between Starboard Marine North West and the sailin' club. Our friend Joris volunteered my services to do the caterin' down there while Iris is away. So I've 'ardly got a moment `arriet. I'm down there tonight. I suppose I'll `ave to be fryin` chips for everyone. I'll tell you somethin`, if that Belinda Oxfordshire comes anywhere near me wantin` `er tea, I'll make sure she gets somethin` on `er plate that will make `er not want to come back. I'll `ave to go `arriet I'm supposed to be startin` tonight. I just `ope `e'll be payin` me double time for all this. `ow can I get on with savin` Venice with all this on my plate? I think that might just be a most appropriate metaphor `arriet. Plate, me serving up. Oh never mind `arriet. Where was I? Ooh I've just `ad an idea. I'll whack the prices up `arriet. `alf for the club and `alf for Venice. That'll give me a good start before Rappin` `ammer's gig. `e'll be comin` just as I finish with all this. I `ope I won't be too tired `arriet. There's no end to the cheek of Joris Sanderson. I might be puttin` somethin` in `is as well. Is there anyone else we don't like `arriet? Oh `ow about Lucinda Lawton? Yes `arriet, I'll see if I can't push `er in! The water would do `er arm a power of good. Talk about snooty. Phone me the minute you get any news on you know what `arriet. At least doin` this will take my mind off that.'

'Too right it will Tricia,' Harriet thought as she pressed play for the next message.

'Harriet, Barry Giordano. I'm over this side. You've got my number. Call me back if you fancy a drink somewhere.'

'Golly gosh Pepper, Barry Giordano. What should I do? See him and sound him out? Or not? Oh let me get something to eat. I'll decide after that.'

Chapter 48

Harriet plopped her plate alongside the mug and everything else in the bowl of cold soapy water just as the doorbell rang. She grabbed the towel. Threw it down. Then dried her hands off on her skirt as she went to answer it.

'It would seem I'm not required down there this evening Miss Glover. Just checking. Needed to pop in anyway to sort out the rudder on Lucinda's dinghy. Mrs. Harrington not missing a trick behind the counter. I see. Till never stopped ringing. A pity she couldn't display the same talent at Starboard Marine North West! May I come in Miss Glover?'

The question superfluous. He brushed past her straight into the kitchen. Slipped his jacket off to sit it on the back of one of the two chairs strewn opposite ends of the table. Then sat himself down.

'Take a seat Miss Glover. Unfortunate interruption for us both back at school. Lucinda chooses her moments. Anyhow it's become increasingly obvious to me you don't want this baby. Now I suggest we....'

'No Mr. Sanderson. No. Most definitely not! I won't hear of it!'

Harriet panicked. Thought. 'He's come to do it. Well he's not doing it here. He's not doing it anywhere. He's just not doing it!' So grateful the only bowl he would find was well utilised. Full of dishes and cold soapy water.

'Won't hear of what Miss Glover? Do me the courtesy of allowing me to finish, will you? I was simply suggesting we talk things through. We have the child's future to think of. That must come before either of our personal feelings.'

Panic subsiding, Harriet flopped back on her seat in relief. Whatever he did to Belinda Oxfordshire at least he wasn't about to to do her. Then she panicked again. Thought. 'No you're not taking my baby away from me on the grounds of incompetence. That's where you're coming from now. That's it.'

'No need Mr. Sanderson. I'm absolutely not pregnant.'

'Ah you certain of that Miss Glover?'

'Absolutely Mr. Sanderson.'

Drawn to the curl resting at the collar of his sea-green shirt, she made herself look away. Neck open. Sleeves rolled up. Elbows on the table. His arms strong, supporting his hands resting under his chin. There was nowhere she could look that didn't send her head spinning.

'This man. Oh this most gorgeous of men. Don't do this to me. Please don't do this to me. This is exactly what you did to Belinda Oxfordshire. Exactly why she still wants you. I know she does. Stop crashing my brain cells will you? Don't look at me like that.'

'Gone quiet Miss Glover and your face has become rather flushed. Now are you sure you're telling me the truth?'

'Absolutely Mr. Sanderson.'

He turned slightly to slip his hand into the inside pocket of his jacket.

'Well I'm not so sure Miss Glover. See your way to using one of these again will you? Pop it back to me in the morning.'

Harriet looked at him. Wondered how she could have read this man so wrongly. Wondered how he could possibly have wanted to take a tiny human life. His own. Wondered how he could so easily move on to Lucinda. Wondered why he hadn't been able to understand her blind panic following his proposal. Wondered why he'd stooped so low as to have them followed by the PM's personal minders. Wondered why he should think she was about to start sleeping around.

She looked down. She could feel his eyes on her breasts. The same feelings, the need for him surging through her whole body yet again. His baby inside her still. For a fleeting moment she was back on the sand. On the wet sand. She could feel his hand slipping away at the blue lace hardly covering her. Opening to him, drawing him in. Lost in exquisite bliss. She hoped she hadn't just painted her face with the aching desire surging her body.

Instinctively she covered herself with her arm. Looked down to the testing kit he'd placed on the table. Watched him stand. Move towards her. Felt him lift her arm away. His hand now moving across just gently brushing against her breasts now rising beneath her top. Unashamed evidence. Her body out of sync with her mind.

' "Give 'im a kiss 'arriet…" '. In her mind, Tricia's words. She moved towards him.

He stepped back. Tossed his jacket from the back of the chair. Lifted the testing kit from the table. She looked up at him.

'Pop that in to me in the morning will you Miss Glover? Let's get this sorted once and for all, shall we?'

He was gone. Harriet couldn't believe she'd just allowed him to do that. Couldn't believe he'd done that and just walked away. Suddenly she was furious with him. Furious with herself. Perhaps he was right. Perhaps it wasn't too difficult for her to behave like a little tart after all. After all she knew about him, she was now no better than Belinda Oxfordshire.

Chapter 49

Relieved the cat hadn't witnessed it she went upstairs to get changed. Shoved the pregnancy testing kit to the back of the top drawer of the dressing table. The folded paper square, falling into her fingers. Mark's note. Brought it out. Put it back. Brought it out again.

'Oh open it Harriet,' she told herself. 'You know what it's all about anyway.'

She sat on the bed. It seemed like ages since Mark had given it her. Told her to open it. Made her promise.

' "Harriet. Try to understand. Please try to understand. Wait for me Harriet. Today is not our day. Not our time for this. If I asked you to sleep in the dark. Would you be able to?'

She remembered the light bulb at university. Breaking the spare she'd collected from supplies. Mark staying the night because she couldn't stand the dark It made her think. She read on.

'If I asked you to use a lift always getting trapped between floors. Could you do it for me?'

'No. I simply couldn't bear that!' She instantly dismissed the thought. Just couldn't go there. Continued.

'They're all phobias Harriet. And I've been battling this one because I met you. Today I just can't do it. Melissa? I took her once. Just once. It meant nothing. It means nothing. It's not how it looks Harriet. If it's not how it looks with you and *him* Harriet then please wait for me. I've only ever loved you. Forgive me Harriet. I know I'm about to give you the worst day of your life. Please try to understand and forgive. Mark" '

'No wonder he thinks I came back. Should have read it straight away. Couldn't. Too painful. Poor Mark. Not his fault. I've let him down. Badly. Oh so badly. I'm *pregnant*. I couldn't go back to him now if I wanted to. Or could I? He admires Bob for bringing up Tricia's child. It's *his* though, Mr. Sanderson's. It might be different if it was anyone else's. Somebody he doesn't know. Now if it was Barry's it might be different. I might even have passed if off as Mark's. Just a couple of weeks out. Not enough to make the difference.'

Harriet put an end to the thought there and then. She couldn't believe she'd allowed such an idea to enter her head. 'But I know I still care for Mark. Still love Mark really. Why would I be so pleased he'd not wanted to proceed with the sale of the house if I didn't still love him? Why am I so pleased his affair with Melissa Scott was as brief and inconsequential as it was?'

For the moment he'd almost put her back on amber. Apart from the baby, of course. She pushed it all to the depths of her mind. Returned to denial.

'A few weeks yet before he'll start noticing the difference.'

She slipped out of her blouse and skirt. Reached for her jeans. Heard the slam of a car door.

'Mark, Pepper. That'll be him now. Same old Mark. Ringing the doorbell even though he's got his keys. He's always doing that. OK, OK no need to play a tune. I'm coming.'

She grabbed her dressing gown. 'In a hurry Pepper. He's probably got to get back to the sailing club. Forgotten something.'

With it hardly wrapped around her she flew to the door. Opened it.

'Gosh Barry I thought you were Mark back. Actually I was going to give you a call. I was just getting changed.'

'Good. You'll come then.'

He stepped in closing the door behind him.

She pulled her dressing gown hard over. 'I won't be a minute Barry. Just go in there. I'll be with you in a tick.'

'Just before you go up there Harriet.'

She turned, puzzled.

'What kind of a greeting is that?'

In an instant she could feel herself being swept off the bottom stair. His arm around her waist. Her dressing gown wide open. He stepped back to look at her. Just bra and pants. His lips covering hers. His mouth warm, wet, exploratory. She'd never known a kiss like it. Too much. Too soon.

'Gosh Barry. You don't waste any time do you?'

He smiled. That gentle artistic, creative smile. Almost reflecting an inner innocence. He slipped the dressing gown from her shoulders. His lips soft, closing over hers. Persuading hers to open apart. She finally pulled away. Dazed she hurried to cover herself up.

'In the lounge Barry please, or I don't go out at all!'

She could hear him laugh as she threw her jeans and clean white top on. She slipped into her sandals. Brushed her hair. A touch of lipstick. Her reflection in the mirror. How did she suddenly get three men in her life in the space of a couple of hours?

'No don't go down that road Harriet. Have a drink with him but make it quite clear he's not on.'

Chapter 50

'So how are things with you Harriet? Everything sorted with the hotel now?'

'As far as I know, thanks Barry. At least I haven't heard any more so I'm hoping so.'

'That guy. That blonde guy, came out as I came in. The first time I called. Your boss. I recognise him. I've seen him before but I'm damned if I can place him. Who does he mix with Harriet?'

'With the high and mighty Barry.'

'You're not talking about the PM are you?' Suddenly he snapped his fingers. 'That's it! That's where I've seen him before. Keep your distance Harriet. Does he need to be calling here?'

'Oh he does it to Tricia as well.'

'You both work together then. What do you do?'

'No, I teach. He's the head of my school. Tricia works for him at Starboard Marine North West.'

'He owns it?'

'Yes.'

'Spreads himself round a bit.'

'And what about you Barry. What do you do for a living?'

'I'm a poor artist Harriet. I pick up work here and there. It all helps with the mortgage.'

'Ah like becoming a gondolier. That's your next job. With Andy of course. "Look don't touch," I think that's what you were both about.'

Barry cleared his throat. Put his glass down.

'I apologise for that Harriet. You looked flushed. Beautiful. I couldn't stop myself from holding you. You've been on my mind a lot.'

Harriet returned her glass of tonic water to the table.

'I haven't been in a relationship since Maria and I broke up. I honestly haven't Harriet. As soon as I saw you at Manchester airport I needed to see you again. Why do you think Andy and I happened upon you both that Sunday morning?'

'Oh, you mean Andy had a thing for Tricia, too?

'No, no, Harriet. She's not his type. He's a clever lad Andy. Does his best to hide it. He's travelled the world. There's nothing he doesn't know about any of it. But Venice. He can give a full blown historical account of every building there! He knows the whole place like the back of his hand. He shrugs it off Harriet but if the truth were known he's far more into art and culture than me.'

'Is that why you both went back to San Marco Barry? Why did you decide to go off on your own, the two of you? We would have been happy to come too.'

Harriet watched him shift a little on his chair. Watched him flick his long dark hair away from his face. Watched him momentarily scratch his head.

'What did we screw up Barry? Why was San Marco supposed to be the end of the road?'

'Just our plans for the evening Harriet. We needed a couple of hours to put it all in place. We were left with a table booked for dinner. Theatre tickets. A gondola booked. You name it we did it.'

'You mean for us Barry? Why would you want to do all that for us? You'd only just met us.' Harriet wondered if Tricia could just have been right after all.

'I've just told you Harriet. I don't go around undressing girls when I've only just met them. I can't explain how I've been taken with you Harriet. Something's happened to me that I've never ever experienced in the whole of my life before. I've fallen in love with you Harriet. Deeply. I'm completely off my head over you Harriet. Will you marry me?'

Harriet opened her eyes wide.

'Golly gosh Barry I can't believe you've just said that! You are joking?'

'Joking Harriet? No I'm not joking. Why would I joke about something like that? I fell for the most beautiful girl in the world in the most romantic place in the world. I could hardly dare believe it when Tricia told us you were each coming out of a relationship.'

'Well, I honestly had no idea Barry.'

'I caught your eye Harriet. More than once. I'm an artist. I'm sensitive by nature. Don't deny there wasn't an attraction.'

Harriet blushed.

'I found you good looking Barry. I was more than pleased you were around. And yes I was attracted to you but I honestly didn't realise you felt that way about me.'

'You're holding something back Harriet. I can sense it. Still I wasn't expecting an answer just now. It can take as long as it takes. There's only one answer I'm waiting for and I'm a very patient sort of guy Harriet.'

He turned to look towards the city across the river. The skyline magnificent in the light of the summer evening.

'In its own way as moving as Venice. Or is it because we're here together like this? Anywhere would be beautiful as long as I'm with you Harriet.'

She could just feel the first shreds of panic running from her stomach through her legs. Felt wobbly. Shuffled on her seat as Barry distanced himself from his proposal. For the next two hours Harriet was more than happy to chatter about Venice. More than happy to keep him on shared but less threatening ground.

'I think it's time to be getting back if you don't mind. It's been a lovely evening Barry. A bit surreal but then it's been that kind of day really. Have you far to go?'

'Manchester Harriet. I'm up here for the moment. I've an apartment now since we sold the house. Maria doesn't think much of it. She said I could have done better than that for myself. Anyway I'm on the move. It's a place to put my head down when I'm up here. Open plan. Enough space for the studio.'

'And what about Andy. Is he from Manchester too?'

'Strangely enough, yes. We were interviewed together. You know? Regional interviews and all that.'

'For what job Barry? Are you both working together still, in some way?'

'That was when we both joined the Foreign Legion. I thought we mentioned that one. Venice was just a bit of a laugh. Well that's how it started out Harriet. It certainly didn't end that way.'

'A confusing answer Barry. I'm none the wiser.'

'As intended. You will see me again won't you Harriet? I'm used to women slipping out of their dressing gowns as you might expect. I don't normally get the urge to help them along though. I apologise for coming on a bit heavy as soon as I arrived. Don't let that put you off.'

Harriet paled. Wanted to run a mile.

'I'm an artist Harriet. Don't let that put you off either.'

'Not in the least Barry. I'll give you a call.'

They parted. So glad she'd insisted on taking her car. She just wanted to get home. Wanted to stroke the cat. Anything to take her mind off the day.

She watched it land on the top of the side gate as she drove her car for enough forward to allow space for Mark to park his.

'Oh let's get in Pepper shall we? Let's just make a nice cup of tea. I've got such a story to tell.'

She closed the front door behind them. Went straight to the kitchen. Filled the kettle then sat down waiting for it to boil.

'Now Pepper, you're not going to believe this.' She stopped. Heard the key in the front door.

'Mark! It all finished down there, is it?'

'Certainly is Hat. Is that a cup of tea you're making?'

Harriet nodded.

'It might boil if you'd switched it on!'

Harriet stood up. Mark on top of her. She could feel herself being drawn very close to his chest.

'Hey Mark. What's this all about?'

'Oh what's the point in us living like this Hat. What's the point? OK so we're free agents but we might just as well be civil to one another.'

'Civil Mark? I'd say this is just a bit more than being civil, wouldn't you?'

'You're looking particularly gorgeous tonight Harriet and I'm feeling like living up to my Bohemian reputation, according to your mother, that is. Same bed Hat?'

'Mark. I don't believe I'm hearing this! What's got into you down there? What did Tricia put in your tea?'

'Oh so *he's* been round here again. You know she's standing in for Iris?'

'She left a message Mark.'

'Pleased to hear that.'

'Anyway how did Tricia get on with the meals?'

'Brilliant Hat. She's a better cook than you. I can't say if she's better than you with regard to the other. Not yet anyway.'

'What do you mean, "Not yet anyway" ?'

'Free agents Hat. You never can tell. Cleavage and chips. I'm up for it any time Hat.'

'MARK!'

'It's getting late. Are you coming up?'

'Yes straight into the back room Mark.'

'But Hat that's not the way to be civil to each other. Let's get it all on the right footing shall we?'

'Well OK, I'll come back but that's all it will be. Don't try anything because I'm warning you. You won't get anywhere if you do.'

'What me Hat? I'm flaked out. I've had enough for today.'

Chapter 51

'Mark. You promised me. You promised me you wouldn't try anything.'

'But Hat. You've never looked lovelier. Like you're in the first flush of youth.'

'Put my strap back Mark. I'm warning you.'

'But it's warm Hat. You don't want to be sleeping in this. There! Isn't that better?'

'No Mark, I said put it back, not slip the other one off as well.'

'Oh Hat. You're not going to turn teacher on me? Not now.'

'Mark I don't believe this is happening.'

'Mmm Harriet.'

'No Mark. Absolutely not. That's enough Mark.'

'But Tricia wouldn't withdraw, to leave me like this. Leave me in this state. You can't do that to me Hat.'

'How can you possibly withdraw from something you never started in the first place, Mark?'

'Exactly Hat. You can't. Not now, we've gone this far. Far too far Hat.'

'Mark. No Mark I'm leaving those on. Didn't I tell you that would be the only way I'd come back to this bed with you?'

'I promise to leave them on Hat.'

'But you dumped me Mark.'

'And you slept with him Harriet.'

'And you slept with her Mark.'

'Free agents Harriet. We can please ourselves.'

'No Mark. No I've just told you.'

'OK Hat. Come just a bit towards me.'

'Only this once Mark. Just this once for old times sake. After all, who's to say not?'

'Exactly Hat. Who's to say not?'

'Mark they won't stretch like that!'

'Harriet let's just take them off shall we? For old times sake.'

'For old times sake Mark.'

Chapter 52

'Tea Hat. If you're feeling like me you'll be ready for it after last night.'

'Thanks Mark, but don't remind me.'

'I didn't get the impression you weren't enjoying it. Good grief Hat I didn't expect you to come back for more. Twice. Then again. Three times Harriet! That made three times in all. Felt like I was on a test drive.'

'Sorry Mark. I can't explain it. Just the way it happened.'

'Oh don't apologise. I'm certainly not complaining. If this is what it takes to enable civility between us I'm all for it. Separate but together. Together but separate. And please ourselves with everything else we do in between.'

'No Mark. Absolutely not! Look, I haven't stopped loving you just like that. How could I after all these years? I've treated you badly Mark. Last night I felt it was almost like there was a deep healing going on between us.'

'You mean like that blue tube of white stuff in the bathroom cupboard. And that one's flat. Nearly empty. I felt like a tube of that last night did I Harriet. An empty flat tube, to boot. Is that why you kept on wanting more, to see if I could improve my performance? Oh that's fine that is Harriet. How to make a bloke feel good and I don't think!'

'No Mark, I'm trying to explain. I was filled with warmth towards you.'

'So I'm a bloody hot-water bottle now am I Harriet?'

'No Mark this is getting silly. I'm just trying to say you aroused all my maternal instincts. I just wanted to knit you a jumper Mark.'

'Oh so it was that bad you'd rather have been getting on with your knitting at the same time Harriet? Well don't do me any more favours will you? There's other fish to fry.'

'Does she do chips as well Mark?'

'Very funny Harriet. I'm going to work.'

'Oh come here Mark. Give me a kiss. For some reason you were fantastic in bed last night.'

'For some reason Harriet? You mean I've never always been fantastic in bed? It just happened that way last night?'

'Of course not Mark. What's the matter with you this morning? Come here.'

'Mmm Harriet, but I've got to go to work and so have you.'

'It'll be OK to be a bit late Mark. Just to show no hard feelings.'

'I'll be exhausted Harriet. I won't have the energy to drive there.'

'Of course you will Mark.'

'Of course I will Hat. You're absolutely right.'

'Lost the urge to knit yet Hat?'

'Too right Mark. This is all down to you.'

'I'm not overheating you like a hot water bottle Harriet?'

'Oh you are overheating me Mark but not like a hot water bottle.'

'And am I giving off deep healing Harriet?'

'You're giving off something Mark and it's not to be found in the bathroom cabinet.'

'So I'm all I know I am to be?'

'You're all you know you are to be Mark.'

'But I thought you said last night was the very last time Harriet?'

'This is the very last time Mark. This is the very last time. As we said, just for old times sake. This is just the way I want to leave it now.'

'But I might not want to leave it like this Harriet?'

'Let's just see how it goes, shall we Mark?'

Chapter 53

Late, Harriet drove into school to be met with Mr. Brown. On the ground. Reminiscent of a curled up hedgehog. Then suddenly stretching forward, his knees somewhere between the soil and the tarmac. Commandeering the end of the only parking slot left. She beeped. He jumped, quickly gathering the trays of plants, his trowel and watering can to clear the way for her.

'`ardly gave me chance to move out of the way Miss Glover! And by the way I've been told by the boss to expect an apology from you on account of you being so rude to me last week. I'm still waitin` for it.'

'Oh Mr. Brown I'm terribly sorry. I really am. Please do accept my apologies. I had no right to speak to you like that.'

'Well I might and then again I might not. I'll think about it.'

'Oh, what are you planting Mr. Brown? You always make the garden areas look so nice. Just look at those over there. They've been a picture this summer.'

'Well you should know what I'm plantin` Miss Glover. Seein` `as you brought me the bloody lot! I've `ad enough of plantin` out for this year. What does `e want to be doin` with toppin` them all up? It will be the `olidays soon. No one will be `ere to see `em!'

'Quite Mr. Brown.'

'`ere hold this a minute. I'll need you to give me a hand with that.'

Harriet took the ball of string he'd just lifted from the ground. Stood waiting. Already late. She suddenly remembered she was supposed to be seeing *him*.

'`ere Miss Glover. Cut a length of string off that will you? `as if I `aven't got enough to be doin`. Now stand on this while I lift it up.'

'I beg your pardon Mr. Brown?'

'`ere. Pass me the key. If I don't get it myself you'll never get round to it.'

'Sorry Mr. Brown I'm not quite with you.'

'That thing `angin` in your car. It's probably `alf dead by now. I don't know what `e wants to be doin` with `angin` baskets.'

'Oh here Mr. Brown. It's tied to the grab handle above the door.'

'Get up on that chair will you and `old on to that piece of string.'

Harriet watched him disappear round the side of her car and then back again trailing the chains from her mother's hanging basket, watching them hitting his knees with each step forward. His brown baggy trousers catching the shreds of falling compost in the folds, before tossing them to his shoes. She couldn't tell him. If he wanted to hang her mother's hanging basket so be it. The less she had to communicate with him the better.

'`ere loop that string through this. I'll `old it while you tie it. Thread it through a couple of times will you? Now pull it up.'

'Miss Glover. What time do you call this? You were supposed to be in my office first thing this morning!'

Harriet jumped. Mr. Brown just turned as she lost grip on the string. Sent it

159

sliding to clout him straight on his head.

'Pull it back Miss Glover. Tie the damned thing up now!'

'I'm trying my best Mr. Sanderson.'

Harriet tugged as hard as she could. Mr. Sanderson, furious, stood watching the basket rising again. Appearing twice the height of Mr. Brown he reached effortlessly. Held his hand under it while she did her best with the string.

'Stay there you clumsy bugger!' Mr. Brown commanded. Nursing his head he stomped off. She watched him struggle back. The spout showering a forward trail as the surplus water sloshed down the sides of the heavy can. Mr. Sanderson had long since seized his opportunity to disappear.

'Get `old of this Miss and water them seein` as you've nearly killed the lot of them off. Leavin` them to dry out in that bit of a basket.' He turned. Raised his finger to her car. 'It gets `ot in there during the day.'

Harriet bent down. Lifted the watering can as high as she could. Wobbled it over the plants only to miss. Spitting water Mr. Brown bellowed. She jumped. Let go. The can clonking his head as it clanged to the ground.

'You menace of a woman. Get out of my way. Oh my friggin` `ead.' His hand now placed firmly on the top. Eyebrows dripping, she watched him stumble away.

'MISS GLOVER get down from there this minute! What on earth do you think you're doing? Mr Brown has just fainted in my office! See me at break will you?'

By the time Harriet got to her classroom someone had already taken her children to assembly. She flopped her bags down. Plonked herself into the chair. Looked out of the window. Instantly jamming her ears with her fingers against the piercing sirens as she went over to investigate.

'Oh no. An ambulance!' She exclaimed out loud. Now Mr. Brown being carried out on a stretcher. Lucinda Lawton, still limping, alongside.

Harriet flew down the corridors and out of the main entrance. She hoped he wasn't dead. She approached to see Mr. Sanderson talking to a uniformed man. Both standing under the hanging basket. 'That'll be the driver,' she thought as she dashed towards them.

'He's not dead is he Mr. Sanderson?'

Then thud. The hanging basket down. A straight thump on the poor man's head.

'No. But he might be Miss Glover. He's out. Stone cold!'

'Get the other stretcher Al.'

'Why what's happened Stu?'

'It's Rodney. Been hit by a flying missile. Dead!'

'He hasn't snuffed it has he Stu?'

Harriet panicked. Never mind Venice. She'd get life for this.

Al jumped out of the back to give Stu a hand. In a flash and double cargo, off they went taking Lucinda Lawton with them.

'Will they be alright Mr. Sanderson?'

'You heard him Miss Glover. I'll see to your class. You'd better follow them and find out. Bring Lucinda back will you?'

'Yes Mr. Sanderson. I'm most terribly sorry. It was supposed to be Mummy's hanging basket anyway.'

'Get going Miss Glover. I've got work to do.'

Harriet ran back. Picked up her bag and took a short cut to her car through the French doors in her classroom. She scrambled for the keys.

'Oh no. Mr. Brown must have put them in his pocket. Oh sod! Now I've got to go back to *him*.'

She ran across the playground. In through the main entrance. She hardly dared knock on his door.

'IN!'

Harriet barely got her mouth open to speak.

'Who else have you killed Miss Glover, between being told to get going and coming back here?'

'No one Mr. Sanderson. It's just that Mr. Brown's gone off with my keys.'

'And what was he doing with them in the first place, Miss Glover?'

'Getting the hanging basket out of the car.'

'Donation Miss Glover? I don't recall sanctioning the purchase of that.'

'Misunderstanding Mr. Sanderson. I didn't want to embarrass Mr. Brown.'

'Preferred to knock him out instead! Collect your children from the hall will you Miss Glover while I go and bring Lucinda back.'

'Huh, flipping Lucinda. What's wrong with a taxi?' Harriet stood behind the double glass doors waiting for assembly to end wondering if she could ever have a normal day.

'Ah Miss, where's the tardis gone?'

'Come on Danny. Keep moving along.'

'We 'eard it Miss. Kevin said a tardis 'ad landed in the playground and the police cars were drivin' in to get it!'

'No, no Danny. No there was an accident. Somebody needed to be taken to hospital. All over and done with now. Now everyone, on the carpet.'

'Ah Miss, she's sittin' in my corner. I always sit there by the books. She knows I do. Come out will yer?'

'Danny stop pulling her arm. Leave her alone this minute!'

'But she's in my place Miss. I'm tellin' Sir of you.'

'Over here. Come here Melanie.'

She sat at Harriet's feet, pulling a tissue from the box wavering under her nose.

'Now wipe your eyes Melanie. Danny out here! Apologise please.'

'I'm not sayin' sorry to 'er. She was tryin' to pinch me banana she knows where I 'id it because she said she was watchin' me Miss.'

'I never said that Miss Glover. It was Kevin that said 'e would pinch it.'

'Oh yeah Kevin so where 'ave I 'idden it? Go on tell me if you know!'

'Danny! Danny that's quite enough. Get your banana now and put it in your lunch box, where it should be.'

Harriet watched Danny sidle his way back to the corner glancing around, fearful of exposing his hiding place. His tough little face, furtive. His expression suddenly putting her in mind of one of the PM's heavies.

'Almost an offspring.' Nervous, she stamped on the thought. Watched him push his hand behind the books to bring out a banana skin.

'Get that off Robert's head this minute Danny!'

'The aliens `ave `eaten it Miss.'

'Miss said it was the police cars Kevin. You've eaten it. `e's eaten it Miss. I'm goin` to tell Mr. Sandcastles of you!'

'You most certainly are not Danny. Now stop waving that around and put it in the bin this minute.'

Danny halfway to the bin suddenly swung his arm Olympian style tossing the strips of banana skin high into the air. Then the door. Peering round, a head like a bandaged football. Harriet panicked. Saw the yellow skin nose-dive like some live exotic missile pulsating straight into Mr. Brown's face. He jerked. Just managed to stop short of skidding on it as it fell forward of his feet.

'Eh Kevin is `e one of your aliens?'

'No Danny I didn't say throw it and don't be so rude to Mr. Brown.'

'Look to yourself before tellin` `im off!' Harriet glanced at Mr. Brown. Caught Danny's grin. Wanted to die.

'Chaos again Miss Glover! Mr. Brown wants a word with you. Take it in the corridor will you?'

'Yes Mr. Sanderson.'

She could feel herself going hot all over. Still in the aftermath of surrendering her body to three men all in one day and then back for more this morning, this was just too much.

Thought. 'On the verge of being done for manslaughter. That man's a gonner. I know it!' Then the thought escalated to something even worse.

'Mr. Brown's come to accuse me of attempted murder.'

Venice and the PM's heavies were fast becoming an irrelevance. It was going to be a long day.

Chapter 54

The three-thirty bell rang. Harriet had never been so relieved to close the door on the day. Until it flew open again. Then he banged it shut.

She took a very deep breath. She thought she'd got away with it.

'Miss Glover. Brown? I took great care in explaining the position to him. Of course we get the exact repeat of last time. He still thinks you've "got it in for him". Quote, Miss Glover. He's convinced you deliberately dropped the watering can on his head.'

'Of course I didn't Mr. Sanderson. It was heavy. He had no right to be asking me to lift it, anyway.'

'Quite Miss Glover. You should have had more sense than to do it. And he should have known better of course than to ask you to stand on a chair. Health and Safety Miss Glover. We've not long been through all of that. I'm sending you both on a course.'

'Not together Mr. Sanderson.'

'Miss Glover they don't tailor these courses to suit *your* whims. There's one next Friday morning at Stetmead Centre. Here photocopy this. Pass it on to Brown.'

Harriet took it, knew what was coming next.'

'I don't expect Brown had a great deal to say to you out there. By the time we'd walked the length of the corridor I think I'd convinced him. He'd pretty much come to terms with the fact it was largely of his own making. Nearly the end of term, can't be doing with that union chap here again. Anyhow, what exactly did he say to you Miss Glover?'

'He said, "If I can't get you that way I'll make friggin` sure I get you some other way. You've had a good go at ruinin` my feet so thought you'd try my `ead this time did you?." They were his exact words Mr. Sanderson.'

'Right. I see! The banana skin wouldn't have helped the position one bit Miss Glover. What was that all about?'

Harriet looked down at her desk.

'Don't bother Miss Glover. Only try to keep some control over your class in future will you? You've been awarded a damehood for goodness sake. Services to education indeed! Try to see your way to living up to it. Now I think you have something to hand over, if you don't mind.'

'Oh no! Sorry Mr. Sanderson, there's been so much going on I completely forgot about it.'

'Well I most certainly didn't Miss Glover. Tomorrow morning without fail!'

She watched him stride off. Couldn't believe he was making her go on a course with Mr. Brown. She vowed not to sit near him. Vowed not to have anything to do with him. Thought.

'There's got to be a good reason why I can't go. Some excuse I can make. Start thinking Harriet. You've got six days to come up with something.'

She gathered her things together. Scrambled in her bag for the keys. Instantly remembered Mr. Brown still had them.

'Oh no. I don't believe it!'

Off she went up the corridor in search of him.

'Lost your way Miss Glover?'

'Actually I'm looking for Mr. Brown. He's still got my keys.'

'Ah, de fumo in flammam, Miss Glover. I've saved you from it.'

'Look Mr. Sanderson. Sorry but I really don't know what you're talking about. I just need to find him so I can get home.'

He lifted the keys from his jacket pocket. Held them in the air.

'Passed them over in Out-Patients Miss Glover. You might also be pleased to know the other casualty, apparently, recovered in the ambulance.'

She thanked him. Basked in the relief.

'Now perhaps you'd like to return the hanging basket, or what's left of it to your mother. Of course you'll have some explaining to do. Mr. Brown's left it in the porch. Minus a few plants now, of course. Not that she'd expect anything else from you. At least you didn't tip them on to my drive this time Miss Glover! Oh and I suggest you borrow a brush and shovel from Mr. Brown on the way out as he's refusing to clear the mess up. Try to do it within the confines of health and safety will you? Or as they say, "Ne quid nimis". Nothing in excess!'

Without even knocking, Harriet was straight into his room. Ugh! Mr. Brown's room. The smell of school again. Wasn't her favourite. She held her breath as she grabbed a yard brush from the corner by the door. It was a full fifteen minutes before she bunged what was left of the hanging basket into the boot. Then slammed her car door shut. Noticed *he'd* got himself away. No sign of the silver Mercedes. No just her car left. Nearly always the last one out. Furious, she drove away, managing not to stop until the traffic lights by Starboard Marine North West turned from amber to red. She looked across. He was in the doorway. Coming or going. Harriet couldn't decide which.

Chapter 55

'I've had a day of it Pepper. Am I glad I didn't marry that man!'

'Now which one were you speaking of Miss Glover?'

Harriet jumped. The key half turned in the front door, she looked round. Didn't know where he'd come from. Been so absorbed in her rage as not to have heard his car. Not even his door closing.

'Come along. Come along. I haven't got all night.'

Harriet struggled with the key. Finally opened the door to let them both and the cat in.

'I notice they still haven't sorted the for sale board?'

'No Mr. Sanderson I've been meaning to give them a call.'

'I should do so as a matter of urgency Miss Glover. It's totally misleading. Now you and Mrs. Harrington, Miss Glover. I've just spoken with her. Tomorrow evening. The PM has a brief space in his schedule. I've arranged for you both to be collected at six tomorrow evening. I've advised Mrs. Harrington to leave her car here. Save confusing the driver. I'm afraid we're going to have to work on this during dinner Miss Glover. The PM has literally only the evening before he has to fly back.'

'Dinner Mr. Sanderson. You mean we'll be dining at Lower Tideside tomorrow evening?'

'That's where I live Miss Glover, as you well know. Mrs. Harris has been instructed to prepare the evening meal for us all. No panic. This is an informal affair. But it's an issue we can't side-step any longer Miss Glover. "De pilo pendet", I'm afraid.'

Harriet couldn't let that go. She needed to know exactly what it meant. He read her expression.

'It hangs by a hair,' Miss Glover. 'We're reaching a critical stage. It's only my intervention that's stopping the pair of you from being called in for questioning. Oh and both of you. Wear something appropriate will you?'

He stood his full height. Went as swiftly as he'd appeared.

With barely a chance to fill the kettle the phone rang.

'Oh `arriet. I was goin` to call in but I saw `is car outside yours so I went `ome instead. `as `e gone `arriet?'

'Just Tricia. I don't believe it. Gosh Tricia we've got to go to Lower Tideside tomorrow night. Dining with the Prime Minister. We're being picked up Tricia so we can't get out of it.'

'Oh I know `arriet. We'll be `avin` the Spanish inquisition while we're tryin` to eat our dinner. I've never `eard of such a stupid idea `arriet.'

'I know Tricia but it must be urgent. Did he tell you it was only his intervention that was stopping us from being called in for questioning?'

'No `arriet. Did `e say that? Oh `arriet I don't like the sound of that. `e did tell me `e was flyin` in though `arriet. Ooh `arriet fancy the PM flyin` in to see us. I'm terrified!'

'Me too Tricia. We haven't got anything to tell them. What do we say? Do we mention Barry and Andy? We can hardly mention his minders, can we Tricia? They work for him.'

'No `arriet. I just don't know. I think we'll say as little as possible `arriet and only speak when we `ave to.'

'That's about it Tricia. I suppose we've got no choice but to get it over and done with.'

'That's if it does get it over and done with `arriet. `ow do we know this isn't just the beginnin`? Oh I do `ope it's not going to get in the way of savin` Venice `arriet. I've been speakin` to Rappin` `ammer. `e's come up with all sorts of ideas to `elp. Do you know `arriet `e's quite nice really. Probably since `e got rid of that cucumber, I would think. It must `ave made `im very `ot and itchy in there `arriet. `e must have been dreadin` `avin` to keep all that in. `e might `ave been better usin` a banana `arriet. One on the turn. Somethin` a bit softer.'

'Don't mention bananas Tricia. Have I had a day of it? It all started with Danny's and things just went from bad to worse. And now this. This has got to be as bad as it gets.'

'Ooh it `as and we've got to think of somethin` appropriate to wear `arriet. What does `e mean by that? Do you think `e means we `ave to dress for dinner?'

'Well he must do Tricia, otherwise why would he mention it? We'll have to find something long I suppose. Something suitable to dine in.'

'As long as it's not somethin` suitable to `ang in `arriet. I do `ope it's not a secret plot to `ave us executed. I `ope `e's not givin` us our last meal `arriet, like they do. Who would know? We could end up like those people who disappear and are never seen again. We're goin` to `ave to tell someone where we're goin` `arriet. We don't want to disappear without trace!'

'You're right Tricia. Look I'll phone Barry. Explain what's happened. I think it would be as well to do that.'

'Oh I would `arriet. At least that makes me feel a tiny bit better. What do you think you'll wear?'

'Goodness knows! I'll go and have a look now Tricia. What about you?'

'I `aven't got anythin` long that would be suitable. Oh I've just `ad a thought `arriet. `ow about that designer gown I collected from Venice? You've still got my case, `aven't you `arriet? It's in there. That will be just perfect. I might need to take up the `em a teeny bit. Can you get your sewing machine out? If I come round now I could `ave it done in five minutes. I need to collect my case anyway. Would that be alright `arriet?'

'Of course it would Tricia. But are you sure that's the right thing to be wearing, given how you came by it?'

'Oh there's no need to worry about that `arriet. `ow will they know where I got it from? There's a couple of posh shops round `ere that sell them. Well not this actual one. But the same designer make. They're all individual you know. No `arriet I don't think I could `ave anythin` better to wear. Do you think we

should wear our shades and `ats as well?'
    'You're joking Tricia. That would be pushing our luck!'

Chapter 56

'Thanks for the tea Mark. Did you have a good sleep?'

'Better than the night before Hat, but I'm certainly not complaining.'

'For old times sake. That's all it was Mark.'

'Old times have never been so good Hat. I can't say I've a problem with this lifestyle. It's working well.'

'Let's just keep it that way shall we Mark?'

'Too right Hat. Too right!'

'Tricia still keeping on top of the meals down there?'

'As well as other things Hat. Do you know if I didn't know better I'd say she's got quite a thing for me.'

'Well she would have, wouldn't she Mark? Especially after the way Bob's treating her. She'll sort herself out. I wouldn't be building your hopes up just yet Mark she's got other things on her mind.'

'Like shortening her designer gown for me? I'm looking forward to seeing her falling out of that one Hat. She's certainly pulling them in down there. A sudden interest in sailing Harriet. You know all those old boats, dried out along the wall in the sheds?'

'Yes.'

'Not any more Hat. The word must have got round. Most of them are on the water now. There's guys down there I haven't seen for ages.'

'Good! She's doing it on purpose to raise funds for her cause. It's not especially for you Mark. She's not shortened her dress for you either. We're both going out tonight.'

'Oh so no one to get my meal. It's about time lard ball took a turn. Tell him I can't make it tonight Harriet. You're bound to see him in school.'

'Sorry Mark. You'll have to go. He won't be able to make it either.'

'And how do you know that? You're not both out with him are you Harriet?'

'No Mark, we're both in with him. We've been invited to dinner. Dining with the PM.'

'Pull the other one Hat. You've got to be joking!'

'Joking I am not Mark. We don't know what it's about either except that it's got something to do with our trip away.'

'I warned you didn't I Harriet? The pair of you getting out of your depth. Especially you. Why can't you leave him alone?'

'I do. It's him. He's insisting on it. It looks like we've got no choice. Just make sure you get the search parties out if we don't come back. That's all.'

'Well I just hope you both realise what you're getting yourselves into. You really don't know what that lard ball of a schemer's up to.'

'Don't worry Mark we'll be on our guard. Anyway you won't starve. There's a couple of ready meals in the freezer and there's rice left over from last night. Just bang them in the microwave. It'll be a quick meal before you go down.'

'Thanks Hat. Oh and you'll need to put that away before Saturday.'

'What away Mark?'

'The sewing machine. We've got viewers.'

'Viewers. What are you talking about?'

'There was a message on there you didn't play.'

'There's a few Mark. Most of them Mummy wanting to know where her hanging basket is, I bet!'

'Yes and I can't understand why you don't just deliver it. We don't want her round here Harriet.'

'Was there one from the estate agent, then?'

'Yes. A Mrs. Moss and her daughter want to see it on Saturday. Unfortunately I'll be down at the club all day.'

Harriet swallowed her tea the wrong way.

'You're not choking are you Hat? Alright now?'

'No! No I'm not alright Mark. It's supposed to be off the market now. I told Mummy. Even Mr. Sanderson said they needed to get the board sorted out. Oh I'm just going to have to phone them. Unless you've put your half back on the market without telling me. Are you worrying about paying your parents back or something?'

'Oh I haven't told you yet Hat. It slipped my mind. It honestly did. I stayed over with them Sunday night. I was there giving Dad a hand with the new fencing. They've had word from their solicitor to the effect that lard ball's formally declared he doesn't want compensation providing the house stays on the market for the express purpose of being sold to him at a time appropriate to all parties.'

'Well thanks for telling me Mark. What's he done that for?'

'Well he said that at the start, in a fit of peak, remember? But you'd better ask him yourself, tonight.'

'He did mention the board coming down. Aren't they stupid wanting to send people round?'

'Anyway shouldn't *I* have had a say in this Mark?'

'Neither of us are in a position to have real say in this Harriet. My parents were prepared to stump up a great deal of money to get me off the hook. You can't blame them for assuming I'd go along with it. And anyway have you forgotten the position you're in? It was different when you were supposed to be marrying him Harriet. Don't forget the minute you pulled out you were legally obliged to settle your side of it all.'

'Gosh no Mark. It never crossed my mind. He's never mentioned it. So he buys it at a time appropriate to us all. Suppose we decide we never want to sell Mark? What then?'

'Well that's it isn't it Hat. It's one of these things whereby he keeps control. He's not interested in the house. His only proviso is that it stays on the market. I daresay he's paying the estate agent an agreed commission for retaining their services.'

'Golly, I had no idea!'

'Quite Harriet. That's exactly it. You don't have any idea how devious he is. You haven't a clue what he's capable of. Well you have now I've told you. Don't be blabbing that to Tricia either. She only has to tell Bob and it's straight back to Belinda Oxfordshire.'

'No of course I won't Mark. Gosh! I wish I had the money to pay him off.'

'Well we haven't Harriet. And isn't it just as well I put my foot down over the sale, in the event?'

'Alright Mark, don't start getting all self-righteous. We both blew it, remember?'

'As it's turned out it's just as well we're still here. At least if we do go separate ways we've got a buyer for this ready and waiting. He's doing us a favour Mark. Let's look at it like that.'

'Could be Harriet. Could be. Separate but together. Together but separate. A cash buyer in the wings. Things are looking up by the minute.'

'I wouldn't exactly say that Mark.'

Chapter 57

'Oh hi Tricia, I'm so glad you've come early. Wow that dress looks gorgeous Tricia!'

'Oh thanks `arriet. You look nice too. Isn't that the one you were wearin` for your weddin`?'

'All I've got Tricia.'

'Oh sorry `arriet I shouldn't `ave said that. It's just that I remember `ow lovely you looked standin` next to `im up the top of that aisle `arriet. I `ave to admit `arriet I was more than a tiny bit jealous of you.'

'Well you shouldn't have been Tricia. Anyway according to Mark you're pulling them in fast at the sailing club.'

'Oh `arriet did Mark say that?'

'He certainly did Tricia. You should have seen his face when I told him we were out tonight. He didn't want to go down there at all!'

'Oh `arriet, you're not jokin` me are you? I must admit I `ave been makin` a fuss of `im lately. But then I find myself doin` that to them all. I never knew we `ad so many men `idin` from us down there `arriet. Do you know I'm getting quite a lot going into my "save Venice tin". Do you know `arriet the more cleavage I show the more goes in, so I've been findin` my lowest cut tops `arriet. I swear I'll go topless before Tarquin Bridgewater gets back at this rate!'

'Good for you Tricia. Now let's have a glass of wine before we go, shall we? Take the edge off our nerves.'

'Now that is a good idea `arriet. I've `ad butterflies all day. I don't know `ow I put up with that whinin` lamp-post fallin` all over Joris. I nearly said to `er "`ow many men do you want at once? Isn't flat-fish-four-cheeks livin` up to the mark?" Oh thanks `arriet that's better. `ow long `ave we got?'

'Oh a couple of hours yet Tricia. We'll get a bit more down us than this.'

'I wonder who'll be comin` for us `arriet?'

'Probably Mr. Sanderson's chauffeur I would think.'

'Oh `as `e got a chauffeur `arriet?'

'Not sure. He probably springs one when the PM's around. Especially when he's arriving by helicopter.'

'Yes `arriet. I'm sure you're right.'

'Just as long as he brings us back Tricia. I've told Mark to send the search parties out if we disappear.'

'Oh I am glad you did that `arriet. So `e knows all about it then?'

'No not all Tricia. I kept it vague, just said it was something to do with our trip away and we didn't know what it was all about ourselves.'

'Well you're right `arriet. We don't do we? And what little we `ave tried to gather we'll keep it quiet when we get there, shall we? We `aven't done anythin` wrong though. Apart from pinchin` this dress of course. Well I didn't really pinch it, did I? It ran after me, didn't it? Ooh `arriet I do `ope that market trader didn't get stamped on. I do 'ope 'e's not dead.'

'Of course he isn't Tricia. As I said, we'd have long since heard about it. Especially as they've pinned us down.'

'Pinned us down 'arriet? I didn't know that. 'ere 'arriet I'm ready for a refill.'

'Hang on Tricia just let me open another bottle.'

'Oh thanks 'arriet. That's much better. Two glasses 'ardly goes anywhere does it? Now what were we sayin'? Oh it's gone now. Gone right out of my 'ead. I don't think it was very important anyway 'arriet.'

'Err. Err I think it was something Mr. Sanderson said Tricia. Gosh he was being pompous. He was going on about how serious it all is. No Tricia. It's gone. I can't remember either.'

'Did you tell Barry about our little dinner invite 'arriet? I think you were goin' to as I recall. Which isn't very much at the moment and the more I drink this the more I'm forgettin' and the better it's all feelin'.'

'Me too Tricia. Now what did you just ask me?'

'Barry, 'arriet. Err now what was it about Barry? 'as 'e mentioned Andy at all? Is that what I was askin' 'arriet? Do you know if Andy fancies me at all?'

'Oh gosh Tricia I'm trying to think. I'm sure he does. Here let me top that up. Now Barry, did he mention Andy? Oh I'm sorry Tricia I can't remember but there was something I was going to tell you about Barry. Oh yes Tricia, now would you have put him down for this?'

'Down for what 'arriet?'

'Oh wait until I tell you this. He rings the doorbell. I go down in my dressing gown thinking it's Mark back. He steps in. It was the night he took me for a drink Tricia. I can't remember if I told you or not.'

'Well I'm sure I can't remember either 'arriet. Anyway what 'appened?'

'I was one foot on the bottom stair about to go up and get changed Tricia and he pulled me down to him. Kissed me one of those French kisses Tricia, then peeled my dressing gown off, looked at me and gave me another!'

'Ooh 'arriet. Did you 'ave anythin' on under it?'

'Just my bra and pants.'

'Gosh 'arriet and 'e doesn't know you very well does 'e?'

'Exactly Tricia and that's not all!'

'Ooh 'arriet 'e didn't 'ave 'is way with you in your 'all did 'e? Well I'll 'ave no inhibitions about goin' topless for a good cause 'arriet, in spite of me tellin' them in Venice I'd never do it. Not after you strippin' naked for 'im out there. Perhaps we're comin' into our own 'arriet. I don't blame you for behavin' in a liberated way. Just wait until I get 'alf a chance. I'm feelin' really jealous 'arriet.'

'No Tricia. I quickly put my dressing gown on and threatened him to stay in the lounge while I went back up to get dressed.'

'Ahh 'arriet I'm really disappointed in you. But then you wouldn't 'ave wanted to be doin' that if you're expectin'. I 'ope you don't mind me sayin' that 'arriet. It's just what you did tell me, that's all. You seem to be 'andlin' it very well.'

'Denial Tricia. Most of the time I just go into denial. I've told *him* I'm not. I've told him I lost it! He's always chasing me Tricia wanting to know what's what. In fact I was supposed to be... Oh gosh Tricia, I've just blanked. I've forgotten what I was supposed to be going to say now.'

'It was about you bein` pregnant `arriet and `im keep wantin` to know.'

'Oh that's right Tricia. Just let me top your glass up again. There, now mine. He doesn't believe me and he's given me a testing kit thing. I was supposed to be handing it in this morning.'

'Well you could `ardly do that `arriet seein` as `e's been down at Starboard Marine North West all day.'

'Well I certainly didn't go looking for him. His car was there first thing and of course it was gone by the time I came out.'

'`e shouldn't be behavin` like that, anyway. I don't think `e `as any right to be that personal with you `arriet. I'd run it past a drop of lemonade if I were you. If you do it the day before, the bubbles will `ave all gone by the time it gives a readin`. What kind is it `arriet? Is it the one with the writin` on like Bob nearly `it Simon Barnes with when `e got the wrong end of the stick from that garage girl and thought I was pregnant?'

'That's the one Tricia.'

'Oh sit it in a glass of lemonade, I don't think it's going to be comin` up with pregnant in its window if you do that.'

'Oh I can't do that Tricia. He's a doctor. He'll know if it hasn't had a proper test. No, I'm just going to have to stall it for as long as I can.'

'Well when you're ready `arriet, just `and it over to me. I'll do the honours `arriet. `e won't know any different will `e? It certainly won't be readin` pregnant when `e gets it back then.'

'Oh thanks Tricia. You're a life saver. Do you know that?'

'I'll do anythin` I can to `elp you `arriet but what will you do when it starts to show?'

'Keep drinking plenty of this and hope he doesn't notice Tricia!'

'Yes, I would `arriet. I think that's a very good idea. It's too far off to be worryin` about it now. Do you know `arriet I was worryin` about somethin` on the way round `ere and now I can't for the life of me remember what it is.'

'Not going round to *his* for dinner by any chance Tricia and meeting the PM? Of course it wouldn't have been that. We're going to have a fabulous time!'

'Oh no `arriet. It wasn't that. I can't wait to get there.'

'Gosh Tricia is that the time already?'

'I think I've just `eard a car door `arriet. It's not our chauffeur is it?'

'`ave I got time to go upstairs `arriet? I've been drinkin` quite a lot!'

'Go on, hurry up Tricia, then answer the door for me, while I go. He can just wait a couple of minutes. Gosh I don't know where the time's gone.'

More than a little shaky, Harriet came downstairs to see Tricia waving her hands frantically towards the front door.

'`e's waitin` in the car `arriet. I don't think I want to go with `im `arriet.'

'Who is it Tricia? Tell me.'

'It's the porkiest one of the PM's two minders `arriet. `e's drivin` Mr. Sanderson's car.'

'Oh no! It can't be. It's probably someone who just looks like him. Come on Tricia, even if it is, at least he can't take us anywhere else. He's got to get that car back.'

'Oh but `e doesn't `ave to `arriet. People like `im don't `ave to do anythin` they don't want to do. `ow do we know we're not goin` to be whisked off to the airport to Venice and end up as `ostages in that `ouse next door to the `otel? `e only `as to leave the car at the airport `arriet.'

'We'll scream for help Tricia. It would be as simple as that.'

'Oh I `ope you're right `arriet. Quick! We'll just throw our coats round our shoulders and keep our `eads down. `obble to the car `arriet. We'll pretend to be old. Listen to `im beepin` is `orn. `ere `arriet just let me `ave a last swig before we go.'

'Pass it over Tricia.'

Harriet threw her coat round her shoulders. Clutching her bag to her side she banged the front door closed behind them. Reality impacting more on her brain than her legs, she wobbled behind Tricia to the silver Mercedes. Tipsy or old? No one could tell. Tricia's suggestion was working just fine now. They noticed the burly man drumming his fingers against the steering wheel as they opened the doors to get in. Heads down, intent on saying nothing.

Harriet sneaked a glance forward to see him reprogramming his satnav.

'What have you been telling them eh?'

Silence. Harriet felt Tricia's nudge.

'I said what have you two been telling them?'

'Telling them? I'm not sure what you mean.' Her voice trembling was somehow commensurate with her newly acquired demeanour.

'We're not telling them anything are we Conny? We do a lot for the old people. We've just been picked. We won this didn't we Conny?'

'What was that you said Onny? `er names not really Onny it's Honorous. Don't know what your mother was thinking about Onny callin` you that!'

'Pardon Conny, what was that?'

'To be `onest we're `avin` the greatest difficulty rememberin` anythin` aren't we Onny? We `ave a lot of trouble `earin` these days. But as I was sayin` she's Conny and I'm Onny. So together we make Connyonny! Like the butty. `aven't you ever `eard of the Conny Onny Butty? You `aven't lived unless you've `ad one of them. Get them to make you one while you're up `ere. You won't get one anywhere else.'

He turned his head back towards Harriet.

'She pissed or just short of a few marbles?'

'Marbles did you say? He wants to know if you play marbles Conny.'

'Well we're not as young as we look but we `aven't given up our bowls for marbles yet `ave we Onny? Do you know they were playin` marbles down at the clinic. We didn't see ourselves joinin` in did we Onny? It would `ave been much too painful stretching forward after `avin` our faces done. You've `ad yours rolled out and trimmed off four times now `aven't you Onny? It's only the third time for me. Oh you wouldn't recognise us now. We've been in there two months `avin` everythin` done. A long time but well worth it. Well we `ad to make an effort for the Prime Minister, didn't we?'

Harriet watched him scratch his head. Dug her elbow into Tricia. Hoping she'd flummoxed him into silence. Along the country roads now and up and over the hill. At least they were heading in the right direction.

Thought about Molly and Percy as they passed their house on the corner. Remembered feeling near demented in the car. Him having to stop. Her head between her knees.

Not long now. Her head starting to whirl. She needed another drink.

'Oh we've stopped `ere Onny. Will this be the `ouse then? Big! The size of the garden Onny, would you believe it? An `ellicopter. Oh `e `asn't come `ere by `ellicopter `as `e just to see us?'

'Zip it you two. Just keep it zipped if you want to get back in one piece!'

Stunned into silence Harriet and Tricia let themselves out of the car. Now only too keen to crunch their feet through the gravel to the front door.

'That fucking gown. A bloody giveaway. We want it back. Give it to her.' He pointed his finger at Harriet. 'You leave it in a bag behind your front wall with our hats. We'll get back tomorrow. Yeah we'll be back up here tomorrow. Don't even think of messing us about.'

'And we'll `ave the police behind the wall waitin` for you, won't we Conny? `ow dare you want to steal my designer gown. If cross-dressing's what you're into you'll be needin` to go to an outsize shop, I would say!'

A frightened Harriet looked across. Knew it was the wine talking. Couldn't deal with the thought of him sneaking around her front garden. She was glad to see Mrs. Harris open the front door.

'A couple of OAP's for you. Conny and Onny. Give them a butty will you?' He pushed Tricia forward. 'Especially this one. Anything to shut her up!'

Mrs Harris cleared her throat.

'Come through dears. Let me take your coats. Now Mr. Sanderson's in the drawing room with the Prime Minister. We'll go through now, but the only protocol we need to observe is the form of address. Just imagine Prime Minister is his name. That's the form of address throughout the evening. Now a quick run though the menu. Is there anything either of you are unable to eat?'

They both shook their heads.

'That's good, now have you any questions before we go through?'

'Oh we are very nervous. You wouldn't be `avin, er `avin` a little drop of somethin` to `elp, to help calm us down first, would you?'

'Yes of course. Come through to the kitchen. There's a bottle of brandy there. I'm sure you need it after that. How very rude of him! Now just take a couple of small glasses from the cupboard below. Help yourselves while I take your coats to the cloakroom. Er would you like to make use of a guest room upstairs to freshen up first?'

'Oh no thank you, I think we'll be alright, but it's very kind of you.' Harriet just about managed to get the words out without slurring them. Thought how much she liked this side of Mrs. Harris.

'ere 'arriet let's get a couple of these down us quick. I'm not goin' back with 'im!'

'I'll take you through now.'

Mrs. Harris stopped as a large stern faced man tapped her on the shoulder.

'Where's the nearest takeaway from here? I think we can spare Dave. Or can we phone it through?'

'No need. I have actually prepared supper for you all.'

'Good of you ma'am but we usually do it this way when we can.'

'That's quite alright. There are four of you aren't there? Oh they'll deliver for that many. Decide what you want and I'll set the table in the kitchen. I'll be with you in just one moment.'

She ushered Harriet and Tricia away from them and along the hall to the drawing room. The two men stood.

'Prime Minister, Mr. Sanderson, Conny and Onny for you.'

Mr. Sanderson stepped forward.

'These are the two ladies in question. May I introduce the Prime Minister. Miss Glover and Mrs. Harrington.'

They shook hands.

'Now we have a lot to discuss in a very short space of time. I want you to be concise in your answers to the Prime Minister during dinner. At the same time you are here to give him an accurate account of all you were party to. You might like to take this opportunity to collect yourselves in preparation.

Ah the drinks Mrs. Harris. An aperitif everyone? A schooner of dry sherry all round before dinner is it? Yes do sit down. I suggest the double sofa under the window.'

Harriet and Tricia simultaneously rocked back into the unmistakable comfort only the most expensive of sofas could afford. The other side of the room now. The last time Harriet was here she was standing in front of him, desperately trying to wriggle her way out of serious questioning. She looked around. The pictures carefully hung against pure white. A testimony to his passion for the sea. The water, each one, different. Every shade of aqua complementing the few tastefully displayed glass ornaments.

'Ah Mrs. Harris. The drinks. Splendid! Now where are you planning on seating the security people for theirs?'

'The kitchen Mr. Sanderson. I'm planning on setting the table in the kitchen.'

Harriet watched Mr. Sanderson side-glance the PM.

'Err I think perhaps the small table in the billiards room Mrs. Harris, if you could lay that. It might be more suitable. We need to maximise the distance if at all possible.'

'That's fine Mr. Sanderson. I'll be serving dinner in a quarter of an hour.'

A quarter of an hour! Harriet could feel Tricia's nudges. She wondered how she could possibly collect herself in that time, in order to meet Mr. Sanderson's request. The house. This would have been her house too. Fear ran through her. It was too big, posh, scary. And Mrs. Harris. She'd seen a kind side, but still calm, efficient, capable. No, she could never have lived here, she decided to herself.

The silence was fast setting like concrete in the room.

Suddenly the PM grinned. Put his glass down. Banged his hands on his thighs.

'Now what did Mrs. Harris call you two? Conny and Onny?'

He flashed a quizzical look at Mr. Sanderson.

'Yes that's right.' Tricia perked. 'She's Conny and I'm Onny. That's right isn't it `arriet?'

'Quite. Mrs. Harrington. Let's start the proceedings the way we mean to go on shall we? We're facing serious issues here.'

'We couldn't agree more Mr. Sanderson. Could we `arriet? It's subterfuge and we're protectin` ourselves `arriet and me.'

'Ah, I see,' returned the PM. Now exactly why do you feel the need to do that?'

'We didn't feel it was at all appropriate to give your bodyguard our real names, did we `arriet? After all we're not very sure why we're `ere in the first place. We `aven't done anythin` wrong as far as we can see, `ave we `arriet?'

'Mrs. Harrington I suggest we save the explanations for the dining room. Perhaps you'd like to tell the Prime Minister a little about yourselves. What you do, hobbies, that kind of thing.'

'Well I work for Mr. Sanderson, Prime Minister. I run Starboard Marine North West. I'm sure you remember comin` to open it last year and trippin` straight off the platform when you got your foot caught in the strap of `arriet's bag?'

The Prime Minister coughed. Turned to Harriet.

'That the one?'

Harriet instantly pulled it closer in to her feet.

'Right, right. It's starting to make sense now.'

His face straight, she watched him down the the rest of the sherry in one. Watched Mr. Sanderson refill the glass. And his own. Not theirs though.

'And you Miss Glover. I know a little more about you. Hopefully living up to your damehood? Not letting Mr. Sanderson down? He went to great lengths to ensure the award Miss Glover. Very great lengths.'

With her mind fogging Harriet thought it safer to just smile.

'We see you've come in an `elicopter Prime Minister. `ow long did it take from London? I `ope it wasn't too difficult to land in Mr. Sanderson's back garden?'

'We're hardly talking about a pocket handkerchief Mrs. Harrington. Now do try to stay focussed with your questions to the Prime Minister.'

'No no Joris. That's a perfectly reasonable question. I'm sure Mrs. Harrington hasn't seen the helipad on the sea side of the house.'

'Oh no I `aven't. We `aven't `ave we `arriet? We `ave seen `elicopters flyin` over `ere. though. I `ad no idea this is where they would be landin`. You're not involved in a teeny weeny bit of subterfuge yourself are you Mr. Sanderson?'

Harriet nudged her. Dreading her next words.

'Certainly not Mrs. Harrington. Whatever are you suggesting?'

'Well `ow about smugglin`? `ow do we know you're not smugglin` drugs that `ave been dropped the other side of the island? There's plenty of ships go past there on the way to Liverpool. `ow do we know there's not someone rowin` a boat full of drugs from one of them ships? We've seen them `elicopters landin` on the island before now `aven't we `arriet? `ow do we know they're not pickin` up crates of drugs and landin` them `ere, seein` as you do `ave an `elipad Mr. Sanderson. After all you do `ave plenty of money. You must be gettin` it from somewhere!'

'Mrs. Harrington. I demand an immediate apology. It's evident to me you've been drinking!'

'Just a teeny weeny bit. We've `ad just a teeny weeny bit `aven't we `arriet? Before we came that is. Just to steady our nerves.'

'APOLOGY Mrs Harrington.'

'Well I'm very sorry Mr. Sanderson. I'm sure there's no drugs bein` flown over `ere. Just bags full of seeds I expect. You do `ave to grow them you know and I believe you've got a very green-fingered gardener and two very big green`ouses.'

She turned to the PM. 'I expect you've come for yours as well `ave you?'

Harriet watched the PM stiffen in his seat.

'Only, as I said, `arriet and I `ave been wonderin` `ow you get all your money Mr. Sanderson, `aven't we `arriet? It's all startin` to make sense now.'

'Dinner is served if you'd like to take your seats.'

Face crimson, Mr. Sanderson stood allowing Harriet to lead the way, following Mrs. Harris to the dining room.

'You'll serve the wine will you, Joris?'

'I certainly will Mrs. Harris, thank you. I'll pop through between courses.'

'Right. I won't disturb you then.' Mrs. Harris closed the door on them while Mr. Sanderson showed them to their seats.

He turned to the PM. Showed him the wine bottle. 'Still going with this?'

The PM nodded.

'You two help yourselves to water. I suspect the both of you have long since past the point of satiation. Not that it will make a great deal of difference. I doubt either of you have the capability to explain yourselves.'

'Time's short, but I can work through the night Joris, if you can. I'm used to it. They haven't yet grasped the gravity of the situation. They'll soon sober up as the night wears on.'

Harriet looked at Tricia fidgeting in her seat. She couldn't believe how she'd managed to drop them both in it, as if there wasn't enough to contend with. She spread her white linen napkin across her lap. From the back of her mind. Could see them both in court. The prison sentence declared. She watched Mr. Sanderson. He was doing this for them. Silently vowed him as much cooperation as she could muster. Desperately hoping Tricia would change tack and do the same.

'Let's start with the latest developments shall we? The grimmest of news I'm afraid.' The PM, momentarily abandoned his pan fried sea bass to place his knife and fork down.

'It looks like we've lost one of our key allies operating in the San Polo area.'

'`ow do you mean you lost `im? Isn't that what you `ave those `eavies for?'

'Mrs. Harrington. I advise you remain silent and just listen to what the Prime Minister has to say.'

'I'm very sorry Mr. Sanderson. I promise to do my very best now. I think this water's startin` to `elp.'

'Do keep quiet Mrs. Harrington!'

Harriet had never seen Mr. Sanderson so enraged.

'We have it on good authority you two were in Venice from Sunday 27th June and returned the evening of Wednesday 30th. Am I or am I not correct?'

'That's right Prime Minister, but we only went away for a short break. It was just a few days holiday. We didn't think there was anything wrong in that.' Harriet looked across. Caught Mr. Sanderson's eye. She knew only too well there was plenty wrong in that. She reached for her glass. Letting the water ease the dryness overtaking her throat, allowing a couple of seconds for Tricia to chirp up.

'Well we will tell you where we went. If you promise not to tell anyone. It was Venice and it was the most beautiful place in the world, wasn't it `arriet? Well it still will be once I've saved it!'

'Mrs. Harrington the Prime Minister's already established that you went to Venice. Have you not been paying attention? Please concentrate. It's vital you do so.'

'Sorry Mr. Sanderson.'

'I would heed Mr. Sanderson's advice if I were you. It would serve your interests better to focus on saving yourself Mrs. Harrington.'

'Well if you could tell us what we're supposed to `ave done wrong it might `elp, mightn't it `arriet?'

Harriet kept quiet. Didn't like the way things were shaping up. Watched the PM raise his napkin to his mouth.

'It would seem Mrs. Harrington you're not averse to accusing us of impropriety. Might that be because it's something you yourself are familiar with? It appears to me more than a little odd the two of you should have abandoned all to arrive in Venice as you did. As you've mentioned Mrs. Harrington you run Starboard Marine North West. How responsible was it to disappear without either requesting time, or informing Mr. Sanderson of your intentions? Very strange. It's not adding up. And you Miss Glover. Given the position you were in on Saturday 26th June, the only logical explanation for your behaviour so far as I can see, most certainly suggests you had a very urgent agenda to attend to, one that took precedence over the disastrous situation you were very fortunate enough to have been bailed out of.'

He glanced at Mr. Sanderson before continuing. 'Now it suggests to me, and I need to be quite clear on this before I'll even consider any further intervention on Mr. Sanderson's behalf. It seems to me, rather than you being unwittingly caught up in all of this, you are a part of it.'

'We'll pause this here, shall we?' Mr. Sanderson declared. 'Let them absorb all you've said for a few moments. I'll just tell Mrs. Harris we've finished the first course. We'll take the opportunity between courses to consolidate between ourselves.'

'If you'll excuse me?'

Harriet and Tricia nodded their heads at the PM as he followed Mr. Sanderson out.

'Did you just hear that Tricia? He's flipping well told the Prime Minister all about me. He had no right to do that. Personal information. I don't want him knowing Mark ditched me. Bloody cheek Tricia! And so patronising. *He* was bailing me out. True colours Tricia. Oh I can see him for what he is now. Mark was so right!'

'Keep your voice down `arriet. They might be listenin` be`ind the door! `e thinks we're involved in whatever's goin` on `arriet. We can't afford to fall out with Joris Sanderson now. If we don't keep `im on board we'll end up bein` arrested. Shush, I can `ear them comin` back!'

'The gentlemen have just told me they'll be retiring between courses. Let me take these plates away. Thank you.'

In silence Harriet and Tricia watched Mrs. Harris gather them to rest on her left arm. Heard the door closing behind her.

'`arriet. `is minder, the one that drove us `ere. Not only is `e after my designer gown, `e's threatened us with our lives `arriet if we say anythin`. What's `e talkin about anyway? `e must `ave forgotten it was them that were followin` us. Ooh my `ead `arriet. It keeps comin` and goin`. `ow about yours?'

'Just the same Tricia. I'll tell you something. We're not going home with him behind the wheel. I'll phone Mark before we do that!'

'That's what I was thinkin` `arriet. Ooh I can `ear them comin` back.'

'In you go Mrs. Harris. Would you like me to bring anything through?'

'No that's alright thank you Mr. Sanderson. You get yourselves seated.'

Harriet watched her place the serving dishes on the table. Didn't know how she'd manage to speak, let alone eat any more.

'All in now. Enjoy!'

'Thank you Mrs. Harris. Splendid!' Mr. Sanderson got up to close the door behind her.

Harriet and Tricia watched the PM lift his glass to his lips. Waited. Knew he was focussed on them.

'Now, this unpredictable behaviour has occurred before. If I may take you both back to last year's opening of Starboard Marine North West. I understand you both disappeared before the function was hardly under way. To come to the point it's somewhat strange your disappearance coincided with that of two of my bodyguards. They eventually returned, however. Apparently you two didn't. Do either of you have any comment to make on this at all?'

Harriet panicked. Thought of Simon Barnes. The ship. The cat. Being on the news. Thought it best to keep quiet. Tricia sipped her water, then turned to the PM.

'Well it was so long ago we 'ardly remember now do we 'arriet? But whatever the reason your bodyguards disappeared it 'ad nothin' to do with us. As a matter of fact we wouldn't want to be 'avin' anythin' to do with them would we 'arriet? We think they're 'orrible!'

'Interesting Mrs. Harrington. Now what makes you both conclude that? You can only make such an emotive statement if you'd had some reason to be dealing with them. So what is the basis for this judgement, exactly?'

'Well, the way I see it Prime Minister, and please don't get me wrong because I'm not accusin' anyone of anythin'. But you might or might not know this but last year I 'ad to carry a bloody big 'eavy case through customs for a certain person not too far away whose name I shall not mention.'

'Oh yes, Mrs. Harrington. Venice again?'

'No it most definitely was not Venice Prime Minister. No it was Switzerland. I 'ad to go on my own from Manchester to Zurich with this big 'eavy case and I didn't 'ave a clue what was in it. I still don't as a matter of fact. I was met by a Johanssen. 'e could 'ave been one of the bodyguards you've got 'angin' around 'ere for all I know. They all look the same to me. 'ow do I know what I was carryin' through for this certain person? It could 'ave been full of drugs flown from the island over there, for all I know. I could 'ave been caught and sent to prison. I was only doin' as I was told.'

Harriet nearly died. Didn't dare look at Mr. Sanderson. Couldn't get her head round why Tricia was saying all this when she'd gone to great lengths to explain it all so accurately to her.

'So can you get to the point here Mrs. Harrington without incriminating yourself?'

'Without incriminating myself, Prime Minister? Mr. Sanderson, you tell 'im what was in that bloody 'eavy thing before 'e 'as me arrested!'

'Now that's quite enough Mrs. Harrington. The Prime Minister is quite au fait with this. Nothing untoward, I might add. Try to focus on the question in hand if you will.'

'Oh yes I will Mr. Sanderson. To be 'onest Prime Minister. I think you've got some pretty dodgy bodyguards if you ask me. We do, don't we 'arriet?'

Harriet's face was enough to pale a beetroot. She looked up in error just to

181

catch a glance between the PM and Mr. Sanderson.

'The dress you're wearing Mrs. Harrington? Italian designer. Expensive? Tell me, how did you come by that exactly?'

'I'm not sure this `as anythin` very much to do with the discussion Prime Minister. Why are you askin` me that?'

'San Polo, Mrs. Harrington. Where we came in. A market trader, a key suspect now fighting for his life in a coma. We have it on good authority two girls identical to your size and height were seen running away. So which one of you tripped him up?'

Harriet watched him glance at her bag sat by the side of her chair. He turned to her.

'Virtually a weapon of mass distruction Miss Glover. Did you give it one good swing?'

'No, Prime Minister. I most certainly did not!'

'You're not denying you were in the vicinity then?'

'Come on, come on Miss Glover. You're here to get yourselves out of this mess. I'm beginning to wonder why we've given you this opportunity. It would be a damned sight easier to let things take their course.'

'But we can't Mr. Sanderson. The bodyguard who drove us here threatened us with death if we opened our mouths.'

'Yes `e did. `arriet's right. So these are the kind of people you've got lookin` after you. It wouldn't surprise me if they weren't all members of the mafia. And these are the people you sent after us to find out where we were and what we were doin`. Very nice and I don't think. I think our friend Simon Barnes would pay us quite a bit `arriet to get `old of this story!'

'Indeed not. I can't over-stress the importance of you both maintaining complete confidentiality as far as the whole of this matter is concerned.' The PM refilled his glass.

'Mrs. Harrington. Miss Glover. You've just heard the Prime Minister. On no account do either of you discuss this with anybody.'

'We understand Mr. Sanderson.' Harriet nodded at Tricia.

'Well yes of course we understand. As long as you understand that we `aven't got a clue what you're tryin` to pin on us and unless you drop the whole thing we'll `ave to sell our story to the press to `ave the money to defend ourselves, Prime Minister.'

Mr. Sanderson stood. 'All finished? Miss Glover you've hardly eaten a thing! Right I'll just give Mrs. Harris the word.' They watched the PM follow him out.

'Oh gosh Tricia. That man, that trader. We did trip him up. What if he dies Tricia? We're not going to get out of this one. What are we going to do?'

'Don't panic `arriet. I've got a feelin` this is all about them `eavies. I've got a feelin` the PM suspects them of corruption. Don't forget we saw them behind us after that `appened. `ow do we know that's why they changed their minds about goin` to San Marco? Maybe they came back to duff `im up `arriet. `e could `ave been an informer. `e could `ave been splittin` on them `arriet over what it is they've been doin`. It's more than likely them.'

'But how will they know it wasn't us Tricia? They might be thinking we've been working with them.'

'Oh you've just taken the words out of my mouth `arriet. That's exactly what I was goin` to say. I think the PM's makin` sure we're not involved with them before he can do any more.'

'But why would they still be employing them Tricia? If they're part of the mafia you'd think they'd round them up straight away?'

'Oh no `arriet. It's probably somethin` much bigger than them. They're probably castin` their nets wide `arriet so they can catch them all at once.'

'Gosh Tricia. You're right. That's got to be it. But what are they doing? What's it all about? What does it have to do with San Marco being the end of the road?'

'I `aven't got a clue `arriet and as long as we don't get done I can't say as I'm too bothered about findin` out. Shush `arriet, the door.'

'I'll just clear these then. Oh Conny you've hardly eaten a thing. Are you alright dear?'

'Yes thank you Mrs. Harris. I think it's the warm weather. I never do eat too much in the heat.'

'That was very nice thank you, Mrs. `arris.'

'I'm glad you enjoyed it Onny. Unusual names. Do you know dear?' She looked across to Harriet. 'Do you know I'm sure I've seen your face before. I'm usually good with names. Just can't place it at the moment.'

Glad about that Harriet saw fit not to come clean. Thought Mr. Sanderson was obviously grateful for the heaven-sent opportunity Brad's introduction had afforded to disassociate. He obviously hadn't wanted to enlightened her.

She gathered the plates while Tricia held the door open until she'd finished coming back and forth to clear the table of serving dishes.

'That's it done. I'll leave you in peace. Thank you very much dear.'

'What shall we do now Tricia? We need to know we're on the right track.'

'I think we just `ave to tell them everythin` `arriet. Everythin` except meetin` Barry and Andy. This doesn't `ave anythin` to do with them and it wouldn't be fair to drag their names into it.'

'No Tricia, you're right. You're absolutely right. I don't think we should mention anything about us tipping those heavies into the water either. We'll leave that bit out.'

'No we won't mention that `arriet or `ow I got my dress, or knockin` over all that fruit from the stall on the corner when we were runnin` out of the market.'

'No Tricia, we'll just tell them we thought they'd sent those heavies to follow us. Oh I can hear voices Tricia. They're coming back.'

'Thank you Mrs. Harris. If you're ready?'

'There. Help yourselves. I'll leave the cheeseboard on the side to save disturbing you again, Mr. Sanderson.'

'Thank you Mrs. Harris. That's very kind.'

The PM began.

'Now what do you suppose Brad meant by threatening you against speaking out? You see this turns out to be a key factor. None of them know the reason for this visit. In fact two of them here very rarely accompany me anywhere now for obvious reasons. They have been deliberately involved in this exercise, particularly Brad for the express purpose of meeting you. It's the reaction I needed to confirm your lack of involvement, to a degree, anyway. I'm referring to your inadvertent involvement now, of course.'

'I thought you'd asked the Prime Minister for his help in trying to find us. They seemed to be following us. Wherever we went, they were there. It honestly looked that way Mr. Sanderson.'

'Yes 'arriet did think that. We both did didn't we 'arriet? They were followin` us all over the place. So to answer your question Prime Minister, they could 'ave thought we'd been watchin` them. That's why they've threatened us not to say anythin`.

'And did you notice anything strange about their behaviour? Anything of consequence?'

'Well we did notice them stoppin` off to talk to a few people sellin` stuff on the pavements. Oh and they always 'ad their 'ats and glasses on.'

'Come, come Mrs. Harrington. Try to stick to the point. The Prime Minister's had a very busy day.' Mr. Sanderson looked at his watch. 'Good heavens it's turned one already. Now do either of you recall anything else?'

'Oh yes we do, don't we 'arriet? Our 'otel was right next to this really spooky 'ouse that 'ad its blinds closed all the time. We saw them comin` and goin` a few times and there was an awful lot of bangin` and clatterin` in the night. It kept me awake didn't it 'arriet?'

'Yes Tricia it did. We thought you'd based them there right next to the hotel to keep an eye on us.'

'You flatter yourselves Miss Glover.'

'Yes, I'm sorry. I apologise for that.' Harriet could feel her face burning.

Mr. Sanderson turned to the PM.

'I'm afraid they have a penchant for being in the wrong place at the wrong time. It's just unfortunate they've stumbled into this mess.'

'Quite Joris. I can see what you're having to deal with. Shall we finish? Take our coffee into the lounge. Catch the rolling news whilst we decide the best way to proceed.'

'I take it everyone's finished?'

'Yes thank you, we 'ave, 'aven't we 'arriet?'

'Go through. I'll bring it along. Nobody interested in the cheese course?'

'Oh no thank you very much Mrs.'arris. Not for me anyway. I think we'll be 'avin` enough nightmares tonight without 'avin` cheese to 'elp them along.'

'Quite Mrs. Harrington. Go straight ahead. The end door on the right will see you into the lounge.'

Harriet followed behind Tricia. Couldn't believe they'd all been here. In this room at Christmas. Couldn't believe how things had moved along. Couldn't believe her folly in falling for this despicable, patronising man. Being outclassed by *him* and all his family. She looked into the empty hearth. No fire. No flames. Just cold and dark, reflecting her thoughts.

'Mr. Sanderson can keep his privileged world. And I'll make sure my baby goes nowhere near!'

She watched him turn the television on. Felt uncomfortable. The last time. Simon Barnes. Her breasts all over the screen. A sticker on each. Rapping Hammer. Cringing like she'd never cringed before. She shuddered wanted to get back home.

'Yes, yes. Just help yourselves to coffee.' Mr. Sanderson, remote in hand switched the channel over as he spoke.

'Now we have some last minute news coming through. Yes we can bring it to you now. Two people, err both female have gone missing feared dead. They'd been attending a local private dinner party with the Prime Minister and failed to return home.

That's all we're getting on that one for the moment I'm afraid. We'll bring you more on that story as it comes in.'

'Oh they're not talkin` about us are they `arriet?'

'We have only one Prime Minister Mrs. Harrington, who else would they be talking about?'

'Oh I can `ear an `elicopter now Mr. Sanderson. You `aven't got more friends comin` `ave you?'

Harriet watched the PM. Virtually a standing corpse. Rigid. White. Silent.

The door flew open. Two of the four bodyguards in a state of shock.

'Brad and Al. Gone. Al grabbed the keys from the table. Something on the radio. We didn't hear.' He stopped, pointed to Tricia. 'Just said something unrepeatable about that dress you're wearing. The chopper's away. I didn't even know Al could fly one! What the hell's going on?'

Mr. Sanderson rose to his full height.

'So which one of you couldn't keep your mouth shut?'

'Sorry gov we didn't know anything about it. Honest.'

Lee pulled out his mobile. Strode from the room.

'No. Indeed not. I wasn't addressing you!'

'Miss Glover. Mrs Harrington. This was supposed to be totally confidential. Now how did this get out?'

'It must have been me Mr. Sanderson. I do apologise. I did tell Mark to find us if we went missing. I'm unbelievably sorry Prime Minister. I was just so frightened about it all. I didn't know why you were sending a chauffeur. What was I to think?'

Harriet, shaking, suddenly felt a hand on her shoulder.

'Quite understandable Miss Glover. We've been holding on to them by a thread. We've been expecting it. We know they've got links with both governments and there's corruption afoot. It would have been better if we could have seen it through. You don't know how near we've been to nailing them. We thought San Marco was the end of the road. No, they'll get them. They've nailed their colours to the mast now. My concern is for you now, err…What was your name again?'

'Harriet. Harriet Glover.'

'Well now Harriet you and your friend here will need to be on your guard.

Mr. Sanderson will keep me informed should you require any assistance. These could be dangerous men. In the interest of your own safety you must avoid the press at all costs and neither of you must discuss our conversation here tonight. Do you understand? If you are unable to do this then to be quite frank I'm afraid the consequences could be dire for you both. You've become embroiled in something far bigger than you could ever have imagined. Mr. Sanderson will be constantly updated and you must now listen and take his advice.'

'Do you know I thought I 'eard another helicopter then. I do 'ope it's not them comin` back.'

Harriet nudged Tricia. The least said now, the better. She felt they were lucky to get the PM on side.

'Your gown Mrs. Harrington. Make sure you get it to Mr. Sanderson as quickly as you can.'

Mr. Sanderson turned to him.

'I'll take these two back home before any more damage is done. Mrs. Harris will prepare the guest rooms for the night.'

'Not the time Joris, unfortunately. But thanks. Sorry. Not the time. Where's Lee? He'll have sourced another chopper. Ah there you are.'

'Just been checking. It left at 1.27. It's on its way.' Lee nodded towards Tricia. 'She was right. That's it. Sounds like he's just landed.'

They silenced as Mr. Sanderson switched the television off. All listening to the whirring blades slowing to a halt.

'Well done Lee. Fast thinking.' The PM turned. Shook Mr. Sanderson's hand.

'Thanks Joris for the offer. I need to get back. A useful evening. Pity we lost them. Don't be too hard on the girls.'

Chapter 58

'Right I'll just see them off. You can watch from the library if you like. Follow me. It'll be quicker for me to go that way in any case.'

They followed Mr. Sanderson to the large room centre back of the house. Harriet watched him. Through the French doors in a flash. Caught them up. Another quick word with the PM. The lights catching his thick blonde hair is it lifted in layers from the draught of whirring blades. Just one hand. The palm of his hand raised flat towards the moving windows. He stood watching its vertical lift to see it nose down and then forward into the night sky.

'How can such a hunk of gorgeousness be so despicable?' Harriet couldn't get the thought out of her head as she gazed round the room rapidly becoming transfixed by the three walls surrounding them. Lined with books of every size imaginable.

'Is it just wallpaper `arriet? You know that wallpaper that looks like books, or do you think there's a door there behind those shelves openin` into a secret passage?'

'Shush Tricia. He's coming back.'

'You are both extremely fortunate the PM's come down on your side. And as for you Mrs. Harrington to make the accusations you did was absolutely appalling. I demand you write a letter of apology to us both. Fortunately for you, though ironic, it was obvious you were under the influence of alcohol and the PM being the kind of person he is put your need for it before arriving down to nerves. Thus you've gained an understanding from him which I consider to be not at all deserved. The suggestion that I would have allowed you to carry a suitcase full of drugs through customs is so ludicrous as to be absurd Mrs. Harrington. Your inebriated state has produced loose talking which is dangerous. I expect a carefully considered written apology tomorrow morning when I'll have the address to which you will send the Prime Minister's. Now, speaking of loose talking. It's absolutely imperative you both retain the confidentiality of the evening. I can't emphasise it enough. It would seem the PM's fairly confident you were not involved with them, by consent, anyhow. Now there are still issues to be dealt with. Keep as low a profile as you can, both of you. And by no means become embroiled with that reporter fellow Simon Barnes. You must not under any circumstances speak to him.'

'Oh no Mr. Sanderson. And I am really very sorry. I will write those letters first thing tomorrow mornin`. We don't want to get ourselves into any more trouble. Do we `arriet? But what about that market trader in San Polo `ow do we know `e's not goin` to die?'

'At the moment we don't Mrs. Harrington. Do you have a particular concern over this, may I ask?'

Harriet nudged Tricia.

'Oh no not at all Mr. Sanderson. It's just that we feel sorry for `im don't we 'arriet? It can't be very nice for 'im 'avin' 'is 'ead bandaged up like that and not bein' able to remember anythin'. I do 'ope 'e gets better. You never know if 'e gets better 'e might not be able to remember anythin'.'

'And would that suit you Mrs. Harrington?'

'I don't see as it would make any difference to me Mr. Sanderson, except if the poor man as 'ad such a bad experience 'e might be better off not bein' able to remember anythin'.'

'Ah right Mrs. Harrington. I see where you are coming from now.'

'I'm very glad about that Mr. Sanderson. Perhaps if we all 'ope 'e gets better then 'e will.'

'Quite Mrs. Harrington. This guy's got to make it now. With the San Marco operation having been blown, it's vital he's interrogated. We'll just have to wait and see. Hope he recovers. Retains all his faculties.'

'What 'ave they all done Mr. Sanderson? We 'aven't got a clue what it's all about. I'm sure it won't do any 'arm just to put us in the picture. It might 'elp us remember a bit more.'

'Remember a bit more? You mean you've been holding back Mrs. Harrington? Haven't you two grasped the seriousness of the situation yet?'

Harriet needed to speak.

'Yes of course we have Mr. Sanderson. Tricia's only wondering if we've missed anything with regard to those two men. I've been thinking hard. They're not nice. They need to be caught.'

'Quite Miss Glover. Should you recall anything at all. Even if you feel it's too insignificant to mention, you must inform me at once. Understand?'

'Yes we understand, don't we 'arriet? Oh and I 'ave to give you this too, don't I Mr. Sanderson? I 'ope you won't be wantin' me to take it off right now!'

Harriet was pleased he'd just ignored the comment as he led them from the library and through the passageway to the large entrance hall. He opened the front door. She couldn't quite make out why Tricia was so keen to hand over what could be incriminating evidence against them. Decided it was a moment of weakness.

'Right, in you two. Let's get this thing over and done with before the law lands on the doorstep. Too late. That's them now. You two get in. I'll turn them round. Tell them it was all a misunderstanding. Let's hope the pair of you don't have to foot the bill!'

Harriet and Tricia watched him flag the police car down. Bent forward. His head in the window. Standing back and then moving forward again. Then touching his chin. Pointing to the house. Waving his hand at something. Then they were gone.

He returned to the car. Banged his door shut. Then silence as he turned the key in the engine. The car crunching its way through the gravel to the gates. Automatic. Opening in advance. He turned left and on up the road. Silent, he got on with the task in hand.

From the rear seat, Harriet watched him. Just the one curl resting at the neck of his collar. Looking right. Looking left. His profile. Strong, handsome, gorgeous. Changing gear, braking. Turning. Slipping the steering wheel effortlessly through his hands. Half turning as if to speak. *Him. The Prime Minister. Him* right up there with them all.

'Oh this gorgeous gorgeous absolutely horrid, patronising man. No I'm not falling for him. All over again. I'm not. I won't let myself go there.' Her thoughts moved to her baby. His baby. She wanted it. His child would be the best part of him. Born of the nice, kind side of him. The only side she'd fully known.

Passing Molly and Percy's house now. They were driving on the top road, about to go down the hill. Mr. Sanderson broke the silence.

'Yes. I must say I'm not thoroughly au fait with the PM's request for the gown Mrs. Harrington. But there you are. Make sure I get it in the morning with the letters if you would.'

'Well, it could be that those `eavies...' She stopped abruptly as Harriet nudged her.

'You were saying Mrs. Harrington?'

'Oh I'm terribly sorry Mr. Sanderson I'm afraid it's gone right out of my `ead now. I'll get back to you with it when I remember, if that alright?'

'I do trust you're not still holding anything back Mrs. Harrington. You heard the PM. This could be a very dangerous game you're playing.'

Harriet was only half listening. Almost there now. She couldn't help herself. Hoping against hope he'd take Tricia home first. Just to give her a couple of minutes alone with him in the car. She wanted it. She needed it. She tried to draw on her fury of the evening to halt the thought. Stem the feeling. It was gathering yet again, low between her hips under her pale blue dress. Her bridesmaid's dress. The one she'd been wearing when she'd stood next to him in the church. In the church when he'd made that beautiful speech. Wished it was this dress they wanted. Wouldn't have had any trouble taking it off for him in the car. Just at this moment.

Her heart sank. The virtually indiscernible click click of the indicator as he turned left into her road. As loud as a time-bomb to Harriet. He drew up. Standing, holding the door. Waiting for her to get out.

'Inform the authorities of your whereabouts will you Miss Glover? Just to make sure they've got the message. We don't want to be held responsible for wasting even more tax payers' money over this damned search.'

'Yes I'll do that straight away Mr. Sanderson. Thank you for the lift. Oh and also for standing by us.'

'Come on. Come on Miss Glover. I need to be getting back!'

Harriet waved to Tricia. Watched him turn the car round and away while she was waiting for Mark to answer the doorbell.

'Oh it's you Hat. Well thanks for telling me! You might have phoned to say lard ball would be bringing you back in the middle of the morning. It's quarter past two, what time do you call this? You warned me to send the search parties out. I've been worried sick. Bob's been going mad. We had to phone the police

Harriet. We didn't know what could have happened to you both.'

'OK Mark. Let me get in please.'

'Turned out to be quite some dinner party, did it?'

'No Mark. That's not fair. We've haven't enjoyed ourselves. Not one bit.'

'Why did you go then Harriet? What's it all about?'

'I can't tell you that Mark. It's just something that's been going on and we got caught up in it. In fact we don't know ourselves. We honestly don't. Tricia asked him just now and he wouldn't say.'

'Oh he's gone on to take her home then?'

'Yes Mark. And then he's going straight back. He's just been really abrupt with me trying to hurry me out of the car. I don't know what's with that man. It wouldn't hurt him to be civil.'

'Come on in Harriet, let's get this door closed. I've had police cars and goodness knows what here since half one this morning.'

'Oh gosh Mark he told me to phone the police. To make sure they'd called off the search. I'd better go and do it before I get into any more trouble. Is that the number you dialled? On this bit of paper here?'

'That's the one Harriet. It's the area number. I wasn't going to be calling 999.'

'Neither am I Mark. I'll try this. See if I can get through.'

'I'll put the kettle on. Tea or coffee?'

'Coffee please Mark. Just let me get on with this.'

'No answer Mark.' Harriet held the receiver away from her mouth. 'Shall I leave a message?'

'Better had Harriet. At least they'll know you tried.'

'Gosh Mark it was on the news. The Prime Minister wanted to see it. Hit it just the minute the television came on. "Missing, believed dead!" That's what he said, the news reader. What on earth did you say to them Mark?'

'I said enough to get them on the case double quick Harriet. We don't know what types lard ball associates with, do we?'

'Did you actually have to tell them where we went Mark? Couldn't you just have said we'd gone out for a meal and disappeared?'

'No I bloody couldn't Harriet. They've better things to do than to be combing the streets for a couple of sloshed over-grown school girls.'

'No need for that Mark. Do I sound sloshed? And we're not over-grown school girls either.'

'Answer to one, evidence of, there! Mark pointed to the wine bottles standing on the window sill. 'And that's *before* you went. Answer to two. Only over-grown school girls would get themselves in this mess. Grow up Harriet. Why don't you?'

Harriet went quiet. Thought. Remembered the threat. Dreaded them coming back to scramble under the hedge for Tricia's dress and those panama hats.

'No Mark you were right. You were absolutely right to do what you did. We could have been in a very tight spot indeed.'

Chapter 59

Although the gravity of the night before went some way towards negating the effect of too much drinking, Harriet knew she'd woken up to a hangover. It was fogging her thinking. There was something else about today. Something she needed to sort.

'I just can't go in today Mark. I feel terrible. I'm going to have to phone in sick.'

'I shouldn't think he'd be in himself today Harriet after last night. I'm in two minds whether or not to take the day off myself. Only I can't. I've got Marcus Cooper after me, trying to test a different hypothesis against all this South Pole data. I don't know how he comes up with them all. The man's off the planet. It's about time he took his retirement package before the government has to go back to quantitive easing. That's a laugh too Harriet. How can we be coming out of this recession when we're billions in debt? We haven't seen anything yet Hat. Believe you me. It might even break lard ball. With a bit of luck. I wonder what scam of his you've both rumbled Harriet? He's got to be thinking them up all the time to keep on top of his lifestyle.'

'I really don't know Mark. I have no idea whatsoever. Watch the news tonight. You never know. We might just find out.'

Harriet lay still listening to Mark getting ready for work. A quick kiss on the cheek and he was gone. She was pleased they were living like this. Together but separate. Separate but together. Glad they'd made love. 'For old times sake, of course,' Harriet thought. It had sealed this new arrangement. It was OK now. She'd been with *him*. Mark had been with *her*. They were free agents. 'Very grown up people now,' Harriet decided. 'Pregnant. But that's OK too. I reserve the right to be made love to even though pregnant and I reserve the right to choose with whom. It's got absolutely nothing whatsoever to do with Mr. Sanderson. How I lead my life. He'll have *his* way with Lucinda Lawton and then move along. Even though pregnant I declare myself exactly the same rights as him. Especially as I'm carrying it.'

She lay on her back. Her hand flat against her stomach. Not showing yet. Counted up the weeks. Uncooperative brain. 'It's got to be four or five.' Then wondered about Mark. His reaction. What it would be. Refused to take that one any further. Thought about Barry. Barry's proposal. Almost lost in the hiatus and drama she was living through. Thoughts interrupted. The phone piercing them to nothing. Stabs of pain like a missile spinning through her head. She reached across to answer it.

'Are you OK Harriet? I caught the news late last night.'

'Oh Barry. Just a tick.' She grabbed Mark's pillows. Propped them behind her.

'Sorry Barry, that's better. It's nice of you to phone.'

'I asked if you're alright Harriet? What's been going on? Dining with the PM.

Going missing. Can I come round Harriet? I want to see you.'

'Oh Barry my head's throbbing this morning. How about this afternoon? I'm taking the day off. Can't face a class full of kids today.'

'I want to see you Harriet. It'll take me about forty minutes to get over. Will that do?'

'From Manchester? You not working Barry?'

'I've got to go back to London today. I'll call in on my way. A bit of a detour but I'll make it up on the M6. Yes, I'm afraid it's going to have to be sooner Harriet.'

'Forty minutes Barry. Mind how you go.'

Harriet rolled out of bed determined not to greet him again, half-dressed. She showered quickly. Threw her jeans and top on and went downstairs to feed the cat. On the way. Looked at the green light flashing itself silly on the answer machine. Pressed play.

'Oh Harriet it's Mummy speaking. Only Violet's got her hanging basket up already and I'm still waiting for you to bring mine round. What with her and Mrs. Jones on the other side ours is looking quite drab. It's not as if we'd had a glorious display of spring flowers Harriet. You know how much I wanted that planter. I think it was very mean of Mark to give Daddy and I the one with the missing bulbs. Just as well he's not under your roof Harriet. Daddy and I would be round giving him a piece of our minds. There's a lot more we'd like to say to him Harriet. Letting you down like that! Now we do hope you've come to your senses and you've sorted a new date out for the wedding Harriet. You'll never get another chance like this one, believe you me. Poor Joris. I can't think what you're playing at keeping him dangling like he's on the end of a piece of string. You know Harriet he won't take too much of your schoolgirl behaviour. I don't feel he's the one to suffer fools gladly. You'll miss your chance. He'll be back with that very sweet girl Belinda before too long. You mark my words! Now Harriet are you going to bring my basket round or will Daddy and I be having to collect it ourselves?'

Harriet was sorry she'd played it. 'No Pepper. I'll stuff it full of those plants and take it round this afternoon. We can't be doing with Mummy here Pepper. That would be the very end.'

She pushed the bowl of food under its nose. Baulked at the smell. Felt sick. Sat down. Looked at the clock on the kitchen wall. There was no point in starting anything. Barry would be here in a few minutes.

'Hi! Come in Barry. Excuse the mess. Gosh you look smart. I'd never have you up for wearing suits.'

'Work Harriet, unfortunately. I can't stand the things. This is a new shirt. Stiff as a board. I'm itching all over.'

'Oh poor Barry. Come in. Tea or coffee?'

'I'll have tea please. Strong, as it is. No milk or sugar.'

He followed her through to the kitchen. Sat himself down at the table. Looked at his watch.

'I haven't got long Harriet. I'd taken leave but I've been called back urgently.'

'Urgently Barry? Why what do you do? I thought you just picked up casual work here and there.'

'That's the way it is Harriet. Casual doesn't imply 'unimportant' or devoid of urgency on occasions.'

'No. Right. Of course not Barry. Sorry. I'm a bit out of my head at the moment. No. wrong phrase. I wish I was. I'm very much in my head and it's killing me.'

'After last night? What happened Harriet?'

'Oh nothing much Barry. Well not really. We were just at a dinner party Tricia and I and Mark got the wrong end of the stick and thought we'd been kidnapped or something because we didn't get home for ten o'clock and he decided to call the police.'

'Not the way it came across on the news Harriet. The PM was involved wasn't he?'

'I don't really know where they got that one from Barry. You know what these reporters are like.'

'Come on Harriet. I need to know. I haven't got much time.'

'But why do you need to know Barry?'

'Concern for you Harriet. Can't we just leave it at that?'

'In what way Barry? Why would you need to be concerned for us now we're home? It's all over. Done with.'

'You can't be sure of that Harriet. Who else was there last night?'

'What do you mean Barry? Who else was there?'

'Where were you Harriet? You were dining with the PM. You must have been invited.' Ah the penny's just dropped. It's that blonde guy isn't it? That's where I've seen him before. Heard on the grapevine he's just been knighted. Fastnet. Yes he's the same guy. Came second in the Fastnet race a couple of years ago. Lives round here. Your boss! You having a thing with him?'

'No. No. Of course not Barry.'

'So what were you doing hob-nobbing with the rich and famous? What were you doing that landed your supposed disappearance on the early morning news? Tell me Harriet was the PM accompanied by anyone you'd seen before?'

'Oh I don't know what you mean Barry.'

'You know exactly what I mean Harriet. Those two thick, heavy set blokes in Venice. The ones that got on the vaporetto thinking they were on their way to San Marco. Did you see them last night?'

Harriet looked straight down into her tea.

'Harriet they're bloody dangerous!'

She panicked. Kept it quiet. The dress. She needed to phone Tricia.

'What happened to them Harriet? Where did they go? I know the PM hitched a lift in a night bird. What happened to his own chopper?'

'How am I to know Barry? You seem to know more than me. How did you get all this information, anyway? Come on Barry. Come clean. What do you really do for a living? What were you really doing in Venice?'

'Let's just say personal interests Harriet. Andy and I have been doing a bit of private investigating on our own account. Keep it under your hat. Be vigilant at least until you know for certain they've been caught.'

'Gosh Barry, what a web we've got ourselves caught in.'

'It's the spiders that bother me. Brazilian wanderers, the lot of them.'

He glanced the clock on the kitchen wall. Checked it against his watch.

'I must be on the move Harriet. I needed to see you, though. To know you're safe. Make sure you'll still be around to tie the knot.'

He stood. Tossed his long dark hair back from his shoulder. Brushed her cheek with his lips.

'I'm not sure how long I'll be away. It might be difficult to phone. Stay safe. You're the inspiration holding the paint to the brushes now Harriet. Don't take it away.' He squeezed her hand hard then hugged her close to his chest. She patted his back.

'You be careful Barry. Think again if it's something you don't have to be involved in.'

'No choice Harriet, I'm afraid. That's the way it is.'

From the front gate she waved him off. Watched the black Lamborghini career down the road. Tried to get her aching head around his feelings for her. She liked him. Liked him a lot. He showed none of the assertive character traits prevalent in Mr. Sanderson. Barry was quietly self assured. Confident within himself. Aligned himself to no one. Sensitive. Intelligent. Quietly serious. Perhaps just a little too serious for Harriet as far as her future was concerned.

Chapter 60

She closed the front door. Went straight to the phone.

'Tricia, Tricia, come on Tricia.'

She caught the side of her face in her hand. Wondered what to do. Ran upstairs. Grabbed a dress that had hung undisturbed in the wardrobe for many years. One of Geraldine's evening gowns her mother had passed along. Expensive but vile. She threw it in a carrier bag. Ran to the front and shoved it hard under the hedge behind the front wall, as near to the gate as she could get.

'Let's hope they grab it without looking Pepper. Better still let's hope they don't come looking.'

The cat played between her feet as she sped up the drive. Glad to bang the front door closed. She determined Barry Giordano would be the last and only one she'd open it for, until she knew they'd been caught. She wanted to tell someone. Didn't have the courage. They'd both been threatened with death. They'd already said too much last night.

'Now what's going on with Barry Giordano? That name sounds Italian to me Pepper. I wonder if there's some family thing going on? Family wars. Something like that. It's got to be Pepper.'

She opened the back door. Decided to lock the back gate. Continued debating with herself the meaning of it all. Couldn't conclude a thing. Only that the PM was satisfied they weren't intentionally part of something huge. Of course he'd only had hers and Tricia's interpretation to go on. As much as they were willing to divulge, that is. Yes they were on the edge, the very edge of it all but she knew full well they were far from the edge. A conundrum. Decided she couldn't hope to make sense of any of it. Looked across to the trays of plants. Suddenly remembered the hanging basket in the car boot. Unlocked the side gate to risk a quick trip down the side to get it.

'That's it! That's what I'll do Pepper. The last thing we need is Mummy coming round, using it as an excuse to pin me to the wall.'

Nursing her head, she struggled. Left it. Went back. Left it. Then a final attempt saw her prodding holes into the reluctant hard dry compost, showering the cat as it nosed into the tray of wilting plants.

'No Pepper. Keep out. It's taken me ages to do this. Oh no, I haven't phoned in. I'll have *him* round next.'

'Precisely Miss Glover!'

Harriet jumped. Hadn't heard a thing. Forgotten to lock the gate.

' "Care quid dicis, quando, et cui", Miss Glover!'

'Sorry Mr. Sanderson. Or maybe it's better you don't translate.'

'Beware of what you say, when, and to whom, Miss Glover. Fortunately on this occasion your only audience was the cat. I trust you've divulged nothing of last night's discussions to anybody.'

'No. Most definitely not Mr. Sanderson!'

'You haven't yet done me the courtesy of phoning in Miss Glover.'

'I'm afraid I'm not too good this morning Mr. Sanderson. That's why I'm out here. For the fresh air. Just needed to get my head together before phoning in.'

'Indeed. A late night. Hardly compos mentis enough to engage, I fear. Do you two realise how grave the situation is you're both in? The pair of you. You seem to attract trouble whatever you do wherever you go. And as far as you're concerned Miss Glover the flippancy with which you've regarded the loss of my child is abominable. The indicator please. I'll wait if I have to.'

'Well I'm very sorry Mr. Sanderson but I've already told you the situation. My head's unbearable and I'm most definitely not into testing kits at the moment. I'm sorry.'

'The scruffy looking guy, the one with the long hair. I'm damned sure I've seen him before. You let him in as I was on my way out a couple of days ago. Damned sure I recognise him. Anyhow what exactly has he been doing here Miss Glover?'

'Here?' Harriet tried to feign confusion.

'Don't try that one on me as well. He called into Starboard Marine North West looking for a quick word with Mrs. Harrington, according to Belinda Oxfordshire. The description fits Miss Glover. You don't see too many brand new black Lamborghini's around here. At least Belinda was smart enough to notice that. Come. Come on. I want an answer Miss Glover!'

'Well I'm very sorry Mr. Sanderson but I don't feel I have to answer you.'

'You don't Miss Glover? Indeed you do! This is school time you are cavorting in don't forget. You're well shaping up for another suspension. Get yourself back in this afternoon, will you?'

Without waiting for a reply he was gone. The side gate banging behind him. She quickly locked it. Covered her face with her hands, sat herself down at the kitchen table. Drawn to him. Repelled by him. She didn't know where it was all going to end.

'No Pepper. I'm phoning in right now. There's no way I'm up to a class of kids this afternoon. Ah there it goes. Someone's beaten me to it Pepper.'

'Hello,' Harriet returned cautiously.

'Oh `ello `arriet. It's only me. I got your message to phone you. I was goin` to anyway, but it's my `ead. I `ope your's is feelin` a bit better than mine `arriet.'

'Oh no Tricia. Golly it's good to hear your voice though. You haven't had *him* round have you?'

'Oh yes I `ave `arriet. `e came about `alf an `our ago wantin` them letters of apology. `e took them both. I don't know `ow I managed to get my `ead round writin` them. I'm sure `e'll be sorry `e bothered. `ow many times can you write "sorry" in a letter `arriet without it soundin` like you don't really mean it? I counted seventeen. I `ope they get the message. Anyway I passed them over and then `e wanted to know what it was all about with Barry.'

'Oh that's right Tricia. Barry's been here. He saw the news.'

'Did `e throw any light on it all `arriet?'

'Only to say those minders are dangerous. For us to be careful. He's been called back to work urgently.'

'Oh I just don't get `im `arriet. We don't need `im complicatin` our lives just now do we? Not unless `e's got somethin` a bit more `elpful to say.'

'No you're right Tricia. Anyway sorry I interrupted. What did you say to Mr. Sanderson?'

'I told `im I didn't `ave a clue `arriet. `e said Barry `ad been down to Starboard Marine North West wantin` to speak to me. Well `ow would I know why? Oh that was as well as tryin` to get me back into work. I told `im I'd `ad no sleep and my `ead was bangin` `arriet. So `e said `e'd `ad very little `imself but `e'd managed to fulfil `is responsibilities. Fulfil `is responsibilities `arriet? `e's got to be jokin` me! `e's been too busy chasin` us up to `ave been workin` anywhere, wouldn't you say?'

'Certainly would Tricia. He must have come straight from yours. He frightened the life out of me. I was trying to clear my head a bit outside. I jumped out of my skin when he announced himself.'

'Yes `arriet `e's really `orrible. `e wanted me to give `im the dress. `e didn't answer when I told `im I didn't `ave it because I wouldn't give it to `im after I'd worn it and it `ad been collected by the dry-cleaners. `e just gave me a very disbelievin` look and told me I was more than `appy to remove it last night, so I told `im I'd `ad just a teeny bit too much to drink. `e said I was bein` very foolish on account of last night's revelations. Well we didn't `ave any, did we `arriet? We still don't know what's goin` on. Do you know `arriet I think you've saved yourself from a fate worse than death not marryin` `im. When I think of the way we used to drool over `im `arriet. `e's not showin` much concern for us wantin` us to be goin` to work with them on the loose. I'm just `opin` we don't `ave to rely on `im to bale us out.'

'Too right Tricia. We'll avoid it at all costs. He's definitely turned out to be a not very nice person.' Harriet could have said more. She sat on the desire to tell all she knew.

'And I bet there's more we don't know about `im as well. Ooh I'm so glad you `aven't locked yourself away in `is big `ouse. I couldn't believe the size of it `arriet. I still don't know `ow anyone can `ave so much money and still be wantin` to go to work. Just why would `e be dabblin` in different jobs? I think they're a cover-up `arriet for somethin` else `e's doin`.'

'No Tricia. If you'd been sat next to us listening to his mother on Christmas Day you wouldn't think that. It did make sense all she was saying. It did explain everything.'

'But `ow do you know she wasn't pullin` the wool over your eyes too, `arriet? Is that a metathingy `arriet? No don't answer. It probably isn't and my `ead can't deal with the prospect of gettin` it wrong just at the moment. No, what I mean is `ow do we know we `aven't stumbled into somethin` `e and the PM are up to? They could `ave been terrified we've rumbled them `arriet. There `ad to be somethin` very important goin` on for us to end up dinin` with them both last night. I would say so.'

'There was something important going on Tricia, don't forget and we're at the centre of it. They were trying to find out whether our involvement was intentional or accidental. At least he told us last night he thought the PM was satisfied.'

'Well at least that's somethin` `arriet, but what if they don't catch those men? We could get kidnapped `arriet. They obviously think we know somethin` about them that would incriminate them. Ooh they could want us out of the way. I'm not sure it was such a good idea to be outside `arriet with them threatenin` to come to your `ouse for the dress and `ats. I'm really sorry they chose yours. That would be because they picked us both up there `arriet.'

'Oh blow. The hats. I haven't left the hats. Oh sod it! I'm not going out there again. But Tricia that's why I was phoning. I've wrapped up an old dress and stuck it under the hedge but I'm wondering if it would be a better idea just to let them have it? It might get them off our backs.'

'Ooh no I don't `arriet. As I said I'm not even lettin` our friend Joris `ave it. We might get accused of all sorts. Don't forget if that man dies I could be up for theft with murder. Well that's what I'd be accused of if they `ave anythin` to do with it. That dress would be evidence. Oh no `arriet, I couldn't be doin` with that. That's why we've got to keep our friend Joris on side to `elp us if we get desperate!'

'Well that might be difficult Tricia if you don't give him the dress. What are you going to do with it now?'

'I'm keepin` it `arriet. Once they've caught them I'll be able to wear it. Who's to know I didn't buy it on `oliday? I'm as much entitled to a designer dress as anyone else, wouldn't you say `arriet?'

'I'm not disputing that Tricia but what will I do if they come round here and find the wrong dress? I'm terrified.'

'Well I'd get it from under your `edge `arriet? If I were you. I'd sellotape it up into separate bags. A bit like pass-the-parcel. If they do come they're not goin` to be `angin` around tryin` to open it. They'll be away. Don't forget `arriet we've already threatened to `ave the police `idin` under your wall. I can't really see them walkin` into that. Can you?'

'Just a minute Tricia, I think there's something going on outside. I think you'd be better staying in too, Tricia. Are you supposed to be down at the sailing club tonight?'

'Oh no `arriet, I won't be goin` down there. You'll `ave to give Mark `is dinner `arriet before `e goes. Tell `im I'll look forward to seein` `im tomorrow night. Now I do `ope you've kept yourself locked inside since your visitors went and don't go near the door or the windows `arriet, whatever noises your `earin` out there.'

'I'll get back to you later Tricia. Put the news on. If you find anything out call me straight away.'

Harriet replaced the receiver. Stood nervously for a few moments not knowing quite where to go.

'Harriet it's me, Mummy. I've come for my hanging basket. Daddy's in the car with the engine running. I'm late. I'm off to my WI meeting. We're having a cake sale and I've promised to be there early. Open the door Harriet. Daddy wants to say a quick hello. I know you're there because of your car. You never go out without it. HARRIET open the door!'

Harriet heard the letter box spring back. Could see her mother on the other side of the door, distorted through the frosted glass.

'Oh there you are Harriet. Here. Delivery men! Can't anyone do a decent job these days? Fancy leaving it under the hedge. Anyone could have picked it up. You see I just did. It could have been anyone! Kiss for Mummy. Now when's the date for your wedding to Joris? I can't think why you're keeping it such a mystery Harriet. Anyone would think you were ashamed to be marrying him! Indeed! The poor man doesn't know whether he's coming or he's going with you. I spoke to him Harriet. Yes I phoned the school to see why you weren't answering my calls. He told me you weren't too good and would be at home. Such a nice man. I asked him if you'd managed to fix a new date for the wedding and he said it was entirely up to you. Up to you Harriet after all you've put that poor man through. What does that say about him? Ashamed indeed. Mark my words Harriet he'll soon come to his senses. The next thing he'll be down the aisle with that sweet girl Belinda and you'll be sorry. You'll rue the day! Here Harriet get hold of it dear. After all I did struggle under the hedge to pick it up for you. Now come and say a quick hello to Daddy and bring my hanging basket with you. I'm going straight back to the car. I'm going to be late.'

'Right with you Mummy.'

'I'll pop that in the boot Harriet. It's good to see you love. My word it seems a long time.'

'George. Do hurry. I'm going to be late!'

'Better go Daddy. Hug!'

'There, there now Harriet. You not too sure about him, this Joris guy? Take your time love. Don't be brow-beaten by anyone.'

'Thanks for that Daddy. I'll come round. See you both soon.'

Glad to be rid of her mother and the hanging basket, Harriet managed a brief wave throwing the carrier bag back under the hedge before dashing in to close the front door quickly behind her. She rummaged in the cupboard under the stairs for as many carrier bags as she could find. With the sellotape between her fingers she proceeded to turn Geraldine's ancient dress into something akin to a pass-the-parcel prize; then crept out to push it back under the hedge by the gate.

She returned to the phone ringing. Hovered for a moment. Then went for it.

'Miss Glover. Change of plan. I request you don't come into school this afternoon. A warning. Mrs. Harris has a gaggle of journalists and photographers outside the house. There's no shifting them. They've been there since late morning sniffing for news. Any minute now they'll split. It goes without saying the Barnes fellow will make his way over to you. Albeit it's the PM they're interested in, nevertheless there's still a story to be had as far as both of you are concerned. Anyhow don't on any account open your door to anyone. Do you understand that? Oh and also, on no account are you to leave the house unescorted until these two bodyguards have been arrested, or at least until their whereabouts is known. They are dangerous men Miss Glover. I personally will escort both you and Mrs. Harrington to and from work for the foreseeable future.'

'But I'm supposed to be going on a Health and Safety course with Mr. Brown on Friday morning, Mr. Sanderson. What shall I do about that?'

'I'll cancel it. Brown can go. At least he'll get to know the rudiments of it without any impairment from you Miss Glover. Now 8.30 on the dot tomorrow morning. I expect you to be punctual.'

Harriet put the phone down. Hadn't said a word. He could have been talking to anybody. Decided it was safer to close the curtains. Didn't want a repeat of last year's run-in she'd had with Simon Barnes. Decided it was going to have to be an afternoon knitting. Besides she needed the space to come to terms with Barry's desire to marry her. Needed to work out why Mr. Sanderson, according to her mother, was only waiting for her to set the date.

Barely surfaced with her knitting from the back of the cupboard in the hall she came out to a voice panicking through the letterbox.

'`arriet. Let me in quick! It's only me.'

'Ooh Tricia. Come in. We're not supposed to be out. Haven't you had a call?'

'No `arriet. I must have been on my way `ere. Why what's `e been sayin` now? `e's becomin` obsessed with us, I would say. Oh no, `e `asn't been on the phone with bad news as `e? You `aven't got your curtains closed because that market trader's gone and died on us, `ave you `arriet?'

'No Tricia. It's not that. He's got the press outside his house and as they're not getting anything there, he reckons it won't be long before Simon Barnes tries here.'

'Oh gosh `arriet. Well I'm glad I've come round. At least we'll be together if anythin` `appens. Oh I'm not stoppin` you gettin` on with your knittin` am I?'

'No, not at all Tricia. I'll put the kettle on. I'm glad you're here.'

'Ooh, I think that was the bell `arriet. Turn that tap off a minute.'

'It was Tricia. There it goes again.'

'`ere `arriet just let me get that knittin` needle. I'll soon get rid of them. Just listen to that cheeky sod Simon Barnes. `e `asn't taken `is finger off the bell yet.'

Harriet watched Tricia fish in the carrier bag to wrap the half-knitted back round both needles. Trailing the ball of wool at her feet she rushed to the letterbox.

'`is bum's just be`ind it `arriet,' she whispered. Then jabbed the needle points straight through. The tall, solid figure the other side of the door simultaneously turning.

Then Tricia through the letterbox. 'Bugger off will you, we're not sayin` anythin` to anyone!'

Suddenly squashed behind the door and the wall she jumped clear as it swung open.

'Ah there you are Mrs. Harrington. Thought as much. And you Miss Glover. Positively dangerous for anyone foolish enough not to see them coming. I get the principle, but poking a pair of knitting needles through the letterbox merely draws attention to the fact you are behind the door. Other than that it serves little or no purpose.'

'`ow did you get in Mr. Sanderson? `ow come you've got a key to `arriet's `ouse?'

'None of your business Mrs. Harrington. Now I'm needing to get back to Lower Tideside. I'd feel far happier if you both came with me. It will give us the opportunity to clarify this incoherent jumble of events and you'll be out of reach of the press. Get whatever you need and come now before we walk straight into them.'

Harriet locked the back door. Grabbed her bag to follow Tricia, leaving him to close the front door behind him.

'It's open. Get in!'

'Where's `e gone now `arriet? I thought `e was in a hurry.'

'Oh blow! Don't look Tricia. He's picked up the carrier bag.'

'Right. On our way. You've some explaining to do Mrs. Harrington!'

As they sped away Harriet could feel the nerves twisting in the pit of her stomach. Wondered if this nightmare would ever end.

Chapter 61

Early afternoon. With little on the roads, they reached the lights at Starboard Marine North West in no time. Harriet watched him pull away to turn right. Gliding away from town now, well into the countryside. He glanced across to the carrier bag on the seat alongside him, finally breaking the silence.

'Managed to get it back from the dry-cleaners Mrs. Harrington?'

Tricia nudged Harriet.

'Oh no Mr. Sanderson. That's something I'd left on the doorstep for charity. It's been there for days. It's obviously been blown under the hedge.'

'Not so obvious Miss Glover as it wasn't there this morning. I've warned you before about lying to me. You know you're both playing a very dangerous game trying to go this alone. It was unlikely they'd come back for it, but nevertheless there was a chance. We still don't know where they are. Oh the PM's helicopter's been found, not far from here. They're either on the run or lying low somewhere. They could be a lot closer than you think Miss Glover.'

Harriet went cold.

'How did you know they wanted it Mr. Sanderson?'

'Mrs. Harris picked it up on the intercom in the hall as you were nearing the front door. That's why the PM and I insisted on it being handed over.'

Tricia nudged Harriet. She looked up to see her shaking her head.

'Anyhow we've got it now. There's obviously something significant about the damned thing.'

'No Mr. Sanderson, that's not it. That's not the dress.' She moved away. Tricia's elbow was beginning to hurt.

'I'll hear no more about it Miss Glover. Mrs. Harrington you've obviously chosen to ignore all advice. If you'd passed it over to me as requested you'd at least spared Miss Glover the embarrassment of trying to cover for you. Most unsatisfactory!'

In the silence that followed Harriet looked out of her window across to the island. This trauma laden route sparked every anxious nerve in her body. She thought about the marriage she'd tossed away. Her mother. Wondered if she'd heard Mr. Sanderson correctly. Wondered if she'd put her own construction on this wedding date thing. He certainly wasn't affording her any subliminal indicators of marriage. Something in her still wanted it. Her emotions were fighting all rational thought for dominance in her mind. She knew him now. Knew of his capacity to flip from charming to the cold and calculating. Knew there could never be a future together. Knowing what she did. Knowing he'd forced Belinda Oxfordshire into termination. She lay her hand on her stomach. Vowed to herself.

"Not my baby. He'll never take my baby away."

She thought about Mark. Together but separate. Separate but together. He wouldn't like it, she knew that. But she hoped there might be enough leeway in the arrangement to accommodate a future change in circumstances. This was the furthest she'd ever taken the thought. And Barry. He'd proposed to her. No messing about. She pressed both hands hard against her stomach.

"Gosh, he wants to marry me. He won't when he finds out about this." Silently reassured she let the thought slide as they passed Molly's house on the corner of the lane.

'Oh eh, just look at that lot!'

'Quite Mrs. Harrington. Prepare yourselves for one long continuous blast of the horn. Hopefully we'll get straight through.'

Harriet watched the gang of press photographers leap from under as he raised the flat of his hand to Mr. Swift and another gentleman standing just inside the automatic gates. They were through. Harriet turned. Watched the gates close behind them. He stopped, wound his window down. Beckoned them over as he reached for the carrier bag. Harriet watched the well-dressed gentleman carry it to his car. He was out faster than Mr. Sanderson was driving in. She turned again to see Mr. Swift walking towards them.

He touched the floppy brim of his sun hat as he held the door open for Harriet to get out. Mr. Sanderson hurried Tricia along. They were back inside the beautiful square hall. The rug at the fireplace. The staircases leading from either side, running their way up to the landing. The massive chimney breast gracefully arching each side to the walls at either end. The gleaming woodblock floor beneath their feet. Tricia looked at Harriet. The look said it all. A different world. She knew exactly how Tricia felt.

'Yes, go through. Go through.'

He held the study door open as they went in.

'Sit down. Sit down. Do sit down.'

He waved his hand at the sofa under the window. Exactly where they'd both sat the night before.

'I'll just organise some tea, or would either of you prefer coffee?'

'Oh I'll be `avin` tea. What about you `arriet?'

'Oh yes thank you Mr. Sanderson. Tea will be fine.'

They watched him close the door behind him.

'He's passed over the wrong dress Tricia. We keep getting ourselves deeper in it.'

'Oh I wouldn't worry about that `arriet. What can they do about it anyway? You could `ave given me that dress and I might just `ave taken it on `oliday with me. In fact `arriet I think you might `ave very cleverly got me off the hook as far as that's concerned. After all `ow do they know what I was wearin`?'

'But what about the market trader Tricia. Suppose he recovers and remembers everything?'

'Well even if `e does `e wouldn't be able to identify us from the back. Anyway it's too late now. I'm stickin` to my plans. I'll be wearin` it to `elp raise funds for Venice, `arriet. I'll be needin` to be wearin` somethin` a bit special when I `ave my photograph taken next to Rappin` `ammer. That Italian designer dress will be exactly right, wouldn't you say?'

'Just as long as they've caught them Tricia.'

'Well they've got another week before then. I don't think it'll take them very long.'

They both jumped as Mr. Sanderson held open the door for Mrs. Harris to go ahead with the tea tray.

She smiled as they thanked her. Without a word she departed, leaving Mr. Sanderson to it.

Harriet watched him swing his high backed leather chair away from his desk to sit centre right of them.

'Help yourselves. Do help yourselves.'

'Oh and 'ow would you like yours today Mr. Sanderson?'

'Same as usual Mrs. Harrington. No sugar, thank you, and very little milk.'

Harriet, grateful Tricia had volunteered, watched her pour the tea. Watched him take the cup and saucer from her.

'I may as well do yours 'arriet.'

'Yes please Tricia. Thank you.'

It was all they could do. The only words they had to say between them. The room filled with a stilted silence hardly broken by the sipping of tea. Suddenly he turned to place his cup and saucer on the desk behind him.

'Now I think it's in all our interest to pool what we know. There may be some happenings seemingly insignificant to you both, but vitally important to this investigation.'

'I think we've already told you what we know Mr. Sanderson.'

'Yes, yes Mrs. Harrington. I'm aiming to give you as much as I can gather from the other side. Between us we might be able to piece something together.'

He flicked his thick layers of blonde hair to the side. Lifted one leg to rest his foot on his knee. Harriet could feel his eyes on her. Felt her face turning a deep shade of pink. Perplexed at how she could be both repelled and attracted at the same time.

'Now, the Prime Minister's bodyguards. Let's get this straight from the start. Unlike many of his colleagues he's an absolute stickler for drawing the line between personal and public requirement. It goes without saying when he's on official business he's covered by those whose specific duty it is to protect him. When he's exercising his choice to attend non-public functions, such as the opening of Starboard Marine North West last year, he uses any of a number of them, obviously well-vetted by the appropriate authorities. These guys are specifically approved to protect him. The only difference is it's not coming out of the public purse.'

'Oh are they the same ones you use Mr. Sanderson?'

'If you don't mind Mrs. Harrington, I'll ask the questions. Anyhow last night was a case in point. He's doing me a favour in many respects with regard to you both, but nevertheless there's a wider reciprocal element to this. I understand the two they're looking for have been under suspicion for some time.'

'Ooh well I'm not surprised. We never did like the look of them two did we `arriet?'

'Quite Mrs. Harrington. Now let me continue if I may. The PM suspects an element of corruption in the house.'

'Ooh you mean `ere don't you? It could be the `ousekeeper Mr. Sanderson. Chargin` more for your groceries than she's payin`. I'd be keepin` my eye on Mrs.`arris if I were you.'

'I beg your pardon Mrs. Harrington. I advise you to hold your tongue. Such accusations could land you in court!'

'Oh I'm very sorry Mr. Sanderson. I was only thinkin` of you. I didn't expect the PM ever suspected `is own `ousekeeper.'

'No, no Mrs. Harrington. You're barking up the wrong tree. I'm referring to the House of Commons. There's a suspected link. That's why the PM's concerned to get this cleared up. Of course none of us are party to the higher workings of state security, but the word is they're dealing heavily in counterfeit goods. Huge cash donations of questionable source have come to light, made to a party I'll not name but it would seem they're trying to ascertain the link. Unfortunately for you both it would appear Venice is their base of operation. Of course they're not ruling out the mafia.'

'I said that didn't I `arriet? I said those bodyguards looked like they came from the mafia. I wasn't wrong then?'

'Please let me continue Mrs. Harrington, if you don't mind.'

Harriet chose to stare at her feet. Caught him repositioning his legs. For a moment she was back on the sand. Him deep inside her. She listened to his voice. Strong. Commanding. Cultured. She felt unreal. Removed from him. As if it had never happened. Desperately she tried to connect. Seeking a look. A gesture. A shred of anything that might indicate all was not lost between them.

'Now they've been under surveillance for some time. They're smart. Very smart. Impossible to nail. It was most unfortunate you managed to get yourselves under their feet in such a way.'

'Oh no Mr. Sanderson, we weren't under their feet. `arriet will tell you. It was them that were followin` us around. That's why we thought you'd `ad a word with the PM to send `is bodyguards after us.'

'Yes yes Mrs. Harrington, I think that point was made last night. I refer to it again because, as far as I understand it, at great expense an undercover operation had been set up in San Marco to scoop the gang leaders, including those two. Now for some reason they didn't turn up.'

Tricia looked across to Harriet. The silence was awkward.

'There's a missing link here do you understand? Vital information missing. Now we know you'd walked from San Lucia to San Polo and stopped to lunch in the square facing the canal by the church you visited. San Giacamo dell' Orio, or dall' Orio as the locals express it. Makes no difference. You recall the place?'

'But `ow did you know that Mr. Sanderson?'

'I'm afraid I'm not at liberty to say Mrs. Harrington. We also know you boarded a vaporetto to the Rialto Bridge and at the same time were joined by the two suspects.'

'What do you mean the two suspects, Mr. Sanderson? We didn't suspect Barry and Andy of anythin` did we `arriet?'

'Barry and Andy Mrs. Harrington? Did you both befriend these people?'

'We met a couple of guys who showed us round, that's all Mr. Sanderson. They were tourists, nothing more than that. It would be very unfair of us to speak of casual aquaintances in this context.' Harriet chipped in.

'Right Miss Glover. I take your point. I have however been given to understand the suspects left the boat at the Rialto Bridge with the intention of picking up another to get them to San Marco. Now, they changed their minds. They were spotted coming back to the vaporetto, the boat you were on, that is, and then they apparently disappeared into thin air! Please, both of you do try to recall your movements and any sightings you might have had of them.'

Harriet looked at Tricia. Didn't know what to do for the best. Didn't know whether it was time to just come clean. Get this whole thing out of the way, once and for all. He sensed it.

'Right I'll just take these through to Mrs. Harris whilst you agree your course of action. I strongly advise the truth. In fact I would go as far as to say this is your last chance to keep yourselves out of the courts. I'll be reporting back to the PM this evening. He's understandably fast losing patience and good-natured as he is, naturally there is a limit to his tolerance.'

They watched him gather the cups and saucers to the tray. Waited until he'd closed the door behind him.

'Tricia, we're going to have to tell him. I can't take much more of this.'

'I know what you mean `arriet, but we still don't know `ow it all fits in with that market trader, do we? If we tell him that it could be curtains for us anyway.'

'Oh gosh Tricia. I don't know what we should do. Should we mention our concerns about Barry and Andy? We did think there was something odd about their behaviour.'

'No `arriet. It's like you told `im. It wouldn't be fair to rope them in.'

'But how did they know what we'd been doing that day Tricia? How did they find out? There was only Barry and Andy oh and of course the boatman, apart from those two heavies.'

'Well we don't know who was watchin` us or followin` us do we `arriet? `e probably doesn't know either. It's like `e said `arriet. We don't know the `igher workings of state security and I don't suppose the PM does either. They're probably as much in the dark as us. `e's only got as much information as someone's been able to leak out.'

'Yes, you're right Tricia. I certainly don't want to get Barry involved in this.'

'Well don't say any more `arriet. We don't know any more do we? We'd only be speculatin` and that would not be very fair at all.'

'No you're right again Tricia. But I wonder why the heavies came back? Why didn't they go to San Marco as planned? Look, shall we tell him about the accident on the boat? It might just help. We don't need to say any more than that.'

'I suppose we could `arriet. At least it would explain that `avin` nearly drowned they wouldn't be much feelin` like meetin` up with their mafia buddies in San Marco after that.'

'Yes OK Tricia. We'll do that. We'll probably feel better for getting that off our chests.'

They could hear him calling something back to Mrs. Harris as he opened the door.

Marched in to his mobile ringing. Closing the door behind him he reached to the inside pocket of his jacket. Walked towards them as he spoke into it.

'Yes Lucinda!'

Harriet glanced across to Tricia.

'Right Lucinda. That's most kind of you. No I imagine Mrs. Harrington won't be in a position to cover for Iris any longer. Yes I'll give you a hand down there. Much appreciated! See you later.'

'Lucinda, Mrs. Harrington very kindly offered to fulfil your hostessing duties at the sailing club. See your way to thanking her will you?'

'Oh and why would that be Mr. Sanderson?'

'You'd be far too vulnerable down there Mrs. Harrington. Let's play it my way shall we until this damned exercise is sorted?'

A quick tap on the door.

'Yes Mrs. Harris?'

'Your private line Mr. Sanderson. There's a call for you.'

'Excuse me.'

Harriet and Tricia watched him stride out of the room.

'ow am I supposed to be raisin` funds for Venice now `arriet? Oh `e's so bossy I'm gettin` really fed up with `im.'

'I know exactly what you mean Tricia but at least it does look like he's genuinely concerned for our safety.'

'Well `e can't be watchin` over us day and night can `e? `ow does `e know them `eavies won't come chargin` into Starboard Marine North West, or your school for that matter. You could be abducted while you're doin` playground duty!'

'Oh don't Tricia. Gosh will I be glad when they're both caught.'

'Shush `arriet. I can `ear `im comin` back.'

'Right! Good news as far as you two are concerned.'

'Oh `ave they caught them Mr. Sanderson? In which case I'm more than `appy to resume my role as `ead cook down at the club. If you wouldn't mind informin` Lucinda. I'll be down this evenin`.'

'Allow me to finish Mrs. Harrington. No they haven't caught them yet, but we do have news on the San Polo merchant. Apparently the market trader's regained consciousness but he's refusing to cooperate with the police.'

'Oh we are very glad to `ear that aren't we `arriet? It couldn't `ave been very nice for `im at all lyin` there with `is `ead in bandages. And will this `elp the police to find them now Mr. Sanderson?'

'Mrs. Harrington I've just told you he's refusing to cooperate. As far as I can make out his stall's been emptied. Apparently they're selling fish on his pitch now.'

'Oh they're sellin` fish all over the place in that market. I'd `ave stuck with the designer dresses if I was `im. They're very expensive you know. `e'll `ave to be sellin` `undreds of clams and eels just to make as much as `e would on one of his gowns, I would say.'

Harriet covered her mouth with her hand. Couldn't believe Tricia had just dropped herself right in it. She could see Mr. Sanderson's eyes narrowing. His face tense. Serious.

'Quite Mrs. Harrington. Yes I can see where it all fits now. This is where you aquired the gown, I take it?'

Harriet could feel her cheeks glowing.

'Don't bother answering that, Miss Glover's doing it for you Mrs. Harrington.' He banged his hand down hard on his right knee. 'Neither of you are leaving here until I get the truth. I want the full story.'

Tricia looked at Harriet. Harriet began.

'This is exactly the way it was Mr. Sanderson. The bodyguards were cursing and swearing when they realised the boat wasn't going to San Marco. They said it was supposed to be the end of the road. So I suppose that fits in. Maybe it was a last big deal for them. I don't know.'

'Precisely Miss Glover. They wouldn't know either. It was the biggest deal they would ever get. They'd never have needed to work again. They didn't know they'd been very carefully set up. San Marco was the end of the road for them but not quite in the way they expected.'

'Oh I see.' Harriet continued. 'I'm afraid I was furious with you Mr. Sanderson. As we already said, we thought you'd arranged with the Prime Minister to send those bodyguards out looking for us. Then we got really scared when it looked like there was a lot more going on than that. We thought they'd followed us through to San Giacamo. That's where we took the vaporetto to the Rialto Bridge. We thought they were going to kidnap us to demand ransom money from you for our return and we were absolutely terrified. The boatman got off and so did we. We knew he was going back up the grand canal to San Lucia so we got back on and lay down on the floor to wait for him. We didn't want those heavies coming back for us Mr. Sanderson.'

She saw a hint of a smile crossing his face before returning to his former demeanour.

'Not beyond the realms of possibility Miss Glover, though I feel even the hardest of criminals would think twice before kidnapping you two! Continue.'

'We must have been lying there for half an hour before we heard their voices. We panicked, jumped up and we don't know how they managed it but they ended up in the canal with the boatman.'

'Rocked the boat violently did you?'

'Well yes, we were frightened Mr. Sanderson. We thought they'd come back for us.'

'I think we got that wrong `arriet. It was their `ats and shades they wanted.'

'Do be serious Mrs. Harrington. They could have picked more of those up anywhere. There's just a chance they could not get a quick enough turn round to San Marco and they'd returned to pay the boatman handsomely for the favour.'

'We never thought of that. Anyway we flew off the boat and down all the side roads, through the market square until we managed to get a boat back to San Lucia.'

'And the market in San Polo. I can't imagine you'd be wanting to stop to buy this designer gown of yours Mrs. Harrington. How did you come by it?'

'On no Mr. Sanderson we were runnin` so fast we tripped up the market trader and there was this trolley of dresses being wheeled to `is pitch and some`ow I managed to get one `ooked to my `at. It was flappin` be`ind me all the time we were runnin`. I didn't even know what I `ad be`ind me until we stopped.'

'Ah, I see. Interesting Mrs. Harrington. So these dresses were being wheeled along on a trolley?'

'Yes, they were all `angin` up, weren't they `arriet?'

'I suspect they were constantly on the move Mrs. Harrington. That's how it works with counterfeit goods. It makes it difficult to get caught.'

'Are you suggesin` my designer gown is not genuine Mr. Sanderson?'

'Indeed I am. We'll know very soon.'

'Well I'd be most obliged if you didn't tell anyone if it turns out to be a fake, Mr. Sanderson. I don't want to put my fundraisin` at risk. I'm tryin` to save Venice and I can `ardly draw the crowds to my cause if I'm wearin` a fake!'

'Oh I doubt if you'll even get it back Mrs. Harrington. Now where were we? Oh yes. You'd boarded a boat to take you back to San Lucia. Then what happened Miss Glover?'

'We got the train back. Packed our bags. Got a taxi to the airport and came home. We'd had enough Mr. Sanderson.'

'Oh and those `eavies did chase us when we were gettin` into the taxi `arriet. Don't forget that. I think they must `ave wanted their `ats.'

'Can we just forget about those damned hats for a moment Mrs. Harrington. There's enough going on here without tossing in irrelevancies.' He turned to Harriet.

'From where did they appear? You must have seen where they came from.'

'It was the house next door to the hotel Mr. Sanderson. The one we told you about last night. It looks like they were staying there.'

'Ah yes, I recall now. Didn't you say something about a lot of activity going on during the night?'

'Oh yes I did Mr. Sanderson. I don't know `ow `arriet slept through it on the first night.' Tricia wanted her say.

Mr. Sanderson turned to Harriet. She felt a fleeting moment of recognition for all they'd had between them.

'Deep sleep can be a natural reaction to trauma, or it can go the other way of course. But you definitely heard activity in the night from the house next door, I understand. Mrs Harrington, can you describe it?'

'Oh there was lots of bangin` and clatterin`. Door slammin`. Vans or somethin` comin` and goin`.'

'Yes indeed. Thank you Mrs. Harrington. Now Miss Glover?'

'I can't add anything to that really, only we felt the place to be intimidating.'

'It sounds like that was their base of operation. The place the goods were delivered to and distributed from. Your misfortune to select a hotel next door.' Mr. Sanderson surmised.

'Oh I don't know about misfortune Mr. Sanderson. If you're right then we will `ave been doin` the world a service locatin` it, I would say.'

'No no, Mrs. Harrington. It will have been well cleared by now. This is the difficulty. This is the misfortune of your inadvertent involvement. Quite frankly it looks like the pair of you have completely blown it.'

'Well we certainly didn't mean to do anything wrong Mr. Sanderson. Yes it was wrong to just go away like that without saying anything and I'm very sorry I did that but Tricia and I have both been traumatised one way or another. It's just the way we reacted.'

He turned to Tricia.

'Oh yes and as your employer Mrs. Harrington might I ask what problem drove you to take absence without leave?'

'Not `as been Mr. Sanderson, still is as far as I know. Maybe you would be better askin` Belinda Oxfordshire?

'Belinda Oxfordshire. What on earth has she got to do with you?'

'Oh everythin` Mr. Sanderson. She's only `avin` an affair with my Bob. She's been after `im for ages now. You must remember `im takin` er `ome from the barn dance at your school last year because those lads `ad done `er tyres in. Remember when she left `er car at Starboard Marine North West because she'd been deliverin` leaflets and it was quicker for `er to carry on to the school than go back there for it?'

'Err quite, quite. Yes I remember.'

'Well that was the start of it Mr. Sanderson. Bob `asn't even bothered to `ide it from me. We're just livin` together for convenience at the moment. I'm in the other bedroom. I'm not lettin` `im come near me as you can imagine.'

'Yes, yes. Quite Mrs. Harrington. I must say I'm most surprised. I'd never have envisaged an attraction there in a month of Sundays!'

'Well I've `ad more of a month of Sundays waitin` for `im to come `ome from a Saturday night, I can tell you. Couldn't you see she was all over `im at Christmas when we `ad Rappin` `ammer as Father Christmas at the centre?'

'Oh good heavens Mrs. Harrington, don't speak of them! My work was well cut out trying to get them out of the place to have noticed anything of that nature. However, I'm very sorry to hear this. It does in some way go towards understanding, indeed excusing your behaviour.'

Harriet sensed what was coming next.

He stood still for a moment. Rubbed his chin with his hand and then briefly put his arm round her. Harriet fizzing could bring only one thought to mind. 'It was me who should have been getting that!'

He returned to his chair. Harriet looked down. Couldn't bear to meet his eye.

'Thank you for your sympathy Mr. Sanderson. You know `e was only worried about me disappearin` last night because `e didn't know what `e'd do with the kids if I `adn't come back. `e wasn't bothered I was missin` feared dead. All `e was bothered about was `ow difficult it would make it for `im to see `er!'

'Oh dear Mrs. Harrington. This is indeed very stressful for you.'

'Yes it is Mr. Sanderson. I think I'd rather `ave Rappin` `ammer any day. Talkin` of `im, did you know `e's changed `is ways?'

'Changed his ways Mrs. Harrington. Is that possible?'

'Oh I believe it is Mr. Sanderson. I don't think it would be very appropriate to go into all the details but `e `as become very interested in savin` Venice with me.'

'What's brought this about?'

'Well `e did `ave to `ave therapy after `e was traumatised at Starboard Marine North West, and since then I believe e's turned `is mind to classical things. Like statues Mr. Sanderson. `e's become very keen on learnin` all about the classics and as `e's always wanted to do a really big concert in Saint Mark's Square `e said before `e's too old. `e said `e would `elp me save Venice as not only would it be preservin` the culture but with `is very substantial contribution made known, `e was surefire certain they wouldn't refuse `im permission for `is gig. Of course `e would then stay in Venice to satisfy `is cultural appetite.'

'Really Mrs. Harrington. You do surprise me. So San Marco will be the end of the road for him, too?'

'Well it could be if `e `as a complete conversion. Once `e gets in all those churches you never know what might `appen, do you?'

'Could only be for the better Mrs. Harrington. Stranger things have happened.'

'Well that's what I think too. I do `ope you won't mind Mr. Sanderson but you know that strip of land they let out sometimes, next to your playing fields? Well `e'll be doin` a gig for my charity there the same day as your school fair. I thought it was a good idea because when all your parents `ave `ad enough of buyin` cakes they can come through to us. All proceeds will be goin` to my charity. It is a good cause Mr. Sanderson. We don't want Venice to sink into all that mud and be gone forever, do we?'

'Certainly not Mrs. Harrington. That would be quite tragic!'

'So you see Rappin` `ammer is mendin` `is ways. If we try `ard enough we might be able to get `im off those drugs. In fact you know `ow `e looks up to you Mr. Sanderson.'

'No. I hardly think so. Not after being chased off the premises like that.'

'Oh no that is most certainly wrong. `e now understands `ow bad `is be`aviour was and `e's more than anxious to make amends. So I said to `im "well I'm sure you'll get the chance to see Mr. Sanderson at the fete. You know `e's a very kind man. `e gave us all such a beautiful speech in the church about love and `ow it runs through our veins like blood and `ow we must all love one another when `arriet got dumped. I'm sure `e'll be only too `appy to take you on board `is boat when `e does that Fastnet race again." Oh Mr. Sanderson you should `ave seen `is face. I've never seen a smile like it. You really do `ave to say yes to `im this time.'

Harriet watched him take a very deep breath. Wondered if Tricia had even seen Rapping Hammer yet. She felt dreadful. Tricia had just made her feel worthless. 'It's obviously gone straight to her head him putting his arm round her like that. I don't know what she's playing at getting embroiled in more lies.' She sank the thought as she caught Tricia's smile. Then realised she hadn't quite finished.

'As you're goin` to the sailin` club anyway Mr. Sanderson if you were to be so kind as to give me a lift there and back again of course, I could carry on with my `ostessin`. You see I've been wearin` my low cut tops and rattlin` my tin at them as they've been carryin` away their chips. They always come back to pop a folded note in my Venice tin. Anyway it would save Lucinda. I'm sure with `er deputy job at school she'll start to get a teeny bit tired working every evening. It's a bit different for me. As you know `er job carries greater responsibility especially when she `as to cover for you if you're not in.'

'Good point Mrs. Harrington. I'll collect you at six this evening and drop you back home again once the dining's over.'

Harriet tried to sit on the spread of envy getting the better of her. Thought, 'Bloody hell Tricia. Can't you leave well alone. It's me he fancies not you!' Then it occurred to her, 'Not any more.'

Mr Sanderson looked at his watch.

'Back to the task in hand. Is there anything else to add to all we've discussed this afternoon?'

'Oh no Mr. Sanderson, we've told all we know now `aven't we `arriet?'

'I would say so. Where does that leave us, do you think?'

'Good question Miss Glover. The pieces are starting to come together. I think once the gown has been through forensics and identified as a fake then they'll have a positive lead with this merchant fellow. We can only be patient now, but I'll relay all of this to the PM for him to do as he will with. In the meantime I suggest you don't go out unescorted. I'll collect you both in the morning as planned.'

'No that's alright thank you Mr. Sanderson. I'll get Mark to drop me in on his way to work.'

'In which case get him to drop you off at the training centre. You might just as well do the health and safety course. Brown can give you a lift back in at the end of the morning.'

Harriet could have bitten her tongue off.

'Just remembered, Mark won't be able to collect me to bring me home, will he?'

'Arrangements as they were Mrs. Harrington. I'll take you two back now. Just let me check.'

He marched to the door. Disappeared. Returned.

'They've dispersed. All clear. Not a damned camera in sight. I shouldn't think you'll catch any of them at your house now Miss Glover. They'll be too anxious to get home.'

'I hope you're right,' Harriet thought as she followed Tricia through the hall to the front door.

She travelled in silence while Tricia twittered her small talk at him. They didn't notice. Waved goodbye as he turned round at the gate.

'You bloody get out from under my hedge will you!' It was Simon Barnes crouched on his hands and knees. She swung her bag hard at his backside and sent him rolling on the grass. From nowhere the cat sprang at his face. 'I'm NOT in the mood!'

From her front window she watched him rush past the top of the hedge.

Chapter 62

'Anything to eat Hat? Oh it's Friday. Usual takeaway is it?'

'It certainly is Mark. Am I glad it's Friday and I've only had one day of it.'

'One day of what Hat?'

'One day of being driven there and back to school by *him*.'

'I recall the days when you'd have enjoyed that Hat. Not anymore?'

'Not anymore Mark.'

'I don't see the need. Once you're in the car, they're hardly going to get you Harriet.'

'No, he thinks they'll be lying in wait under the hedge like Simon Barnes last night or behind the school railings. He just wants to make sure we're not at risk until they've been caught.'

'Simon Barnes still scraping around. That news reporter? Oh no you're not on TV again Harriet. I don't believe it.'

'No Mark. He scooted. The cat flew at him again. After I'd clouted him one with my bag.'

'You want to be careful Harriet. The next thing you'll be done for assault.'

'He wouldn't dare. Anyway I've got far more to worry about than him.'

'But I thought it was all over. Why the concern if it's all over Harriet? They're not likely to come back here. It's just lard ball's excuse isn't it to be with you?'

'No, it's the same for Tricia. I think he just feels a sense of responsibility. As if somehow it's his fault.'

'Well it is Harriet. Everything's his fault. If he hadn't been so damned quick to jump in at the church it might have given us both time to collect our thoughts. I'll never forgive him for that.'

'You don't have to Mark. He's not part of our lives.'

'Oh but he is. He's hanging round our necks like a line that ties a ferry to the landing stage. He wants first option on this don't forget.'

'Only when we come to sell it Mark.'

'No Harriet I still feel like we owe him money while we're here. I don't like it.'

'But I thought he'd dropped that?'

'On the face of it Harriet.'

'What happens if we sell to him? He wouldn't be expecting compensation then, would he?'

'Oh I bet he would Harriet. He's probably only delaying taking it until he buys it. He'll find a way to add it to the asking price, I bet.'

'I must have got the wrong end of the stick on that one. I thought he'd drop it if we agreed to sell to him.'

'On paper Hat. Don't believe a word. The more I've thought about it, the more I've realised that wouldn't have worked for him. He doesn't want this place. He's keeping us or at least you here.'

'Well we can't sell now. By the time we've paid him we wouldn't have enough to get anything half decent.'

'Precisely Harriet. He'll force the price up so we can't move.'

'Now I take your point Mark. Oh what a mess! Why is life so perverse?'

'Don't ask me Harriet. Let's lose it all in few glasses of red shall we? I'll pick up a couple of bottles on the way past.'

'What about the sailing club. Aren't you going down tonight?'

'No. Let that fat arse of a lard ball do it for a change. Let's make it a night in shall we?'

'As long as you don't start getting any ideas Mark. That was a one off remember?'

'A one off Harriet. At least a five off, as I recall. And then there was the next morning.'

'Oh you know exactly what I mean Mark. It was for old times' sake only.'

'OK Hat. Suit yourself. Melissa wouldn't be saying that.'

'Oh bloody Melissa. Go round there then. I've just about had enough!'

She heard him close the front door behind him. From the small window in the hall she watched him back off the drive. There was something she had to do. She couldn't remember. It was something to do with the conversation they'd just been having. There was too much spinning round in her mind. She needed the weekend to clear her head. At least there was nothing on. No arrangements. Not until next Saturday at least. A week to go before the summer fete.

'Oh gosh Pepper and then I'm supposed to be going to see Molly and Percy in the evening, with *him*. We've been invited for dinner Pepper. How can I get out of that? At least I've got a week to think about it. At least this Saturday's free.'

Then she realised.

'Oh no Pepper. That was it. I forgot to phone the agents. Mrs. Moss is supposed to be viewing the house tomorrow morning with her daughter.'

She checked her watch.

'They're closed now Pepper. I'll have to phone Mummy. Get her to pass the message along. I can't be doing with them in the morning.'

'Oh hello Harriet. This is a nice change to have you call us. Do you know Daddy's hung the basket by the front door. It looks awful but he went to so much trouble I don't like to ask him to take it down. What kind of plants are they Harriet? They keep wilting. Daddy's having to water them constantly.'

'Don't worry Mummy, they'll all come out soon. All pretty pastel shades. It will look stunning. Just be patient and give it a couple of weeks.'

'I'll take your word for it Harriet. Now you're phoning with your wedding date, aren't you? I've been telling Violet all about you marrying a knighted gentleman. I told her we're just waiting for the date.'

'No sorry Mummy I'm not phoning about that, I'm actually wondering if you can do me a big favour?'

'A big favour Harriet? You'd be doing Daddy and I a big favour if you could decide when this wedding is to be. I'm warning you he won't hang round waiting for long.'

'No Mummy. I just wondered if you could pass a message on to Mrs. Moss please. If you could tell her there is already a buyer for the house and the agent made a mistake arranging a viewing for tomorrow morning.'

'You what Harriet? After me telling her how suitable it would be for Avril. The poor girl's pregnant Harriet. They're desperate for space. They can't afford anything better than yours.'

'But that's nothing to do with me Mummy. I'm telling you again the house isn't really on the market. Not the open market anyway. There's no point in them coming here tomorrow.'

'Whatever are you talking about Harriet? I don't know about you these days. The menopause is certainly causing very strange behaviour. No Harriet I'm not passing the message on. If an appointment has been made then the least you can do is keep it! You're not very good with appointments Harriet. You're going just like that Bohemian partner you used to have. Breaking promises is becoming common place with you. Try to remember what it was like being pregnant Harriet. The least disappointment can set you back. Anyway I must go. Daddy's waiting for his dinner. Now you call in soon. Another of your promises Harriet.'

'Oh gosh Pepper what am I going to do now? Mummy's really mean. I hope that basket lands on her head! No Pepper. Didn't mean it. Now Mark's gone. I don't know whether he's coming back or not. Oh sod Pepper. I'm going to get mine. I'm having it and I'm going straight to bed.'

Chapter 63

'What time did you creep in last night Mark?'

'Does it matter? Free agents Harriet.'

'Oh yes! Meaning?'

'Meaning just that Harriet. As you reminded me last night. I can't live on memories. We're under the same roof Harriet. What do you expect? A one off for old times sake! Get real Harriet.'

'Oh so you went to Millington. Melissa second best was she? I bet she didn't know that when she took her knickers off!'

'No Harriet. I went down to the club. Just had a late night, that's all.'

'A very late night Mark. I didn't hear you come in.'

'You were flat out that's why.'

'So who was down there?'

'Lard ball. He was hanging round for some reason.'

'That would be Tricia. He was going to give her a lift home.'

'Well he didn't. He asked me if I'd mind. He said Lucinda wanted to get back so he'd have to take her.'

'What? Did he give her a lift down as well?'

'Seems like it. Tricia was livid. She said she didn't want to go back with him anyway.'

'Where was Bob?'

'Looking after the kids. He's hacked off. Ever since Tricia's been helping out he's had to stay in. He only gets to go out at the weekend now.'

'Yes he goes out and forgets to come back. I think he's being a bit of a swine to Tricia to be honest.'

'So do I Harriet. It's all over between them. They're a bit like us. Living together because it's convenient. There's no relationship there now. Apparently Tricia sleeps in the back room.'

'So how do you know all that?'

'Because she's been telling me Harriet. I gave her a lift back remember?'

'Is that all you gave her Mark?'

'I don't think it's got anything to do with you what I do Harriet.'

'Well you were certainly up for it last night Mark.'

'And you were certainly not interested Harriet.'

'No I was not. But it wasn't very nice going looking somewhere else Mark. That's hardly the way to win a girl over.'

'Changed circumstances Harriet. Or can't you handle this arrangement?'

'Oh I can handle it Mark. Just don't tell me. I don't want to know.'

'I wasn't going to Harriet. Until we decide to become partners again we're free to please ourselves. Or are you wanting to commit right now?'

'Not just at the moment, thank you. Life's already too complicated.'

'There you go then. Now go and make me a cup of tea.'

'Oh go and make your own Mark I'm getting up. We've got viewers this morning.'

'Viewers, how come?'

'The agent left a message to tell us they'd booked an appointment for this morning and it went straight out of my head.'

'Phone them. They're only supposed to be holding it. Not selling it for goodness sake.'

'You phone them Mark. You're in this just as much as me. I'm going out.'

'Not before me. I've got to get all the Toppers ready for the kids. It's Saturday morning don't forget. We've got sailing lessons on the hour until one o'clock.

'Well they can just ring the doorbell then because I'm going out. I'll see you tonight sometime whenever I decide to get back.'

'Please yourself Harriet. Oh and by the way Tricia's not my type. I was just winding you up. She was in a foul mood when lard ball went off with "that Lucinda Lawton". It's him she fancies, she never stopped rabbiting on about how he put his arm round her this afternoon. Make love to her? You've got to be joking. No wonder Bob found solace in Belinda Oxfordshire.'

It wasn't nice but the words were sweet to Harriet's ears. She lent forward to kiss his cheek. 'See you later. Don't worry I'll let myself in if you're in bed,' she smiled. Decided to phone Barry. Wanted to place him somewhere in the puzzle.

Chapter 64

It was almost ten o'clock. Harriet looked out of the window waiting for the black Lamborghini to arrive. Barry had immediately responded to her call of only an hour ago. He was back in Manchester. Managed to get home for the weekend hoping for a break.

She didn't let him get out. Banged the front door closed behind her as she walked to the car in her tight jeans and skimpy top.

'Very chic Harriet. You're looking absolutely gorgeous as usual.' He opened the door for her, bending to kiss her cheek as she sat down in the car.

'Thanks. You're looking good too Barry. How's it been going?'

'Not bad at all Harriet. I think we're getting there.'

'Family wars Barry. Is it something like that you're involved in?'

'Can't say Harriet. I suggest we both have a day off from it all. What do you fancy doing?'

'I don't mind Barry. You say.'

'Well how about we shoot up to the Lake District? Do a bit of a tour then come back to my place in Manchester. We can go out for a meal if you like, or I could play chef.'

'Sounds good Barry, but no, I don't want you cooking. Let's go out shall we?'

'Fine Harriet. That suits me just fine.'

He started the engine. Harriet covered her face with her hands.

'Oh no that's Mr. Sanderson turning in. Quick Barry put your foot down. I don't want to get involved with him!'

It was quite some experience. With wings it would have been in space by now.

'Gosh Barry it doesn't hang around, does it?'

'Certainly doesn't Harriet. Knocks *his* well into the shade! What's he doing anyway?'

'I honestly don't know. I certainly wasn't expecting him. I wouldn't have phoned you if I'd known.'

'You mean you'd rather have been with *him*?'

'No Barry I really rather wouldn't. I've had enough of him over the last couple of days.'

'Oh pontificating is he?'

'Well in his own way but I think he's just trying to help.'

'He should butt out. It's this cronyism that's fouling the whole thing up.'

'What do you mean Barry?'

'Absolutely nothing Harriet. We said we weren't going to talk about it, remember?'

'You know Barry you're a bit of a mystery.'

'Not really. I'm quiet by nature. It's not intentional.'

'You know Barry at one point Tricia and I thought you and Andy were working for MI5.'

'Over-active imaginations.'

'Well you were behaving rather mysteriously at times. Non-verbal communication. Rushing off and wandering round and then returning as if you both hadn't been doing it.'

'Doing what Harriet? I think I've lost the thread.'

'Oh so have I Barry. You're right. Let's have a day off from it all.'

They were nearing the tunnel entrance. He tossed the coins into the basket as the automatic barrier lifted.

'I can't say I'm too fussy on tunnels. Still this is better than the old tunnel.'

'What's the problem Harriet? They're open both ends. We could always walk out if we had to.'

'I suppose you're right. I'm the same with lifts. I suppose it's confined spaces that do it.'

'You don't like the thought of being trapped?'

'No I suppose I don't, but then I don't suppose anyone does.'

'Too right Harriet. But like you, most people manage to keep it all in perspective. There's a risk in everything we do in.'

'Tell me about it Barry!'

'Why did you and Mark never get married?'

'There's loads of people don't Barry. It's a question of choice.'

Relieved to see the flashes of daylight against the semi-circle walls ahead she leaned back and stretched her legs forward to watch him find his way out as the tunnel exit roads splayed out ahead. Up and along the flyover now, she looked down to the city. Recalled her coach trip to Southampton to board the Christiana on her own. Recalled how Mr. Sanderson had tried so persistently to give her a lift. How deeply she regretted refusing him. The mini-cruise where she'd met Molly and Percy. It was only last year. She could hardly believe all that had happened.

'Whose choice Harriet? You look the marrying kind to me.'

'Well we were very young. I'd barely started my first year at university before I got pregnant with Rachael. Mark was in his final year. Fortunately he got a job straight away. I think the whole think traumatised him, especially as I very quickly fell pregnant with Clare soon after Rachael was born. Yes, to be honest I did want to get married. That never changed but Mark seemed to develop a phobia about it.'

'Ah, I see.'

'And you Barry. I'm sorry your marriage didn't work out for you.'

'Our circumstances were unusual. It was me that always wanted kids. She didn't. She didn't want anything to spoil our relationship. That was the problem. It became stilted. Too intense, suffocating. We both reached the point where our space was more important to us than the relationship we had, though she wouldn't admit it. In the end we had to call it a day. We're on reasonably good terms though, Maria and I. She's got someone else now. She's a lot older than him. He's got the time and the money to keep her happy.'

'Do you miss her Barry?'

'At first it was strange suddenly finding myself with too much personal space. It wasn't long before a few nibblers appeared.'

'What do yo mean, nibblers?'

'Just former female aquaintances starting to take my time. Good friends actually. Casual relationships, so to speak. I wasn't interested in tying myself down. Haven't been until now.'

He took his hand off the wheel to rest it on hers.

'Four junctions to go Harriet. How do you fancy heading to Grange-Over-Sands for lunch? Then wending our way back in a circle over the mountains. It would be good to get a sniff of the sea though the sea grass has encroached for miles way beyond the coastline. Artists' country Harriet. We'll see if we can't get a window view to enjoy whilst we're eating.'

'Sounds lovely Barry. That's what's happened to the Dee estuary. There are some quaint little restaurants looking straight across the marshes to the Welsh hills.'

'You'll have to take me Harriet.'

'Yes I will. Of course I will. Gosh Barry I reckon you've been doing at least a hundred miles an hour. I don't believe we've come this far.'

'It soon goes when your thinking. Chatting.'

'Oh I love this part. I love the smooth high domes of the mountains. Look you can see them over there. Thank you for this lovely day Barry. You don't know how good it is just leave everything behind.'

He squeezed her hand. In silence they continued. Harriet taking the opportunity to collect her thoughts. Sitting next to Barry. So different from the tension, excitement of being this close to Mr. Sanderson. She felt Barry was probably younger, closer to her own age. His look, swarthy. His eyes dark. Masking his inner-self. He gave little away. Just enough for Harriet to feel confident in his company.

'Tell me about your Italian roots Barry. How did you end up here?'

'I'm of Spanish Italian extract. My mother's Spanish. My father's Sicilian. They came over here when I was very small. Settled in Kent. I was actually christened Basilio, Spanish of course. Somehow it transmuted to Barry. It must have been my parents, I've never bothered to find out. Kids don't like to be different, do they?'

'No, certainly not. It was very forward thinking of them. So that's where you get those good looks from. Are your parents still there?'

'No. Not any more. They've gone back to where my mother came from, Andalucia.'

'Do you manage to get to see them much?'

'It goes in spates. If I'm working in and around there, then yes. I last saw them in April.'

'Gosh you certainly get around.'

'It's what I like to do. I've got the freedom to go where I please now. I've been making the most of it. Now according to this, it's taking me down here. That's the way Harriet. That should take us down to the promenade.'

'Now that's an idea, a satnav. I could have got Mark one of those for Christmas.'

'You and Mark did Christmas together?'

'We did. Just about. It's a long, long story. You won't want to hear it.'

'You mean you don't want to tell it. Too painful?'

'You could say that. Though I know I asked for everything I got.'

They continued along the promenade then climbed as the land rose to overlook the sea.

'There's a hotel somewhere along here, I think. The higher we are the better. It's a limited view otherwise.'

They pulled into the car park. Harriet tossed her bag over her shoulder. Followed him into reception. They were shown to the dining room. Their table in the window. Harriet smiled at the waiter as she pulled her chair in. She glanced at the menu.

'What do you fancy Harriet? Anything there?'

'The fish sounds nice Barry. "Haddock and Pancetta kebabs: bringing a taste of Sicily to the table".'

'I'll go with that Harriet. I'm not sure about the connotation. Still, they're trying.'

The conversation light. The experience pleasant. They explored a little then returned to the car. Harriet happy to go with the mountains and lakes. On this sunny day a delightful detour before joining the motorways leading them to Manchester.

'I'm actually not too far from here Harriet. Just a couple of left turns. The apartment overlooks the park just here. I'm on the far side of it.'

The apartment block, modern. Set on brick stilts to allow for parking. Barry pulled into his spot. Held the door open as she got out.

'It's nearly six Harriet. Do you want to walk into town to find somewhere to eat?'

'Oh no thanks. It feels like I've not long finished lunch. What about you?'

'No I'm fine, too. I've got some bits of salad and deli stuff in the fridge. We could work our way through that later with a glass of wine.'

'Perfect, thank you Barry. What floor are you on?'

'Right at the very top. I've got one of the four penthouses.'

She looked up.

'Stairs or lift? I don't mind a climb.'

'Right here Harriet. See this strip of glass goes all the way to the top?'

'Yes.'

'Glass sided lift. Goes straight up. You can see everything.'

He smiled as she relaxed. It was very reminiscent of the lift on the ship.

'Wow, this is luxurious. These carpets are sumptuous. We could be on a cruise liner.'

'One day Harriet.'

She wished she hadn't said that. The thought disorientated her.

'Right, this is mine. No over here Harriet. We're facing the park on this side.'

She followed him in.

'Gosh, I thought you said it was small?'

'I said it was open plan Harriet. Come through.'

'Ah I see. You've got this side set up as your studio. Oh it's very nice Barry. It's lovely looking across there. Your paintings. Wow, this is serious stuff. You've quite a collection. Wow that's a sketch of San Marco. When did you get chance to do that?'

'It's not finished yet. I've been working from a shot I took while we were there. Oh and that reminds me Harriet I must give you the second CD of the shots.'

She smiled. 'What's your favourite subject to paint? You seem to have a range of pictures. I must say they are absolutely brilliant. No wonder it's so important to you.'

'Thanks Harriet, not as important to me as you though. Glass of wine? Here take a seat. Let me get you a drink and I'll just empty the fridge of this lot. We can help ourselves as and when.'

Harriet sat on the end of the sofa. Looked around. A massive space. Almost of warehouse proportions. Her side carpeted in ivory. Both sofas black. Everything black and shades of white. Furniture glass and stainless steel. It was smart. Very smart. She sipped her wine. He sat next to her.

'Enjoyed the day?'

'Very much thank you Barry.'

From nowhere, music. Just gentle background stuff. Some her favourites. She relaxed. This was one of her better days of late.

'Does it still hurt Harriet? Or are you coming to terms with your split from Mark?'

'That's a difficult one. At the moment it's convenient for us to stay under the same roof. Together but apart. Apart but together if you know what I mean?'

'Yes I do Harriet but you may be making life unnecessarily difficult living like that.'

'Well I haven't seen a great deal of him really. To be honest I've been so caught up in this Venice thing it's dominated everything.'

'So you haven't given any thought to my proposal?'

'Oh Barry, do you know I can hardly believe you have proposed. It's just not the way it works for me. Decisions like you've made don't land very readily on my lap.'

'You're beautiful Harriet. You could have anyone in the world.'

'Rose-tinted spectacles, I fear. For some reason I can't get my head round that one.'

'No no Harriet. That's why you've got that Sanderson guy after you.'

'Not anymore I haven't. Anyway how did you know that?'

'I made it my business to find out.'

'What else do you know about me Barry?'

'Only one thing Harriet. Apart from wanting to marry you, that is. I know I want to paint you. I want to paint you so whatever happens I've got you for the rest of my life.'

'Gosh Barry, I didn't realise you felt as strongly as that.'

'Love at first sight Harriet. I spotted you at the airport. Couldn't believe it when you came through to the departure lounge. I just knew I wanted you. Something in here and here clicked.' He moved his hand from his chest to his head. 'How many ways can I say it. I'm off my head about you!'

Blushing again. Alarmed. She felt it swamp her whole body.

'Have you ever done any modelling Harriet?'

'No I can't say as I have. Why do you ask?'

'Would you, please, let me sketch you while you're here? Would you lie across the sofa for me? It won't take more than ten minutes. If you can't say you'll marry me today, please just do that for me Harriet. Here, let me top up your glass first.'

Harriet could see no harm in it. She liked him. Liked him a lot. Wanted to please him. He was already a good friend. She emptied her glass, placed it on the small table alongside as Barry stacked some cushions against the other end of the sofa.

'There's a dressing gown on the bed, through there, if you'd like to slip your clothes off.'

'Pardon? Oh no. Gosh I didn't realise you meant that!'

'It's no problem Harriet. Honestly it isn't. It's art. I've done it that many times. I paint you, or in this case sketch you with an artist's eye. I promise you. Once you've come through and slipped the dressing gown off you'll just be lying there. You won't give it a second thought.'

'Oh but I will Barry. I do understand that's what artists do. From your point of view you're not asking me to do anything out of the ordinary. But I'm afraid I just can't do it. I'm sorry. I'll lie across here with my clothes on for you though. Will that be alright?'

'Yes Harriet that will be just fine. Don't worry about it. I'd never have asked if I thought it was going to upset you. You're different. Most girls can't wait to get their clothes off.'

'I'm afraid not. I just don't know how they do it. Now which way do you want me?'

He smiled. Rolled her slightly backwards as he gently eased her legs apart.

'There, let's just put that hand on your belly and let this arm fall down a bit. Gently down, just like that.'

He reached for the camera.

'Just let me snap that. Get a couple of angles. Right. Stay still. I'll be as quick as I can.'

Harriet lay very still. She watched him. Those dark brown eyes first on her and then the paper. Sketching away. Looking down. The soft 2B graphite pencil transferring every inch of her body to the sheet of white fine grain paper pinned to his board. She felt uncomfortable in her pose. Vulnerable. Couldn't for the world have lain there naked. Hoped he'd nearly finished.

'That's it Harriet. Thanks for that. All done. With the help of the photographs I can get that painted now.'

'Can I see it Barry?'

'Sure.'

'That's absolutely brilliant. You've captured the likeness. Gosh you're good. In that short time, too.'

She was pleased. Felt so much better for having seen it.

'Come through Harriet. Help yourself. We can munch our way through this lot.'

'Mmm, looks good. Where from Barry?'

'Oh there's an excellent delicatessen on the edge of town. They know me. I've always got this kind of thing in.'

They took it through. Nibbled and chatted.

'I want to marry you Harriet. I've already said. I'll wait for just as long as it takes. You must at least *like* me. You wouldn't have phoned me this morning if you didn't.'

'Of course I like you Barry. I actually like you quite a bit.'

'I'm relieved to hear it. Is it to do with this mess you and your mate have got yourselves in? Is that holding you back?'

'Well you're right. I'll feel a lot better when that's out of the way. Mr. Sanderson's very concerned. He insists we don't go anywhere unescorted.'

'He's absolutely right Harriet. They haven't caught those two yet.'

'But how on earth do you know that Barry and what's it all got to do with your family? Are they in politics any of them? Mr. Sanderson said there seems to be corruption in both governments. It's more than family wars, isn't it Barry?'

'I thought we were leaving this alone Harriet. Oh yes sorry. It's me who raised it. Marry me and I'll tell all.'

Harriet went very quiet. Thought for a few moments, long and hard.

'Barry there's something I must tell you. It's only fair you should know. You really won't want to be marrying me anyway once I tell you this. It's very confidential. Please, please don't say anything to anyone. Promise?'

'I promise Harriet. It won't be difficult. I'm in the business of keeping secrets.'

She pressed the crumbs left on her plate to her finger then dropped them to make patterns.

'You're stalling Harriet. Is it that difficult to say?'

He put his own plate down. Moved across. His arm around her now, drawing her close.

'Come on Harriet. Spill the beans. It's obviously something I need to know.'

'Barry I'm expecting a baby. You needed to know that, didn't you?'

He gasped. Stood for a moment and then resumed his position.

'Does Mark not know Harriet, or is that why you're both still under the same roof?'

'It's not Mark's, Barry.'

'Do you want to tell me whose it is Harriet?'

'It's Mr. Sanderson's Barry. And no Mark doesn't know.'

He brushed his hand across his face, tossing his hair back. His brown eyes melting into hers.

'Is it over with Sanderson then?'

'It looks like it. He's not turned out to be quite as expected, actually.'

'Does he know?'

'He did but I told him I lost it.'

'And you haven't?'

'No I haven't yet. As far as I know I'm still pregnant.'

'How far gone are you Harriet?'

'It must be getting on for two months now.'

'Time to be getting checked out. Have you done that yet?'

'Not yet Barry. Too much going on.'

'You must. You really must. You know Harriet this makes no difference to me whatsoever. Well it does. You need looking after, protecting if you like. I've always wanted kids. You know that.'

'Yes but this isn't yours. I couldn't do it. I couldn't burden you with all of this. I think too much of you for that.'

He kissed her forehead.

'We own nothing Harriet. Not even our children. We are all part of the same universal soup. We are all children of the ether. This child has originated from the dust of the stars, as we all have. You merely carry it Harriet. But it will need two parents. I'm a firm believer in that. A secure home and a good start. We'll get married and I'll adopt it at birth. I'm here for you Harriet. Maria never wanted any. It broke my heart. Has fate taken this final twist to turn up a trump card at last? I'll believe and hope it has Harriet. Don't turn me down now. Think carefully before you say no.'

She brushed at the tears welling in the corners of her eyes.

'Oh sorry Barry. Yes I'll think on those beautiful words. Would you mind taking me home now, please? I'm sorry to end such a lovely day like this.'

'Yes, of course I'll take you home. I'm glad you told me Harriet. I'm so glad you told me.'

Chapter 65

'I walked straight into your mother last night Harriet.'

She pushed the rack towards him as she watched the honey dripping long and slow into the butter on the toast from the spoon in her hand.

'You mean you met her? Where?'

'No the phone started ringing as I opened the front door. I made a grab for it.'

'What did she want?'

'You Harriet. But I got it. Going on about Violet Banks, or Green or somebody or other. I can't remember.'

'That would be Violet Moss and her daughter. The viewing Mark. What did she say?'

'She said it was nothing whatsoever to do with her and it was very unfair of you to treat them like that. Avril had managed to turn up inspite of her morning sickness and Mrs. Moss has been very bad on her feet lately and it didn't do them any good whatsoever standing on the doorstep ringing the bell for half an hour.'

'Did you tell her the house wasn't for sale?'

'No I did not. There's no way I was going to get embroiled. Oh and she said something about the poor woman already having had a tussle with the travel agent. Something to do with them thinking she'd withdrawn a complaint and her swearing blind she hadn't.'

Harriet swallowed hard. Wanted to move it along.

'How did you leave it then?'

'I banged the phone down when she decided she could hold back no longer. She was just starting on how I'd ruined your life.'

'Golly. I do wish Mummy would mind her own business for a change.'

'Oh and she said something about some very strange looking buds gathering on the plants in the hanging basket. She wants it down but your dad won't hear of it. She wants you to take it away.'

'That's gratitude for you. Well I'm not. I've had enough of sodding hanging baskets.'

'Pass the honey Harriet. Anyway where did you go?'

'I had a day out with Barry, a guy I met in Venice. He lives in Manchester. He's actually taken quite a shine to me.'

'Oh yes. And where did he take you Harriet? I would have thought you'd have been better staying close to home with this mess you seem to have got yourself into. Still that's up to you.'

'Precisely! You really did wind me up making me think you'd slept with Tricia. Why should I believe you didn't? I don't know the truth, do I? I rang up Barry because I'd had enough and as it happened it was the right thing to do. We went to the Lake District. Had lunch in Grange-Over-Sands and then went back to his penthouse in Manchester.'

'Oh yes and then what?'

'And then nothing. Just a pleasant evening chatting before he brought me home.'

'At some unearthly hour.'

'This time you were asleep so you wouldn't know what time.'

'What time was it then?'

'It wasn't late. Well before midnight, anyway.'

'So this guy, what does he do?'

'I'm not too sure. He's an artist, I do know that. He does sell his work. But he also does contract work I think. I really don't know.'

'Dangerous Harriet. You don't know what you might be getting yourself into again. I do wish you'd grow up once and for all. One of these days you're going to come really unstuck, if you haven't already.'

'Thanks for your concern Mark. You haven't exactly been protective of late.'

'Why do you think we're still under the same roof Harriet? Think about it will you?'

Harriet looked down. Felt very uncomfortable. Wondered if this would be a good time to tell him about the baby. Thought better of it.

'How do I know you didn't go with Tricia?'

'Because she's got Bob back hasn't she? In any case what do you take me for? I wouldn't touch my best mate's wife.'

'What do you mean?'

'Bob was down there yesterday, too. He told me it's all over between him and Belinda Oxfordshire.'

'He did? Did he say why?'

'He puts it down to not being able to get out in the evenings. But there's got to be more to it than that.'

'Yes you're right. What about Tricia, is she taking him back?'

'Tricia doesn't want to know. Apparently she's giving him a hell of a time.'

'Why did he go with Belinda Oxfordshire in the first place? They always seemed happy enough to me.'

'I think Bob had had it up to here with lard ball. It was probably more to do with challenging him.'

'Oh come off it Mark. He must have fancied her.'

'Of course he did. She put herself right in his way. I don't suppose many men could resist that temptation. But I'm sure he wanted to score one over lard ball. Wanted to let him know he wasn't the only one who could get her into bed.'

'And she was trying to show Mr. Sanderson that he wasn't the only fish in the sea. She was trying to get him to go back to her, hoping to make him jealous. Well it didn't work.'

'Whatever Harriet. It shouldn't make any difference to you anyway. You've not long turned him down. Or have you?'

'And what's that supposed to mean Mark?'

'Sounds like you're starting to get wound up about it all to me.'

'No. I was just making an observation, that's all. I don't get Belinda Oxfordshire still wanting him after what he did to her.'

'That's the measure of him Harriet. The guy's a twister. As I keep reminding you, you're well out of it.'

'And what about Melissa Scott, Mark? Am I to presume it's all over between you?'

'It's all over between me and her mother.'

'That's not an answer.'

'I don't feel the need to give you one Harriet.'

'Then you're in no position to dictate to me.'

'She's not like lard ball. She hasn't got an evil bone in her body. She's no guile Harriet. Naïve in many respects. She certainly didn't realise what she was letting herself in for with Geoffrey.'

'Oh don't go any further Mark. It's obvious you haven't finished with her. I don't know what this talk about protecting me is all about.'

'On the contrary, reading between the lines, it sounds like you're ready to commit to renewing our partnership Harriet.'

'About as ready as you are Mark!'

Chapter 66

Monday morning. Up early. Harriet wasn't looking forward to being taxied by *him* to school. It was open-ended.

'They might never catch those heavies Pepper. Just keep those little paws crossed. Ah the phone. Good he can't make it. Get down Pepper, let me get to it.'

'It's just a quick one `arriet before `e comes. Bob's just left for work. `e's as miserable as sin. `e's mopin` around like one of those dogs with them sad eyes. `e actually told me it was all finished with `er. As if I'm interested `arriet. I've got used to sleepin` on my own and I can tell you it's much better than `avin` `im in bed with me. Pinchin` all the covers when it's cold and shovin` them all over me when `e's too `ot. I told `im `e needn't think I'm sharin` `is bed again after `e's been with `er. `e's tainted goods now. Then `e `ad the bloody cheek to tell me `e'd asked `er to marry `im `arriet and she'd turned `im down. We both know why, don't we? It's `im she's still got the `ots for, our friend Joris. Talkin` of which `arriet I've done a test with one of them thingies for you. It's not saying pregnant, as if it would. I did it properly so there won't be any come-back. It made me go all maternal though `arriet. I was wishin` it was me, for real. Quite out of the blue it was. I never expected to feel like that. Anyway I've put my new white lace panties away `arriet. I'm savin` them for someone special.'

'Who's that Tricia?'

'I don't know yet. I'm still waitin` to meet `im. Anyway I'll slide this thing over to you in the car `arriet.'

Harriet submerged herself in the sense of relief overtaking her. Trying to match her with Mark hadn't been such a good idea after all.

'Thanks Tricia. You didn't go out and buy one especially. I've got *his* here you know.'

'No I didn't buy one. Remember when Bob blew `is top at Simon Barnes? When `e thought I was pregnant. Well `e bought all sorts of them `arriet, trying to find out if they all read the same. No, this one was left in the cupboard. There was a couple `e'd missed.'

'Oh thanks for that Tricia. That'll get him off my back for a couple of months anyway. I'm not thinking beyond that at the moment. Fortunately there's the summer holidays coming up. I won't need to see him. I'll get out of the school camping trip.'

'Oh I will too `arriet. More's the pity. Starboard Marine North West doesn't do school `olidays. But you know what `appened, don't you?'

'No Tricia, what?'

'Well it was me and my big mouth tellin` `im Belinda Oxfordshire `ad stolen Bob off me. `e's had one of `is words with `er `arriet. Probably taken `er back or promised `er somethin` to pack it all in. I'm furious with `im `arriet. `e was supposed to be givin` me a lift `ome and `e goes waltzin` off with Lucinda

Lawton. I don't think Mark was very pleased gettin` roped in like that, either. I do know `e's gettin` fed up standin` in for Tarquin Bridgewater. `e doesn't need to be doin` taxiin` for me as well.'

'Oh I'm sure he didn't mind Tricia. He was asleep when I got in. I had a day in the Lake District with Barry.'

'Oh very nice `arriet. Did you find anymore out about them?'

'Not a thing Tricia. I tried but he closed like a clam. I can only gather he and Andy have been doing a spot of private investigation into some kind of family wars. He hasn't actually denied it anyway.'

'`e's no `elp then. I wish they'd `urry up and catch them. I can't be doin` with `*im* escortin` us to and from work. I don't fancy bein` on my own with `im either when you break up. Still it could be worse. Better than `im escortin` me to jail `arriet. I'm very relieved that market trader `asn't died.'

'You're not still thinking of wearing that gown are you Tricia? It's this Saturday you know.'

'Oh I do know that `arriet and I'm really lookin` forward to it. I'm wearin` my panama `at and shades, too. I'm goin` to look the part `arriet. I forgot to tell you it will be in Wednesday's paper. Well both of them actually. I've used my stage name again `arriet, Holly Berry. I left it a bit late really but I was waitin` to `ear if I'd got permission. Still once everyone reads about Rappin` `ammer they'll all be there. Look at last time. Our Adam can't wait!'

'Yes the girls are coming up at the weekend for that, too.'

'That will be nice `arriet. Do they know about the weddin`?'

'They do Tricia but they don't know anything else. They think things are just as they were with Mark and I. I'm not saying anything yet. Let them enjoy married life without having to worry about their mum and dad. I think they've got more sense than all of us put together Tricia.'

I think you're probably right `arriet. Oh there `e is. I can `ear `im blastin` away on is `orn. I'll see you in a couple of minutes.'

Harriet gathered her bags. Dumped them by the front door and waited until she could hear the car.

'Good morning Miss Glover. Here let me put those in the boot.'

He opened the rear door. Tricia seized her opportunity to pass the testing kit over, then launched into the weather as he sat himself behind the steering wheel.

'Oh I `ope it's goin` to be better than this on Saturday, `arriet. We don't want the day to be a flop, do we?'

'No, Tricia. It won't be much fun in the rain.'

'Not a problem. We have contingency plans Miss Glover. We'll set it up in the hall if need be.'

'What about Rappin` `ammer Mr. Sanderson? I don't suppose you'll be able to find a little corner for `im? Especially as the last time we spoke you was startin` to `ave goodwill towards `im.'

'Really Mrs. Harrington? I can't say I recall.'

'Oh you most certainly were. Don't you remember `ow I told you `e needed therapy after the Christmas do at yours and as a result `e's changin` `is ways?'

'I have a vague recollection Mrs. Harrington.'

'Oh good because if I remember rightly you did promise `e could crew for you on your next Fastnet race Mr. Sanderson. I've already phoned `im and told `im. `e sounded so `appy. `e said `e was gettin` lovin` vibes from you and it `ad moved `is `ealin` along no end.'

'Really Mrs. Harrington I do wish you wouldn't put words in my mouth. I've got far more on my mind than any of that at this time. I'm surprised you've got the inclination for all this, given the circumstances.'

'Of course I `ave Mr. Sanderson. That's what's keepin` me goin`. I told you about my marital troubles, didn't I? Savin` Venice `as given me a real cause to focus on.'

'Has Mr. Harrington not told you the affair is over yet?'

'Oh yes `e `as Mr. Sanderson. `ow did you know that? You `aven't been `avin` just a teeny tiny word with Belinda Oxfordshire `ave you?'

'I've spoken to her Mrs. Harrington. Warned her about getting involved in extra-marital affairs. Apparently she'd already decided to call it off.'

'Oh I see. My Bob not good enough for her then? Snooty little tart!'

'I think we'll refrain from using that kind of language Mrs. Harrington. Her behaviour is not to be admired. She knows well enough she's been doing wrong. It's a case of "conscientia mille testes", Mrs. Harrington.'

'And what might that mean Mr. Sanderson?'

'Conscience is as good as a thousand witnesses.'

'Well it's taken `er long enough to discover she `ad one.'

'You must try to be forgiving. I know it must be very difficult for you Mrs. Harrington but life has never been particularly easy for her.'

'And you haven't helped,' Harriet stormed to herself.

'It's all very well you sayin` that Mr. Sanderson but `ow would you feel if you'd been badly let down by someone you loved.'

'Tricia shut up PLEASE.' Harriet's mind was in a whirl. Thought again. 'What's she going to say next?' She caught his glance in the rear mirror. Could feel herself blushing to the roots of her hair. Didn't realise they were already pulling up at the traffic lights outside Starboard Marine North West. He turned right and into the car park.

'Try to maintain a professional stance Mrs. Harrington since you'll be working with Ms Oxfordshire until I collect you sometime between four and five.'

'In the front Miss Glover?'

Tricia managed a quick wave as Mr. Sanderson reversed to drive forward out of the car park. He wasn't hanging around.

Harriet felt strange. In the front again. This was the first time she'd sat next to him since he'd brought her home from the church. She sneaked a glance. His strong profile. Handsome. His mop of blond hair just shifting as he turned his head to look right. The blonde curl at the pristine white collar of his shirt. Its usual resting place. His suit finely tailored from charcoal worsted. His cuffs, edging the sleeves of his jacket in broad white bands. The gold cufflinks. His hands, strong, purposeful. A shiver went through her. The very hands that took away Belind Oxfordshire's baby. His baby. 'How could this gorgeous, gorgeous man do that?' The thought stiffened her resolve. She lay her arm across her lap as if protecting her own. Thought about the testing kit. Had no doubts about handing it over. Thought about Barry. Felt easier. 'He's wanting to stand by me. Wanting to marry me. I don't need to deal with this on my own. I don't have to.' She looked across at him. 'If you could read my thoughts!'

Chapter 67

'You managed to get out of it, I see.'

'Pardon Mr. Brown, I really don't know what you are talking about. Look I need to get in. I need to see Mr. Sanderson.'

'You've only just got out of `is car as far as I can see. Oh yes.'

Harriet watched his mouth twist into a knowing little smile.

'And you're wantin` to be talkin` to `im again? While you're at it ask `im why I `ad to do the `ealth and safety course and not you. That's discrimination that is. I'll be `avin` a word with Mr. Potts about that. You `appen to be the dangerous one around `ere. I've been gettin` bad `eads ever since you landed me one with that `angin` basket, I'll `ave you know. And talkin` about plants I don't think much of them there you brought into school. They're shapin` up to `ave right funny lookin` `eads on them they are.'

'Sorry Mr. Brown. Must go.'

Harriet threw her bag over her shoulder, hurried through the doorway and marched along the corridor to her room. Irate, she hastily pulled the day's lessons plan from her drawer then thought better of it. Today she'd loaf it if she could. Get the children to make things for the school fair on Saturday. Then a brilliant idea. She'd noticed a stack of photo frames by the checkouts at the garden centre. She'd ask the children to paint portraits of each other. She'd frame them herself and get the parents to buy them at the fete.

'That's it! I'll pick up the frames on the way home. Oh! No car! Flipping heck *him*. He's taking me home. I'll ask him. I'll ask him a favour. I'll go and do it now.'

'Ah you want your bags Miss Glover. Just let me open the boot.'

'She followed him out to the car.'

'Oh so there you both are!'

'I beg your pardon Mr. Brown?'

'I'm just saying there you both are. So Miss Glover told you I wanted to speak to you, did she? I don't know why I `ave to do it in front of `er.'

'Whatever are you talking about Mr. Brown?'

'Oh so you `aven't told `im then. Thought you could get out of it did you?'

'No Mr. Brown. I haven't had chance yet.'

'What is going on between you two now?' It was not difficult to detect the impatience in Mr. Sanderson's voice.

'I want to know why I `ad to go on that `ealth and Safety course and she didn't. After all it was `er that dropped the `angin` basket on *my* `ead.'

'Come come Mr. Brown. I don't think it's necessary to get quite so upset over this. I don't think it warrants this reaction.'

'It might not to you, but it wasn't your `ead that got it. I've been `avin` `eadaches non-stop since she clouted me with that. She needs to go on a course more than me! I'm takin` this to the union. I'll be `avin` a word with Mr. Potts and goin` on strike if you don't send `er on a course too.'

'Miss Glover had good reason to be absent from the course Mr. Brown I can assure you. And as you did attend it I suggest you join her in her room at three thirty this afternoon and relate all of the course contents to her. It will prove excellent revision for you Mr. Brown and I'm sure Miss Glover will retain every vital aspect from your specific interpolation of the course content.'

Harriet glowered at them both. Thought. 'How can *he* do this to me? So much for wanting to go to the garden centre.'

Mr. Brown scratched his head.

'Err if you don't mind Mr. Sanderson. I'm not back on duty `til four.'

'Just get back at three thirty will you.'

'Mr. Brown can't do that Mr. Sanderson. He's just been saying how awful the flowerbeds look and he's wanting to go to the garden centre to get some more plants to spruce the place up for the summer fete on Saturday. I think you said that. Am I right Mr. Brown?'

'She needs `er ears testin` that one. I never said no such thing. See `ow she lies Mr. Sanderson.'

'Alright, alright. I think she's got a point. Call in at the garden centre on your way in. See if you can't pick up some half-price plants to perk it all up.'

'Well I'll not be givin` `er `ealth and safety lessons as well. I'll be in late. School time is this.'

'Quite, quite, Mr. Brown. Just make sure you get the place tidied up before the fete.'

'If that's a criticism of my gardenin` I'll be takin` that one to Mr. Potts too seein` as it's outside my contract.'

'I think you'll find site maintenance in all its forms is very much part of your contract Mr. Brown. You'd be well advised to adhere to it.'

Harriet caught Mr. Brown's smirk. He pointed to the bedraggled leaves dotting the flower beds behind them.

'These are the weird plants she left for me a couple of weeks ago. I `ad nothin` to do with choosin` them weedy lookin` things.'

'They were only the ones Mr. Bridgewater told me to collect and deliver to you

Mr. Sanderson. He said you wanted them for the school. Actually some were for Mr. Swift. Did he get them?'

'Unfortunately yes. They're in the greenhouse. Pretty much said the same thing.'

Mr. Brown's smirk instantly revived.

'So it's not just me then. It's `er, probably cast a spell on them.'

'I'm sorry Mr. Sanderson but I think Mr. Brown should apologise for that.'

'She owes me more apologies than I owe `er!'

'Right that will do you two!' He turned to Mr. Brown.

'So you don't now feel it's a priority Miss Glover should partake of your health and safety knowledge?'

Mr. Brown shook his head. Looked down at his feet.

'Mr. Sanderson would it be alright if Mr. Brown bought me twenty-eight photo-frames while he's at the garden centre this afternoon? It's the large ones, the largest they sell and they're right by the checkouts.'

Mr. Brown seized the preferable option. Turned to Mr. Sanderson.

'They'll go on the back seat. I'll do that. You can give me the money for it all.

'Exactly how much are we looking at Miss Glover?'

'Oh let's see. I think they were £4.99, so it's twenty-eight times five. Let's see that's one hundred pounds plus eight times five which is forty, so that's one hundred and forty pounds and you'll get twenty-eight pence change.'

'And what exactly are these for Miss Glover, if I might ask?'

'The fete on Saturday. Don't worry they'll more than double that in profit.'

'What, empty frames?'

'No Mr. Sanderson. The children are going to be painting portraits of each other to sell at the fair.'

'Oh I see. It's a large investment Miss Glover. Are you sure of a return?'

'Guaranteed Mr. Sanderson, art never fails.'

'I just hope you're right Miss Glover. How much did you say?'

One hundred and forty pounds Mr. Sanderson, but there will be 28p change.'

'Very magnanimous of you Miss Glover. Here take these bags. I want a word in my office just as soon as I've seen Mr. Brown out.'

Harriet returned to her room. Plonked her bags down. Pleased Mr. Brown had fallen into cooperating to get himself off the hook. Pleased she'd decided on a day of painting for the children. They could do as many as they liked as far as she was concerned. She just wasn't in the mood for teaching a class of kids.

She removed the testing kit from the inside of her bag to the zipped pocket on the back. Good old Tricia. He wouldn't be bothering her after this. By the time her baby was showing she'd have well worked something out. No this would get her to the summer holidays. At the moment this was all she needed to do. Get to the holidays and away from *him*. Space to collect herself. Space to work out the best way forward.

She knocked on his door.

'IN!'

A familiar response. Loud. Clear. Uncompromising.

'Take a seat if you will Miss Glover.'

She sat down. The chair opposite his desk.

'I'm not sure the school funds can stand such an investment Miss Glover. I'm afraid you rather wrong-footed me there. Just make sure we get a decent return will you?'

'Oh you know how much parents love their children's paintings. They'll go for at least ten pounds each Mr. Sanderson.'

'That remains to be seen Miss Glover. Still you've given Brown a mission. Got him off our backs. The man's an absolute pain I'm afraid. More trouble than he's worth bleating on about this, that and the other to the union every five minutes.'

Harriet watched him now. He was standing, tall. She fought the urge to fling herself into his arms. Explain. Explain just why she'd disappeared with Tricia. Just how she'd been so overwhelmed she couldn't handle it. She'd completely flipped. Thought. 'He's a doctor. Why can't he work that one out for himself?' Then it occurred to her. The only thread of hope. 'But Mummy said he's waiting for *me* to make the date. No he can't be. Not a hint of it. Mummy probably got it all wrong.'

'I'm sorry Mrs. Harrington's been through such a bad time recently.'

He paused. Looked at her. Waiting for her response.

'Yes. She took it very badly, especially as Bob had the gall to tell her he'd proposed but she'd turned him down.'

'Good heavens. What a thing to say! Not forgetting the fact he's not free to marry her!'

'Yes, I'm not sure Tricia and Bob will be able to pull their relationship round after that.'

'Certainly a tall order. I feel extremely sorry for her.'

This was overdoing it. Harriet started to feel irritated.

'Mr. Sanderson you did say Belinda Oxfordshire hadn't had a very easy life. Did something really awful happen to her that you know about?'

Harriet determined to get this despicable act of his out in the open.

'Largely medical problems Miss Glover. Things a young woman should never have to go through.'

'Oh that doesn't sound very good. In what way?'

'Well I'm not at liberty to tell you that. Indeed it would be breaking confidentiality to do so. Just take my word for it Miss Glover, she's had a lot to cope with.'

Harriet had lost. She knew she could persue it no further. Although he'd as good as admitted it. She could hardly believe how he'd somehow distanced himself from it all. As if he'd never played a part in it.

'Speaking of medical conditions Miss Glover. I'm still waiting for the testing kit. Are you still losing? You have had time to have one normal period should you not be pregnant. I'd appreciate an answer Miss Glover.'

'Oh it's here Mr. Sanderson. I've got it here for you. Did it yesterday. I think you'll find I'm not pregnant, as I told you.'

She jumped to the knock on the door. He took the testing kit, looked at it. Put it in the inside pocket of his jacket.

'Thank you Miss Glover. That will be all.'

'IN!'

Harriet brushed past Lucinda Lawton as she left the room and closed the door behind her. Relieved to be rid of it she made her way to her classroom. No assembly today. It was Monday. She called the register then gave the children free reign with the paints.

'Ah Miss he's drawn one of me and painted my tongue hanging out.'

'Alright Melanie. He can start again.'

'She's started paintin` my `air Miss. Put it on the paper not on me `ead. That's why I've made `er tongue `ang out.'

'Melanie please don't....Robert. Stop that this minute!'

'I'm tellin` me mum of `im. My ears don't stick out like that and I `aven't got blobs of green comin` down the `oles on the end of me nose.'

'Well he's painted my teeth black at the front with yellow bits round the top. He said I don't clean them Miss and I do.'

'Alright Robert. That's no reason to blob his jumper with yellow spots. Whatever is his mum going to say?'

'Ah Miss she's joined my eyebrows together. I've only got one now and it looks like a caterpillar wiggling across the top of my `ead Miss.'

'Your eyebrows *are* nearly together. Look.'

'No Florence! Stop it now! Get that brush away from his face!'

'My `air doesn't stick out like that. She's makin` me look like an `edgehog Miss. I'm tellin` my mum of you. I will if she doesn't stop it Miss. Make `er stop. GERROFF will you.'

'That's quite enough Charlotte. Leave his hair alone NOW!'

'Stop it will yer. I don't want my nose painted red. He's not doin` it on the paper Miss. Tell `im `e's not supposed to be paintin` me.'

'Paul. You're getting it on Simon's shirt. Look it's dripping off his nose. Put that brush down. WILL YOU NOW!'

'Ah `e's made my `ead look like a mug with two `andles Miss. Ah I'm tellin` Miss of you. My mum won't buy that now. I'm tellin` my mum you called me mug face.'

'Look Miss she's put blobs of blue down my cheeks. She said it's because I'm always cryin` and I'm not. THERE. `ave that yourself.'

'Miss I've got blue paint on my face now. I'm tellin` my mum of `er.'

'Cry-baby.'

'Come here Andrew. Get it wiped off. You'll end up with it in your eyes. Helena STOP IT THIS MINUTE.'

'Ah eh. Why's `e painted me a yellow mouth? I `aven't got a mouth like a banana, you.'

'Oh yes you `ave Danny. Look I've just given you banana arms and banana legs.'

'Ahh. I'm tellin` Miss of you. We're only supposed to be doin` faces.'

'Right everybody STOP! I've had this all day. Write your names in pencil at the top and the name of the person you've painted underneath. Do it now, then put your paintings on the window sill to dry. Clear up then wash your hands outside in the sinks. Be quick and then line up by the door. The bell's about to go. Do it NOW!'

Harriet was glad to see the back of them. She'd managed a bit of reading. Had the children to her desk one at a time on and off throughout the day. Sent a few over to the science corner to record their observations. Had a couple more tidying the classroom. Sorting the books out in the class library. Things like that. Only added to the chaos really. She was in the full flow of yawning when the door swung open.

'Miss Glover, a word if you don't mind. Indeed a word if you do!'

She didn't like his tone. Hoped he wouldn't notice the paintings on the window sill. Didn't want to be accused of wasting school money, on top of everything else. He pulled a chair round the side of her table. Sat himself on hers. She sat down. Opposite.

'Miss Glover, that wasn't the pregnancy testing kit I gave you!'

Her cheeks flushed to scarlet. It hadn't crossed her mind. Thought they'd all look the same.

'Don't try to find excuses Miss Glover. I noticed Mrs. Harrington sliding across to you, passing you something, when I closed the boot lid this morning.'

Harriet took a deep breath.

He reached to his inside pocket. Held it up then placed it on her table.

'It really is of no interest to me whether Mrs. Harrington is pregnant or not. Return it to her will you?'

Harriet bit her lip. Looked down. Couldn't meet his eye. Didn't want to pick it up.

'So why the need to do it Miss Glover? Might it be because you are indeed still pregnant?'

No answer. She couldn't bring herself to answer him. Then felt the need to try.

'I'm not terribly sure Mr. Sanderson.'

'So it looks very much like a case of "adversus solem ne loquitor", Miss Glover.'

She looked up. His eyes deep, deep blue. Like pools of sea reflecting the light of a summer's day. His brows raised, then one lowered to frown. His lips apart, drawn back to allow a massive intake of breath. Just a glimpse of his teeth, white against his sun tanned face. His blonde hair tousled from running his hand constantly through it. She felt the same, same need rushing in, surging upwards towards her tiny growing baby.

'Literal translation Miss Glover? "Don't speak against the sun." '

'Sorry Mr. Sanderson I still don't understand.'

'Don't argue an obvious fact Miss Glover.'

She didn't answer.

'Antenatal care. Get it organised will you!'

Harriet turned to the classroom door opening. Saw Mr. Brown backing his way in, loaded with photo frames.

'Oh I beg your pardon Mr. Sanderson. I didn't realise you were both in 'ere. Where do you want them Miss Glover?'

'Just leave them on top of the cupboard please Mr. Brown. Thank you for getting them.'

He put them down. Fished in his pocket. Brought out twenty-eight pence.

Left it on top of one of the piles.

'That's to be returned to school funds and don't anyone try to accuse me of `avin` a mind to pilfer it!'

He went. Closed the door with a hefty bang behind him.

'The last thing I need is that damned paranoid caretaker winding that Potts fellow up. Is it not within your capability to steer clear of the man? I'm not sure I go with colluding for your own ends.'

'I beg your pardon Mr. Sanderson. I'm trying to raise funds for the school fete.'

'Quite, quite, Miss Glover. Gather your things. We'll need to be on our way to Starboard Marine North West to collect Mrs. Harrington.'

He picked up the testing kit.

'You prefer *I* return it?'

She took it from him. The colour returning to her cheeks.

'Meet me outside the main door Miss Glover.'

Chapter 68

'`ave you `ad your paper yet `arriet?'

Harriet carried the phone to the lounge. She'd forgotten it was Wednesday. Having spent the last couple of days to and from work, sat next to her in the back of Mr. Sanderson's car, the call was unexpected.

'Oh hi Tricia. Hang on I'll just go and have a look.'

'Get off that Pepper. Shoo, get down.'

'`Is that your cat attention seekin` again `arriet? You could do with trainin` it to `ave a go at our friend Joris. Do you know `arriet `e `ad a right go at me this mornin` over that pregnancy testing kit. I know you told me that you never said a word to `im and I do believe you `arriet but I thought I was off the `ook with `im not `avin` mentioned it yesterday. Fat chance! `e really laid into me as soon as I got in `is car. I was like you `arriet. I didn't admit to anythin`.'[

'Oh I'm sorry about that Tricia. I thought you were a bit quiet this morning. I feel awful because you're always so willing to help me out. You're such a good chum Tricia. Take no notice of him. He can't prove a thing.'

'No `arriet, you're right. I've got better things to be doin` than lettin` `im upset me. Anyway `ave you got the paper there?'

'Oh I have Tricia. You're on the front page. Well not you but they've got a big picture of Rapping Hammer. Oh you've got your byline too. "Holly Berry". Just a minute. Just let me read it through. "Rapping Hammer and the Ironing Bards are back in Stetmead this coming Saturday helping Holly Berry to raise funds to save Venice……..." Oh they've given you a good piece Tricia.'

'Yes `arriet, I'm ever so pleased. All I did was tell `er what it was all about on the phone. She's made a good story `arriet. I'm sure it will draw the crowds like last time. Especially as, read that bit a bit lower down. In the middle `arriet. `ave you got it? The bit about me doin` my fortune tellin`'

'Oh yes, I see it Tricia. "Veiled in mystery the psychic Holly Berry will be there to tell your fortune. Let her be your guide to happiness and success. You won't go wrong with Holly's crystal ball." Gosh Tricia. I didn't know you were psychic!'

'Neither did I `arriet but `ow will they know if I'm makin` it all up? They're bound to go away with a smile on their faces if I tell them nice things.'

'Well I certainly hope so Tricia. Hang on a minute. What's this down at the bottom here? "……and Holly Berry will be wearing her latest Italian designer gown, with one or two surprises up her sleeves!" Gosh Tricia what have you got planned?'

'I `aven't got anythin` yet. I was just gettin` my `ead together when I came out of the `ouse this mornin` and `e put me right off my stride. `e's an `orrible man `arriet. Can't you set the cat on `im like it went for Simon Barnes on your doorstep last year?'

'Oh gosh Tricia, I forgot to tell you. The other afternoon when he brought us both home from his.'

'Ooh what `appened `arriet?'

'Well Simon Barnes obviously broke loose from the pack. I opened the gate to find him hiding behind our wall. I hurled my bag at him. Sent him flying and then the cat landed on his face. I ran in and he flew. I don't know where his car was.'

'Ooh `arriet. I'm glad you were alright. I mustn't laugh `arriet but that's really funny. But come to think of it I thought I saw `is car down the end of the next road. You know `arriet where I left mine when we spent the night in your shed before we went to Venice. `e's got a pale blue `atchback `asn't `e?'

'Yes, that's right. Oh well he had a bit of a run then. Serves him right!'

'I do `ope `e doesn't turn up on Saturday `arriet.'

'He's bound to Tricia. We'll just have to be ready for him. Make sure we give him better than we get!'

'Yes, I'll start thinkin` about that. At least it will take my mind off that very `orrible man. Do you know `arriet I've `ad more than enough of `orrible men. Bob's now decided `e's in recovery. `e brought me flowers last night, so I pulled the `eads off and put them in `is salad. `e's tryin` is best to get me back in `is bedroom. Must be missin` all the activity. I said to `im "You'll `ave to do better than a bunch of wiltin` flowers if you're tryin` to win me over." And then do you know what I said `arriet?'

'No. Go on Tricia.'

'Well I said I don't do less than twenty-one centimetres any more and that's unaroused, and if `e cared to get the tape measure out, you know the steel one that twangs back and `its `im `arriet, `e could measure `is and see if it's up to the mark. I told `im as I recall `e never made a quarter of that and that was on `is better nights `arriet. I said to `im no wonder Belinda Oxfordshire finished with `im, I `appen to know that Mr. Sanderson's exceeds twenty-one centimetres and that's on a bad night. I said she was only puttin` up with `is little one because she was desperate.'

Harriet exploded. Could hardly speak. Falling about laughing.

'Oh Tricia what….. What did he say to that?'

'Nothin` `arriet. I `eard `im rummagin` in my knittin` bag while I was pullin` the `eads off the flowers. I knew `e'd got the tape measure. `e must `ave gone up to measure `imself because `e yelped `arriet. `e can't even `ang on to a tape measure without `it `ittin` `im back. Serves `im right I say! Anyway I can `ear `im comin` in. I'll see you in the mornin`, `arriet.'

Chapter 69

'I'm glad it's Friday night Hat.'

'Me too Mark. I've never known a week to drag like this.'

'I'm not doing any more down there, either. Tarquin Bridgewater can go and whistle. When's he back anyway?'

'Oh it should be soon. They were only going for a fortnight.'

'Bad week. Bad week at work, too. It might have helped if the conference hadn't been cancelled. We've been depending on these talks with the Europeans. We're only second guessing the true effects of global warming as far as land mass is concerned. They're far ahead of us on this.'

'Well you've been more involved with the water and ice side of it, haven't you Mark?'

'Well spotted. Top marks!'

'No need to be patronising. Anyway why couldn't they make it?'

'Volcanic dust Hat. Where have you been all this week? It's been in the news, all over the papers. The planes aren't flying Harriet.'

'But the girls are coming up tonight. We haven't heard they're not.'

'That could be the call now Hat. Go and answer it.'

'Oh Rachael. That's a coincidence. Your dad thought it might be you. It's lovely to hear from you again. Are you all OK? I hope this isn't a call to say you can't make it up after all.'

'Sorry Mum it is. Volcanic dust! We've been hoping the wind would change direction but it's not forecast. We've got as far as Portugal but there's not a flight to be had. We've decided to extend the honeymoon rather than scramble around trying to get a ferry. We're all doing another week here.'

'Oh I see Rachael. That's disappointing but I think it's a good idea to do that. Make the most of every opportunity while you've got the chance. So we'll hear from you at the end of next week, will we?'

'Yes Mum. Are you and Dad OK? Got over the shock of having to live together after all? You wouldn't like marriage Mum. You're far too much of a hippy to like marriage. You and Dad. Clare and I knew you didn't have the commitment to go legal, either of you. It's different for Clare and I. We're just going to love being one up on all our friends that can only manage to live together. Keep bucking the trend Mum.'

'OK Rachael. I think your dad and I have got the message by now.'

'Can't stop. Must go. Oh Mum do you think you could get someone to video Rapping Hammer for us? We're a bit hacked-off to be missing it.'

'I'll do my best Rachael. It might be filmed for TV anyway, in which case I'll record it for you.'

'Ah thanks Mum. Love to you and Dad. Talk soon.'

'Love to all.'

'There, what did I tell you?'

'Well it was hardly the most amazing prediction of the year Mark, given it was in the news and all over the papers. Anyway they're in Portugal. Staying on for a week. Extending their honeymoons. Gosh I wish I was in my early twenties and knew what I know now!'

'Well most of us would. But yes, you more than most I would think Harriet.'

'And what exactly do you mean by that Mark?'

'I don't think there's another person on the planet could dig so many damned big holes for themselves as you Harriet. And when you've finished one and made it as deep as possible you don't leave it there, do you? No not Harriet! You go on to start digging another hole even wider and deeper than the last. And so it goes on. Is it any wonder I've ended up with a phobia about marrying you? Oh I could just about hear Rachael wittering on about marriage. Well it's sure fire certain to get my back up coming from her. What do they know about life? I'm pleased for them. Very pleased. I'd never have wanted to see them end up like us Harriet. But the trouble is they don't know the half of what it's been like living with you. Hurtling from one disaster to the next. And this latest sounds like you and Tricia are in it up to your eyes. I'm amazed it's gone as quiet as it has. Anyway back to the point. I'm not having our kids weighing it up. Making judgements. I presume they think we're back together again, as before.'

'To be honest Mark I haven't wanted them to think anything else. Why spoil their honeymoons? They'll get to know soon enough. They're married now. Got their houses to find. They'll make their own way. What we do will hardly impinge on their lives now. As long as they come up, we go down. We all get to see each other. What's the point in telling them anything we don't need to?'

'So it's sounding a bit like you're happy to go with the status quo then Hat? Maybe we could try settling back a bit now. It's been a hell of a time for us both. At least I'm not getting lard ball rammed down my throat every five minutes. Dare I hope at long last you've got him out of your system? It might take me a bit longer, I can tell you. Still he lost you Harriet. Lard ball failed. Serves him bloody well right! We might just as well reinstate our partnership.'

'That sounds a bit clinical Mark. Certainly not conducive to sex if that's what you're after. No I'm not ready for that if that's the best you can do. You've been just as unfaithful to me but at least you know Mr. Sanderson and I are finished. No Mark I'm not being one of two in your life.'

'No Harriet. You've got that wrong. It was just the once. Once only with Melissa.'

'Do you know just how that makes me feel Mark?'

'I ought to Harriet. That tells us something about our feelings for each other, don't you think? Indifference never did produce anger Harriet.'

'I know. I know Mark. I know exactly what you're saying. I was pleased. I am pleased you came back. So relieved you didn't want to part with the house. He brought me back here. I held your jacket to my face. I hated the hole I'd dug for us.'

'There it is then Harriet. There's the answer. If we both swear to remain faithful to each other we can start again. We'll get through it. Find a new place. Let him have this. We'll find the money. We lived like that before without being married. We can do it again. We don't need marriage for that. We've proved it over many years Hat. The issue is whether or not that's what you really want now.'

'That's the issue Mark but it's not quite as straightforward as that. Sit down a minute.'

'What's this Harriet? What's this that you've got to tell me now?'

Harriet sat down. Took a very deep breath.

'Go on Harriet. Spit it out. For goodness sake tell me what's on your mind.'

'I'm having a baby Mark. I'm just so sorry to be having to tell you this but I'm expecting a baby.'

She watched the colour drain from his face. She went to hold his head to her chest. He moved his chair away.

'No Harriet. It's *his* isn't it? We've been under this roof together for all this time, you knowing that and you've only decided to tell me now?'

'I'm sorry Mark. I'm just so, so sorry.'

'When did you first find out Harriet?'

'The morning of the wedding Mark. Our wedding.'

'You mean if I'd gone through with it you'd have just let me think it was ours?'

'No Mark I could never have done that. I was planning on taking you to the vestry to tell you. I knew we'd never get married that day. You just made it easier for me, that's all.'

'And that's why *he* jumped in. Proposed. He knew all along.'

'No he didn't Mark. He honestly didn't. I told him after that. I told you just now I didn't find out until the morning of the wedding. Anyway Mark, it's sometimes the consequence of having affairs. It could just as easily have happened to Melissa.'

'Oh no it could not Harriet. I made damned sure I took responsibility for that. What the hell was that fucking great ball of lard playing at?!'

'Oh come here Mark.'

'No Harriet. I'm no saint. But this is certainly the end of the road for you and me!'

Chapter 70

Harriet heard the door bang shut behind him. Heard the engine start. He'd gone. She went back to sit herself at the kitchen table. Flopped her head in the space her crossed arms had made against the hard pine wood. Couldn't believe she'd come out with it. Gone against her plans. Felt there would have been a better time to tell him once she'd had space in the summer holidays to get her head round it all. No tears. She couldn't cry. Just a numbness, a sense of disbelief at what she'd just done. Hoped against hope he'd come back. Drive safely. Wondered whether to drive down to the club. Decided against it. The cat jumped up to her lap. She could feel its rough little tongue licking at her neck. She lifted her head. Stroked it.

'He's wrong Pepper. He is a saint for putting up with me all these years. Saint Mark Pepper. He's a saint for putting up with Mummy too. Not a Lord, or a Sir like *him*, not one of those titles you can buy like Mr. Sanderson did Pepper. No he's a Saint. He said it's the end of the road Pepper. San Marco the end of the road. Gosh Pepper why is it all falling away like this?'

Chapter 71

Saturday morning. Harriet awoke to the bed empty alongside her. She felt sick. Wondered what had happened to Mark. Looked out of the window. Her car. Not his. Rushed to get showered and changed. She needed to know if he was alright. Wanted to drive somewhere. Desperately needed to see him. Grabbed the phone.

'Tricia you haven't seen Mark have you? He's gone. I've got to find him Tricia. I've just got to.'

'Where's 'e gone 'arriet?'

'I don't know Tricia. That's why I'm asking you.'

'Well fish-feet-four-cheeks did go down to the club last night 'arriet. I'll wake 'im up and see if 'e knows anythin'.'

It felt like forever. Her mind racing, running through each and every conceivable disaster possible that might befall him.

''e was down at the club 'arriet but then 'e left after about 'alf an 'our. 'e didn't say where 'e was goin' though.'

'Oh thanks Tricia. Thanks for that.'

'Why 'arriet. What's been goin' on?'

'I told him about the baby Tricia and he stormed out. I just need to know he's alright.'

'Oh 'e'll be alright 'arriet. 'e'll 'ave gone to Melissa Scott's 'ouse in Millington. Don't forget 'e's still got 'er. 'e was tellin' me on the way 'ome the other night what a pain in the arse 'er mother was gettin' in the way of their relationship. It didn't sound to me as if 'e'd gone off 'er though. Quite the opposite I would say. I wonder if that's why 'e came back to live in your 'ouse 'arriet because of 'er mother?'

'You could just be right Tricia. I know he hasn't stopped seeing her anyway. Oh gosh Tricia I bet that's why he's not in a full relationship. You're right. They probably never get the chance to do it if her mother's around all the time. And there's me believing him when he's telling me there's nothing between them. I bet he's burning with frustration for her. I don't mind Tricia. No, I really don't. I just hope that's where he's gone. I'm worried sick about him. I don't care as long as he's still alive.'

'I wouldn't be quite so worried 'arriet. 'e'll be alright. 'e's probably just 'ad a bit of a shock, that's all. Look I'm goin' to tell you somethin' I've never told anyone. Promise you'll keep it a secret?'

'Promise Tricia.'

'Our Adam isn't Bob's child you know.'

Harriet felt bad. She knew. Mark had already told her. From the turmoil she was now forced to feign surprise.

'Gosh Tricia. He looks so much like him!'

'Well, I've always been glad about that. And to be fair to Bob 'e's always treated them both the same. At the time `e must `ave loved me enough to go ahead with the weddin` and we `ave been `appy until she came on the scene. I think it's `ad somethin` to do with `is age as well. `im be`avin` like that. But I'm not forgivin` `im `arriet. It was a long time ago when I went off the rails and `e `ad the choice. It was `im who wanted to marry me.'

'No one could ever have guessed you'd both been through all that Tricia. And there's me in exactly the same boat, but of an age when I should have known better.'

'`ow can you know better `arriet? Life doesn't work like that. But you `ave got yourself into the same mess as I did and all I'm tryin` to say is I do think Mark will get over it. It'll most probably wind down to a sulk after a while, if e's anythin` like Bob was, but you never `ave been married to Mark so in a way you've always been free to please yourself. Anyway `arriet don't you worry, `e won't be doin` anythin` silly.'

'Oh thanks for that Tricia. You've made me feel so much better. You're right. He'll be with Melissa Scott, no doubt offloading his fury. Anyway I'll let you go. Sorry to have called so early.'

'No, that's alright `arriet. I'm meetin` Rappin` `ammer down there at nine o'clock. `e's settin` up the tent for me and fixin` `is stage. `ave your girls arrived yet `arriet?' 'Volcanic ash Tricia. They're stuck in Portugal.'

'I wish our Adam was. `e's been playin` me up somethin` awful since `is Dad's been avin` it away. I just `ope `e doesn't cause any trouble down there this afternoon. See you later `arriet.'

Chapter 72

Grateful to Tricia for having put her mind at least partially at rest, she tried to focus on the day ahead. Her stall. She suddenly remembered. Every teacher was supposed to be selling something. Then she remembered the frames. The paintings. Then decided she needed more than that. She had most of the day to fill. In all the hiatus it had completely slipped her mind. She rummaged in the wardrobe. In the drawers. Panicked. Found a couple of Mark's old ties. Bits and pieces from their Christmas sacks shoved in the bottom of the wardrobe. Went into the office. Grabbed a couple of paperbacks from the shelf. An old unused ink cartridge. A few CDs. Then into the spare room. Pulled her suitcase out from under the bed. The panama hat. The shades. She didn't want those. Certainly didn't want to be reminded of those two heavies. Threw it all into a bin-liner. There was still not enough. Decided to make cakes.

Above the sound of the whisks whizzing through the mixture she thought she could just hear the phone. She switched the blades to silence.

'It is Pepper. Quick it might be Mark!'

'Good morning Miss Glover.'

'Oh good morning Mr. Sanderson. I'm just busy making cakes for the fair.'

'Yes, yes. I won't keep you a minute. Mrs. Harrington. I'm not able to get hold of her. What were her arrangements for today exactly?'

Harriet looked at her watch.

'She'll be there by now. She was meeting Rapping Hammer at nine.'

'Foolish girl. I expect she's arrived unescorted.'

'I really wouldn't know Mr. Sanderson. She didn't say how she was getting there.'

'Quite Miss Glover. Totally incomprehensible that she should have exposed the both of you to danger today.'

'I'm not sure what you mean exactly Mr. Sanderson.'

'Publicising her event in the way she did. Fund raising for Venice. Wearing that damned designer gown. We still don't know where they are Miss Glover. If ever anyone could lay themselves open, she most certainly has. Anyhow be ready for ten thirty. I'll collect you then. Oh and I hope you haven't forgotten we're dining at Molly's tonight.'

He was gone. Without so much as a goodbye. Harriet rushed back to the kitchen. Banged the first three trays into the oven and blobbed the rest of her mixture into the remaining trays of cake cases. Looked down at the cat. Completely splattered.

'Sorry Pepper, you'll have to lick it off. I used to like licking the bowl when I was little.'

She ran upstairs. Changed into her tight jeans and skimpy top. Thought about Barry. She'd been wearing those the last time she'd seen him. Looked at her watch. Could smell the cakes. Nearly ready. Took them out. Underdone. Flat and soggy on the top. Banged the rest of them in. Then the phone.

'Oh no Pepper he'll be here in five minutes.' Grabbed it. Sat on the bed.

'Barry Harriet. I'm free this afternoon. Any chance?'

'Oh no terribly sorry Barry. I'm on duty. It's the school fair today. You know, the summer fete. He'll be here any minute. I'm sorry Barry I can't talk just now.'

'Who's *he* Harriet? No, I don't need to ask. It's that Sanderson bloke isn't it?'

'Only because he's insisting on escorting Tricia and I everywhere Barry. To be honest I could well do with out it.'

'And me Harriet? Could you well do without me? You haven't phoned since I last saw you.'

'Gosh Barry. It's not as if I haven't been thinking about you. It was such a lovely day out, too. Sorry, I just haven't had chance.'

'I've been waiting for an answer Harriet. You haven't decided, I take it? I take it you're not certain.'

'Oh gosh Barry, the cakes are burning and that's him now. I can hear the key in the door.'

'Umm, the key in the door? I'll let you go.'

'Something's burning.'

'Oh Mr. Sanderson. I can't say we're too happy about you still having a front door key.'

'I rang the bell Miss Glover but you were obviously otherwise engaged.' He pointed to the phone. 'That's still connected. Here let me.'

'Thank you Mr. Sanderson.'

'I should rescue whatever it is you've got in the oven before the house catches fire.'

He followed her to the kitchen. Watched her grapple with thirty-six hot cinders sinking into brown crinkled-edged smouldering paper cases. She grabbed a couple of carrier bags.

'You can't put them in these Miss Glover. They'll melt the plastic!'

Rushed out to the shed. Returned with two square tins. Tipped them out onto the sink drainer. Fished out the last couple of nails wedged into the corners where the seams meet. A quick wipe with kitchen towel. One tin of burnt cinders. One tin of soggy flat-middled cakes. Pulled the rest of the cakes from the oven. Left them in their trays. Mr. Sanderson raised his eyebrows. Then scratched his head briefly. Decided against comment.

'Please could you put all these in your boot while I get the black bag from upstairs? Mind those. They're a bit hot yet. That's all. I'm coming. I'm ready now.'

She dragged the bin-liner down the stairs. He was in again to take it from her.

'Turn the oven off Miss Glover. It might help. I don't particularly want you burning down my portion of collateral in the property.'

She ran back. Grabbed her bag. Closed the front door behind him and rushed after him to the car. She waited for him to close the boot. Then followed him round the side as he held the door open for her.

'Not a bad day Miss Glover, though we're threatened with rain later on. Let's hope it keeps dry. There's nothing worse than having to set it up twice to accommodate the weather.'

'No Mr. Sanderson, especially once the tables are set up. Not easy carrying them all into the hall.'

'Quite Miss Glover. Now I trust you haven't forgotten about this evening. I've had a word with Molly, explained we might be a little late in view of today's agenda. She was fine about it. In fact she said that would give her chance to pop along with Percy. She feels she'd like to support the school now she's part of the local community. A splendid woman Miss Glover. Full of good down to earth common sense. I must introduce her to Mother. They'd get along famously.'

'Not like mine Mr. Sanderson. I can't see anyone getting along that well with mine.'

'On the contrary Miss Glover it would seem my mother and yours get on extraordinarily well. I'm delighted. They appear to have a routine established now whereby they visit each other once a week.'

'Mummy didn't say. That's strange. That's just the kind of thing she'd be falling over herself to tell me.'

'You may have strained the relationship Miss Glover. As you have with more than a few of us. You can't expect people to be open with you when you choose to create a trail of deceit.'

'I'm not sure what you mean Mr. Sanderson.'

'Oh I most certainly think you do Miss Glover. You've gone well out of your way to try to deceive me into thinking you're not still carrying my child. Still! This is neither the time nor the place. You're going to have to face me head on I'm afraid. It's inevitable you won't be able to keep up this charade for too much longer.'

He looked across and down to her lap as they pulled to a halt at the lights outside Starboard Marine North West.

'Certainly won't be feeling very comfortable in those in a couple of months time.'

She could feel herself blushing. Kept quiet. Couldn't think of a thing to say.

'Indeed you're going to find it difficult keeping it from everybody Miss Glover. What about your job? How do you propose to deal with that? I take it you are back with Mark. Some kind of loose arrangement between you both, I expect. You can hardly hope to maintain that once he discovers you're carrying my child. You see Miss Glover I'm concerned here. I don't particularly want my son or daughter growing up in impoverished circumstances. Even if you're planning on returning to school after the birth, er once your maternity entitlement runs out, you're going to need childcare to enable it. You do appreciate that these are going to have to be joint decisions. You have this facility to bury your head in the sand Miss Glover. Rest assured I'll be fighting every inch of the way for my child Miss Glover. For my child and its mother.'

Harriet couldn't believe he'd just said that. There was something about being next to him in this car that sent all rational thought through the window. He was speaking of his child. His baby. Of being with her. She was back on the sand. He was slowly undoing the buttons at the edges of the blue lace on the bodice of her dress. This time different. He was slipping it from her shoulders. Taking the buttons out of their loops all the way to the hem. He was slipping away the hooks of her white lace bra and taking it from her breasts. Then her blue lace panties. She arched her back against the car seat to allow him to slip them down to her feet and away to the sand. He was looking at her. Pregnant but he'd never seen her completely naked. His lips soft against hers. She was feeling him exploring her mouth she was needing him, wanting him. She shifted on the car seat. Felt the belt tighten across her waist. Knew she was moving her legs just slightly apart. Tried to stop the thoughts as she watched his hand strong on the gear lever. His hand now on her breasts, brushing across her stomach and down, down. Her head spinning. Both lying in the evening sun. Her back warm against the sand.

'Right Miss Glover. We're here. You've gone very quiet. Indeed I've given you a great deal to think about. I'll park this round the back and give you a hand to carry your stuff across the field.'

She jumped. Hadn't meant to go there. Tried to remind herself of just how terrible he was. 'How could he do that to Belinda Oxfordshire?' She kept the words ringing in loud silence to herself as she followed him across the field to her table.

Chapter 73

He led her to the table at the end of the row backing onto the narrow strip of land behind. She'd not been able to make out the boundary as they'd walked towards it. Filled with tents of all shapes and sizes. Things of every description hanging over the wire netting fence. Already the band was on the go. She was glad Tricia was in there, somewhere.

She turned round to Mr. Brown stumbling towards her. Struggling trying to push his trolley through the grass. Then she realised. The picture frames. In his trolley. She needed to get to her classroom to gather the paintings.

'Don't walk off Miss Glover, my feet are killin' me. They've never been the same since you stamped on them with those 'igh 'eeled boots the night of the barn dance. I wouldn't 'ave struggled over 'ere like this but I've been told to by Sir. 'e made me bring this lot over. The picture frames. I don't see as 'ow those paintin's on the window sill are goin' to fit these. They look a bit too big too me. You'll never sell this lot without pictures in them. Well you might get a penny each. You might get your twenty-eight pence back. That's if you're lucky. These 'ere plants. You can 'ave them back. Spoilin' my borders. I counted 'em. Twenty-eight as it 'appens.' He pointed to the trolley. 'You'll need to be sellin' them for £4.98 each to get your money back on them!'

'Well done Mr. Brown. Go to the top of the class.'

'And I don't want any lip from you either. A thank-you wouldn't go amiss.'

'Sorry Mr. Brown. I'm supposed to be selling cakes on this table. It's not going to be that good trying to handle those as well. Health and Safety, that sort of thing.'

'Don't talk to me about 'ealth and safety, not with that lot over there. Wires trailin' everywhere.'

'That's nothing to do with us Mr. Brown. Rapping Hammer's doing a gig for charity.'

'Aye and what's the bettin' they won't all be climbin' over the fence? I've locked the gate but it won't stop the little beggars.'

Harriet changed her mind. Watched him push his empty trolley back towards the school. Decided to collect the paintings once he was out of the way. Opened her black bin liner. Arranged all the bits and pieces around the panama hat in the middle. Put the cakes to the right of it all and the plants, wilting from the roots, to the left. At least they filled up the table.

'Oh 'ello 'arriet. 'ow are you gettin' on? Rappin' 'ammer and I 'ave been gettin' on just fine. Ooh 'e is keen on savin' Venice 'arriet. I do 'ope everyone read my bit in the paper, I do 'ope it's a good turnout.'

'I'm sure it will be Tricia. Just look what Mr. Brown's lumbered me with. Tarquin Bridgewater's plants. As if these are going to sell.'

'No they are a bit funny lookin' aren't they 'arriet? I put ours in the front garden and they're comin' into bud just like those. They're remindin' me of

somethin' 'arriet. Ooh I must tell you this. Rappin' 'ammer's been tellin' me
'ow 'e's come to be able to forgive me 'arriet. I found it a bit embarrassin' after
what I did, but 'e's been tellin' me 'ow much better 'e feels without that
cucumber in 'is pants. Oh 'e said 'e only did it for the televised gigs. Wanted to
look good for 'is world-wide fans, but sometimes 'e couldn't get 'old of any
little ones 'arriet and 'ad ended up 'avin' to cut one in 'alf. Once 'e 'ad terrible
trouble when the skin started to split and the cucumber started slippin' over to
one side. 'e said 'e could feel it under 'is leathers and 'e 'eard some girl shout
up 'ow 'e 'ad two! That was what finally sent 'im into therapy. 'e became
convinced 'e'd grown another one because 'e'd been so over-sexed 'arriet. I'm
glad it wasn't all because of me. Anyway I told you about 'is therapist making
'im understand little didn't really matter and most men were 'is sort of size
anyway. And 'e's on a mission to make men feel much better about themselves
now, instead of tryin' to make them jealous. You remember that don't you
'arriet?'

'Oh yes I do Tricia.'

'Well you wouldn't believe it 'arriet but 'e's now worshippin' Leonardo da
Vinci since 'e found that drawin' 'e did. Vitruvian Man. That's what it's called.
You know the one 'arriet. It's a man drawn in a circle. 'e's got an extra pair of
arms and an extra pair of legs all stretched out. A bit like a clock with extra
'ands, or maybe it's more like a cartwheel. Anyway, 'e 'asn't got an extra one of
them. If you know what I mean. 'e told me it 'ad 'elped to sort 'is mind out
'arriet and 'e's brought loads of them to sign so people can buy them.'

'Gosh Tricia. He has been severely traumatised. No wonder he's so keen to
help you save Venice.'

'Well that's it 'arriet. 'e showed me the picture and asked me if I thought 'is,
if you know what I mean, was about the same length as 'is thumb. Well it's very
difficult to make that kind of judgement from a picture. So I told 'im Bob had a
very long thumb and 'is was only 'alf the size of it and that was when it was in
full use. You should 'ave seen the look of relief in 'is eyes 'arriet. 'e said if that
was the case when 'e goes to Venice to measure those 'angin' off the statues
and they're the same, that will confirm 'is therapist 'asn't been 'avin' 'im on.
And then 'e went just a tiny bit too far 'arriet. 'e asked me if I 'ad experience of
any others and what length were they? That's when I said "Excuse me!" and
came over to see you. 'e's obviously obsessed with 'imself 'arriet. I'll think I'll
tell 'im to talk to Belinda Oxfordshire about it. She'll 'ave a better idea than me.
Oh and there she is 'arriet. Wobblin' along on those 'igh 'eeled shoes. Just look
at 'er talkin' to 'im. Our friend Joris. Look at 'er fallin' all over 'im. What's she
wearin' 'er 'igh 'eels for in the grass? Not very sensible I would say 'arriet. With
a bit of luck she'll land in a cowpat!'

'No cows in here I'm afraid Tricia.'

'Except 'er! Anyway it's startin' to fill up now. I 'ope our friend Joris won't
mind them all comin' through 'ere. Rappin' 'ammer's put 'is tent right across
that main gate. 'e's got 'is stage in there and all 'is electrics wired up so 'e won't

want to be movin` anythin`. Oh look, there's our Adam leadin` the way. Gosh `arriet I think `e's brought the `ole of `is school with `im.'

'That gate's locked Tricia. How did you get through?'

'That bit of loose wire netting by the railings on the road `arriet. Anyway the fence is low enough. I'm sure they'll be able to jump over it. I'm goin` to get changed. That's my own little tent in the corner over there. Come over when you get chance. I'm just dyin` to show off my designer gown. I've just got to be wearin` it when I'm rattlin` my tin for Venice.'

Harriet smiled. Gave her a quick wave. Suddenly thought about Mark. Hoped he was with Melissa Scott. Turned round. Mr. Brown again. Loaded with paintings.

'I wasn't expectin` to be `avin` to come over `ere again. If `e'd told me, they could `ave gone in the trolley before. `ere take them. Just look at those little buggers jumpin` over that fence. They'll `ave it down! HEY! STOP IT! YOU CAN SEE THE GATE'S LOCKED!'

Youth in all its exuberance now rushing past them both. In droves. All leaping over the fence. Some not making it now. Catching it on their heels. Peeling it back. Treading on it. Flattening it to the ground. A load of tattooed skinheads finishing the job for the rest of them. It was beginning to look like one of those rock concerts where every blade of grass in every farmer's field is flattened under foot.

Then Belinda Oxfordshire, struggling to catch Mr. Sanderson as he strode towards them.

'Mr. Brown that's positively dangerous. Give me a hand to clear them will you and roll it all back out of the way. The last thing I wanted was to be part of Mrs. Harrington's save Venice mission.'

'YOU! ALL OF YOU BACK. AT ONCE! NOW! GIVE US SPACE TO GET THIS FENCE CLEAR. NO! YOU BOY. GET OUT OF THE WAY THIS MINUTE!'

Suddenly silence as the front mass halted. Metamorphosed to a mass of lumpy statues. As far as the eye could see, the rest tumbling over them to roll the wire netting back, pummelling it towards the railings by the road. Sheets, jumpers, jeans. Everything hanging lost to the wiry spikes as the old wire cracked and split under the force.

'Good grief. It's turning into Glastonbury. Crikey! Look at that lot coming from over there. You shouldn't have any difficulty selling your cakes Miss Glover. Some of them don't look as though they know what day of the week it is. We'll be looking for an exceptional return on the day's trading just to pay for the damage.'

He turned round.

'Ah, Miss Lawton.'

Harriet watched him march off. His thick blonde hair lifting and settling in sync with his stride. She tried to sink the blade of jealousy cutting at her throat as he placed his left hand on her back to signal his presence. She watched

Lucinda turn to catch his smile. She'd seen enough. Turned to watch Mr. Brown doing his best to pull the draped roll of wire fencing clear of the crowds. Frowning at Belinda Oxfordshire as she pushed some kind of notice under his nose. Then watched her totter her way towards the single story canteen building on the far side, stopping at the gate to weigh up just where to pin her large oblong notice.

Harriet jumped.

'Oh sorry `arriet I didn't mean to frighten you. It looks like we're all going to be together after all. I feel a bit safer with that fence out of the way. I `ave been thinkin` I wouldn't fancy bein` captured by those `eavies from behind my tent. I wouldn't `ave been able to jump that fence `arriet. Still we `aven't `eard any more of them. What do you think?'

'It does look good Tricia. I just hope we're not tempting fate.'

'No, we `aven't `eard any more of them `arriet. They're most probably back in Venice by now. Findin` another `ouse for their counterfeit goods. Do you know, I don't think we'll be `earin` any more about any of it. After all `arriet I drove myself `ere and I'm safe as `ouses. I don't know what `e's been fussin` about myself.'

'Yes Tricia, he was a bit miffed he'd missed you. I got caught for a lift.'

'Oh well I wouldn't be worryin` about `im. I'll take you back home if you like.'

'Oh thanks Tricia. What do you think? Shall we grab something to eat now before it all gets under way?'

'Yes I think that's a very good idea. `ang on a minute. I'll see if the boys want me to bring anythin` back for them.'

'No `arriet they've brought their own. They'll `ave theirs in the van over there. Is that where we go? What's she doin` messin` about with that notice? Just a minute, you go on. Just let me get my carrier bag.'

Harriet went from one foot to the other, waiting. Watching. Parents. Children. People in all their variety already wending their way to the canteen. Caught a wave.

Mrs. Bustard marching Danny by the ear to somewhere he didn't want to go.

'More trouble,' Harriet thought. Some of her class now. Kids running around. Excited. She started walking slowly towards them. Then turned to see Tricia grinning, swinging a carrier bag at her side.

'I'm just goin` ahead `arriet. I'll catch you at the gate.'

'Not more trouble, I hope. Tricia please DON'T!' Harriet's thoughts were whirling as she moved forward to join the lengthening queue.

Then like a jack-in-the-box Tricia's head popping up. Harriet could just see her waving her carrier bag up as she pushed her way towards her.

'What did you do then Tricia?'

An instant screech. Harriet looked round.

Belinda Oxfordshire rolling in horse dung. Fresh, hot and steaming.

'You didn't did you Tricia? You didn't plop that lot under her feet.'

'I'm not sayin` anythin` `arriet!'

'Where did you get it from?'

'See that light brown `orse in the field behind us? It was doin` it right by the fence. I couldn't believe my luck!'

Chapter 74

'Ah there you are Mrs. Harrington. Would you mind putting that pie down whilst I'm speaking to you? What's the meaning of all this?'

'I'm sorry Mr. Sanderson, I can't `onestly say as I know what you're talkin` about. It `ad nothin` to do with me.'

'I would refute that statement Mrs. Harrington.'

'Well it's `ardly my fault if a big `orse jumps over the fence and drops a dollop by the canteen door is it? I can't understand why I get blamed for just about everythin`.'

'What *are* you talking about Mrs. Harrington? I'm referring to your need to advertise this whole affair in the paper. Exact repeat of last time. Hiding behind a pen name will afford you no protection whatsoever. It's even more foolish of you to advertise the fact that you'd be wearing an Italian designer gown Mrs. Harrington, given the suspicion surrounding it. Given you'd relented to pass the responsibility of its disposal to Miss Glover. And as it's with forensics at present it can hardly be in two places at once! Very foolish to have alluded to it in such a way. Totally unnecessary.'

'I beg your pardon Mr. Sanderson but this is the genuine thing I'll `ave you know. I'm surprised someone as `igh up as you can't even recognise it!'

Harriet cringed. Thought. 'Tricia shut up. Just leave it, *please.*'

'That's enough Mrs. Harrington. That's quite enough.'

He turned looking towards the door.

'What's the matter with that blasted woman now? She's not crying for goodness sake!'

Belinda Oxfordshire limped round the tables towards them.

'Whatever's happened to you Belinda? What's that you're covered in? It smells disgusting.'

Harriet looked down to her plate. Took a deep breath. Didn't dare look across to Tricia. Her shoulders shaking already. Trying to contain an explosion.

'It wasn't there before *they* came along. I've been there a while fixing that notice to the gate. I'd have seen it and smelt it. It's definitely got something to do with them Joris.'

'Tell me `ow can it possibly `ave anythin` to do with us. We `aven't seen any big `orses in `ere `ave we `arriet? And if we `ad we wouldn't `ave been able to stop them from doin` what come natural would we `arriet? I don't know what she's talkin` about Mr. Sanderson but I don't think it's a very good idea for `er to be in `ere like that where there's food. She smells `orible!'

'Come come now Belinda. No need for tears. I suggest you drive yourself home. Ah Mr. Brown have you a large black bin liner we could cut holes in just to pop over Miss Oxfordshire to get her home?'

'Right back Sir. I got a stack in ready for clearin` up the rubbish.'

'Good man! Come along out of here Belinda. I'm afraid I need to stay. I can't risk leaving this lot. I should have a hot bath and call it a day if I were you. We could ask Brown to run you home if you prefer.'

'No thank you Mr. Sanderson. I'll manage,' she sniffed.

Harriet could see Mr. Brown through the window, fiddling about with a pair of scissors and a black bin liner.

'`e's cutting` `oles for `er arms and `ead `arriet. Well isn't life funny. There's me wearin` my designer gown and she's bein` measured up for a black bin-bag!'

Her shoulders started shaking again. Uncontrollable now she screamed 'Oh look at `er now. `er `ead won't go through the `ole `arriet!'

Everyone turned to look. Mr. Sanderson tried to pull it off and both her arms shot up into the air.

The tears were streaming down their cheeks as they watched Mr. Brown with his scissors cutting round the hole trying to make it bigger.

'Ooh `e's cut the `ole too big now `arriet. Look it's dropped down to `er bum. Now `e's tryin` to sellotape it all back. Oh she's just `it `im `arriet! `e's got it all caught up in `er `air!'

The low level roof above their heads barely contained the laughter as it pulsated its way to the open window. Tricia fished under the table for her carrier bag. Brought her save Venice tin out.

'I'll catch them while they're laughin` arriet.'

'Tricia it's covered in it!'

'Oh the `andle's alright `arriet. They won't be gettin` `old of the tin. They'll only be `avin to drop their pound coins down the slot. From the air `arriet.'

'Why did you put it in there Tricia with all that lot in it?'

'Oh I'd scooped it all in before I realised it was in the bottom of the bag `arriet.'

Harriet sat back. The canteen crowded now. The place darkening as howling faces trying to get a better view blocked the light from the long line of windows opposite. Tricia made for the door. Went for the kill. In an attempt to get it rattling, swung her tin hard above her head then lost the action to gravity as someone pushed the door open hard into her back. She gasped then tumbled as her heavy missile in full flight swung back to clout Rapping Hammer at the zip of his black leather pants. Harriet, eyes streaming, watched him double up in agony as he tussled with Tricia on the floor.

'You swung that on purpose. Fuckin` `avin` another go at me Chick-Lips, after all I've told yer?'

'Oh no I did not. You rammed the door into me, don't forget. What were you doin` `ere anyway? You said you were `avin` yours in the van. I didn't know I was goin` to `it you with my tin.'

'I bet she did!'

'Oh no I did not Rax!'

'She's tryin` to slice your cucumber off now Rappin`.'

'Sod off Rix. This friggin` `urts.

'`as she belted `im one?'

'What does it bleedin` look like Rux?'

'It bleedin` look like `e's gonna need surgery. That's if `e's got anythin` left.'

'Eh Rex. Don't just stand there lookin` like a fuckin` coat `anger. `elp `im up.'

'Get lost will yer Rux. Look what `e's landed in. It's all over `er and `er friggin` tin, It stinks!'

'She stinks. You could mash the mush on `er alright. Be `igh with the cows.'

'Oh I `eard that! Bloody cheek! It was a complete accident. `ere!'

She swung the tin hard at Rex as he jumped back. Caught Mr. Whittle's bottom just as he stepped ahead of Mr. Sanderson coming in. Stunned, Mr. Whittle turned.

'You vermin! Joris you haven't sanctioned the presence of this scum again? Not after the Christmas fiasco?'

'Get up boy this minute! Get back to your tent and take your band with you before I call the police!' He turned to Mr. Whittle.

'Indeed not. This performance is totally independent of the school. They're on the strip adjacent to the field.'

'Look `e's covered in it. It's all over `is fuckin` arse!'

'It's off `er, Chick-Lips. Look at that gunge round the bottom of `er tin. It's `er that swung you one.'

'Mrs Harrington, will you kindly remove yourself and that damned tin from our presence. Come, come Mr. Whittle let's see about cleaning you up. I hope you all know Mr. Whittle is the Area Chief Inspector for Schools. You would be well advised to return to the ground you are renting before he considers prosecution.'

Harriet watched Tricia scoot. All eyes had long since turned from the window to the door. She needed to get back to her stall but wondered if her jelly legs, too weak from laughing, would make it. She took a deep breath. Tried to sink the look on Mr. Whittle's face. Decided it couldn't have happened to a better person.

'Well, maybe Mr. Brown,' she thought, walking straight into him. His roll of sellotape. His bags and scissors.

'`ere take these will you while I clear that mess up in `ere and out there. `ealth and safety! We can't be `avin` anyone else slippin` on it!'

Harriet gladly obliged, only too pleased to escape.

'Oh `ello Miss Glover. Our Danny's over there. Oh I see you've got the roll of bags and scissors. `e wants one our Danny. `e wants to look like `er. That glamorous one who fancies `erself from the coffee shop. What was `e doin` puttin` that on `er? Fancy dress I suppose. We'll know soon enough. Well I `ope that's it. I don't want our Danny takin` a fancy to wearin` frocks. At `is age anyway. I've given `im 10p to buy `imself one. Don't cut the `oles too big for `is arms. `is are only thin. DANNY OVER `ERE!'

'Right Mrs. Bustard. I'll see he gets one. My table's the last on that row backing onto the tents.'

'Thanks Miss Glover. You're a good'n you. By the way `ave you `eard any more? Is `e still `avin` an affair with Miss what's `er name, Lawton. You know, the deputy? I wonder why she dumped `im at the church? I'll soon get to know. Someone's bound to `ave `eard what's goin` on.'

Harriet forced a smiled. Hurried off to her table and the din from the tents. Wondered if Rapping Hammer would be up for it all now. Finished her table off with the panama hat and shades. She wanted rid. Turned round to see Danny.

'ere's me 10p Miss. Make sure you cut the `ole for me `ead in the middle.'

Then the rest of the class. Small hands thrusting money at her. Harriet constantly tearing and cutting. She was of a mind to increase the price. Hardly a dent in the roll. Mr. Brown had handed over one of those mammoth things packaged especially for caretakers. Enough for the whole school. Before she knew it she needed them. She looked up. Masses of eager faces. Black bin-liners everywhere running amok. Heads, arms and legs poking out In between brushing the flies off the cakes, Harriet had done nothing else.

She rubbed her fingers, sore from the scissors. Watched them circle the field in droves. Now like flocks of huge blackbirds, small arms becoming wings. Screeching and squawking. She hardly noticed the gang gathering to her left.

'`e's cool in there.The best gig `e's ever performed man. It's almost like `e's `ad a rebirth. A renewal. `e's takin` the full routine to Venice. Saint Mark's Square. We've been waggin`. `e's off with `is band tomorrow mornin`. We're all goin`. It's free! We'll be sittin` right there on them steps watchin` and we won't be payin` a penny. Not to `im anyway. For each one of us that turns up `e's donatin` ten quid. All we `ave to do is put somethin` in `er "save Venice" tin while we're sittin` there.'

'Oh!' Harriet declared. 'Very good. Has he been performing then?'

'Are you off the planet or somethin`? That's what we came `ere for.'

'Yes, of course. He must have recovered. Have you booked your flights?' Harriet replied.

'Give us a chance will yer, we've only just found out about it! `e's gonna be there for the week.'

Harriet watched his mates trailing towards him from the tents. The straggly youth turned to them.

'We're thinkin` of hitchin` our way over aren't we lads? We're not riskin` bein` dumped on by a load of cinders. What do them people do up there anyway to keep settin` off these volcanoes? I thought it was supposed to be all ice and water. Why don't they just fill the `oles with snow? They've got plenty of it.'

'Quite!' Harriet declared. 'Now is there anything you wish to buy from my table?'

'I wouldn't mind the `at and the shades. `ow much are you chargin`?'

'No I'm very sorry `arriet's not sellin` them. They got mixed up in the bag didn't they `arriet?'

Harriet jumped. Startled to see Tricia in hers, coming out from behind.

'Oh yes. No these are not for sale. Sorry! Definitely not. In fact I should be wearing them. Not good too much sun.'

She put them on, not quite knowing why she'd automatically gone with Tricia's line.

'Arrh, eh. *I* wanted them. They would 'ave looked cool on me.'

'Eh Daryl never mind them, just look at these 'ere!'

The lads swarmed round the plants.

''ow much?'

'They're well on now. Ten pounds each.' Harriet returned.

''ow much 'ave we got between us then?'

'I'm not fuckin' payin' that for them. We might not be able to do anythin' with 'em.'

Harriet didn't like the look of the bruiser that had just pushed his way forward.

'Ten pounds the lot. Sorry that's what I meant to say.'

He scrambled in the back pocket of his jeans. Waved a crumpled tenner at her. She turned to tear off a bin bag. Felt a tap on her shoulder. A uniformed officer. The arm of the law. She nearly died. Thought her moment had come. Tricia had vanished. Wondered if she was already on her way to jail.

He beckoned. Two more police officers rushing across.

She watched the gang being hauled in. Wished the man in the black uniform would move out of her personal space.

'Cannabis Miss. You been growing it?'

She took her shades off.

'No! The school caretaker wheeled them over for me to sell.'

'Which one's that?'

'Over there. Mr. Brown's over there. He's standing by that notice with the arrow that says "Canteen".'

Trembling. Her legs barely able to take her weight. She looked across. All but collapsed. Simon Barnes following him with camera on shoulder.

Looked over to the tents. No sign of Tricia. Then the other way. Her mother and Violet Moss striding towards her.

'HARRIET, THOSE PLANTS! They are just the same as those in my hanging basket before the police took it away. They asked where I got it and I told them I'd asked you to buy it for me from the garden centre. I sent them down there. I felt like a criminal Harriet. Are you sure you didn't take the pretty ones out for yourself and then fill my basket with these horrible things hoping I wouldn't notice?'

Harriet couldn't answer. Felt the onset of a nightmare.

'You see Harriet I didn't realise Daddy had taken a couple out and passed them over to Violet here on account of them being unusual. Cedric planted them in the tub right outside your front door, didn't he Violet? And the police marched off with those. Of course you had no choice but to tell them how you got them did you Violet? I understand perfectly. But we got accused of spreading them around Harriet. I don't know what things are coming to. We're pensioners. Daddy and I are hardly going to be growing those horrible things to be smoking the leaves in the garden shed!'

'No Mummy. I'm sure it will all sort itself out.'

'It better Harriet and I think you also owe Mrs. Moss an apology, leaving her standing like that on your front door step. Go on Harriet do as Mummy says.' She half turned.

'Ah there's James and Geraldine talking to Joris. I think they're on their way over.' Harriet hardly heard. Trembling and flummoxed she turned to Mrs. Moss.

'It was a misunderstanding Mrs. Moss....'

'Not another one Miss Glover!' She turned round. Mr. Sanderson just ahead of James and Geraldine. The carrier bag in his hand. The one she'd left under the hedge with Geraldine's dress in.

'My mistake. You left it out for charity Miss Glover?' He pulled it out. 'I suggest you sell it along with these.'

'But that's my dress James. That's the one I gave to you Frances to give to her.' She turned to Harriet. 'Don't you like it? She's never liked anything of mine. Or me for that matter. I don't think she likes anyone only herself.'

Harriet watched James steer her away. Watched Mr. Sanderson take yet another deep breath.

'Over here if you will Miss Glover.'

He lead her some distance away from her stall.

'Brown. He's throwing it back to you. Got the police thoroughly confused. Where did you say these damned plants came from?'

'Remember Mr. Sanderson? It was the day Mr. Bridgewater went away with Iris. He asked my to collect all the plants from one side of his greenhouse. They were mostly for Mr. Swift and of course here, the school. But he also said I could keep some, so I gave a few away.'

'Oh that damned man! There's no way out of it other than to drop him right in the mire. You obviously cleared the wrong side of his greenhouse Miss Glover.'

He marched her back. Called out to Tricia coming towards them.

'Ah Mrs. Harrington. Keep an eye on this lot will you while Miss Glover and I join Mr. Brown and the police.'

'That won't be any trouble Mr. Sanderson. Where's your money pot 'arriet?'

'That's her Frances. That's her! She's the one who attacked me in the hotel in Venice. It's no good wearing those things. I recognise your voice. And you of course.'

She turned to Harriet. 'You were just as bad. The two of you together. Cedric and I filed a complaint immediately. At the time. We're still waiting to hear. We'll be looking for compensation.'

Harriet watched her mother pale from shock.

'Oh Violet, how dreadful. It's the company she keeps I'm afraid. I've warned her repeatedly about mixing with this common girl.'

'Oh I beg your pardon Mrs. Glover. Just you watch who you're callin` common. I'll `ave you for slander if you're not careful.'

'No Mummy, Tricia's right. You have no right to judge any one like that.'

'Well it's not you I'm referring to. It's simply the kind of behaviour you choose to indulge in.'

She pointed to Harriet and then turned to Tricia. 'She's no different you know. Living with that Bohemian boyfriend all these years. No manners. Common. She's probably influenced you Patricia. Such a pretty name to match your pretty face dear. Though I could never understand why it gets shortened.'

Tricia smiled. 'Fallen for the flattery,' Harriet thought as she watched her mother fidget.

'Now Mrs. Moss, exactly how much compensation were you looking for?'

'Cedric suggested three hundred and fifty pounds would get us a new greenhouse. You know we had to leave the other one behind when we moved.'

Harriet's mother opened her bag. Pulled out a pen. Then the corner of her cheque book. Mr. Sanderson stepped forward.

'No no Mrs. Glover I simply won't hear of it. I have to take a certain amount of responsibility for this. Here…'

He pulled his wallet from his back pocket. Counted out the twenty pound notes on top of the heap of photo frames.

'Here Mrs. Moss I think this is one matter better dropped, don't you?'

'Well that's most kind of you, but I don't think it's in order to accept money from a stranger, albeit a very kind stranger, Mr. Sanderson.'

'Oh just take it Violet. He's not a stranger. He's supposed to be marrying this harum scarum, though I can't think for the life of me why. When she gets round to making her mind up to fix a date, that is. You wouldn't believe she's already reneged on one date. Venice that's where they were. I ask you? Venice! They were supposed to be in church together hearing the banns read for three Sundays and then the wedding. I ask you and the good man still wants her! That's an indication of the calibre of Sir Joris Sanderson, Violet.'

'Oh, *Sir* Joris Sanderson.'

Harriet, mortified watched her. She almost did a courtesy. Her mother went off again.

'Well that's right isn't it Sir Joris? You're just waiting for her to say the date?'

'That's correct Mrs. Glover, now if you'll excuse us we need to be getting over to Mr. Brown. As I said. Keep an eye on this lot if you will Mrs. Harrington. Hopefully we won't be very long."

Harriet caught her breath. He'd just publicly declared his intention to marry her.

'No. It was Mummy. He just said it to shut her up.' Her thoughts turned to Mark. Uneasy all day she'd tried to convince herself he'd be alright. He'd be with Melissa. 'Most probably telling her I'm pregnant. He'll be getting oodles of sympathy, no doubt. He'll end up marrying her, in spite of what he said.' Conscious her thoughts were spiralling she wasn't quite able to convince herself. Her stomach churned at the prospect of having got it all wrong. Of no one ever hearing of him again.

'Come. Come. Do come along Miss Glover. The police haven't got all day.'

Harriet barely glanced at her mother and Mrs. Moss as she followed him across the grass towards Mr. Brown and the police officer as they hurried towards them.

'Explain Miss Glover!'

'I'm terribly sorry I got mixed up. I was asked by someone to deliver plants from his greenhouse to Mr. Sanderson here, at the school. That's all I did. Well not quite actually. He told me to take some for myself so I did and of course I gave some away.'

'Can I have the name of the gentleman in question if you don't mind, please?'

'Its Bridgewater young man. Tarquin Bridgewater. It's better Mr. Bridgewater explains this himself. He's away. Due back any time now. Am I correct Miss Glover?'

'That's right Mr. Sanderson.'

The young officer scratched his head. 'We're trained to spot the stuff.'

'Fair enough. You report it. I'll have a word with Brian Andrews just to put him in the picture. Bridgewater's been asking for this for some time, I feel. I suspect you're on security here, young man. I would advise you to do the necessary quickly so as not to be distracted from your duty.'

Harriet watched the young police officer's face. In awe of Mr. Sanderson at the mention of his boss. She recalled the name. Recalled her car sitting with flat tyres near the estate agent's office. Recalled his intention to speak to Brian Andrews then about the spate of it. Recalled how impressed she'd been. Feeling just like this young officer looked.

'Get on with reporting it young man.'

'I think that one's yours Sir.' The policeman walked away.

Mr Sanderson reached for his mobile.

'Right. Yes Mr. Swift. It's all been a misunderstanding. No, don't worry. Just clear the lot from the greenhouse. Tell the policeman we've declared the source. No, no Mr. Swift there's absolutely no question of you going to jail.'

He returned his phone to his back pocket. Looked at Harriet. 'Let's hope we can say the same for Tarquin Bridgewater. Now Miss Glover relieve Mrs. Harrington will you?'

Harriet turned. Rapping Hammer bounding across the grass, coming towards her. Orange and purple chiffon tails flapping about, getting caught between his black leather-clad legs as he started shouting.

'Well if it isn't Mummy-Mamma causin' trouble again. What the fuck are you doin' sellin' roots all over the show?'

'Roots? What are you talking about?'

'The place will be heavin' with them now. You've well set the fox on the `ens.'

'Pardon. I'm not sure what you mean?'

'Put the frighteners up the band. That's what I mean. See them takin' that

265

tent down?'

'That's Tricia's tent. What are they doing that for?'

'Because they're puttin` it inside that one. Inside the one inside. Get it?'

'No. That's the tent Tricia's using to get changed in. She needs that.'

'Don't start flappin` Mummy-Mamma. Chick-Lips owes us one.'

'Owes you what?'

'You thick or somethin`? Owes us a favour.'

'A favour? Why?'

'Come off it Mummy-Mamma. You tell her did you to swing one at my fuckin` poker? We saw you laughin` in there. Gettin` your own back for `avin` your tits on the telly were you? Just for `avin` a couple of friggin` labels stuck on the knobs.'

Harriet coloured. Bright red. She struggled for words as he continued.

'They'll be dopin` the rope in that. Well out of sight. She'll be tellin` a few fortunes in the doorway keepin` everyone out. She won't be lettin` anyone through the back. At least they'll be able to keep the mush mashin`.'

'Oh you're not doing drugs again are you?'

'You're the only one who's doin` drugs round `ere. I've come to tell you to get those frickin` cauliflowers off your table. Oh and get back to it will you. Chick-Lips is waitin` to get dressed up.'

'Well I'm sure she won't be wanting to change out of her designer gown to please you!'

'She's doin` it for fuckin` Venice isn't she! She's puttin` `er jeans back on and I'm lendin` `er this to drape over `er tits.'

He grabbed the ends of his nylon scarf. Waved them at Harriet.

'Oh Tricia would never do that. You haven't been forcing her into whiffing that stuff, I hope?'

'CHICK-LIPS GET IN! SHE'S `ERE. ON `ER WAY BACK!' Harriet jumped as he yelled over the top of her head.

Harriet watched her wave as she shot across to the main tent.

'She's doin` it for Venice ain't she? She's gonna let them lift this up. For a pound a go. Venice is full of them statues. Tits all over the fuckin` place. She's a great gal Chick-Lips. She's really passed the smoke around. Let loose man. We're doin` it together for the sake of the crumblin` gods.'

'Well I hope she doesn't regret it. I hope you haven't talked her into this Wayne Hammer and I certainly hope you're not considering revealing anything of yourself.'

'Mummy-Mamma fraught and frigid. Can't drop your drawers, pegs too rigid!'

'I don't believe I'm hearing this Wayne Hammer. I thought you were supposed to be a changed man?'

'Changed for the better. Changed for the good. Suits Miss Prim and Proper. Nothing else would! Fuck you!'

Harriet was incandescent with rage.

'Not with the little one you've got. I know all about it. I doubt it would fill a thimble!' She stormed back to her table. Looked across to the large tent. Just caught his two fingers jabbing at her before he disappeared inside.

Furious she stood watching, wondering whether or not she ought to go and save Tricia. Saw Simon Barnes and his crew clutching their cameras like haversacks over their shoulders rushing towards the huge tent. Nervous now. In two minds she looked around to see Danny followed by what looked like a mass of running bin-liners swarming towards her.

'We wan` our pictures Miss. We wan` them stuck to `ere.'

He was rubbing his hand up and down his chest.

'No Danny these are to go in those frames, look. They'll look nice in there, especially hanging on the wall.'

'Our mums `ave already been round `ere Miss. They said those pictures won't go in them frames because they're too big and they told us to come and get them if we want. Can we `ave a cake Miss?'

She brushed the flies off again. Nodded her head. Then made a swift decision. Reached for Mr. Brown's roll of sellotape, fished out Danny's portrait from the pile and stuck it across four corners to the bin bag covering his chest. With the children crowded round. One by one. Sticking and watching until the last painting had been done and the last cake had disappeared. People in dribs and drabs moving past and then in gathering crowds. All on their way to Rapping Hammer's tent. Quiet for a minute. The children gone. She stepped back. From nowhere she felt Mr. Sanderson tapping her on the shoulder.

'Not the brightest of ideas Miss Glover!'

Harriet blanked.

'I fear a fight may break out back there. Your class. Parents. Those damned paintings you've stuck to the bin bags the children are wearing. Terrible pictures. Parents are being insulted. Grabbing kids right left and centre demanding apologies. They're hot. Boiling in those things Miss Glover and they won't take them off. Next thing we'll have them all collapsing from heat stroke.'

Harriet stayed quiet. He weighed up the picture frames dumped in a heap alongside the bits and pieces she'd gathered in a hurry.

'A lot of money Miss Glover. Another of your foolish ideas. The school fund can hardly bear that kind of loss.'

His words fast sinking. Drowned by the noise of screaming louts now rushing towards them. Waving their signed prints of Vitruvian Man.

'Come here young man. Let me have a look at that.'

Mr. Sanderson shot a glance at the image on the paper. A man standing naked in a circle. With four arms and four legs spaced apart, stretching to its circumference.

'Yes indeed. I'd expect nothing less. This masterpiece of Leonardo da Vinci vandalised! I see someone has elongated his penis to a long balloon in order for that scum boy to stick his signature in. Disgusting. The man's perverted. I want him and his band out of the place immediately. Goodness only knows what else is going on in there!'

Then a competing bellow of delight.

'Fuck 'im. Look at these. Just made for our pictures, them.'

Mr. Sanderson walked away.

By the time he'd returned Harriet had cleared the table of photo frames.

'Good heavens Miss Glover. Sold the lot! What did they give for them?'

'Five pounds each Mr. Sanderson. Refused to take the change. They told me to put the penny in Tricia's "save Venice" box.'

He scratched his head. Then glanced behind.

'Crikey that's not Belinda coming back is it? Is that Mr. Harrington with her? Yes indeed it is. You'll find her in there Mr. Harrington. I certainly didn't expect you to return Belinda!'

Bob nodded. Without stopping they continued towards the tent.

'I came over to tell you Miss Glover. That guy, the dark-haired swarthy looking chap forever at your house.'

He pointed to Geraldine's dress still sitting on the table.

'As well as returning this he brought us a wedding present. It's in the boot of my car. We'll open it later on our way back from dining with Molly and Percy.'

'Barry, Mr. Sanderson? You don't mean Barry Giordano do you? Where is he? I didn't even know he'd been here. Is he still around? But why would he be giving you this dress? What's it got to do with him?'

'I can't be one hundred per cent certain but I suspect he's an under-cover agent of some description.'

'Oh gosh, that's a shock! No wonder he's been so evasive. But why would he bring a wedding present for us?'

'Because we're getting married Miss Glover. It's as simple as that! Now follow me over will you?'

Chapter 75

Harriet, stunned, didn't want to follow him over. She watched him stride towards the tent. Couldn't believe he'd just said that. Couldn't believe Barry had found his way to the school fete. Left a wedding present. Gone without even looking for her. She needed to see him. Needed to explain. All she needed was the time he'd first promised her. She wondered if Mr. Sanderson was right. Why else would he have delivered the dress? It had come back from forensics. How else would he have got hold of it if he wasn't in the thick of it?

She slung her bag over her shoulder. Reluctant. Waited for Mr. Sanderson to disappear then sauntered over. Noticed Tricia's designer dress, hat and shades strewn on the grass at the opening of the huge tent. It was noisy in there. Very noisy. Rapping Hammer and the Bards banging it out for all they were worth. She changed her mind. Picked everything up. Didn't want to see Rapping Hammer after that. Didn't want to see Tricia making a fool of herself. Walked back to her table. Engrossed in Mr. Sanderson's words. Head down she hardly noticed someone standing there. Waiting to be served. A short guy, stocky. A rough brown beard curling its way to the arms of his dark glasses. Wearing a panama hat, not dissimilar to the one on her head. Just like the one she was carrying.

He watched her place the dress, hat and shades on the table. Then he picked up the couple of paperbacks and one of Mark's ties.

'How much?' His accent different. Not one she could recognise. He was deliberating. She felt vulnerable, uneasy. Needed to do something. Decided to stack the six, empty tin cake trays into one. Hot now from sitting in the sun. She slid them across, propping them up to rest her hands on the top edge. She watched him. He put the books down. Picked up the shades.

'How much?'

'Oh terribly sorry those are not for sale. Belong to my friend. Let's just move them along.' She put them with the hat to one side.

'This then?'

She started to feel uncomfortable. Suddenly felt threatened. There was something strangely familiar about this man. Couldn't put her finger on it. Wanted to get rid of him. He put the dress down. Went back to the hat and shades.

'How much?'

Decided Tricia wouldn't mind. She'd give her hers. The place was deserted. The noise was deafening. She wished she'd carried on to the tent where everyone was.

'Just a pound. You can have them both for a pound.'

He reached in his pocket. Kept his head down. Then her legs almost went from under. Sudden realisation. He was one of the PM's heavies.

She passed the hat and shades over then dropped the pound coin to grab her six baking tins as he snatched at the dress. Then with a full force wham she hit him on the head. Sent him reeling to the ground, bashing him again and again, then ran as fast as her legs would take her straight into Mr. Sanderson's arms.

She turned to see him stagger. His ungainly body falling back as an officer struggled him into handcuffs before three or four of them carried him away.

'Miss Glover I thought you were in there. I told you to follow me. Crass stupidity to my mind. You could well have been hurt!'

'It's you they should be arrestin` Miss Glover. I saw you `it `im over the `ead with those cake tins.'

Harriet jumped to Mr. Brown shouting into her ear.

'There Mr. Sanderson. What did I tell you about `er? She's a menace. Can't keep `er `ands or `er feet to `erself. I'm goin` over to tell them exactly what you did.'

'No no Mr. Brown. You've got it quite wrong. They've been here on the look out most of the day. I think they felt they were on a bit of a red herring. I'm loathe to praise you, but in the event well done Miss Glover! I think on this occasion your instincts have served you well.'

Glowering, Mr. Brown pushed his way past, stomping off in disgust.

Harriet looked up at Mr. Sanderson. Managed a wobbly smile. Her legs shaking.

'I didn't recognise him at first. But then it clicked. One of the two bodyguards. Did you say they'd caught them both?'

'I believe so. I've been furnished only with the briefest of detail. It was quite incidental Miss Glover. As I thought, the police weren't here looking for Bridgewater's rubbish. No, they were acting on intelligence. They knew them still to be in the area and obviously this place this afternoon was somewhere they needed to target.'

'But it could have been dangerous Mr. Sanderson.'

'Precisely Miss Glover. As soon as they were spotted the crowds were gently shifted towards the tents here. You weren't supposed to be out here all on your own. Very foolish Miss Glover. For all we know they could have been armed. But it was essential they were left to their own intentions without them suspecting the net was closing in.'

They reached her table. A police officer walking towards them.

'Clean. It couldn't have been cleaner. They've gone now. Away! We'll all sleep better in our beds tonight.'

'Gosh I can't believe it. Was he alright? I didn't stop to think. There was only me and him about and I got very scared.'

'You made the arrest a lot easier Miss, though I'm not recommending you attempt to do our job again. I wouldn't worry. It doesn't seem like he's going to be in a position to take you through the courts for assault. There's got to be too much on him. Of course we don't get filled in with the detail. Just follow instructions. Oh and I'll take this one too if you don't mind.'

He lifted the panama hat from Harriet's head.

'And the shades. Sorry Miss, forensics will be taking a look at these. It could be all the evidence they're looking for.'

They watched him walk off.

'Golly Mr. Sanderson. When you think of the mayhem there could have been. People might have been killed.'

'Including you Miss Glover. You're probably right. They would be armed without doubt. Of course they'd be wanting to claw back the evidence with minimal intrusion. I expect they would only have used firearms as a last resort.'

'But how did they know we were going to be here? How did they know Tricia's gown would be here?'

'They obviously read the paper in exactly the same way as we did.'

'Gosh they've been close to home.'

'Intelligence pointed to that Miss Glover. Hence my insistence you were both constantly escorted.'

'But how would they have escaped?'

'Did you not see the helicopter flying low and disappearing somewhere behind there?'

'No I can't say I did Mr. Sanderson. There was so much noise coming from over there, just like it is now. I wouldn't have heard it.'

'Anyhow they surrounded it. Picked another of them up I believe in the process. But to answer your question they'd have probably backed their way out guns blazing. Could even have taken a hostage. It could well have been you Miss Glover.'

'Oh I can't bear to think of it!'

'I'd try not to now it's all over. Fortunately we're on our way to Molly and Percy's this evening. Try to relax and look forward to the evening. Ha! Simon Barnes in there with his crew. Missed the lot! Indeed I suppose we should be grateful to Mrs. Harrington for arranging the event and even that Hammer boy for waking the dead! No it's worked out extremely well Miss Glover. No one hurt. The PM will be most relieved. No doubt I'll get to know all the details.'

He turned back towards the tents.

'Ah people are starting to drift out. There's nothing like a topless young girl to draw the crowds. Or so I've heard. Someone in there decided to make a spectacle of themselves. I understand. Probably one of these hyped-up orange-haired, tattooed jezebel's been strutting around anyway in next to nothing all day.'

Harriet looked down. Took a deep breath. So relieved he hadn't seen Tricia. Then in the doorway of the main tent. Tricia in her jeans, orange and purple chiffon tails falling from under her arms folded across her chest.

'`ARRIET. MY TOP'S BEEN ROLLED UP IN ALL THAT FENCIN` AND MY DESIGNER GOWN'S GONE. `AVE YOU GOT SOMETHIN` FOR ME TO PUT ON?!'

'Good gracious me Miss Glover, I might have known. Get this to her this minute!'

He pushed Geraldine's dress into her hands and as if next in a relay race she shot between the crowds to get it to Tricia.

'Where's my designer dress gone 'arriet? Ah thanks! It'll do. I'll be with you in a tick.'

Harriet hurried back to Mr. Sanderson.

'Last time it was you, as I recall. Breasts filling the screen.'

'I beg your pardon Mr. Sanderson but I was certainly not naked!'

'Quite, quite Miss Glover. Your nipples never the less most crudely exposed. Simon Barnes having a field day, as now. Still what Mrs. Harrington chooses to do in her own time is totally her business. Fortunately she hadn't tried to link the occasion to ours in her Holly Berry feature. I'm thankful for small mercies Miss Glover.'

He marched off. Harriet still shaking from the experience looked across to see Geraldine's dress rushing towards her, Tricia lost somewhere inside.

''arriet I've just spotted Bob with Belinda Oxfordshire in there! Oh I do 'ope 'e didn't see me 'arriet. I'm really enjoyin' the moral 'igh ground at the moment. But 'er 'arriet. What's 'e doin' with 'er? It's supposed to be all over between them. Anyway I'm surprised she came back after that. I think I'll just be lookin' out for a bit more 'arriet. Get both of them this time! Ooh I see you've nearly cleared your table 'arriet. It was me who told them to 'ave a look at your frames. I was surprised Rappin' 'ammer drew a big one though to write 'is signature in. Especially after 'im startin' to come to terms with 'is own. 'e was supposed to be makin' men feel better, wasn't 'e 'arriet? It looks like somethin''s 'appened to upset 'im.'

'Well you did clout him one Tricia.'

'Oh I know 'arriet. That's what made me go topless. I was so frightened of 'im refusin' to 'elp my save Venice cause I felt I 'ad to offer. Although I did 'ave it in mind all along. I'd 'ad plenty of practice wearin' those very low tops.'

'It was probably me as well Tricia. When he came over to get me back to the table. He was just so unbelievably rude. I ended up telling him his was so small it wouldn't fill a thimble.'

'Oh dear 'arriet. I do 'ope you 'aven't undone all the good work of 'is therapist. I thought 'e was in a bad mood when 'e started singin' the loudest most 'orrible songs 'e could think of. 'e never looked more like that evil picture of 'im on our Adam's wall.'

'Don't worry Tricia. It won't make any difference. The yobs that bought the frames can't wait to get to Venice to see him. You'll make a fortune for your "save Venice" fund. He's donating ten pounds for each one there as long as they put something in your tin. Anyway that's what they said.'

'Oh yes 'e did tell me that. 'e's always wanted to do an open air concert in Saint Mark's Square. No, you're right. 'e'll get over it 'arriet.' Tricia's shoulders started shaking. 'Ooh 'arriet I wish I'd 'ave been there to 'ear you both.'

'He's revolting Trica. I hope he didn't lead you astray in there.'

'Oh no 'arriet. It's like I just said. I've been wearin' plungin' necklines at the sailin` club. Remember I told you the lower they were, the more money went in the tin? Well I could `ardly let an opportunity like that go, could I `arriet? I did ask `im for `is scarf though but it was `is idea to let them lift it for more money. Anyway it ended up on the floor. I didn't mind at all `arriet. I felt like one of those statues in Venice. Proud to be doin` it to save them. Anyway it's no worse than bein` a Page 3 girl is it `arriet? I wouldn't `ave taken my jeans off though.'

'You might be a Page 3 girl yet Tricia. Simon Barnes and his crew were in there.'

'Oh they weren't were they `arriet? I didn't see them. I'd `ave seen them if they'd been filmin` me.'

'Don't bank on it Tricia. Gosh I hope he didn't. I had to tell you though. I couldn't not let you know he was in there.'

'No, I know `arriet and thanks. Anyway I don't know where my things are. `ave you seen my dress? We `aven't got our `ats either `arriet, or our shades. Where `ave they gone?'

'Off to wherever Tricia.'

'What do you mean `arriet?'

'He was here Tricia. Standing just here!'

'Who was `arriet? Oh you `aven't gone and sold them `arriet? `ow much did you get for them?'

'No Tricia. It was him. One of the heavies, the bodyguards. Grown a beard, kept his head down under his hat, and sunglasses. There was just something about him. He wanted to buy them. I got scared. I took a pound off him and hit him on the head with my cake tins!'

Tricia started off. Her shoulders going again.

'It wasn't funny Tricia. I've still got wobbly legs. The police swooped in. Took all the stuff with them.'

'Oh `arriet you wasn't lettin` `im `ave my dress as well and only chargin` `im a pound?'

'No he snatched that Tricia. That's when I hit him on the head!'

'Oh don't set me off again `arriet. What about the other one, did they get `im as well?'

'It looks like it Tricia and the one from the helicopter.'

'Where was that then?'

'According to Mr. Sanderson in the field the other side of you.'

'Gosh `arriet I never `eard anythin`. We could all `ave been shot. Did they `ave guns?'

'Mr. Sanderson seems to think so.'

'Oh `arriet I'm so glad you're alright. You weren't `ere on your own with `im were you?'

'Too right Tricia. I was on my way to the tent but changed my mind about going in. I picked up your stuff off the grass by the entrance and came back here.'

'Oh I wish you'd come in `arriet but `ow did my stuff get there? Oh I think I know. One of those Ironing Boards thought `e'd be clever. They were all doped again in there. In my tent in the corner. It's a good job the police `ad better things to do.'

'Certainly was Mrs. Harrington.'

'Ooh you made me jump then Mr. Sanderson. I didn't see you come up behind me like that. Oh and there's Bob with `er. Just look at that. Got the cheek to be comin` over `ere.'

'Oh no, Mummy and Violet Moss back again.' Harriet grabbed the scissors. Ducked under the table. Couldn't bear to see them again. Unrolled the bin bags at her knees on the grass. Rolled off the top one. Cut the arms and head holes far too big. Slipped it on anyway. Draped the rest of them across and over her head.

'Oh Sir Joris, Harriet was here just a second ago. Where is she now? She couldn't have vanished into thin air.' From under the table Harriet cringed. Irritated. Thought. 'Stop calling him Sir Joris, Mummy.'

She could hear Geraldine and James back again. Mr. Sanderson talking to them. Then her mother's voice.

'There, there Geraldine. Look, doesn't Harriet's friend look a picture in your dress?'

She turned to Tricia.

'I hope she didn't charge you too much for it dear. Not that it was a cheap dress.'

She turned to Geraldine.

'You don't buy cheap dresses do you Geraldine? No it's a high class dress that's just what this girl needs to lift her social standing.'

She turned. Tricia grabbed the stack of tin trays. 'Oh don't hit me on the head with those dear, I wasn't trying to be offensive.'

'Shut up Mummy. Just shut up!' Harriet was so glad to be out of it. Unable to contain herself Tricia waited her moment. Bob turned his back. Swiftly she swung them full force aiming for his head.

'Ow! My nose. You've just hit me on my nose! Bloody hell Tricia!'

'Serves you right for turning round. Oh don't worry Bob. I `aven't finished yet!'

'Put those trays down this minute Mrs. Harrington before you do something you might regret.'

'Oh I know I won't regret this Mr. Sanderson. `scuse me.'

'Ow my arse! Joris she's just clouted my arse. Get those baking tins off her will you?'

'That's for pinchin` my `usband back again!'

'I haven't pinched him back again. I met you coming in didn't I Bob? You tell her why you're here. Go on.'

'Nice ploy Tricia. Trying to get me arrested. Planting that lot in the front garden. They've been in the loft. Convinced there was a cannabis farm up there. Did I know they were in the front? Thought someone was trying to blow my cover. I've had a swine of an afternoon thanks to you.'

'Oh I wouldn't blame this sweet young lady! Your dear wife...'

'Shut up Mummy! Just shut up!' Harriet could see her legs from under the table. Tempted to brush them with the nettles sitting alongside her.

'No! We've had exactly the same. Had the police round investigating our hanging basket. The same for your flower tub in the front wasn't it Violet? Oh no we've all had a taste of the long arm of the law today, thanks to Harriet. Where is she? I wouldn't be in the least surprised if she'd had the police round to you, either Sir Joris. That poor man of yours Mr. Swift. Heaven help him after her throwing all those bulbs on your driveway at Christmas.'

'Yes, I slipped on those.' Belinda's voice now.

'Yes poor dear. I know you did. And can you still believe this charming man still wants to marry her. Waiting for her to make the date indeed!'

It was too much. She tore off a bin liner. Wrapped it round the nettles and broke them off.

'Just shut up Mummy will you?' she thrust her arm forward waving it straight at her legs.

'Ouch. I've been stung!'

'Oh dear, Violet. It must be a horsefly,' came her mother's voice. 'Here let me look.' Instinctively Harriet swept the nettle back.

'Ow! It's got me now!' Belinda Oxfordshire wailing. 'Everyone but Mummy,' Harriet thought. More voices.

'Cool man rock!' Rapping Hammer

'Oh good afternoon young man. Successful concert?' Mr. Sanderson now.

'It was until frosty kecks put her oar in.'

'I beg your pardon young man. To whom are you referring in that disrespectful manner?'

'Mummy-Mamma! Pulls `er drawers up. Never takes them down. Ties them with a rope. `ardest fuck in town!'

Harriet could see his legs pushing in just at the side of the table. Open toed sandals! She brushed the nettles against his feet.

'What the fuck!'

'I do beg your parden young man. I suggest you watch your language. There are ladies here should you not have noticed.'

Harriet retreated as Rapping Hammer bent down to rub his feet. His backside steering towards her. The black leather pulling away at the base of his spine as he rubbed away.

'A good place for this,' Harriet decided. Then the nettle. Straight in. Yowling he shot up. Banged himself on the table then flew back to his tent.

'It looks like `e `ad somethin` like a plant wavin` from `is bum,' Tricia observed.

'I expect it was growing by the table leg Patricia. He's caught it in his belt as he's bent down. And he's been unfortunate enough for it to have popped in. We're better rid of him. He needs poetry lessons I'm afraid. The language of today. Quite shocking. Goodness knows who Mummy-Mamma is? Probably someone trying to befriend him. A fan. An older fan looking for a toy-boy and ended up with cold feet. You know we older ladies ought to think very carefully before we mix outside of our generation.'

'Quite Mrs. Glover. I think Mr. Brown's trying to move every one along if you wouldn't mind. Oh and Mrs. Harrington, if he thinks he's on for next year's Fastnet race tell him to forget it will you? He'll be needing to spend the money getting that fence reinstated.'

'I think I'll find out what went down 'is backside first Mr. Sanderson. 'e might need a teeny weeny bit of sympathy. I dropped my 'olly down there last Christmas don't forget. 'e's not 'avin' a good time with the little bit 'e's got round the front just at the moment and now 'e'll be thinkin' there's somethin' out to get 'is bum! 'e is supposed to be goin' to Italy tomorrow. 'e is doin' a big concert in Saint Mark's Square to 'elp save Venice you know. 'e 'as gone quite cultural since 'is therapy. 'e will be on the road tomorrow. On 'is way to San Marco.'

'Let's hope he stays there Mrs. Harrington. Let's hope San Marco is the end of the road for all our sakes.'

Chapter 76

'Good luck 'arriet 'avin' dinner with 'im tonight. I'll look forward to 'earin' all about it.'

'Wish I didn't have to go Tricia. Still no sign of Mark. Well his car at least. Look, thanks for the lift, I'll give you a call tomorrow. I hope everything's alright with you and Bob after whamming him one like that. I heard the clang.'

'Oh 'e won't be 'ome tonight 'arriet. 'e went off with 'er didn't 'e? I'm goin' to lock 'im out. I've 'ad enough for one day.'

Harriet smiled, waved. Relieved to be able to walk up the drive to the front door knowing those men had been caught.

'Hi Pepper. Hang on. Just let me get the key in the door. That's better. Ah, a couple of messages. It might be Mark. Let's play them.'

'Bryce Rae Roberts here. Please call the office at your earliest convenience.'

'No Pepper. He can just sod off. I've had enough of Violet Moss for one day.'

She moved on to the next.

'Harriet it's Mummy. Violet and I looked everywhere for you on the way out and you were not to be seen. I do hope you haven't done one of your disappearing acts again. You know I tried very hard to like that common friend Patricia you insist on going round with Harriet. I'm finding it difficult. What she does to her husband, poor man is her own affair. I don't think dear Belinda would for one minute have stolen him from her. Such a nice girl. Not his type at all. I think it was most uncalled for that she should have hit her on the bottom with those cake tins. She was obviously badly jolted. You know Harriet.......'

'Shall we just delete this now Pepper? I've had enough of Mummy too, for today.'

Her finger on the button. Suddenly she stopped. For some reason decided to let it run.

'.....Olivia and I were having afternoon tea together last week and she told me something Joris had spoken of with regard to Belinda. Of course I'm supposed to be keeping it confidential and I expect you to do the same but I think you should know for the next time you and your common friend are of a mind to upset her. She's a young woman Harriet and she can't have children. Can't have any of her own that is.'

Harriet took a deep breath, wondered what Mr. Sanderson had managed to do to her.

'No Harriet, apparently that poor girl suffered some kind of congenital deformity. Went through terrible surgery which meant she had to have a hysterectomy at a very early age. At the age of twenty-one. She was only twenty-one, I ask you? Try to be kind to her Harriet. She's had such a lot to put up with one way or the other. Do you know Harriet I could see it in her eyes. She's still in love with Joris. I do think you should drop that common girl for good and settle on a date for your wedding. You'll lose him. He won't be able to resist going back to her. You mark my words Harriet.'

What a revelation. Harriet was so glad she hadn't wiped the message off.

'So it had all been lies,' she thought. 'She's been telling lies about him. Telling Mark lies in the hope they'd get back to me. Banking on me breaking it all off.'

She filled the kettle. Decided she needed a cup of tea. Went upstairs to find the blue two-piece she'd worn for Clarissa's wedding. Pulled out her blue lace panties and white lace bra from the drawer. Knew *his* ring was there somewhere at the back. She brought out Mark's diamond engagement ring with his note. Sat on the bed. Read it again. Blinked hard on the tears watering her eyes, his words running into magnified distortions. Hard to read. Wished she hadn't told him. Couldn't believe she'd blurted it out like that. The thought setting every nerve in her stomach on edge. She wondered what had happened to him. Lifted the phone. His mobile. Switched off. Tried Millington. No answer. Bit her lip. Hoped he hadn't disappeared. Vanished. Like people sometimes do. Folded the note back into four. Slipped the diamond ring into the small square of space inside the paper. Screwed it hard to the inside of her hand and placed it back in the drawer. Brought out Mr. Sanderson's ring. Slipped it on and off her finger. First the right hand, then the left. Couldn't decide what to do. Didn't know whether to wear it at all. Then decided she'd better. Didn't want to embarrass Molly and Percy. After all she'd pretty much agreed to go along with the charade. It was the least she could do now, after that. After believing all those lies about him.

She looked at her watch. Mr. Sanderson was picking her up at six thirty. She had less than an hour. The kettle had long since clicked itself off. Her mind everywhere. Couldn't even focus on making tea. She didn't bother. Went to the bathroom. Pulled her skimpy top off over her head. Slipped her jeans and pants off together. Undid her bra. Stepped in the shower. Let the tepid water seep into her hair. Roll down her face. Fall from her shoulders to her breasts all the way down her legs to her feet. She looked down to the drop glistening, resting in her naval. Spread her hand below and across. Thought about him. Closed her eyes. Back on the sand. The start of their baby. His baby growing. The water showering her body. Each droplet his fingertips. Touching, caressing every inch of her body. Tonight he would see her like this. Tonight he would take her like this. Tonight she would set the date for her wedding. Just as long as she knew Mark was OK.

Chapter 77

'You're looking very attractive this evening Harriet, especially in view of the day you've had.' He held the car door open for her.

'Thank you Mr. Sanderson. You're wearing your sea-green shirt again. It looks nice with that aran sweater.'

She watched him stride round the front of the car to his side. Thought. 'What a stupid thing to say. Of course he knows he's wearing it!' She could feel herself going pink already. Nervously twisted the ring around the base of her finger. Didn't look across as he sat down closing the door.

'We've had a bit of a day of it today Harriet.' He looked across. A brief smile but his eyes just that fraction behind.

'Certainly have Mr. Sanderson. The relief I feel now they've all been caught is unbelievable. I do want to thank you for your concern. The lifts. And of course having a word with the PM. Getting us off the hook. Well you know what I'm trying to say. Tricia and I could have ended up being arrested.'

Silent she watched his hand firm on the gear lever. Forward. A quick reverse up the slope. Then away. In his car again. In this top-of-the-range silver Mercedes. Gliding. Just gliding along. Sitting next to this gorgeous, gorgeous man. She was ready to marry him now. No longer caught in the shock of the wedding day. The ache of desire. The need for him forcing her hand to her lap trying to quell the exotic mix of embarrassed excitement as she waited for him to speak.

'Well there'll be ends to tie off still, but as far as you two are concerned I understand it's the end of this particular road for you both.'

'San Marco the end of the road Mr. Sanderson. When Barry first said that I had no idea how significant those words would turn out to be.'

'Quite Harriet. It's not an episode I'm particularly interested in having regurgitated. You know you left me in a complete state of discomposure. Embarrassing to say the least. Having to explain your absence and the change of plans. Not to mention the worry of it all. The only relief came in the knowledge that both you and Mrs. Harrington had disappeared together.'

'Oh I know Mr. Sanderson and I'm most terribly sorry. I really am.'

'Well I'm a doctor of course. I'm not without a certain understanding of stress and the sometimes bizarre reactions associated with it. Nevertheless you've continued to lead me more than a bit of a dance Harriet. Certainly as far as this baby's concerned.'

Harriet went quiet. She'd managed to put all that from her mind. Didn't want to talk about it. Didn't want anything in the world to stop him taking every shred of clothing from her tonight.

'In fact, to be perfectly honest Harriet, I wouldn't know whether you are pregnant or not!'

'But you still want to marry me Mr. Sanderson? I think that's what you said this afternoon.'

It slipped out. Hadn't planned on saying that at all. Held her breath. Couldn't bear the thought of him having changed his mind.

'I see you're wearing the ring again. Does this mean you are now ready Harriet?'

About to speak. His mobile instantly prioritising his attention. He pulled into the side.

'Ah Molly. We didn't notice you at the fete this afternoon. Everything's well with you we hope?'

Harriet watched him. The hint of dimples elongating as he spoke and smiled. Thick layers of blonde hair brushing against the phone as he moved in his seat.

'Oh we're terribly sorry to hear that Molly. Of course we understand. We hope Percy's soon feeling better. Give him our best and we'll see you both soon.'

'I'm afraid they've had a bit of an afternoon of it. Percy's got a violent migraine. Anyhow she's had to cancel it.'

'Oh dear. I'm very sorry to hear that Mr. Sanderson. I wonder what brought that on?'

'It seems Swift passed them a few plants Harriet. I'm surprised he didn't recognise the damned things when he saw them but I suppose that's what comes of focussing entirely on the propagation of tomatoes.'

'You mean…?'

'Yes I do, unfortunately. They searched the place top and bottom. Were there all afternoon. Poor Molly and Percy. Convinced they were going to be arrested. Anyhow it's all off, for the moment at least. We're on our way Harriet. We've got the house to ourselves tonight. We might just as well spend the evening at Lower Tideside.'

Harriet sank into her seat. She wished Percy well but couldn't have heard better news.

She watched him swerve the steering wheel to the right as the lights changed to green outside Starboard Marine North West. She watched him. His black denims stretched tight across the top of his legs to the side seams. She knew the strength in them. She knew the strength in his arms. Burnt brown by the sun seizing the light from the water he'd sailed. Along the country roads now. A warm summer evening. Climbing. She could see the river now, opening to the sea. The hills running down. The sky blue, paling to shed just a hint of mist over the still water. She wanted this man. She needed this man. He could take her any way he liked. Almost there. Just waiting to hear the crunch of gravel under the wheels of his car.

'Right that's it Harriet. In we go.'

He drove through. Stopped just short of the large porch. Opened the door to let her out. Waited. Then walked slightly behind him to the large porch and beautiful old door. In. They were in. She stood on the gleaming parquet. Looking at the grand fireplace central to the staircases. Her eyes taking her up to the banisters disappearing behind the chimney breast. She could feel him next to her. She looked down to the ivory flokati rug set against the hearth in front of her.

'Shall we dial something in Harriet, or would you prefer to eat later?'

'Later if that's alright with you Mr. Sanderson.'

She felt herself being drawn into his arms. Close against his chest now. His lips hard against hers. Laying her down. Gently brushing her hair from her face. Slipping her from her jacket. Her dress. The long zip undone to the very end. Easing her out. She arched her back. Wriggled the rest of it away. She lay, arms relaxed, outward at her sides. Felt the deep pile wool from the rug against her bare skin. He pulled back. Only her bra and blue lace panties remaining. Looking at her. Just looking at her.

'My beautiful, beautiful Harriet.'

'I'm yours Mr. Sanderson. All yours now. Whichever way you like.'

She felt his hand slip the strap away from her shoulder. Ease away the white lace cup from her breast. Held the fullness, soft to his hand. Could feel his lips resting gently against her nipple.

'The field of flowers Harriet. I'm in the field of flowers. Only two buds in the field of flowers now Harriet and they're both mine.'

Her head spinning she could barely handle the waves of desire surging through her body. Weakening to the full flood opening her mind, her senses, every part of her for him. She whispered.

'Now Mr. Sanderson. Take me now. Any way you like.'

'You still want me Harriet. You still need me.'

'I do. I do.' She reached down, touched at her panties. Wanted to pull them away. Felt his hand firmly against hers.

'No Harriet!'

'Not the field of flowers all over again Mr. Sanderson. That time you didn't want to get me pregnant.'

'And this time I fear you might be pregnant Harriet. I'm taking no chances.'

'But I'm not pregnant Mr. Sanderson. Honestly I'm not!'

'I'm not too sure about that Harriet.'

Chapter 78

'Well now, we've had a good evening Harriet. I must say you took me rather by surprise. I thought we would at least have made it into the lounge.'

She covered her face with her hands. Knew she was blushing.

'It's just the way it happened Mr. Sanderson after you held me close. I hope I didn't make you cross.'

He smiled her that smile. Opened her again to the need for him.

'There's nothing wrong with making love properly even when you are pregnant Mr. Sanderson. You should know that. You're a doctor.'

'Yes but you've already indicated blood loss Harriet. Or have you forgotten you told me that? You haven't been lying to me again, have you?'

'No.' She knew her face had just turned crimson. Didn't quite know how to get out of the lies she'd been telling. Suddenly felt a bit cross with him for leading her on. Like that.

He put his arm around her.

'It wasn't easy for me either you know Harriet. Best thing we can do is get this thing settled once and for all. I don't even think you know what's properly going on yourself.'

He kissed her forehead.

'The wedding date. Just let me make some coffee and I'll bring the diary in.'

Harriet sat back on the sofa. Couldn't believe this is where she'd been sitting at Christmas alongside his mother. Her mother at the other end. Newly engaged to Mark. She thought about him. Felt uncomfortable. Wanted to know he was safe.

'Right Harriet. Just let me put these down. Oh, by the way, certain information has come to light.'

'Barry Giordano. So he *is* working for MI5 then?'

'Highly unlikely Harriet. Not exactly their area of operation. No, not him, he's obviously an undercover agent. Anyhow the source is irrelevant. However, it would seem Mrs. Harrington was right after all. Those two criminals would certainly have panicked at losing their panama hats. That's why they returned to the boat.'

'But why, Mr. Sanderson?'

'A double lining in each. One filled with notes...'

'What kind of notes?'

'The kind that get spent Harriet. The other was full of lists. Contacts, rogue traders. Corruption far wider than anyone could possibly have imagined.'

'Golly that's scary. Us getting embroiled in all that.'

'Well Harriet, there's certainly a lesson to be learned from all of this.'

'What about the market trader selling the designer dresses. What happened to him?'

'Selling fakes you mean. Well, it would appear he had the authorities run ragged. A very devious character indeed. They've got all the evidence they need now to nail him.'

'Oh gosh, no wonder he went wild when Tricia accidentally ran off with that dress.'

'Quite Harriet. Quite. Apparently he was managing to sell the fake goods by constantly switching dress racks.'

'And what about the boatman Mr. Sanderson? He said he hurt his back when he fell against the boats into the water; not that we noticed. He was wanting compensation. What happened about that?'

'I paid him off Harriet. That was one way I could be of help.'

'Oh golly. I can't thank you enough Mr. Sanderson. Wait until I tell Tricia. That was so very good of you. Particularly given the circumstances.'

'Yes, the circumstances Harriet. I trust you're fully aware of all you've put me through?'

'Yes, and I'm just so, so sorry. Everything got out of hand. Tricia and I just needed some space. We had no idea what we were getting ourselves into. We just wanted the whole affair resolved.'

'Yes Harriet, I would say it pretty much is. Now we've an affair of our own to resolve, wouldn't you say? Speaking of which, I'll just nip to the car, get our first wedding present out of the boot.'

She'd forgotten all about it. Wondered what it could be. Wondered what Barry was playing at.

It was huge. She watched Mr. Sanderson lifting it through with both hands.

'Looks like a picture of some description. I wonder if he's done it especially for us? I recall someone telling me he's a bit of an artist. Might just as well unwrap it Harriet. Then we can get our thanks out right away.'

She put her hand across her mouth as he pulled the paper back to lift the whole thing clear.

'Good Gracious! What's this? *Harriet* is this you? Is this *you* draped across the steps of Saint Mark's Square, legs apart, utterly naked and looking distinctly pregnant. Is that what you got up to in Venice when you were supposed to be sitting alongside me hearing the banns read in church? I'm appalled Harriet. Absolutely appalled! Here what does this say along the bottom? The title. "San Marco the End of the Road". Well he's got that right Harriet. He most certainly has. This is the last straw. I'm taking you straight home this minute!'

Chapter 79

Harriet woke the next morning, her pillow damp from the tears getting in the way of her sleep. Still no Mark. She felt sick to the core with worry. At the same time furious with Barry. Sunday. The only good thing about the day was it started the summer holidays. She wouldn't be having to see Mr. Sanderson for six weeks. Oh apart from the school camping trip. She decided she's certainly get herself out of that one.

She pushed the cat off the bed to go down to make a cup of tea. Then rushed upstairs to answer the phone. Her mind dazed. She never even thought to take the call in the hall.

'Hi Tricia. Survived the night with Bob alright?'

'Oh no `arriet `e didn't come `ome. I told you `e wouldn't. No `arriet I'm phonin` to ask a really big favour.'

'If I can Tricia. What is it?'

'`arriet you wouldn't come to Venice with me, would you? Rappin` `ammer's concert in Saint Mark's Square. `e's goin` over today and `e's asked if I'll be there for `is first show. I could `ardly say "No" `arriet but I'm not very keen to go on my own.'

'When are you thinking of going Tricia?'

'Today `arriet. We'll only be away for two nights. I'll be takin` a couple of days `olidays. I'll tell `im when we get back. We'll be flyin` `ome on Tuesday.'

'Gosh Tricia. That's a bit short notice.'

'Same as last time `arriet, remember?'

'I do. And I was desperate. You've certainly been a good friend to me. OK Tricia. Just for you.'

'Oh thanks `arriet. I've already booked the flights and we'll be stayin` in that very posh `otel.'

'Oh you mean the one we saw when we turned left into the Grand Canal just before we got to the Rialto Bridge?'

'No `arriet. I found it. The one Barry told us about. The romantic one that looks right over the sea. I've got us a double room each. You never know who we might meet `arriet.'

'Gosh Tricia. I bet that cost a fortune.'

'No it's alright `arriet. I've paid for it out of the fund. We can `ardly save Venice from `ere can we? It's all part of the good cause. Oh and we'll be able to buy some masks this time `arriet. We can be lookin` all mysterious while we're passin` the tin round. Can you pick me up in an `our `arriet? You won't need to pack much.'

'Golly Tricia. I'll do my best.'

'No sign of Mark yet Pepper. Oh gosh, I'm not sure I should be doing this. I hope he's alright. I'll leave him a note Pepper. Tell him where I am this time. It's just a couple of days. I can't really let Tricia down. Oh gosh Pepper. How did I ever manage to dig the three men in my life into this whopping big hole I've made? And a baby on the way. No father for my baby. Oh Pepper it looks like it's just you, me and him. Or her of course. She stopped to count. 'We'll know around the 12ᵗʰ March. We'll manage together. The three of us. Plenty of single parents do. I'm off now. San Marco the end of the road, Pepper. I might just as well be there.'

Chapter 80

Harriet looked at her watch as she backed off the drive. Barring any hold-ups she should just make it in time. Moved to drive forward. Could hardly believe her eyes. A black Lambourghini pulling hard over, screeching to a halt. Barry. Head on. He stopped. They lowered their windows.

'Thanks a bunch Barry!'

'It did the trick then?'

'What else would you expect? The least you can do is put him straight.'

'Now why would I want to do that Harriet? I'm saving you from yourself. One day you'll thank me. Sanderson's just not your kind of guy.'

'Don't you think that's for me to decide Barry? Anyway you're chancing it. Why are you here?'

'Coming with me Harriet? There's nowhere else for you now.'

'No! Wherever it is I most certainly am not!'

'Come on Harriet. Don't tell me I've got to take Andy. Don't make me share a double bed with him. The flights are booked. Just a couple of nights at The Cielo Misterioso. The one that looks straight over the lagoon to the Adriatic sea. Remember I told you about it? I've booked the room Harriet. You've got to come.'

'OH NO I HAVE NOT. Not after what you did Barry Giordano. Sorry but NO. San Marco the end of the road for you!'

She watched him speed away. Turned the car into the drive. Felt the cat brushing against her legs as she opened the front door to let herself in. Picked up the phone.

'Sorry Tricia. I just can't do it. Not after last night.'

'Oh `arriet, what do you mean, "after last night"?'

'It's a long story Tricia, there isn't time. Look I'll drive you to the airport. I'll explain on the way. I'm just so sorry to have to let you down. It's Barry Giordano Tricia. He's turned out to be despicable. Revolting. It turns my stomach just to mention his name. I'll explain but just to say he's booked a double room in the very same hotel. He wanted me to go with him, now. Oh just how much has he got to be joking?'

'Oh is `e waitin` there for you `arriet?'

'No Tricia. I've just sent him packing.'

'Oh I see `arriet. Just a minute. Oh `arriet Bob's just come in. `ang on a minute.'

Harriet could hear his voice. Gathered he'd spotted the suitcase. Now shouting. Unsure, she didn't like the feeling of eavesdropping. 'YOU BLOODY GO THERE AGAIN AND THAT'S THE LAST YOU'LL EVER SEE OF ME AND THE KIDS.'

'Oh `arriet. Don't bother comin` for me. I can't leave `im like this. Rappin` `ammer will just `ave to get on with savin` Venice for me this time. I'M

COMIN` BOB! See you `arriet.'

Harriet replaced the receiver. Flopped onto the sofa. Beckoned the cat to her lap.

'You're the only one who hasn't crashed into this big hole of mine Pepper. Come on up you stupid cat. I need you now.'

For a moment, all vision lost to a ball of black fur and a long curling tail. The cat pressed its head hard against her hand, pausing only to scramble its tiny pink tongue against her cheek. She felt the tears well. With no will left she allowed them to roll then stream in torrents down her cheeks. Her shoulders shaking now as her rib cage lifted and fell catching her breath sideways just as it did in Mr. Sanderson's car on the morning of June 26th.

She gazed round the room. Tried to draw comfort from its familiarity. It wasn't working for her.

'I still love him Pepper. It's a different kind of love, but I can't shake it off. I can't help myself from loving him.'

Then a sound. She pricked her ears to a slight click. The key in the door. Opening. Allowing only a split second of doubt as to whom it might be.

'Oh no, not *him*. Please, please let it be Mark, please let it be Mark.'

'He's not taking you from me Harriet. I'm damned if I'm giving in to his final stunt.'

'Mark. Mark you're alright. You're OK. Mark I've been worried sick about you.'

'Come here Hat. Nothing's worth all this.'

She pressed hard into his chest. 'I still love you Mark. I can't help myself from loving you.'

'You're crying my tears, too, Harriet. I've bottled them for far too long.'

'Oh Mark I'm just so glad it's you. But the baby. What about the baby?'

'Well, I've thought long and hard Hat. In all these years I've never had the guts to commit to the girl I love. You've put up with it Harriet. You've put up with me and my phobia. You've always been free to go your own way and in the back of my mind I've kind of known it would happen. I can't blame you. I've got to take my share of responsibility. Neither of us can help the way we are.'

He relaxed his hold. Looked straight into her eyes.

'Will you take me back as I am Hat?'

'More to the point Mark. Will you take me back as *I* am?'

Now pulling her in he kissed her cheek. Swallowed hard on the tears filling his eyes.

'We'll always be a Hat and a pair of Glovers, no matter what. A little mitten won't change that.'

'Do you really mean that Mark?'

'I do Hat.' He squeezed her hand. She buried her face in his jumper. Spoke softly.

'San Marco the end of the road. No. Saint Mark at the end of the road.'

'What was that Hat?'

'Oh nothing really. Just thanks for being there Mark.'